The Woman
Who Knew Too Much

A CORDELIA MORGAN MYSTERY

The Woman
Who Knew Too Much

A CORDELIA MORGAN MYSTERY

by B. Reece Johnson

CLEIS

Published in the United States by
Cleis Press Inc., P.O. Box 14684, San Francisco, California 94114.

Printed in the United States.
Design: Karen Huff
Cleis logo art: Juana Alicia
First Edition.
10 9 8 7 6 5 4 3 2 1

Library of Congress Cataloging-in-Publication Data

Johnson, B. Reece.
 The woman who knew too much : a Cordelia Morgan mystery /
 by B. Reece Johnson. — 1st ed.
  p. cm.
 ISBN 1-57344-045-0 (trade). — ISBN 1-57344-078-7 (cloth)
 I. Title.
PS3580.037172W66 1998
813' .54—dc21   98-8717
                CIP

ACKNOWLEDGMENTS

My thanks to all those gun experts at the rec.gun newsgroup site for their informative and highly entertaining replies to my questions concerning firearms. For information about New Mexico water issues and acequias, special thanks to Nicasio Romero and Albert Padillo; any errors of fact in the manuscript concerning water issues, however, are entirely my own. And to Joy Alesdatter—friend and veterinarian extraordinaire—thanks for the read.

For Jude

Morgan

*I*N NEW MEXICO, *the desert lives outside of time. Scorpions and rat-tlesnakes and coyote flourish, winding their way among piñon-studded mesas, cutting paths through vast plains of cholla and mesquite and flow-ering yucca. Mindless and ancient, impervious to human revision, the desert endures millennium after millennium—a timeless panorama of sudden electrical storms and flash floods, of killing droughts and deep smothering blankets of snow, of shrieking winds that tear through the arroyos and across the mesa tops, howling among the cottonwoods that follow the rivers. At night, the land becomes a boundless ocean of dark-ness, its chill air pricked above with stars, the earth below the last domin-ion of restless spirits—playground of kokopella and cursing desperadoes and fugitive misfits, where it is said that the shade of La Llorona still haunts the riverbanks, weeping in endless grief and searching for her lost children.*

And I, one of them, have returned.

Tonight, clouds hide the moon. The darkness is unblemished save for the cones of light cast by the headlights on the gravel road and, in the dis-tance, the solitary knot of lit windows at the foot of a mesa. I shut off the headlights and coast past the first entrance to the parking lot. When I come to the second, I enter along the edge where the surveillance cameras do not quite reach. In the corner office of the second story, Cruz's window is a pale illuminated rectangle. I ease the car into a parking space exactly below the rectangle, switch off the ignition, breathe deeply and lean my head against the seat, watching the window above. The MG's engine pings as it cools. Through the wide glass entry doors, I can see one edge of the security desk where the night guard sits reading.

It is the dead time. The guard's name is Mike, and he will not look up for hours during the ordinary passage of the night. But for a moment, just as I enter, the ordinary is suspended. We will face, our eyes locked. He will recognize me, and as his handsome features relax, the fifteen years between our last meeting and this moment will disappear as circles on a pond. There is nothing so simple to accomplish as that which the world believes impossible.

And then I will walk through the security doors, down the long hallway, up the stairs. Through Cruz's locked door.

In the shadows above the pool of light from the desk lamp, his head, which has been bent over the contents of an open folder, snaps up. Yet he is a miracle of composure—which, after all, is but the reduction of response time between one event and another. It is a skill, acquired through time and practice, like riding a bicycle or using a typewriter. Like learning to hit a moving target the size of a man's head with a .45 at a distance of fifteen yards. Cruz's miracle is that he has narrowed the interval almost to nonexistence. Almost.

"Cord." His voice is casual enough for friends, neutral enough for strangers. We might have last parted over lunch at a local restaurant. The pale eyes are dark, dilated.

I settle into the leather chair in front of his desk. It is deep and comfortable as a glove. I press my weight into it. My legs are very long, so long that I can stretch them beneath his desk, my boots near enough to his ankle that I can feel his heat.

"Cruz." My tone matches his exactly, cut from the same air. I toss the syllable to him, cool and low-slung, a volley of a word.

I have left the last fifteen years tied and bundled in the seat of his MG parked below the window behind him. But outside the black glass, the wind moves. It seeps through the pane like a winter chill, an insidious drift of déjà vu laced with the odor of his shaving cream, the texture of his skin and shape of the bone behind his ear, the sound of his glasses being folded and placed on the nightstand after the light is out, a ragtag of scrapbook intimacies that flood the air. It is the kind of attic memory that will sneak up sideways, sap your attention, leave you reeling off balance as though you have leaned against some treacherous wind.

Cruz's face hovers above the circle of light, an enigma of shadows. Lit from below, the hollows of his eyes and cheeks are deep as a cadaver's behind the glasses. Yet even at this hour, with no one except night security employees on site, he wears the immaculate grey suit, faintly striped shirt, the tie knotted in place, his hair silvered, elegant—an arrogant, lethal man.

A ripple of familiarity winnows in the air between us. It is a great temptation to reenter the old sepia-colored times, to attend the ghostly images of my younger self and a younger Cruz, lying naked in a shaft of late-afternoon sun as in the distance doors close at the end of a workday. The sun sinks behind the mountains, and the light in the room evaporates, dissolves, turns the color of ashes as we lie there on the burgundy carpet. There, just where the desk now sits, where Cruz sits.

He snaps shut the folder, and the pale lovers disappear. He places the folder on top of the stack to his right, caps the silver fountain pen, aligns it exactly perpendicular to the edge of the desk. He makes a steeple of his hands and rests his chin on the fingertips. His eyes, the color of steel, narrow. I watch as his thoughts emerge like small bright spiders, a neon aura of words and images which leap around him, pirouette across the desk. I read them as easily as you might read a more traditional text. Such is my gift. I see that he is in that other August night, fifteen years ago, when I told him I was leaving. But it is not only my disappearance that has put the steel in him. He ponders the vintage silver MG which disappeared that night as well.

I lean my head farther back against the chair. I smile at him and savor the way the soft leather caresses my ass, and I shift my feet nearer to his so that my left boot rests against his ankle. I feel his muscles pull at his bones. He is eager to rise, to stand at the window behind where he sits so that he can look down to see whether his silver car is parked there. But, you see, he has mastered the art of composure. He retracts his ankle slightly.

"If it were anyone but you, Cord, who just walked through my locked door at midnight, I might have been surprised." His voice is dry, almost a whisper. The light from the lamp shoots off his glasses.

"But not you, Cruz. You weren't surprised," I lie. Almost all the body's so-called involuntary reactions can be controlled, given the appropriate strategy. An exception is adrenaline, that Judas juice that floods a pupil black, a dead giveaway. Cruz had been surprised. Even, yes, afraid.

"Well, let's just say that I was not expecting you." He takes up the silver pen and rolls it between his thumb and forefinger. "I suppose I should ask poor Mike at the security desk just how you floated past." The chair creaks as he leans farther back and crosses his legs, placing the two of us at an equal distance from the pool of light cast on the desk.

"Do that." Because Mike is even now staring off through the glass doors, the air hanging with my perfume, the old fragrance I wore all those years ago. Tomorrow he will explain to Cruz why he admitted me without first ringing. But the truth is much simpler—old habits live on. The past never dies. That much is certain.

Cruz and I square off across the light as though we are opponents in the ring, competitors over chess. Yin and yang. On the black window behind him, my own reflection stares over his shoulder, and I remark as of old how closely we resemble one another. Alike as sun and moon, as though I were his dark and younger self—the both of us slender, fine-boned, with the hint of foreign about the eyes and the high cheekbones. He is still the color of pewter—his suit, his hair, the ice-colored eyes. And I still hold to black—jeans and sweater, jacket and boots, dark-eyed, dark-haired.

"Midnight," he says, checking his watch. "Your idea of social etiquette, tea perhaps?"

"Mmm. Not tea. Anything stronger?"

"Would that I could offer you a shot of hemlock, Cord. Pity. Might there be something else that occasions this visit?" He holds the pen as though it were a dart, tipping his head slightly.

"Strictly business, sweetheart. Pity." I offer him the slow smile, higher on one side. "On assignment. Paso gave me the Pecos Water Development case, need the background work-up on it."

His pupils dilate again. "Now, Cord, tell me why Mr. Psichari would have done that." He spaces his words evenly, articulating them as though speaking to a child.

"Because," I say, mimicking, "I asked him."

"And just why, my dear, did you do that?"

4

Dark angry clouds fill the space between his words, and I feel now as I once felt riding one of my father's spirited stallions who had thrown me for the last time. I have fought the animal, driven him into the bit so that he is under control, set along the path according to the course I have chosen for him. Cruz moves restlessly in the chair, tapping the silver pen on his desk several times, and for a moment I see him as a petulant child. And then, quite as suddenly as the stallion has been mastered, reined in, and set along the path toward home, I am overwhelmed by boredom and a sense of utter futility. It is an irrational, inexplicable feeling, a black despair descending out of nowhere. It strikes from behind, surges over me like an ocean wave. Boredom and impatience: provocateurs, those fatal sisters. It is they who lean me close to the stallion's neck, their hands who guide mine, who bring the crop down hard behind the saddle.

"Just give me the fucking file, Cruz." From the inside of my jacket, I extract the folded sheet of paper, Paso's directives, and toss it to him.

Imagined victories play sweeter. He scans the document, glances at the stack of manila folders, and tosses it back. We rise together—exactly the same height.

"I can't imagine why you'd want this case," he says, moving toward the file cabinet, the same one where I lifted the MG keys. He jerks open a drawer while keeping up a clipped, brisk monologue: "I won't pretend to fathom your motives because I know they won't be those of a sane human being—no one knows that better than I—and I suppose, given the hour, I should thank you for saving me the time of perusing the rest of these folders." He pulls out a dark red portfolio and spins on his heel. He yanks open the office door, stands beside it with the file extended. His lips are thin, compressed. Bloodless.

The burgundy carpet is deep and voluptuous under my heels, but I no longer want to lie down on it. I take the folder and cock an eyebrow at him, give him the one-sided smile. And as I walk down the hall, I am gratified to hear that he cannot resist slamming the door.

AUGUST 7, 1993

SATURDAY MORNING

I FIGURE THE GODDESS would have made us all hack lawyers, necrophiliacs, or poor relatives if she'd expected us to enjoy funerals. Happily, I'm none of the above. Nevertheless, there I sat, listening to the old pastor mutter on, letting a pretty good Saturday morning get away from me—maybe not sitting up front with a hankie, but then neither was anyone else. That long first pew was as empty as the pastor's words bouncing around the adobe white-washed walls.

From my corner near the back door, I counted seventeen spectators, mostly natives from the New Mexican village surrounding the church. I doubted any of them had known the deceased. But they didn't have to—they tiptoed up to death's threshold like a rookie Don Juan holding a bouquet in one hand and crossing his fingers with the other. Whenever the church held a ceremony, the locals cruised in for a song and a prayer. Villagers aside, it was a pretty meager turnout for Jasper Blankenship, the guy lying in the wooden box up front; not enough folks to make Juan Falcon, the county sheriff in the corner opposite mine, take out his pad and pen. Besides me and Juan, I counted three nonvillagers—Kit Willis, my best friend and next-door neighbor; Metzo Almanzar, a gallery owner from Tortuga, the nearest town of any size before you hit Santa Fe; and Marguerite Sanchez, an artist who bartends nights at the town's only serious tourist attraction—a historic inn where, so the story goes, both D. H. Lawrence and Greta Garbo had slept. Separately.

The pastor was winding down, nodding to the organist who began fingering the opening chords of "Amazing Grace." Metzo and several other men in the congregation stood up, shuffled their way between the pews, and filled up the center aisle toward the corpse. Hoping for a quick exit, I backed my way to the entrance, eased open the heavy wooden doors, and slipped quickly onto the porch. I turned straight into a blinding August sun, sweltering heat, and a profusely sweating woman who blocked the stairs and shoved a microphone in my face. Parked near the edge of the churchyard was a white van with a logo from an Albuquerque television station.

"Ms. Butler. You're Jet Butler? You found the body?"

I stepped sideways to put her between me and the fellow with the camera perched on his shoulder.

"Could you just tell us how he died? What was your relationship with Jasper Blankenship?" The woman had a manic glint in her eye, flitting from me to the camera to the church door that had drifted closed. She leaned her body sideways to give the cameraman a shot. I took the stairs two at a time while she kept pace, maneuvering the cracked concrete on her spike heels with the expertise of a seasoned high-wire artist.

"Is it true Blankenship was working for the Pecos Water Development Project, Ms. Butler? Is there any connection between that and his death?" The cameraman had circled around with the lightning speed of the passionately ambitious and now stood at the bottom of the stairs blocking my exit.

"I never knew Jaz Blankenship to work at all," I said as I leapt sideways over a deep crevice in the stairs and landed on solid ground. "You'll have to ask the authorities. Jaz and I were just acquaintances." I sprinted toward my truck parked at the other end of the church while the woman and cameraman rushed back up the stairs where the pallbearers had emerged with the coffin.

The Jaz was at last finding the infamy that I imagined he had dreamed about in life, although I was mystified about why his death was attracting statewide news coverage. I slammed the door on the hoopla in the churchyard, started up my truck, and torqued the air conditioner to warp speed. The temperature outside was already sweltering, and it wasn't even noon. In the rush of cool air, I watched the circus in front of the church at a safe distance: the woman with the microphone, flanked by the cameraman, had cornered Sheriff Falcon outside the church doors while the pallbearers hefted the box from their shoulders and slid it onto the bed of an old pickup backed to the bottom of the stairs. The congregation filtered out of the church and gathered around the television crew. The truck started up with a cough, died, started again, and pulled away, bumping down the dirt road toward the small graveyard on the outskirts of the village. Slowly, the men walking in front, the women and children behind, the group followed.

I sat there in the cab of cold air for a while, staring out past the dusty courtyard and the village that circled around the church, thinking that reaching the midlife hump had its good and bad points, but one thing was certain—you had some perspective from this angle. Death and funerals have a way of pulling you around so you can see back across the years, and if you haven't cultivated a good, solid stash of irony to soften the blow, the view can just about kill you.

Take Jaz Blankenship: effete, a confirmed elitist, a San Francisco native whose only positive words I could recall were about The City—its restaurants, writers, history; its music and wharfs and the chill wind that blew up and down the streets in every season. I had never asked, nor had he told me, why he left California in the seventies to come to New Mexico, or why he lived in a primitive cabin without electricity or running water. What I did know was that he had put in a short stint teaching at Berkeley, and that for the last fifteen years or so he had been working on his immortality, writing The Great American Novel. I also knew what everyone else in the area knew—that he spent lots of time drinking beer and cheap wine, or mescal if he could get it. But Jaz's greatest distinction, to my mind, was that he ranked as the single most unlikable human being I had ever met. This was a fellow who could argue for hours on end about the efficacy of the Nazis' extermination of the Jews, the economic value of ethnic cleansing, the physical and intellectual superiority of the Caucasian male—all while sitting in a locale where the white residents comprised only twenty percent of the total population. And now he was going to be lowered into a grave a few yards from the AmTrak rails where the sole reminder of his existence was the slim metal marker that the county puts up when the deceased cannot afford a proper gravestone.

The television crew had packed up in a sudden flurry of slamming doors, and their van disappeared down the road toward the freeway, leaving the churchyard completely deserted—except for Sheriff Falcon who was walking my way.

A tall man with slender hips and an inscrutable face, Juan Falcon was the new kid on the block. In the last election, he'd ousted the incumbent sheriff who had held office since the fifties— a prime example of rampant old-school nepotism who appointed every male relative in his sizable family to various local positions. Falcon, known less for the horses he bred on his ranch outside of town than for his crusade against drunk driving after his wife and child were killed on the highway, attracted voters of a younger generation. He wore faded Levi's, a plain leather belt, scuffed boots, a short-sleeved white shirt, and a battered tan cowboy hat—no conchos or feathered hatband or chunks of turquoise, no jewelry of any kind except for the plain gold wedding band on his left hand. His shoulder length hair was pulled back in a ponytail, his face in shadow under the hat. I rolled down the window to a blast of heat as Juan propped his elbow over the door and leaned down.

"Hey there," he said in the deep bass voice that always reminded me of Sam Elliott's. "How you doing?" Up close, his face was a miracle of flawless dark skin and the kind of eyes that keep the imaginations of post-pubescent women working overtime. I had been paler and shakier the last time I'd seen him Wednesday night, at Jaz's cabin.

"Hanging in," I said. "You?"

"Hot."

But he didn't look hot, not from the weather anyway. His white shirt was crisp, no circles of sweat under the arms or dusty smudges along the front where the top three buttons were open. I could smell the odor of soap and leather coming through the window.

"You be around in a little while? Thought I might drive up," he said, in a voice as neutral as his expression.

Whether Juan was as imperturbable as he appeared was impossible to guess—he had been this way the night he walked into Jaz's cabin. He had been this way a couple of years back when I came to his ranch to take weekly riding lessons from his wife, Grace. Often, as I rode in the training ring while Grace called instructions at the center, I could see him working a young horse in a corral, or sometimes he dropped by and sat on the top rail, watching his wife. Their daughter, Jamie, was seven then, and in the summer when school was out, she was a whirlwind of energy—brushing the horses, oiling saddles, helping rake the manure into piles while her father followed behind and shoveled them into a wheelbarrow. The little girl had always worn plaid shirts and jeans and scuffed cowboy boots, and she had not yet lost her baby fat. After the collision with the drunk driver, she had lingered for over six months in a coma.

"I'll be home. What's up?" I said, knowing this wasn't a social call.

"Few questions. Routine." He looked past me, toward where the small crowd had disappeared. "Got to go down to the burial, then I'll be by." He straightened up, gave a slight nod, and began walking after the others.

I adjusted the air conditioner louvers to get the full blast of cold air moving in my direction, then pulled away from the church toward home. The village road was unpaved, spiraling out around the church and bordered by ancient adobe houses. A few leaned crumbling and abandoned, their mud bricks eaten away by years of rain and wind and sun, but most of them were neatly kept though shabby, fronted with porches shaded by tin roofs propped on wooden uprights. Some of the houses were set back from the road, surrounded by waist-high walls of flagstone or higher walls made of adobe with only the rooftops of the houses visible. But recently, the face of the village had begun to change—the Southwest had been discovered, had become a mecca for California burnouts and disenchanted yuppies. Real estate prices, even this far from Santa Fe, had skyrocketed, and many of the local residents were selling out for figures they had never imagined. Shiny new realtor signs had sprung up in front of the Martinez place and, farther down, beside Martin Lux's little trailer by the arroyo. One home I passed, recently purchased, had last year been surrounded by an inlaid rock-encrusted wall that was now smoothly stuccoed and painted pumpkin orange.

As I started up the incline toward the mesa, the village fell away below, its gentle patina of old tin roofs circling around the white adobe church at the center like a swirling mosaic, stippled here and there with splashes of sparkling turquoise or brick-red Pro-Paneled roofs, dabs of textured clay tiles, shards of new glass skylights reflecting the sun.

On a small rise overlooking the village perched a squat metal water tank, with an incline on one side leading to the graveyard where the pickup, its bed empty, sat next to a fresh mound of red dirt and the gathering from the church service. On the other side of the truck, a silver sports car was parked next to a piñon too small to offer shade, and in the distance the figure of Juan Falcon walked steadily up a dirt path toward the assembly. While some niggling sense of loyalty had brought me to attend Jaz Blankenship's service this morning, a combination of claustrophobia and irreverence kept me from watching a human being, albeit dead, lowered into the earth and covered over. I passed the turnoff to the graveyard with relief, feeling that I had left the nightmare of Jaz Blankenship behind me.

Ahead, a dirt road ran alongside a set of railroad tracks for several miles. This was the road I pictured last week all the way from California, driving east on I-80 for twenty-four marathon hours, as the sun rose over the Nevada desert and set behind Salt Lake City, rose again over Cheyenne and then, as I headed south on I-25, sank behind the Sangrias. I drove seeing not the endless asphalt of the freeway, but this red dirt aisle between borders of purple asters and nodding sunflowers and silver-green wedges of chamisa that would turn a mustard color with the first touch of chill September air. But a drought lay across the Southwest. Throughout the spring and summer in California, though I had followed the daily reports of record-breaking temperatures and parched grazing land and failed crops, I had not been prepared for this change, as though the brilliant colors of the earth and the sky had been drained away, leaving behind this burned landscape, this dusty road flanked by nothing but dead weeds. Behind the barbed wire fences where cattle once grazed stretched deserted fields of cholla and dusty, gnarled piñon pines. But to the west, the mesas still abutted the western sky, rising highest at the center with the point of the Rowe Mesa, the longest mesa on the continent, and descending on each side along the horizon like steps left behind by some long-extinct race of giants.

At the side road that led to the mesa top, I turned left, beginning the steep drive up the mountain with switchbacks threading alternately across exposed surfaces of granite boulders and through dense stands of piñon. Here and there, ravens hunched in the branches. By the time I reached the top, the heat gauge was closing in on red. I passed a narrow road on the left, a driveway that led to the small guest house a few hundred yards behind my own place. My friend Kit had been staying there during her prolonged visit, nearly three years now, and I almost turned in for a quick hello until I remembered that she would still be at the funeral. In fact, knowing her distinct dislike of Jaz Blankenship, I had been very surprised to see her there.

I pulled into my own driveway and nosed the truck into a bank of juniper beside the tack shed. Jones, a wolf-sized Siberian husky, leapt toward me as I opened the door into a hot blast of air. Behind him, Fresca tossed her mane and kicked up a flurry of dust racing around her corral. Jones stood on his hind legs now, his front paws gripping my shoulders, staring into my eyes with his own strange, pale blue ones that could make the blood of a stranger run cold. I nuzzled my face into his deep, thick fur while the horse, a dappled grey Arabian filly, stood with her neck stretched over the top rail, her ears pricked toward us. She nibbled the handful of oats I dug from the sack inside the shed, and I stroked her neck and breathed in her musky horse smell.

I followed behind Jones, taking a narrow flagstone path to the front entrance of the house where the patio extended to the edge of the mesa that overlooked the Pecos River two hundred feet below. Inside, I poured a glass of iced tea and returned outside, climbing the stairs to the upper second-story deck where I sat under a shady bough musing for a while over the river and valley spread below. In the pasture across the river, behind groves of cottonwoods, the fields were brown and cows huddled near the watering trough beside a decrepit barn. Several goats spotted the field, and I imagined them feasting on the dead grass, content and forever chewing as their odd slotted amber eyes scanned the horizon. The heat lay like a blanket; my mind wandered, slowed, drowsed. Somewhere a crow screeched, and I woke with a start to drumbeats coming from the direction of the guest house. Kit was home from the funeral.

From my angle, I could look straight down into the river which was much lower than usual because of the drought, and across the tops of some piñons I could make out the edge of Kit's garden where she often sat. But she was not there. I lowered the back of the chaise, lay in the shade, and closed my eyes to the sound of the running river and the drumbeats, the rhythmic staccato notes that Kit used as a kind of mantra against whatever demons she fought to paint the works that she was just beginning to sell in local galleries.

Even though she was my closest friend, she kept her demons private—whether from embarrassment, jealousy, artistic perversity I didn't know. For Kit was something of an odd duck, even in the lackluster halls of academia where I'd first come across her. My thoughts went back five years, to when I had taught a one-semester creative writing course at a small Southern California college besieged by all the familiar gadflies of higher education—budget cuts, administrative incompetence, faculty rivalries. I was sitting in the back corner at the monthly faculty meeting held by the humanities department, swatting at a fly with a roll of handouts, checking my watch, and wondering whether the dean, who was droning on behind the podium up front, was as deadly boring to his students as he was to faculty. My money was on yes. As he began to enumerate the third reason for the art department's decline in student retention figures, he held up three fingers on his right hand, which made him look more like an elderly boy scout than an administrator. Someone snickered.

The woman in front of me with the Audrey Hepburn neck, however, was not amused. She jerked at the string of hair she had been twining around her finger, plucked from the knot twisted on her head and battened with long bobby pins. Pins, I began to notice, that were easing their way out, so that the knot had begun to sink slightly down the back of her head. Between reasons three and ten, I watched first one pin, then another, then still another spring out, the woman snatching them as they began the long slide down the back of her neck, stabbing them violently into the knot again. The dean, one eye on the clock, had revved up his drone and was racing to the finish line with his tenth point: he relinquished his grip on the podium and spread his arms wide as he held up both hands with five fingers spread on each. Though he was not a very good dean, and probably no better at teaching, he had the earmarks of a born traffic cop. Again, the anonymous snicker.

Again, Long Neck bristled—her skin had mottled red and white, and her jaw was clenched so tightly that her swan's neck was a column of tendon and bone. The diatribe ended; the meeting adjourned. She rose from her chair and unfolded to a spectacular height, as the old fellow who had been sitting next to her made awkward patting motions at her shoulder, quite a stretch for him, and muttered softly up to her. I filed behind them toward the door. From what I gathered, the woman held the dubious honor of being the department's toughest grader, provoking not only the wrath of the students who were dropping her introductory art classes like the proverbial flies, but also the wrath of the dean who had more than likely already been hauled into the president's office on the retention issue. This was a common enough scenario in schools across the country, and teachers everywhere were feeling the whip. The message was simple: lighten up and keep students, even if it means giving them the grades they want rather than the ones they deserve. Most teachers had given up the battle, having learned that tenure was little protection against joblessness in this era when there were hundreds of qualified applicants waiting for their positions.

But this woman, Katrine Melpine Willis, was having a tough time of it. I could see even in the poorly lit hallway, deserted of both students and staff at this hour in the late afternoon, that her skin had gone from mottled to white. The old fellow had fluttered off down a staircase, and she was bent over at her office door, fumbling with a large ring of keys. Just as I passed by, she hauled back and gave the door a whooping kick that would have made kindling of the one on my rented apartment.

"Trouble?" I asked. Call me subtle.

She peered around at me over a set of wire-rimmed glasses with murder in her eye. Then she collapsed against the door with a deep sigh. "I think I'm so mad I can't see straight," she said, extending the wad of keys, "I can't seem to find the right one."

Even seeing straight, it was a stretch in the dim hall with her impressive number of keys. I finally found the chunky bronze one stamped "Do Not Duplicate" and swung open her office door. She had furnished her space in Kitsch Clutter—every square inch designed to offend the sensibilities of the nineties yuppie. She fell into the nearest chair, an overstuffed rocking concoction covered in pink-flowered chintz. It looked like the hot spot where her irate students usually sat, for on the table beside it were a box of tissues and a pink-flowered lap desk that matched the chair. Her office had the same institution-issue laminated desk, set of bookcases, and grey filing cabinet as my own, but the walls were thumbtacked with posters, drawings, graffiti, note cards, newspaper clippings, and snapshots. From the ceiling dangled objects swaying in the air—origami fish, clothes hangers bent in the shapes of cranes, empty bottles painted with turtles, frogs, and other animals. Two large oil paintings on plywood covered one wall. They were slashes of primary colors and bold black lines from which sprouted surrealistic figures that combined the reptilian and the human. She caught me looking at them.

"They don't much like my painting here any more than they like me." She snatched a tissue from the box, took off her glasses, and dabbed at her eyes. Then she gave her nose a loud blast. "Motherfuckers. I hope they roast in hell." No longer shielded by the glasses, her eyes were a spectacular combination—the right one a deep chocolate brown and the left a greenish hazel. Before the days of enlightened science, she would probably have been called a witch and disposed of by fire. These days, the methods were more subtle, even if the results were pretty much the same. "Sons of bitches," she spat and gave her nose another blast.

I liked her Teamsters' diction, but it probably hadn't helped her case much here where tastes ran less to four-letter words than to four-syllable ones. As a campus brat reared in this tepid atmosphere, I knew the rules and could dance the dance. But part of me had always yearned for a wilder place—the same part that wanted to switch off the Beethoven and crank up Patsy Cline. The same part that twenty years ago left Berkeley for rural New Mexico. The same part that knew this spicy Amazon, Katrine Melpine Willis, was never going to fit neatly into the academic mold.

I leaned one shoulder against her office door, taking in the place, watching her wad the tissue into a wet ball and hurl it toward the wastebasket. Missed.

I said, "So fuck 'em if they can't take a joke," managing a pretty good Valley Girl imitation.

She looked up, startled. And then we both laughed. Later, we sat over towering hamburgers thick with onions and dripping with mustard at the local pub, and she gave me the full story, one that carried her through six beers by the time she finished up. She didn't know it yet, but her description of the campus fit colleges everywhere; only the names changed. I knew because every two or three years, depending on the slim royalties that trickled in from the books I wrote, I taught a course at various colleges across the country to keep my checkbook out of the red, and this story was as familiar as overcrowded classrooms and low pay. Another thing she didn't know yet was that if she ever managed to shove herself into the contortions necessary for a tenured position, she wouldn't have much of herself left over to paint with. But by the time I left campus that semester, she suspected it. And by the time she arrived unannounced in my driveway a year and a half later, she had accepted it.

She pulled up in an old green rusted-out Jeep truck, dragging behind it a trailer piled with everything she owned, including several unfinished oil paintings wrapped in an aquamarine tarp. This time her hair was loose and electric. This time she was laughing. She jumped from the Jeep, startling Jones who was used to strangers staying in their cars when he told them to. As I walked up the flagstone path toward her, she was holding herself in her arms and spinning around and around across the mesa. She'd done it, she said, left tenure, retirement, security, and was risking it all for Art.

The memory of her arrival always made me smile. I had stood watching, surprised less by her visit than by her hot pink Spandex body suit, the June sun touching it with silver as Kit swirled around the mesa with her hair spread around her like a wild cape. After all those years of twisting and pinning and spraying her unruly hair into a tight bun, camouflaging her extraordinary eyes behind thick lenses, and heaping several layers of fashionable long skirts and high boots over her body, even after doing her level best to weed out the colorful words from her vocabulary, Kit had failed to fit the academic profile. That evening over dinner, I set out my prohibitions against alcohol and drugs on the property and offered her the guesthouse in return for minimal caretaking during the mercifully infrequent times I was off teaching, and we left it at that.

In fact, I had driven the freeways last week not only with my brick-red road in mind, but with Kit in my thoughts. And the azure sky and the mesas and the way the wind tears across the high country and the river runs through it and ties it together and makes sense of it. I had pulled in from California late last Tuesday—red-eyed from lack of sleep, high from No-Doz, and not expecting to see a light on. But it was.

Kit had been waiting, and as soon as I pulled up she was running up the flagstone path with Jones, her hair flying behind her.

"I knew it," she said, hugging me, dragging suitcases out of the truck bed and lugging them both down the path. "I knew you'd drive straight through. I'd have bet any money on it," she said, talking over her shoulder as I followed along behind, fussing over Jones.

Inside she bustled around the kitchen, heating up the meal she'd prepared, and I tracked through the house to chat with the twelve cats I'd acquired over the years. Later, we sat in the living room balancing wooden bowls of rice and mushrooms and broccoli on our laps, eating with chopsticks, surrounded by the cats and

Jones who sat among them with a look of disgust as they edged closer to sniff the bowls.

Kit rocked in the bentwood and talked nonstop: "....and then the asshole, can you even believe it, tells me to mind my own business. I mean here he is, so *fucking* drunk he can barely sit on the stool, and...You want some hot oil...?" She leapt up, sprinted to the kitchen, and returned with a small bottle. Her hair had grown nearly to her knees, and she was wearing a Day-Glo orange leotard topped by a purple leather jacket with long cowboy fringes. She sprinkled oil over her rice and passed me the bottle.

"...and he's telling me, *he's* telling *me*, that I have an attitude problem. He's just the kind of son of a bitch that gives the whole race of men a bad name, he's..." She stopped mid-sentence. Her long neck stretched up several more impossible inches as she looked past me. "*Shoo!! SHOO....!!*" A tremendous clatter issued from the kitchen. "Shit, Jet, why in hell do you let them all over the table and counter? I was just getting them trained, and then the minute you walk in the door..." Kit leapt up again. I sprinkled oil over my rice and twisted around to see her aiming a spray bottle at a particularly large yellow cat streaking above the table with something dangling between his teeth. "I just can't believe it," she said, bringing the spray bottle back to the living room with her and setting it beside the rocker.

"You can't believe Jaz is a son of a bitch?" I asked. Innocently.

"No," she glowered. "I can't believe how you let your cats behave. Everyone knows Jaz is a son of a bitch." She made a sour face and sat down, working the chopsticks over her bowl, talking in between bites. "This latest little escapade of his is just more of the same. Someone saw him out behind his house fiddling with one of those thingy-ma-jigs that the Lab's installed in the river. It just figures that he's low-down enough to help them make this whole valley a wasteland." She paused to chew, setting her bowl back on her lap. A tortoiseshell cat who had been waiting beside the rocker stood on its back legs, peering into the bowl. "So anyway," Kit continued, swallowing, oblivious to the cat, "I was curious about it, so I asked. He acted like I asked him the size of his dick or something. He just started in raving like some fucking nutcase lunatic." The cat fished with its paw in Kit's bowl, snagged one morsel, sniffed, dropped it back, tried another.

"Well," I said, using the chopsticks to feed bits of mushrooms to the cats who had chosen me over Kit, "consider the source. And, anyway, it's not like Jaz or any one person is responsible for this whole water business." I lifted out a chunk of broccoli and tried it on Jones. He glared at it and then at me. Ever the wolf.

"Christ, Jet, we're all of us responsible. We...*hsssssttt!!!*" Kit snatched her bowl up and aimed flat-tire sounds at the mottled cat who stalked away with her tail waving and leapt on the couch. I burrowed through the rice and offered her a mushroom. She took it gingerly, shook it, and began to chew.

"That stuff's not good for them, you know," she said, making another sour face. "But anyway, if we band together on this, we'll attract enough attention to make them stop. And there's not much time left. Next week, a week from today, August tenth, is D-day. Then it's a done deal. There'll be no stopping them after that, no matter what."

I vaguely recalled some details from Kit's letters over the last few months. Between updates on the animals and scuttlebutt about the neighbors, she had written about the Pecos Water Development Project. But the details had deteriorated into a long and dense political diatribe that I had scanned briefly and set aside. Nor was this the time for an update. The No-Doz was wearing off, and the weight of the last twenty-four hours was settling on me like lead. I ate what was left in my bowl and stretched out on the couch. I dimly remember Kit covering me with a blanket.

I HAD FALLEN ASLEEP on the chaise listening to the flow of the river, lost in thought about my return home last Tuesday night. But this was Saturday, and I knew when I woke with a jolt to the sound of a vehicle approaching that it would be Juan Falcon. I sat up and shook my head, feeling disoriented from the nap and the heat. In the distance, Jones was barking full tilt, and I forced myself reluctantly from the shade. When I reached the driveway, Jones was running ahead of Juan Falcon's white Dodge truck, a huge, high-powered affair with a crew-cab and a diesel engine.

"Hey," he called, getting out and squatting to ruffle Jones's fur. I gave a wave, and while he went over to visit Fresca, I returned to the house where the cool air had collected inside the thick adobe walls. I took a tray of ice cubes out of the freezer and was filling two glasses with iced tea when Juan appeared at the door, followed by Jones.

"Not ruining your Saturday, am I?" he said, removing his hat and leaning against the door frame as his eyes scanned the house.

I set the two glasses of tea on the table and nodded for him to come in. "Not yet," I said. "But it started with a funeral, so you're probably not going to do too much damage to the rest of it."

He entered the house, hat in hand, still looking around. I was used to this from people who had never been here—the place was unusual, to say the least. Some said it had been built by a man who ran guns, others said drugs. Whichever story you bought, there was no doubt that someone had designed the perfect hideout. Backed against the cliff and facing the mesa, the house wrapped around its own center with huge windows set deep into the adobe walls. A narrow, precipitous staircase curved up to where a trapdoor opened to the second story, and then finally a third story unfurled with a slender, multiwindowed loft that was a spectacular place to be when the frequent electrical storms lit the nights. The house, viewed from a distance, had always struck me as looking shiplike, its broad bottom story anchored into the red New Mexico soil, bearing the weight of the smaller upper stories. Through the years, as I'd discovered its secret places, the house became so familiar that I felt myself connected to that distant maverick who had built it. I imagined him a crude man, driven by expediency and circumstance, yet oddly graced with a poet's sensibilities. He had cut the boards and mixed the adobe and pounded the nails like a man in a hurry, one who uses whatever materials lie close at hand, so that the windows were mismatched, the boards of the walls and floors gaping with cracks, the flagstone ground-level floor uneven, and the house itself out of plumb and tipped slightly back toward the river. And while the restless mesa winds sometimes drove cold air around the window casings in winter, and dust seeped into the house and drifted around its halls and up its stairs in summer, there was about the whole a sense of primitive elegance in the curving walls and the ceilings' rough vigas that flared out from the house's center like spokes from a wheel. Juan, too, seemed to have fallen under the spell.

"Want a tour?"

"I would. Maybe some other time," he said, pulling his attention back to the kitchen. He placed his hat on the table, and we both sat for a moment, sipping at the tea and clinking ice cubes. "I didn't expect to see you at the funeral. Not much of a turnout, was there?"

"Jaz wasn't the most popular guy around," I said. "It would really have been bad without the villagers, though."

He nodded and pulled a pen and a spiral-bound pad out of his shirt pocket. "I've gone back over what you told me and Scott that night at Jaz's place. I was hoping maybe you'd go over the details with me again. That okay?"

"Sure. Anything in particular?"

He opened the pad and thumbed through several pages. "Well, one thing. I was wondering about that day, why you rode over to Jaz's. I was thinking about your filly out there, little Arab isn't she? I was thinking about how hard it must have been to get a young filly like that across the river. Most of them are crazy when you want them to get their feet wet. Your filly like that?"

"Like I said before, I really didn't think much about where I was headed, you know? I'd been stuck in California for too long, and maybe it was me who was crazy. But you're right. She was a handful to get across the river, even with it low like it is. I was just riding, that's all."

He nodded his head and laid down the pad with the pen across it. He reached over to his hat and traced the stitching where the crown of the hat met the brim.

"What, do you think I went over there and killed him?" I said it as a joke, but Juan didn't crack a smile. He stopped fiddling with the hat and looked at me with his dark, impenetrable eyes. I felt my stomach turn over, but now was not the time to think why. I shrugged and rattled my ice cubes.

"Nope, I don't think that. But I don't think it was just coincidence that got you there, either. I was wondering about your neighbor, whether she might have mentioned Jaz to you."

"Kit? Good lord, Juan, what's Kit got to do with this?" I was beginning to feel surly. I sipped at the tea and set the glass down in front of me a little too hard.

"Well, that's kind of what I wanted to talk to you about." Jones sat with his ears on alert by my side, his head tilted sideways at Juan. A couple of months passed. Finally, Juan continued. "I guess she and Jaz got into it one night last week over at the Inn. They say she was pretty mad, say she threatened to kill him."

"Are you serious? You think Kit…?" I stared at him, unable to finish. He patted his leg and Jones walked over to him.

"I don't think anything right now. I'm just asking questions, Jet. This isn't personal, okay?" Juan looked at Jones and ruffled the dog's ears. When I didn't say anything, he went on. "I don't want this to go any further, but I'll tell you because it might explain why I've got to ask these questions. We got the autopsy report back.

Looks like it might be poison that killed him, but we can't be sure yet. There's some chemical that Jim can't identify, so we've sent what we've got on up to Santa Fe. It'll be a day or two until we hear back, but meanwhile, I'm finding out all I can about anybody who knew Jaz or had contact with him recently."

"And Kit did."

"Well, it's not much of a secret. Lots of folks in the bar that night. I didn't have to be Sherlock on this one." He gave Jones a final pat and drank the rest of the tea. I reached for the empty glass, but he put his hand over mine and shook his head. He didn't move his hand, and I felt it warm and heavy over my own. My heart did some double time, which only meant that I wasn't made out of concrete. "Let's talk," he said in a voice an octave or two lower than the one he'd been using. He withdrew his hand, and I took back my own. I got up and took the pitcher of tea out of the refrigerator, filling my own glass and setting the pitcher in the middle of the table, more to ease my thumping heart than to quench my thirst. He waited until I had sat down again and gripped my eyes with his own. "I think your friend Kit asked you to pay Jaz a visit. I want you to tell me if I'm right."

"I don't know what's going on here, Juan. What's this about?" My nerves were starting to fray. I got up again and stood by the window in the kitchen, looking out over the same brown fields that I had been watching before I fell asleep, before Juan had come. They hadn't changed. They still looked desolate and foreign and burnt. I turned to him. "Are you seriously suggesting that Kit could *murder* somebody, even someone as eminently murderable as Jaz?"

"She's a woman with a mean temper, Jet. Are you seriously suggesting that she couldn't?"

I thought about that for a minute. When it came to questions of who could kill and who couldn't, I wanted to get in my truck and head for a simpler country, a gentler era than the one we lived in. I went back to looking out the window. Across the river, the cows had lost their shade and stood clumped with their heads lowered together. I couldn't see how I could get much more isolated than I was here, what mountain I could climb where the violence couldn't reach. I thought of Kit kicking her office door all those years ago, and the nights during that semester when we met at the local pub and she drank herself senseless, raving about her colleagues. She no longer drank, so far as I knew, but what person among us cannot be brought to murder under the right conditions? I thought of the sixties and the Vietnam War and Kent State—all of us who had grown to adulthood during that era could tell you that all it took to make a killer out of the boy next door was to stick a rifle in his hand and shrug. So was I suggesting Kit was any different?

"Sure, Kit *could* have. I *could* have, you *could* have. Anyone *could* have. What I'm saying is that I believe she *didn't*."

"You know that for a fact?"

"Of course not. You don't even know yet, for a *fact*, if he was murdered."

"That's why I'm just asking questions. Like this one: Did Kit say anything to you about Jaz? Is that why you rode to Jaz's Wednesday?"

Nothing's ever simple, is it? I was not going to lie to Juan, but why bore him with all the details either? I started to do some fancy dancing. "Kit told me she thought Jaz might be helping out on the Pecos Water Project. I guess that's a pretty hot issue right now with a lot of people around here."

"Depends who you talk to. The Lab folks can give you all the figures. The way they've got it laid out, there will be as much water as there ever was." Juan narrowed his eyes. "Course, Kit doesn't see it that way, does she?"

"No, she doesn't. Do you?"

Juan looked past me to the kitchen and then up to the ceiling where the vigas flared out like rays. "Don't matter what I believe. But I've seen the reports. They're public record. No reason to think the valley's going to turn into a desert wasteland."

"Well, then."

"Well, then, I guess maybe you did decide to check out Jaz for yourself? Going on Kit's perspective of the situation?"

I sighed and drew squiggles in the frost of my tea glass. Jones walked over and pushed his sharp muzzle in my lap, and a grey-striped tabby leapt from the top of the refrigerator to the table and began rubbing her ears against my forearm. "I don't know that there was anything that premeditated about it, Juan. Kit had mentioned him, but I didn't consciously set out to visit him. You know, I'm one of the few people Jaz could talk to in any sane way, so maybe on some level, after hearing Kit's view of the water situation, I did think I could sound him out." I paused, waiting for Juan to respond. His head nodded slowly over his empty glass, and in the silence I listened to the sounds in the room—the cat purred, the refrigerator behind me hummed, the wall clock ticked. Jones panted for a moment and then stretched his lanky body beside my chair, gave a prodigious sigh, and began a nap.

"Well, let's come back to that." Juan took up the pen and thumbed through the notepad again. "I'd like you to go over the whole thing with me, leading up to finding the body. Start anyplace you want to." Juan laid the pad out on the table and clicked the pen.

I closed my eyes and tried to think. Finding where to start has always been a problem for me, and talking about Jaz Blankenship, even a dead Jaz Blankenship, was about the last thing I wanted to do with the tail end of a Saturday afternoon. But, in fact, the Wednesday in question had started off pleasantly enough. It was nearly noon when I woke on the couch where Kit had left me that night after we ate. I was covered with a blanket, pressed under the weight of three cats, buttressed by several more, and the tip of Jones' muzzle was nearly touching my chin. When I opened my eyes, I was staring straight into his pale blue ones. He gave a happy yelp, sending terrified cats in all directions.

After a shower that used up every drop of hot water, I pulled on a pair of jeans and a T-shirt and with Jones eagerly following, went to visit Fresca. She nickered, raced around the corral several times, and came to a sliding stop where I sat on the top rail, watching and waiting. Although Kit had taken care of the morning feeding, Fresca stretched her long neck, first checking for treats, then lifting her muzzle toward my wet hair, sniffing and blowing loudly when she touched it. The sun was scorching, but I dawdled over her, talking softly and brushing her mane and tail until they ran like silk through the comb. I had left her unshod, knowing that she would not be ridden until I returned, so after saddling up and heading out, I chose the path with the fewest rocks.

It was a narrow route, winding down behind Kit's house and then steeply declining in a zigzag pattern through juniper and piñon until it leveled out in a sandy arroyo that led to the river. Fresca picked her way carefully through the brush and trees, tossing her head when we reached the arroyo, dancing sideways and chewing at her bit. She was young and eager to run, fretting angrily against the reins. Ahead of us, Jones barked and leapt through the bushes, chasing the occasional rabbit. I relaxed the reins, felt the filly walk into the bit, and leaned forward, tightening my legs as the horse charged ahead. I held her to an easy canter, feeling her muscles move beneath me, the rhythm of her stride as her hooves drove into the sand, the two of us slicing through the hot parched air. As we neared the riverbank, Fresca slowed into the jarring, rib-splitting trot that Arabs seem prone to, and Jones raced by us and splashed into the river where he stood lapping at the water.

The Pecos was low, shrunk to a mere stream in places, leaving a dusty white residue where the water used to run. In spite of the media coverage I had seen on television about the drought, I was not prepared for this—the remains of dead fish littered the banks, the skeletons farther back and the rotting carcasses nearer the water, covered with hordes of flies that rose and descended in black clouds as we passed. The stench was overpowering. Fresca snorted and danced sideways, rolling her eyes toward the river. I leaned over her neck and talked softly to her, fighting back the nausea that rose in my throat as we traveled the path alongside the stream bed, toward the crossing where the river grew narrowest. But the crossing, too, had changed. It was mostly dried sand with a few narrow branches of water trickling through, and as I urged Fresca up to the first rivulet, she reached her muzzle to the water and blew loudly, refusing to drink. She balked and danced backward and tossed her head, not wanting to cross. Here, actually standing on the riverbed where water had once run, I could see the small fish stranded in pools cut off from the main flow, swimming madly, and larger fish, half-beached, lashing with their tails as the water was absorbed by the air and sand. Suddenly, Fresca faced the river and stood absolutely still in the hot air, her nostrils flaring as the sun pounded down. I began to see that, in fact, we were surrounded by a slowly churning turmoil of life struggling to live. The air was loud with the whine of flies; the ground was moving with suffocating fish, crawling with insects feasting on those already dead.

I tried to recall what Kit had said, and what she had written, about Jaz Blankenship's involvement with the water project, something about seeing Jaz in his backyard. I saw her face rise up before me, her anger bubbling between the words though she was trying to keep her voice modulated. Blankenship's cabin was somewhere in this direction, and although it wasn't near the path I usually took along the river, I had some general sense of its location—some three or four miles on up the trail, I figured. So what I'd told Juan was true, as far as the literal truth went: I hadn't urged Fresca across the river with any particular plan to visit Jaz, but once on the other side, I decided to swing by his place to take a look around the river where Kit had mentioned seeing him. In fact, since it was common knowledge that Jaz had spent much of his time the last couple of years drinking at the Inn, I had some notion that the odds against running into him were in my favor.

I guided the filly along the shady trail that ran through a wide fringe of cottonwoods, bordered on one side by the river and on the other by a gravel road. As we came to dirt roads veering toward the river, I followed them, thinking each might lead to Jaz's place. One led to a deep arroyo filled with heaps of garbage, rusted vehicles, scraps of furniture, refrigerators; another brought us to a trailer with its roof weighted down against the wind with old tires and two dirty, naked children staring out the open door at me as I turned the filly back up the road. One road merely ended at the edge of the riverbed where piles of beer cans, broken bottles, scraps of clothing, and a record number of used rubbers lay scattered. It was late in the afternoon when I turned Fresca down the road that led to Jaz's place, Jones panting along behind. By then, the sun was edging close to the mesas along the western horizon, and I was charting my route home, opting for the main road through the village, even though it was hard-packed and rocky in places, in order to cut the riding time down to a couple of hours. Besides, I reasoned, trying to ignore the aches in my back and legs, the moon was full, and the ride would be cool and pleasant.

Such were my thoughts as I rode along a narrow, deeply shaded road and rounded a bend, nearly running into the rear bumper of the old Rambler that belonged to Jaz.

Startled, Fresca leapt backward and sideways, nearly unseating me while Jones disappeared in a great rustle of underbrush, in hot pursuit of some wild creature. I righted myself, steadied the horse, and recovered the stirrups I'd lost. Beyond the car, parked where the road and forest ended, was an immense circular clearing with a small structure in the center and the river running along the far side behind it. The cabin, made of rough boards and plywood scraps, topped with mismatched pieces of rusty tin, might have appeared rustic, even picturesque had it been nested in the shade of trees and the whispers of the forest, but this one stood naked, its patchwork construction exposed in the brutal glare of the New Mexico sun. I was puzzled by the clearing in the midst of the cottonwood forest, and then I saw that the entire expanse was dotted with the stumps of cut trees.

I urged Fresca forward, toward the cabin, but when she began to back nervously, snorting and tossing her head, I dismounted and led her back among the trees where I tied the reins to a low branch. Jones was nowhere to be seen, so I walked alone toward the footpath leading to the cabin, calling out Jaz's name even though the place looked deserted. The last rays of the sun were disappearing behind the mesa, and the air which had been cool among the cottonwoods, grew hot in the parched flat clearing, rising from the earth like a hot breath. The tree stumps dotting the field gave it an odd, unshaven appearance. I wondered why Jaz had cut the trees, and then I noticed that the more distant trunks around the circumference of the clearing were pale, more recently cut. I realized that during the past fifteen years, Jaz had gradually cut away the protective forest in order to keep himself warm during the winter months.

As I walked along the footpath, I began to notice that a pervasive silence filled the clearing, so different from the woods with its trilling birds and scurrying fauna. The sky had taken on a deeper turquoise hue, with the faint glow of pink edging the horizon of mesas to the east. I stopped to listen to the sound of the river running in the distance, but I could not hear it. Ahead, the path ran in a straight line to a piece of flagstone at the cabin's front door and then veered sharply left, probably leading to the river behind. I wanted very much to avoid the cabin and follow the path, but it would be tough explaining that if I happened across Jaz. Yet the clearing felt empty, the cabin deserted. As I came closer, I saw that a ragged cloth hung across the window inside, and a ditch of raw, red earth edged the ground around the cabin where, over the years, rain had flowed off the corrugated tin roof. The front door stood slightly ajar, and the hairs at the back of my neck began tingling, sending a chill down my spine.

"Jaz? Hey, Jaz, you in there?" I gave the door a knock, and it swung open a few inches with a loud squeak of the hinges, shooting a blade of light across a floor made of hard-packed dirt. "Hello?" I said in a high voice that did not sound like my own.

I stuck my head inside, waiting for my eyes to adjust to the dark and picking up the heavy, stale smell of alcohol and cigarettes. A metal-framed twin bed sat in the far corner, its single mattress heaped with a knot of filthy sheets. A wooden crate had been turned upside-down to serve as a bedside stand. Crowded on it were a kerosene lamp, a jumble of paperback books that had spilled off and covered the floor in heaps, an ashtray overflowing with ashes and filters, and a glass with red liquid in the bottom. Surrounding the bed and lining the floor around the walls were stacks of paperbacks and magazines, some leaning precariously, others overturned and sprawling across the floor, mostly of the Louis L'Amour and naked lady variety.

"I was surprised at that as much as anything else," I told Juan, who was making an occasional note. "I knew he'd taught at Berkeley. We exchanged some faculty hate stories now and then. I guess I expected to see James Joyce, Shakespeare. Hillerman, at the very least." I was pruning my story for Juan, having decided to start with the walk up to Jaz's place and the events that took place after I entered the cabin.

I had been marveling at Jaz's taste in reading when I had my first hit of adrenaline—a pair of legs and boots sticking out from the space between the wall and the bed. My heart was still racing as I tiptoed across the floor to discover a pair of empty jeans and boots that Jaz had apparently shed before going to bed, with a hefty pile of dirty clothes stuffed back into the corner.

I should have known then, as I stood trembling at the foot of the bed with my back to the door, that the best place to go next was back down the road and out of there. Maybe I was getting ready to do just that as I stood looking down over Jaz's dirty laundry, taking in the dirty bed and the dirty magazines, the cigarette butts and empty wine bottles and beer cans scattered across the hard-packed dirt floor. Maybe I stood there for only a second or two, maybe longer. What I remember next is that suddenly the room seemed to darken, and I felt him behind me, his shadow across the doorway, the shaft of daylight obscured.

I had the second hit of adrenaline then. I whirled to see Jaz coming toward me, naked from the waist up with his long, bony arms stretched out, and for a moment I had the dizzying sensation that he was going to hug me. But his eyes, pale and protruding, were vacant and looked straight through me as he took one lumbering step and then another, leaning forward, and then his knees buckled. He seemed not so much to fall as to fold, coming to rest on his knees with his arms still stretched out and his hands grasping. His mouth was working, opening and shutting, so close that I could smell his foul breath against my face.

"Did he look drugged? Choking? Did he say anything?" Juan asked.

"No," I said, looking across the table at Juan, but seeing Jaz instead, kneeling and staring through me with his wide, pale eyes bulging. "He just...," I shrugged, "just fell over."

I stood there frozen, looking down at the back of Jaz's head. He lay spread-eagle in the swatch of daylight coming through the door, his hair covering one side of his face in oily strings. It was strange hair, the kind that babies have, fine as spider webs. Most of the time it hung straight and limp over his forehead, his mad eyes gleaming through, like some lurid psychopath escaped from the local asylum. Other times, more rarely, combed neatly to one side, his hair was golden, and I could imagine the handsome man he might once have been—blue-eyed, aspiring and in despair, too intelligent to believe even his most carefully constructed delusions. Jaz had not been a likeable man, but he had been an interesting one. As I leaned over his body, I could see his eyes behind the strings of hair, not gleaming now but dulled over in the patina of death.

I felt for a pulse at his wrist, and then his neck, but found none. I didn't have to be a medical doctor to know that this man was dead, yet there was no wound, no blood, nothing to indicate what had happened to him. Heat stroke? Cirrhosis of the liver? Heart attack? My firsthand experience with death was minimal. I knew that Jaz was somewhere around fifty years old, so thin that he looked anorexic, though I had always taken this as a symptom of his alcoholism. He definitely wasn't a Type A. It would have been hard to find anyone who expended fewer calories in a state known for the slow life. He was dressed in a pair of dirty cutoff jeans barely hanging from his hip bones, no shoes or socks. While the day had been hot, it wasn't heat stroke weather.

My own pulse had slowed considerably, and even though I was in a room with a corpse, I felt an odd calm. I stood up, took a couple of deep breaths, and tried to call up a semblance of sorrow or regret. Nothing happened. The room was growing quickly darker; evening descended fast across the valley. I looked around, thinking that I must call someone, but of course the place didn't even have running water or electricity, not to mention a telephone.

The other side of the cabin was a kitchen. It had a propane camping stove, a large foam cooler, a double sink dropped into a hole cut in what appeared to be a door, and a wooden table with two unmatched chairs. Among the litter of bottles, beer cans, and several overflowing ashtrays, I spotted a wrinkled pack of generic filter cigarettes. I knew I wasn't as calm as I thought when I struck a match and lit up. My hand was trembling. It had been two weeks since my last one, sitting in the tiny kitchenette apartment on the college campus in California, land of sunshine and bad dreams, thinking of New Mexico, and it had been ten years before that one.

The smoke burned my throat as I inhaled deeply. Coughing, I looked for something to drink—bottled water, a warm beer. Nothing. From the light in the window above the sink, I saw a rusted spigot sticking through the wall. When I turned it, a stream of brown water came seeping out and disappeared down the drain. It didn't look like anything I'd want to drink, so I kept the cough, doused the cigarette, and shut off the water. Along the windowsill were several potted plants growing in old cans—flourishing cannabis, well tended by the looks of them, and just budding. Next to the sink was a cardboard box full of small bottles like the ones used for artichoke hearts and small-sized condiments. I held one up to the window against the early evening sky and jiggled it slightly, watching a gelatinous substance rise from the sediment at the bottom. In another tiny bottle, I examined the delicate tentacles of some plant that waved gracefully as vines touched by a breeze, the soft pinkish fibers beckoning like tiny fingers. I couldn't resist—who would miss this one small bottle among the other twenty or so on the counter? I stuffed it into my pocket just as Jones came loping to the door, his hair bristling along his spine as his eyes fastened on the body.

"So, you didn't see anyone else while you were there?" Juan was resting his chin in his hand, but he was watching me closely.

"Are you kidding? You think I wouldn't have told you if I'd seen anyone there?" I had left out a few details, to be sure—like the cannabis plants and the bottles beside the sink. Juan and his deputy, Scott, had arrived there shortly after I'd left on Fresca to use the nearest phone at the village liquor store a mile or so from Jaz's cabin, and later, after Scott had driven me back to the scene, Juan hadn't seemed interested in my blow-by-blow description as he questioned me. Why should he be? He and his deputy had doubtless gone over the place with a fine-toothed comb. "Do you think someone else was there?" I asked.

"Mm. Well, we found some tire tracks. Someone was there after Jaz parked his car." He hesitated, looking at his pad. "And after you left there on your horse."

"Who?" How much time could have passed between when I left and when Juan arrived? Forty-five minutes, maybe an hour at the outside. Plenty of time for a drop-in visit. But who, and why hadn't anyone besides me reported Jaz's death?

"Dunno." He clicked his ball-point pen several times. "You see anything in the cabin somebody might want?"

"Well, there were some marijuana plants. And the bottles." I couldn't recall anything else in the cabin that anyone would take on a bet. I was sure Jaz had scarfed most of it from the village dump.

"Bottles? What bottles?" Juan said quickly, too quickly. I realized that he must not have seen the bottles by the sink. And that could only mean that when he got there, the bottles must have been gone. For some reason, I wasn't ready yet to share the information, not till I had had time to think about it.

"Bottles, you know. All those wine bottles he had stacked around the kitchen. They looked pretty scummy, that's all."

"'Scummy'? You think Jaz would wash wine bottles?" Juan raised his eyebrows at me.

"I just thought he would use them to store drinking water from town, that he'd need to wash them out first." This sounded pretty lame, even to me, but then Juan was under the impression like everyone else in the region that anyone from California was at least partly crazy to begin with, no matter if she had been living in New Mexico for twenty years. I looked at Juan wide-eyed, as though to say that after all I was female, Californian, Caucasian, and therefore mentally at high risk. I felt a small pang of shame at using so clichéd a stereotype, but what's a girl to do in a pinch?

Juan glared at me. "We found the marijuana. Low-budget stuff. He probably made a few bucks." He clicked the pen again and wrote something in the notebook. Wildebeest, the stripped tabby, rose from her petting position near me and stretched with her rump in the air. She padded to Juan's side of the table where she sat beside the notebook and watched him write. She raised her right paw delicately and batted at the top of his pen until he paused to stroke her ears with the tip of it. She rose up on her back legs, trying to catch it as Juan waved it past her whiskers. "This isn't a game," he said, stroking the cat and slipping the pen back in his shirt pocket. He pinned me with his eyes, his face dark and serious above the immaculate white shirt. "A man is dead, maybe murdered. If that's what happened, you could be in danger. I want you to be real clear about this. This is not about a fellow that everybody loved to hate. If it's true he was killed, then there's a killer running around loose." He slapped the notebook closed, stuck it in his pocket behind the pen, and stood up.

What he said was true, and it frightened me, but I didn't like his tone. He was taking the air-head female stereotype I'd used too far. I glared back at him from where I sat. "I've told you what I know Juan. What else do you want?"

He put both hands on the table, leaning toward me. "I'll tell you what I want, Jet. I want your cooperation on this. Your best friend is at the top of my suspect list. You were the last one to see him alive."

"You're serious about Kit, aren't you?"

"Very."

"Look, I'll make a visit, okay? I'm as sure as it's possible to be that Kit's got nothing to do with this." I paused, running a quick mental tape of everything I knew about my friend. I didn't believe she was involved, and I was willing to back it up with a little research for Juan. "I wouldn't go so far as to say Kit didn't celebrate a little when she heard the news, but you're way off the mark on this one. I'll check it out and give you my number one, honest opinion. Deal?"

"That's all I'm asking. I'll remember the favor." When Juan smiles, it's like seeing the sun come out after a long rain. He took his hat from the table, and Jones sat up, yawning loudly.

"Hey. This isn't for you, it's for her," I said, walking him to the door and down the flagstone path to his truck. The air outside was still hot, though the sun was headed west. Juan started up his truck, his arm resting on the window and his eyes shaded by the brim of his hat.

"Something else," he said. "You said Jaz was writing a book?"

"Yeah. For years."

"We didn't find any writing there." The truck was a diesel, its idle loud. "Don't you think that's odd?"

"Well, kind of odd, I guess." I thought for a moment. "Writers can be pretty strange about their habits. I mean, he could have been writing somewhere else. Or maybe he didn't keep his stuff at the cabin because he didn't think it was safe."

"He thought it was safe enough to grow marijuana in."

"Maybe he wasn't writing at all. Maybe he was just talking," I said. Juan cocked his head at me, and I went on. "I don't think that's it, though. I'll see what I can find out." We both knew that his new status as sheriff had some limitations. He had won the election by a very narrow margin, and lots of people in town had strong ties to the former sheriff, people who would be less than forthcoming about whatever information they might have.

He began to back his truck out the drive and then stopped and pulled forward again. "One other thing," he said. "You know anything about Jaz's love life, past history?"

Whatever sexual life Jaz might have had probably wouldn't be considered, by any standards, a love life. "I don't have a clue— why?"

"Real pretty lady at the burial. Says she's Jaz's ex." Juan tipped his head down and looked up through his eyebrows. "Come all the way from Caly-forn-eye-ay." He lifted his eyebrows and gave his second smile of the century before disappearing in a plume of dust.

I STOOD WATCHING the empty driveway until the dust had settled, but my head was still spinning. I wandered over to where Fresca stood eyeing the oat sack through the open door of the tack shed and let her nuzzle oats from my palm as I thought about the missing bottles, the manuscript that might or might not exist, the possibility of murder, and the presence in the world of someone who was Jaz's "ex." Ex-wife? Ex-girlfriend? I decided that now was as good a time as any to drop in on Kit, so with Jones trotting ahead, his tail curled over his back, I followed the precipitous footpath that ran along the cliff behind my house and led to Kit's backyard. When we came to the huge boulder that jutted out over the river below, I stood on it for a moment looking down across the valley. To the northwest, where the Rowe Mesa came to a peak at La Punta, a black fist of clouds had collected. I listened for thunder, but there was none. Below where I stood, house-sized boulders dotted the steep decline, stacked together at crazy angles, with piñons jutting from the patches of earth among them. Gradually my ear tuned to the valley sounds as they rose—the flow of the river seemed to grow louder as I watched it rippling around the small island and the bony shoulders of rocks in the center. A raven who soared on outspread wings a few feet from where I stood gave a flap and squawk of surprise as it passed. An invisible plane hummed faintly, a cock crowed, and somewhere in the far distance came the mournful call of a train whistle.

I continued along the path that wound over and among the boulders, under the branches of piñon trees and around cacti, passing the cutoff that led down to the river, and made my way slowly toward Kit's backyard. This was the "scenic route" that connected our two houses and offered the quickest access to the river. It was as familiar and well used as our living rooms—full of shady bowers with lawn chairs and tables made of wooden spools where I often went to write, sprinkled with flat-topped stone plateaus where Kit set up her easels or stretched out naked in the sun, or where we made fires and sat around them at night, playing drums or guitars and singing with friends. I lingered in the recesses, stroking Jones and puzzling over the mystery of Jaz Blankenship's death.

Someone had visited the cabin after I'd left to call Juan that night. Someone had found a dead body, had taken the bottles but left the marijuana, and had possibly taken Jaz's manuscript as well. As I had ridden Fresca home by moonlight, turning down Juan's offer to ride the horse back while Scott drove me home, I had felt relatively calm, considering the day's events. The huge orange moon rising above the eastern mesas would not have been nearly as mesmerizing if I had known that somewhere, maybe in the valley below, was Jaz's murderer, possibly someone who had seen me at the cabin. On the other hand, I reasoned, feeling my heart race, it was possible that there was no murder at all, that the chemical analysis would show that Jaz had experienced an allergic reaction or was taking some type of unusual medication or had eaten an exotic plant—wouldn't someone who was so poor that he cut the trees around his home for firewood be just as likely to experiment with eating the indigenous plants, perhaps unwittingly eating something poisonous?

Yet taken together—the unidentified substance in the autopsy report, the mysterious visitor, and the theft of the bottles—these elements suggested a less encouraging picture. I still had the tiny bottle I'd filched from the cabin; whatever was in it was something that someone had wanted badly enough to steal. A friend of mine taught in the science department of the local university, and although tomorrow was Sunday, he often spent his weekends working in his office. It was worth a drive into town tomorrow to see if I could enlist his help in identifying the bottle's contents.

Meanwhile, I wanted to touch base with Kit, just so I could report back to Juan and get her off his suspects list. Ahead, Jones was already taking the flagstone steps that led up to Kit's backyard two at a time. I called a loud hello as I reached the top, letting her know I was coming. Like me, Kit had opted to live without the dubious benefits of the telephone. For one thing, the cost of bringing the phone line this distance was prohibitive, but even with the advent of the cell phone, we had both decided to sacrifice convenience for privacy. Good manners on our mesa demanded that friendly outsiders on foot give a yell, drivers a beep or two of the horn. Along the flagstone walk leading to her door, the yard was tidy and flourishing, in spite of the drought. In fact, Kit had constructed it with an eye toward water conservation—instead of grass, there was a mosaic of cacti and other succulents interspersed with rocks painted to resemble animals—a menagerie of stone cats, armadillos, a beaver, frogs, turtles, rabbits, squirrels. Here and there, Kit had painted wooden sticks to create mock reptiles and arranged them strategically among the other animals and plants. In the garden between the house and the cliff, she used all types of natural mulches, to which Fresca herself unwittingly contributed, and she grew herbs, vegetables, and even a string of willows farther along the back, which she used to make baskets. A wheelbarrow piled with horse manure sat alongside the chicken-wire fence separating the garden from the yard. Several peahens clucked about, Kit's answer to the grasshopper problem during the drought.

As I reached the door, Jones was standing on his back legs, peering through its window and barking. I cupped my hands and looked, too, knocking loudly. On the third knock, the door flew open. Kit stood shining with sweat, six feet tall and stark naked, her hair wrapped turban-style in a white towel. Rivulets of sweats coursed between her melon-sized breasts.

"Hey, bud," she said, wiping the sweat out of her eyes with the back of a hand. "What's up?" She stepped back, inviting us into the house. It had been a decrepit, crumbling adobe until she'd moved in, braced the walls with new supports, and room by room reconstructed the old place. As always, I marveled at the black walls, mystified by how the light from the windows bounced and danced through the house. We followed her through the tiny kitchen with its hand-laid brick floor and into the front room made mostly of several floor-to-ceiling windows that Kit had installed herself and a floor of earth-colored Saltillo tiles. She took up a cross-legged sitting position on a towel in front of the open door of her wood-burning stove. The temperature in the room had to be at least a good twenty degrees above the ninety degrees outside. She leaned back, bracing herself on her arms, pointing her chin squarely at the ceiling. Jones took a step back from the heat, turned, and left the room. I followed him through the kitchen and let him outside.

Returning, I asked: "Is this some kind of ad hoc sauna, or are you doing penance?"

Motionless in front of me, Kit might have been posing for a steamy men's magazine. Though just on the upside of fifty, I guessed, she could give Tina Turner a run for her money. She opened one eye at me, the hazel one, and said, "Penance for what?"

"Got me." I leaned against the doorway, watching.

She closed her eye and pointed her chin back at the ceiling. "Cleansing. Indian stuff. Sweat lodge."

"Oh?" I was interested. "What's the occasion? You been to the big bad city lately?"

"Not a chance, bud," she quipped. "You're the one that deals on that scene. I was just feeling fuzzy, out of focus."

"Oh yeah? How come?"

"You writing a book?" she snapped. I hated her sarcasm.

"It wouldn't have anything to do with being at Jaz's funeral, would it?" I asked.

"That scumbag?" She bolted upright, opening the chocolate-brown eye as well as the hazel one. "Good fucking riddance. I went just to make sure he was really down for the count."

"Yeah, well." I wandered over to the window and sat on the wooden chaise Kit had built last year. On the other side of the glass, a yellow-striped stone tabby crouched over a tortoise whose back was painted in bright green squares. Perched on top of the tortoise sat a kangaroo mouse looking up at the cat with a jaunty grin. "Juan was just by."

Kit stood up, marched into the bathroom, and slammed the door. The shower came on for a few minutes, and then she returned with a blanket-sized white towel, wiping herself roughly.

"And he mentioned me?" She tucked the towel around her waist, Indian style, banged the stove door shut, and opened the bottom panels of the windows. Sitting on the floor facing me, straight-backed and cross-legged, she pulled her long hair across one shoulder and began braiding it.

I stretched out on the chaise, feeling soggy and hot in the jeans and shirt I'd worn to the funeral. I thought about taking them off. On the other hand, given the purpose of my visit, it seemed a little dishonest to get too comfortable. I could smell the odor of eucalyptus coming from Kit's body.

"Not exactly," I lied. "But I picked up that you and Jaz have not been the most agreeable of friends lately. I'd like to know more about it."

"Why is that, Jet?" She was still braiding, her head tilted back as she watched me through narrow slits.

"Hey, I have some vested interest here. I found him, you know."

"So?"

"So. I want to know how he died."

"Why? You didn't give a rat's ass about Jaz."

She was right, I didn't. But I did give a rat's ass about a murderer on the loose. And I gave a rat's ass about her. I wasn't at liberty to share Juan's information, though, so I parried. "I guess I'd just have to stick it in the category of loose ends. My obsessive-compulsive side coming out."

"Mmnh." She was using her teeth to pull a rubber band from around her wrist and wind it around the end of the braid, leaving a paintbrush tuft at the end that she tossed back over her shoulders. "I can tell you what I know," she said, looking up toward the corners of the ceiling. She brought her gaze back to me. "But I don't like talking about him or even thinking about him. And I'd be lying if I said I wasn't happy that he's not taking up space on the planet anymore. If you get my gist."

"Got it." Kit was starting to wind up. Any other time, I would have been searching for ways to divert her into calmer waters. But considering my assignment, I kept quiet and listened.

"You remember when you were gone, I wrote you about the Water Project, how I heard they were setting up measuring devices along the river?"

"Mmm-hm. Not clear on the details, though."

"Well, it's simple enough." She was sitting lotus-style, her back perfectly straight, eyes closed. The towel had fallen from around her waist, and her pubic hair was a nest of light-brown curls between her legs. I was trying to imagine her on the witness stand. "Two things were going on at the same time, overlapping, so that it *seemed* very complex when, in fact, I don't believe it's this gigantically complicated issue that every one thinks. My theory is that this 'complication factor' is just smoke." She inhaled deeply several times, exhaling slowly, her breasts rising and falling. I recognized the routine as part of the biofeedback and imaging techniques she'd been using for a couple of years now, methods for controlling her anxiety—and her temper. "First, there's what's called the Pecos Water Development Project. It goes back a ways, to when the United States took some water from Mexico, via the Colorado, and now it's payback time. It's coming out of the Pecos though, because people in California have more moxie."

"Kit's opinion or fact?"

"It's a crap shoot, isn't it?"

I sighed. "Never mind. So then what?"

"Well, they looked around at some other options—the Rio Grande was the obvious choice. But the bottom line is, it got shoved over to us because we're the poor cousins. Like in the old days when they decided southern New Mexico was just a dandy spot for the first nuclear test site, or like lately when it's just perfect for the nation's first nuclear waste dump. Same old shit. It doesn't change, it just gets deeper."

"So you believe there's a water shortage problem ahead?" I said, drawing Kit back to the subject at hand.

"You don't have to be a scientist to look at the river and see how bad things are already. What do you think a thirty percent decrease will do?"

"Thirty percent? Holy shit!" I remembered the piles of dead and rotting fish I'd seen along the riverbed.

"You're *so-o-o* articulate." She frowned at me and snorted. "But for articulate, read the official stuff put out by the government or whoever writes that baloney. Schmaltz. Pure bullshit. According to them, you won't even know that thirty percent's missing. I got a stack of stuff on it, if you're interested in the details and the whos and whens. But it's pretty much water under the bridge now, so to speak." She pointed at a stack of papers beside the chaise. On top of the pile was a letter written on Sangre de Cristo Laboratory letterhead with a black jagged line that could have been a bolt of lightning or the silhouette of a mountain skyline, overlaid with the Zia, the New Mexico state symbol.

"This Tuesday they'll be signing the final papers. Then it's a done deal. The fat lady sings and all that."

"Maybe I'll take a look at the stuff you've got on it. So what's the rest of the story? Where is Jaz in all this?"

"The plot thickens. Begin part two," Kit said. I waited for her to quit inhaling and exhaling. "The government had to show that water could be taken from the Pecos without damage to the countryside and the communities. So they employed a local research company outside of Santa Fe, the Sangre de Cristo Laboratory, to make a study of the river. The water level had to be monitored at various points to document the rise and fall as adjustments were being made to irrigation flow and to limiting community access. Water quality had to be tested. Stuff like that. So the Lab went to work doing all the research and presented their assessment. According to them, no problem."

"But you don't believe it. Why not?"

"Lots of reasons. But start with this one. I wanted to see the official statistics, the actual studies that were done, a list of when and where and all that, and not just the bullshit summaries the government sent around. Those statistics are supposed to be public record. I went through all the proper channels," she said, making a sour face, "to get them. Guess what?" She looked at me expectantly. "I'm still waiting."

"What's the problem?"

"You name it. There's a long list. First, I had to fill out several days' worth of forms. In person. They sent the request back a couple of times asking for clarification, just crap. Then my request was lost, so I had to start over, do it all again. This took about three months. When the materials came through, it was the wrong stuff. So I had to put in another request with more details. Then the request was lost again, then sent to the wrong address, then...get the picture?"

"Red tape. It happens." I thought about the problems I had in California trying to get the paperwork straightened out on my job contract which required an actual, original social security card that I hadn't seen in years. That created all kinds of problems, and finally, in order to receive my paychecks, I had been forced to apply for a second, temporary card. That issue was still unresolved.

"So they say," Kit went on, "but the fact remains, the public has been *told* that the reports show the decreased amount of water won't have any visible effects, but to my knowledge, no one has seen the actual studies and figures. No one."

"Well, someone must have seen them. Surely there's a way." I'm a die-hard rationalist, which sometimes makes me very naive, but I knew that whatever Kit's shortcomings in some areas, she was extremely thorough and maddeningly persistent.

"That's what I thought. I got together a grassroots movement, I wrote you about it, and we caused enough ruckus to get the attention of the media. The Channel 4 news even sent out a reporter to one of our demonstrations, and I had my moment on the telly." She smiled broadly at me, the tendons of her long neck tight as piano strings as she twirled the end of her braid like a lasso.

"And?"

"What you'd expect. They followed our spot with a thirty-second response from Whutzit Cruz, the head honcho at the Lab. He said the reports were available to anyone who wanted them, and that he'd personally make sure I got a copy."

"But you didn't?"

"Oh, I did, I did. When Cruz speaks, God listens. That was the material with the wrong stuff. Well, it was kind of the right stuff, but not really, not the updated figures, not the locations of the checkpoints, not anything that would prove their contention about the water loss being harmless. Not the information I'd asked for.

But by then, we'd had our day. We couldn't get the media back. We couldn't get jack shit."

"So where is Jaz in all this?"

"I'm getting to him," Kit said. She stretched her arms above her head, doing side bends, leaning to one side and then another. "When we couldn't get the list of the checkpoint locations, we started combing the river, trying to find them." She stretched left, her arm curving in an arc over her head, then gave a couple of extra bounces toward the floor. "You know how hard that is?" she said, stretching straight up and then right. "Try following the river for even a mile, not to mention several hundred." Her eyes, which had been closed, flew open, angry and accusing, as her torso lay nearly parallel to the floor.

"And you found a checkpoint at Jaz's place?" I asked, beginning to feel dizzy as Kit came upright again, then stretched left, bounce, bounce.

"Well, I saw him foxing around out there, messing with some kind of gizmo he had by the river behind his house." She closed her eyes. Up, stretch right, bounce.

"You saw him? You just drove over there, caught him in the river, said 'Hi Jaz'?" She put her arms akimbo behind her head, still doing side bends, aiming her elbows toward the floor. "Not exactly." Bend right, bounce. "I was hiking on the mesa above the river where he lives, and I had a pair of binoculars."

"You've been *spying* on him?"

Her eyes popped open again. "I wouldn't call it spying, exactly," she said, dropping her arms and sitting straight up. "I just happened to be walking by. And anyway," she paused, wide-eyed, her voice suddenly shrill, "how the fuck are we supposed to know the checkpoints, what's supposed to be public knowledge, if we can't even get the list? We have a right to know." Kit was screaming, her face red with anger.

"All right, all right," I said, holding up a hand. She started in on her breathing exercises. "So you *suspected* Jaz of working for the Lab. I mean, for all you know, he might have been raising guppies back there or something, right? And even if he was working for the Lab, so what?"

44

"So *this*. Lots of folks are damned pissed about losing their water. Some buy the Lab's story, some don't. But anyone actually working for the Lab on this water issue isn't going to win any Brownie points around here. And something else," she said, pausing for drama. "Think about it. Think about someone like Jaz doing work requiring exact measurements. He's sloshed to the gills ninety percent of the time. Is this the kind of data the Lab is basing their studies on?"

"Okay, I can see why you're concerned." I could also see holes as big as the Grand Canyon in her reasoning.

"But wait. That's not the end of it," she said, as though she'd read my thoughts. "We have reason to believe there is also some kind of...mmm," she said, looking around as though the word she wanted might be written in the air, "...experimentation on the water going on."

"Oh, *we* do? And just *why* do *we* believe this?" Sweat was trickling down the back of my neck, and my T-shirt was dark with sweat. The room was still sweltering hot from the stove and the sun slanting through the passive solar windows.

Kit smiled a little. "Lots of people around here don't bother to put up curtains, you know."

Time to worry—when Kit resorted to non sequiturs, trouble was close by. I sat up and faced her. "Are you saying you've not only been using binoculars to spy on people, but you've been peeping in windows as well? Is that what you're telling me? I hope you got some photos while you were at it, because if you didn't, you're on pretty shaky ground here."

"Well I wasn't exactly putting a case together for the grand jury. I was just trying to find out what was going on," she said, her voice rising with an edge of defensiveness.

"And?"

Kit shrugged and looked crestfallen. "It's hard to tell, Jet. We got the media to ask them about any other experimentation, but you can't expect them to come right out and say, 'Oh yeah, sure, we're adding a little plutonium and radiation to see how far into Mexico it goes.' "

"I have to tell you, this sounds pretty far-fetched," I said, standing up as she started in on forward bends. "Where did you get this idea about water experiments?" I went into the kitchen and fixed us some iced tea from a jug sitting in the old round-cornered refrigerator. I knew that this wouldn't be anything as common as Lipton. Kit preferred mysterious teas made from her own herbs. As I gathered two glasses and filled them with ice, I noticed the small plants flourishing on glass shelves placed across the window near the sink. Some looked like furry grey mosses, with minuscule yellow flowers; others had a fountain of purple spore-like growths shooting up from the center. One specimen had dusky green leaves with purple veins and looked very much like belladonna, a highly lethal plant more commonly known as deadly nightshade. Just looking at it gave me the willies. I poured the pale tea over ice and carried the glasses back into the living room where Kit was talking and bending forward like some crazed supplicant.

"...and while I had the binoculars out, I just happened to see some kind of something along the river over behind that guy Becker's place, and then I remembered hearing about him being connected way back when to the Sangre de Cristo Lab, and..."

"Hey, break time," I said, handing her the glass of tea. "And I vote we move outside."

"Good idea." She snagged a long, gauzy, gold-colored dress hanging by the door and tossed it over her head as we left the house. Outside, the late-afternoon sun cast long shadows, leaving us a broad section of shade along the edge of the cliff beside the garden. Kit and I sat facing out over the river and valley below.

"See, right over there," she said, bending forward and pointing north.

"What?" The knot of black clouds had grown larger, more menacing, and toward the east a trail of dark smoke drifted up along the horizon.

"There, where the trees have started to turn yellow, down by the river?"

"Mmm." I took a sip of the tea and felt every taste bud in my mouth wither. When I tried to swallow, the tea stopped halfway down and expanded to hairball proportion.

"That's just this side of Becker's place, on down past where Jaz lives. Lived. That's where I found out about the experiments." Kit raised her glass and sipped the tea as though it were some rare velvet liqueur.

I was beginning to understand that Kit's method of inspecting the river had not involved walking every foot of it. "You saw him doing experiments through the binoculars too?" I asked, my voice reduced to a whisper.

"Well, that required an on-the-spot inspection," she said with a smile. "I couldn't get a really clear view through the glasses, and I was curious. So I just kind of wandered by his house, you know, hoping maybe he wouldn't be there and I could get a closer look at the river."

"I take it you found him home?" I said. My mouth was dry and pulsing, and my head had begun to ache.

"Yup," she said, "and that is one weird dude." Kit gave a shudder and rolled her eyes. "I think I gave him quite a shock when I knocked on his door that day." I was trying to imagine Becker, infamous for his reclusiveness, opening his door to find a six-foot Amazon out in the wilderness where he lived. This was a fellow who frightened small children in the aisles of the grocery store on his rare visits into town, and who had allegedly shot at local reporters who sought him out after his daughter's suicide several years back.

"I can't believe you actually dropped in on Jim Becker," I said, shaking my head. "You really need a keeper."

"Well, before he had a chance to push me back on the porch and shut the door behind him, I got a glimpse inside his place. There was this kind of weird apparatus set up in his kitchen. Like here's Doc Frankenstein out in the New Mexico outback, you know?" Kit downed the last of her tea and set the empty glass on the ground by her chair, giving me a look of great satisfaction. "It was only later that I put it together. There's something in the river behind his house, and he's got some kind of experiments going on inside. It has to be for the Lab. Don't you see?"

"What I see," I said, watching a peahen clucking our way, her head turned to fix us with one beady yellow eye, "is that your imagination can get you in a world of trouble." The hen stretched her neck toward Kit's glass, pecking among the ice cubes. Suddenly her speckled lid dropped over her eye and she stood stock still. Then, with a great flapping of wings, she recoiled backward as though she'd been shot before reeling off toward the garden. "What the hell do you put in this stuff, anyway?" I asked, holding up my glass of tea.

She snatched it from me and took a large gulp. "Goldenseal, among other things, grown from my very own stock," she said. She downed the rest of the tea, threw out the cubes, and pulled a small drum from under her chair. She gripped the instrument between her thighs and began tapping out a staccato rhythm across the drumhead.

My throat was parched, I was sticky with sweat, and the drumbeats were roughly in the same measure as the headache at the base of my skull. I leaned my head back against the chair and tried to remember what I'd come for. "Okay. So basically you think Jaz was working for the Lab, and maybe Becker as well. And that's it?"

"Yeah," she said, drumming as she spoke. "When I saw Jaz in the bar the other night, I decided to ask him what he had in the river behind his house. He was pretty tanked, there's a surprise, so I thought maybe I could get him to talk. He was sitting over at the end of the bar, next to the popcorn machine where he gets his free meals, and Metz was sitting next to him, so I sat down next to Metz and kind of worked myself into their conversation. Such as it was." Kit did a drum roll that lifted my headache to somewhere around the level of the lower cerebellum.

"Apparently it was pretty memorable. Juan heard about it, anyway."

"Yeah, it escalated." Kit had put down the drum and now lounged in the chair with her long legs stretched out in front of her, slapping the end of her braid against the palm of her hand. She was looking down with rapture at the pigtail.

"I hear you threatened to kill him."

"Might have," she said. She plucked the rubber band off the braid and began unraveling it, meticulously separating each of the three strands. Somewhere above, a high-pitched *skree-e-e* tore through the silence, a hawk cruising for supper. Kit finished unbraiding her hair and combed her fingers through it. When she stood up, she towered over where I sat, facing me with her back to the cliff and her hair flying electrified around her. "It's no secret that Jaz and I disagreed on everything from apples to zeitgeist, and last week's fight wasn't any worse, or any better, than the last ten or twenty. It was just business as usual."

There was a certain amount of truth here—I had witnessed Jaz in his cups at the Inn more than once. He had probably been drinking mescal, those were the worst times. It was then that his mad pale eyes would shine like fire through the dirty hair hanging over his forehead. But he never slurred his words as he held his glass up like some ancient Latin pontificator, spewing forth his opinions in the sonorous tones of Truth. Unwitting tourists sharing after-dinner drinks would stop talking, look up, watch this man, and later tell their friends in California and New York and Wisconsin about the mad poet, the evil maestro of New Mexico who described a planet free of polluting blacks, browns, reds, women, Jews, and whatever else tweaked him at the moment. And sooner or later, someone would rise to the bait.

"He said that my painting was contrived, my lifestyle inconsequential, and my sexuality questionable at best." Kit was beginning to pant slightly. "That miserable fucking windbag has the sensitivity of a lead brick."

"Had," I ventured.

"What?"

"Had," I said, "past tense. As in, 'no longer living.' "

"Fuck tense. Fuck 'no longer living.' Fuck that crazy bastard and good riddance," Kit said, her voice shrill with hysteria. The sun had dropped behind the mesas, casting a red glow across the valley and the mountains to the east. Kit towered over me, her hair sizzling in the blood-colored sunset.

I cleared my throat and started to speak.

"Just don't say it, Jet." She held up both hands, palms out. "I didn't kill the motherfucker, if that's what you think. And if that's what Juan thinks, he'll just have to find something better than that night in the bar." Jones had come leaping up the stairs while Kit was talking. He sat panting beside the flagstone path, his strange colorless eyes watching us both.

"So that's it, that's all of it?" My headache climbed another couple of notches till it was right behind my eyes, and I was having trouble concentrating.

Kit paused, drew herself up in a long intake of breath, and glowered. "Well, what do you think? I took my voodoo doll out and put a hex on him?" She sighed and sank back into the lawn chair. Jones stretched out by the stairs, his muzzle on his paws, still watching from the black mask surrounding his eyes.

"What I think is that Juan wouldn't make a trip out here for nothing, would he?" I asked. Kit stared out over the valley, her jaw set in a hard line. "Would he?" I asked, more loudly.

"Okay, one more thing." Kit leaned her head back, her eyes closed and her long throat bared to the sky. She sat that way in silence for a moment, and I waited. The light was draining from the day, and the horizon above the eastern mesas was turning dark. The peahens had left the yard for the day, clucking back toward the shelters that Kit had built for them behind the house. I watched the exposed flesh of Kit's neck, and I saw her swallow before she spoke. "I had heard, through the grapevine let's say, that Jaz might have some mushrooms, some really good stuff that he was growing, you know?" Kit rolled her head slightly toward me, checking my reaction. We were on dangerous ground. Our agreement was no alcohol or drugs on the property. Kit picked up the drum.

"First, let me say this." She worked the drum skin softly under her fingertips, trilling out a gentle rhythm. "I was right in the middle of something really good, the best piece I'd ever done. But last week I got stuck. I felt I needed something at that point." She stopped drumming and reached over to lay a cool hand over mine. "I wanted to see that vision again, the one I'd started off working on. Like the Indians and their peyote, you know? Maybe I didn't need it, but I thought I did. And..." she looked sideways at me from under the canopy of hair. Her hand squeezed mine tightly.

"Go on." I pulled my hand away.

"Well, I heard something about Jaz having some major great stuff. I was *desperate* to finish this piece." She was biting her bottom lip. Her teeth were very white, with a gap between the two front ones. Her lips were full and the color of pecans. "I dropped by his place thinking he might sell me some. You know he never remembers what he says when he's drunk. I figured the worst that could happen was that he'd say no. You've got to see how important this piece was to me, Jet."

"Oh, Jesus. You went to Jaz's place? When?"

"Well, last Sunday night was our main event at the Inn. So it was the next day, Monday."

"You *drove* over there?" I remembered Juan telling me someone had visited Jaz after I left. He would have examined all the tire tracks, and he had probably already matched up the set that belonged to Kit's Jeep. Was hers also the set that came after I had left Jaz's cabin the night he died?

"Yeah, my broomstick was in the shop." She looked at me curiously for a moment before continuing. "He was there, but 'most indisposed,' as he put it. He was sitting on the bed when I walked in, drunk as a fucking skunk, and said that first he wanted a 'piece of *my* action' to 'seal the deal.' Nobody ever accused him of being stupid—he knew his secret would be safe if that was our method of payment. But I wasn't that desperate. He got raunchy, abusive, even started for me. He wasn't much to put down; he's thin as a stick, plus he must have been drinking all day to get that wiped out. So I left. That's all. That's it. Nada, nothing else."

I believed Kit—imagining her and Jaz as the two-backed beast was a comedy in itself, about as likely as seeing a coyote mating with a snake. Still, this had happened Monday, just two days before Jaz's death. It was possible that Kit was the last person, besides me, to see Jaz alive. I put the issue of drugs on hold for the time being. We would have to thrash that out later. Right now, my head was pounding unmercifully, and all I wanted to do was go home.

"Okay," I said, getting up and wandering toward the stairs where Jones lay. I didn't want to say what I had to say next. "Kit," I said, turning to face her. She was tapping on the drum again. "I have to ask you this. It's the reason I think Juan showed up today."

"He thinks I might have done old Jaz in?" Her voice was joking, but our eyes locked. She banged the drum loudly a few times, shooting hot pains through my head.

When she finished, I walked back to her. "Yeah," I said, "I think that just might be the direction he's going."

Kit sat quietly, her hair glowing in the sunset. She turned her face up to me, and I reached down, smoothing the damp hair from her forehead. Her hazel eye glittered green and moist.

"Do you think it might get serious?" she asked in a low voice.

I paused, stroking her forehead. "I think it's possible," I said.

"Oh fuck!" She gave the drum a sharp bang and leapt out of the chair in a blaze of wild hair, stomping toward her garden.

I descended the stairs, Jones at my heels, and from behind me, through the sharp, searing pain at the base of my skull, I could hear Kit humming "Amazing Grace."

Morgan

*O*N THE TOPSIDE OF THE EARTH, *there is no such thing as true darkness. You can only get that if you go down under, into the caves. The same is true of people.*

Tonight the sky is black, thrown with clouds. The landscape that had seemed invisible after I switched off the headlights gradually returns. At first it is just the edge of objects that bloom, but if you are patient, you can watch them fill with detail after detail. Patience is the thing. And time.

Sound is another myth—it is not present unless it is invited. It comes from touching. There is nothing more effortless than silence. So that easing myself from the MG, closing its door, making my way through the terrain, sifting between trees and rocks and cacti, among the ravens and the night animals which sleep and the reptiles and the night creatures who don't, ascending the side of the mesa toward the woman's house, none of this took effort. Only patience and time. The one limitless, perhaps the other as well.

I stand at the head of the sloping driveway, kneeling to stroke the husky, and together we watch the house below, where the woman sleeps. It is strangely shaped, as though moving through the earth toward the river whose running sound is eloquent and embroidered in the air. We watch the shadow, man-shaped, drifting from one window to another, approaching and regressing, like a moth testing a flame, at once clumsy and agile. He is working his way toward the door.

I begin to descend along the path with the husky alongside, and we stop beneath a tree, a few yards before we reach the man who is crouched before the door. I pat the husky along his shoulder, and he walks on farther, sitting on his haunches behind the man who is turning the doorknob. He growls, deep inside the wolf part of him. The man freezes. He turns and sees the dog—but he does not see me.

5

"WHO IS IT?"

I flew straight up in bed, showering cats in all directions, staring into the darkness. My mind was a panic of empty space, a free fall of nameless, faceless pandemonium. I couldn't remember who I was or where I was—and then I began to grasp the contour of the windows, the faint panes of the French doors, and to place myself firmly on the mesa in New Mexico.

My ears still echoed a mysterious sound that had cut through my sleep. Jones, who usually slept across the foot of the bed, was gone. I threw my legs over the side of the bed facing the French doors and the sun deck that circled the second story. I sat perfectly still, waiting for the sound to come again. Nothing. I tiptoed to the doors and cupped my hands against the glass. The night was black, and I could make out only the vague pale shapes of the white table and chairs on the deck. I opened the doors, letting in the cool night air, and listened again. There was the river, of course, always the river, but nothing else—not the blood-mad shrieking of a coyote pack or the drowsy stomp of horse hooves, no barks or hoots or feline caterwaul.

"Jet? Jet Butler?"

I suppose my heart must nearly have stopped in shock. But my first thought was pure vanity: what a picture I cut, standing in the doorway of my bedroom, holding open the French doors, stark naked. And then I saw Jones—sitting, facing me at the head of the stairway that led up to the deck, with a pale hand stroking his head.

"Who's there?" I fought to keep my voice from shaking and my body from slamming shut the doors. I stretched backward and snatched the top sheet off the bed, covering myself.

"My name's Caroline Marcus." It was a woman's voice like those of women in old movies, the silver-screen sirens with dark hair draped across one eye. "Sorry if I've frightened you." A shape began to materialize out of the darkness, a tall column standing next to Jones who padded over to me and shoved his cold nose at the palm of my hand. "It's very important that I speak with you. If I could just have a few minutes, I can explain."

The voice floated, disembodied, a voice that could calm a nervous horse or seduce a cowboy. Jones leaned against my leg. I wound the sheet around me, toga fashion, tucking the end over my breasts, and stepped barefoot across the threshold onto the deck, the sheet trailing. I kept the table between us. My pulse had slowed, but my hands still trembled, and although I strained to see into the shadows, I could make out only that she was tall, thin, apparently dressed in tight-fitting dark clothes, and either dark-haired or wearing a cap. Her face hovered, a pale smudge in the night.

"I didn't mean to frighten you," she repeated in her smoky voice, as we stood facing each another across the deck for what seemed like a long time. And in some ways, that first moment between us seems caught in a frieze, outside of time, so that I can recall it as though it were a photograph: she, dark and slim below the great creamy cornucopia of stars; me, wrapped around and trailing folds of white sheet as Jones stood between us, looking first at one and then the other.

"There didn't seem to be any other way to speak to you privately," she said, breaking the silence and moving forward. I heard her pull out a chair from the table.

"Who are you?" My own voice flew out, too high and skittering around the deck like a mad bat. She sat down, and I was no longer frightened, only curious. I pulled out a chair and sat facing her, waiting. Noche, a small black Manx, leapt to my lap and began scratching at the folds of the sheet. I stroked her head while she made a nest for herself and curled into it.

"New Mexico's beautiful, isn't it? Magical, even," said the voice as though we were having afternoon tea. It was well past the cocktail hour, and New Mexico was dark except for a scattering of lights in the valley below and an occasional headlight from the freeway. I repressed a testy response, trying to figure whether my visitor was simply nervous or perhaps deranged, drugged, or some eccentric air-headed tourist. I remembered that she had known my name, so I curbed my irritation and started counting. I was well past ten when she said, "I nearly came with Jasper when he moved here, how long ago? Ten years? Fifteen? A long time ago."

"Jasper?" I asked, but I knew she was referring to Jaz. And in that same instant, I knew she would belong to the silver sports car I had seen at the funeral, and that she would be the visitor from California Juan had mentioned, "Jaz's ex."

"Jasper, Jaz you call him. He was a beautiful man, like a god."

By the sound of her voice and because my eyes were adjusting to the night, I could tell she was gazing away from me, toward the river. I saw that she was wearing a dark turtleneck that fit tightly under the chin. Her profile revealed a high forehead, a straight nose, and a strong chin that she propped on one hand. She was not wearing a cap; her hair was dark, pulled back tight at the back of her neck. And then suddenly I heard what she had said.

"Jaz? Beautiful?" My last image of Jaz came to mind. His madman's eyes glittering behind strings of greasy hair. His emaciated body stretched across the dirt floor of his cabin.

"I'll never forget the first day I saw him," she said. This time the voice was full of distance and nostalgia. "It was 1974, and I was a freshman at Berkeley. He was teaching the world literature course I had signed up for, and the way he talked about the course, the writers we would read, made the whole room light up. Then he told a personal story about reading all seven volumes of Proust one summer in Paris. It was a late-afternoon class, and there was a window on one side of the room where the sun was coming in. His hair wasn't just yellow, it was golden, and every girl in the room was spellbound." Jones had gone to lie across the top of the stairs, and the cats were coming out of hiding after their fright. The yellow tiger-stripe leapt into my lap, setting Noche off into a hissing fit.

After the yellow cat had been routed, Noche shook herself and set-tled back in. Caroline Marcus barely paused. "After class, I went up to where he was talking to students at the head of the classroom. When he discovered I was a freshman, he explained that I needed a prerequisite, a freshman composition course, in order to take his class. He was very nice about it, almost apologetic, standing behind the podium, pointing out to me the section in the catalog where the composition courses were listed. I told him I was already enrolled in one of those, the one he taught right after the lit class. He laughed then, and he let me stay in. I knew he was wonderful that first day."

She recited a long story, punctuated with pauses, silences. Put unkindly, male professors like Jasper Blankenship seduce female students like Caroline Marcus on every campus across the country, where a certain percentage of the professorate have wives who were once their students. With mind-numbing regularity, like that of lemming making their run to the sea, each semester unfolds this weary melodrama—so familiar that most faculty have ceased to be embarrassed, and most wives no longer bother with divorce. In this version, one of the common variations, Student did not marry Professor. Instead, Jaz had taken to his heels, disappeared into the outback of New Mexico.

"He said that this rift in his life, when his wife left him and took their son, was a good time to break away from all the things he had bought into and had come to regret." She had turned away from the river toward me, her hands clasped on the table. "So he quit his job, said he was going to write. He just disappeared."

My attention had wandered, and I repressed a yawn. No mat-ter; I knew my cues. "But you were in love with him?" I asked rhetorically, trying to scrape away the surface of the Jaz Blankenship I remembered and see him as she described. It was a stretch. When I tried to wrestle him down into the Adonis position, he fought back. More realistic was the Jaz Blankenship climbing the stairs to join us, perching on the guardrail behind Caroline Marcus, and leering foul-breathed over her unsuspecting shoulder. His legs dangled; his burial clothes reeked of the grave, and their tatters waved in a sudden breeze that carried the odor of rotting flesh in my direction. I gagged.

"Yes, I loved him," she said, oblivious to the ogling face just inches from her own. "But I couldn't get through to him..." Her voice had turned soggy. Somehow, maybe reinforced by the propaganda of television and cinema, Caroline Marcus had kept her dream of young love pristine. I was amazed—not so much at how long the past could keep its hands knotted around your neck, I knew too well how that could happen, but at the shabbiness of her shrine and the empty years and wasted energy she must have devoted to preserving it.

Jaz leaned in closer, cheek to cheek with Caroline, fixing me with his mad, bulging eyes. I felt a sudden chill. In spite of the sweltering days, New Mexico nights are cold. But it was more than the night air that was poking an icy finger at my bones, and it was more than talk of Jaz Blankenship that was calling up memories of my own that wouldn't stay buried.

"...by then, and with Jasper gone, Berkeley seemed empty," Caroline Marcus was saying, "so I decided to transfer someplace with fewer memories. I finished up my degree in L.A. and got on as a junior editor at *Western Writers*, a small magazine that specializes in contemporary west coast writers. That's kept me pretty busy over the years."

Another cue. "Husband? Kids?" I asked. Jaz's image was beginning to dissolve, leaving behind the odor of putrefying flesh.

"No," said Caroline, impervious to the ripe, empty air, "just your garden-variety professional. No time for anything but work. But it's interesting and demanding and I like what I do. I think maybe some people are meant to live solitary lives, and I'm one of those." A coyote howled in the distance, and Jones sat up at attention, looking through the slats in the guardrail. Noche shifted position in my lap, and when the howl became a chorus of high-pitched yips, she stood with her front feet on the table and peered out into the darkness. Jones joined the chorus, turning his muzzle to the sky and launching into a bone-chilling wolf's howl that stretched across the valley. Caroline Marcus was lost in her own thoughts, deaf to whatever tragedy was in progress out on the mesa. She stared down at her hands clasped on the table. Her voice had sounded tired, and I realized that, like me, she had also recently come from California, possibly driving with the same breakneck urgency that I had just a few days before. Another foul-smelling breeze drifted past, and I had the fleeting notion that Jaz was now leering across my own shoulder, ogling this morsel from his past.

"So how did you find out about Jaz? About his death?" I asked. The back of my neck was tingling, and my skin had turned to gooseflesh.

"I already knew he was living somewhere in New Mexico," she said. "A couple of years ago, he sent an article in to the magazine where I work, not knowing I was there. By then, I was reviewing most of the fiction and poetry when it came through, so I saw his piece. I wrote back, and we've been in touch off and on ever since. Strictly business. We kind of pretend," she paused, "...pretended that nothing had happened between us."

I listened while I pried Noche carefully from my lap and set her on the table. Like most Manx cats, she had the jungle still running in her blood, and more than once she had demonstrated her dislike of being treated like a domestic tabby with a slash of her claws. She especially disliked being picked up and moved about. I felt my way into the bedroom where the red numbers on the digital clock showed 3:39, grabbed a blanket, and threw it around my shoulders. "You cold?" I asked, returning to the table. "Want a blanket?"

"I'm fine," she said, both hands engaged in kneading Noche's ears. The tiny cat was curled on the table in front of her, purring with the delicacy of a tractor in mud.

"Well, I'm sorry about you and Jaz," I said, dumbfounded by Noche's sudden docility. "He never talked about his past, so I imagine you'll be quite a revelation to anyone here who knew him." If she was intent on seeing where Jaz had lived, or maybe was waiting for a cut of the will, there wasn't much I could say to prepare her. She seemed like the hot water and central heat type to me. I pulled my legs up under the blanket and rubbed at my toes to warm them, wondering for the first time just how Jaz *had* written all those years. In spite of the fact that this was the most frequent question that writers get asked, I had never thought of how Jaz had managed to write in his cabin—pen, pencil, chalk and blackboard? I dimly recalled seeing a kerosene lamp sitting among the litter on his table. But no paper, no writing instruments at all.

"Did he, uh..." Caroline began, apparently at a loss to continue. I was trying to figure out what was coming next. "Did he have a...uh, girlfriend, anyone...you know?"

Ah, the green-eyed monster. "Not anyone I knew about," I said, remembering Kit's last experience with him. "You should know, I wasn't particularly close to Jaz. We talked when we ran into each other, maybe once a month when I saw him at the Inn, the local bar where he hung out. But I've been gone since January, so I'm not your best source of information. In fact, I'm not sure why..."

"Why I'm here?" she asked, finishing my sentence. She was hugging herself, her hands caught under her arms. "Well, first, I knew from reading the paper that you were the last one to speak to him, that you were there when he..." She paused, searching for a word.

"Died." I helped her past mortuary euphemisms.

"Yes. Well, as I said, Jaz and I had been in contact off and on for a couple of years. In fact, I've been putting together a special issue for the magazine, a feature on writers in exile. A few months ago, he sent me a chapter from the book he's been writing, thinking I might be able to work it in." She stopped as though waiting for a response. I shrugged.

"You see," she continued, "after I read the chapter he sent, I understood that he might be calling it fiction, but actually he was writing his memoirs. The chapter he sent me was about me and him, about his wife and his marriage, about leaving it all and how he was able to do that. It wasn't particularly flattering, not at all the way I remember it. But, worst of all, it was a harrowing portrait of his marriage."

"Really?" The skepticism burned like acid in my voice, and I could almost hear Jaz's scathing diatribes against the autobiographical novel as he and I, over mescal and Perrier respectively, sparred off in our separate writerly camps: to my passionate belief that the best writers must write themselves, as Joyce and Lowry had proved, Jaz would fly into a condemnation of "confessional school schmaltz." Had Jaz been lying all these years, or was Caroline Marcus lying now? And if so, why?

"Really," she said. "I was hurt and offended by the way Jaz presented our relationship. But if his wife, or rather ex-wife, ever saw it, she would be crushed. Worse, if his son saw it, that would be the end for him." Noche stood up and arched her back, rubbing herself against Caroline's arm as though she were in heat. Before I could stop her, Caroline picked up the cat and tossed it across her shoulder like a baby while she left the table and paced along the guardrail. I waited for the inevitable, for Noche to slash out at this great insult. But the cat remained docile, drooping like a pelt as Caroline patted her back. "You see, I've kept in contact with friends we had in Berkeley," she continued. "I know his wife had a breakdown, was in an institution for several years, and that the son, just starting college himself now, has had a tough time of it. In fact, the magazine's published some of his poetry, and we've become friends in our correspondence. He doesn't know I ever knew his father, of course. He's, well, he's delicately balanced. He doesn't need to read Jasper's version of reality back then. He doesn't have a clue about where his dad is, or that he's dead. And, believe me, he doesn't want to know."

There was probably no particular reason why he had to know—it wasn't like he was losing a big inheritance or missing out on knowing some great paragon of virtue. In addition, if a relative did pop up somewhere, probably what he'd get was a bill from the state for burial expenses. "I see your point," I said carefully, "but I still don't understand why you're here."

"You mean in New Mexico, or here tonight, with you?"

"Both."

"When I didn't hear back from Jaz about the article, I gave a call to a number he'd given me. A fellow named Metz. That's when I found out he'd died. I...It was a shock. You know, some people you just think you'll see again." She shook her head, and I saw that her hair was very long and she had tied it back into a ponytail that hung down past her waist. Noche was still draped over her shoulder, purr motor roaring. "Before I could even think, I was in the car and driving. Now that I'm here, it seems crazy, but that's how it happened. I got here just in time for the burial, so I really didn't get to see him again, even dead."

"And here, tonight?" I pulled the blanket more tightly around me. It had just occurred to me that we could have been sitting inside, out of the chill, but now what I wanted first and foremost was to be back in bed. I was sleepy and getting grumpier about it by the minute.

"Well, I've talked to the sheriff about me and Jasper," she said, turning to me, stroking Noche. "I told him I'd been waiting for a piece Jasper was doing for the magazine, but he said he doesn't know anything about it. He acted a little strangely when I brought up the manuscript, and I realized that whatever information he had might be confidential. So then I thought maybe, since you saw him last and the newspaper said you're a writer, too, you might know something about the manuscript for his novel, or at least have seen it when you were there at his place that day. I just, you know, want to make sure it doesn't fall into the wrong hands."

"I see." The manuscript again. It was then that I remembered the noise that had awakened me. Had it been Jones barking? Maybe, but I didn't think so. Whatever the sound had been, I wondered what would have happened if I had slept through it. Had this woman dressed in black standing across from me, whose face I could still not clearly make out in the dark, intended to search the contents of my house for a manuscript? "So, you want to find Jaz's novel," I said. "Want to edit it a little, is that it?"

"I wouldn't put it quite that way," she said. She lifted Noche from her shoulder, leaned over to place the cat softly on the table in front of me, and I caught the ghost of a smile flicker across her face in the darkness before she leaned back. "I would just hate to see the manuscript read by the wrong people." I had the uneasy feeling that she was watching me closely from where she stood by the railing of the deck.

Noche wobbled unsteadily on the table for a moment, then shook herself before leaping down and disappearing.

"Afraid I can't help you. I knew Jaz was writing, of course, but I didn't see the manuscript that day. I don't have any idea where it could be. Sorry." I was shivering again, and I stood up and walked toward the stairs.

"I understand," Caroline said, following my lead. "I just thought I might be able to save the boy some grief just in case it turned up. But I guess if no one's found a manuscript, there's no problem, is there?" Jones had followed, too, his tail curled over his back and wagging. Even as we stood only several feet apart at the head of the stairs, her face was still a patchwork of shadows—a wide forehead, hint of high cheekbones below the dark pockets of her eyes, a strong chin. "Still, surely it will turn up," she said, descending the stairs. "Maybe if you're in Tortuga next week, we can get together. I'll be here a few days, taking a break from California. I'm at the Inn, room 218."

I had just remembered the sound that woke me, and I leaned over the rail, intending to ask her if she had made it. Or heard it. Only a few seconds had passed and there was no sound of footsteps along the walkway, yet before I could utter a sound, Caroline spoke from the far end of the driveway:

"You know, you really should lock your doors at night."

And then she was gone.

Complacencies of the peignoir, and late
Coffee and oranges in a sunny chair,
And the green freedom of a cockatoo
Upon a rug mingle to dissipate
The holy hush of ancient sacrifice.

AUGUST 8, 1993

SUNDAY MORNING

IT WAS A STEVENS MORNING, my first Sunday home in seven months, and the early morning sun was falling like honey over the valley—the day couldn't have looked more delicious to me if there had been angels crowding the sky and strumming harps. Reciting a few lines of Wallace Stevens and juggling a steaming cup of French Roast, a plate of sliced oranges, and a blueberry bagel, I left the kitchen and headed for the sun deck. On my way out the front door, I nearly tripped over my favorite azalea lying overturned on the patio. I stepped over it, climbed the stairs to the deck, and after arranging my booty on the table, went back to look over the railing at the ruined plant and the mess below—the earthenware pot that had been sitting on a large stump beside the door was scattered in pieces, the red-blooming azalea splayed with its roots in the air.

That explained the mysterious sound last night. Sipping coffee and nibbling on an orange slice, I strolled around the deck and savored the morning as I considered Caroline Marcus's parting words. She must have tried to enter by the front door; otherwise, how had she known it was unlocked? And if that were the case, she had intended to enter the house while I slept, but then she must have knocked over the plant in the dark. On the other hand, I thought, maybe she had merely tested the door out of some compulsive curiosity, accidentally overturned the plant, and was on her way to knock on the bedroom door upstairs when I had discovered her on the deck. For reasons that I hadn't yet examined, I was intrigued by the woman—in spite of the fact that I didn't trust her and probably wouldn't even recognize her in broad daylight. But for all the excuses I could devise in her defense, there were loose ends and unanswered questions. For example, how would she have known I slept upstairs? And why had Jones left the house and taken up with a perfect stranger? And if she had knocked over the plant, wouldn't she have mentioned it, knowing that I would discover it this morning?

From the west side of the deck, past the driveway, I could see Fresca stomping and switching her tail as she nuzzled through the dregs of yesterday's alfalfa, the dapples on her grey coat catching the sunlight. I longed to saddle up and spend the day riding along the top of the mesas, but soon the heat would be sweltering again, and besides, I was eager to drop off the bottle I'd pillaged from Jaz's cabin to my friend Mac who taught in the science department at the local university. The bank of dark clouds that yesterday had been accumulating on the horizon to the north had drifted east, along with any rain they might have carried, and the trail of smoke had broadened into a column in the direction of Taos. As I followed the deck around to where I could see the tip of Kit's roof poking up through the piñon trees and the edge of her garden, I began to feel the beginnings of a gnawing anxiety, the kind that will eat like acid straight through that complacency Stevens was writing about.

So much for the green freedom of this Sunday morning. Swallowing the last of the bagel, I shifted into gear—swept up the shards of pottery, gave the azalea a quick repotting and a squirt of water as I placed it back on its stump, took a quick shower, and tucked the bottle from Jaz's cabin in my jeans pocket. I gave a whistle to Jones and tossed Fresca a flake of alfalfa as I headed toward my truck.

Tuning the radio to a Santa Fe station as we zipped along I-25 toward Tortuga, I discovered the smoke I'd spotted belonged to a fire burning out of control in the Carson National Forest. According to the newscast, it had already destroyed two small mountain communities, though luckily the residents had been evacuated and no lives had been lost. "Now, however," continued the report, "local residents in the Taos area are preparing to evacuate if the fire has not been brought under control within the next twenty-four hours. The storm front which the Forest Service had hoped would help stem the flames has failed to materialize, and local firefighters are asking for volunteers across the state to help in their efforts to control the fire..." I switched off the radio as I took the off-ramp into town, the hot morning air whipping in through the window.

Tortuga is a funky small Hispanic town of seventeen thousand that harbors hopes of becoming the next Santa Fe. And if the price of real estate at the mecca of Southwest glitz keeps rising and the great exodus of Californians, who don't bat an eye at commuting fifty or sixty miles to and from work, keeps sliding this direction, then eventually the two-acre junkyard beside the freeway off-ramp with its mile-high stacks of bellied-up vehicles will give way to the shopping mall the mayor has been chatting up for several years now. Me, I'm voting for the junkyard.

I took a left on Guadalupita, a shortcut to avoid the strip of fast-food joints and motels along the freeway frontage road, and angled back through the old residential section where most of the town's Hispanic poor still lived in patched adobe houses and rusted-out trailers. Here the streets were cracked and narrow, without curbs or sidewalks, but with enough potholes to keep the kids who played there safe from speeding vehicles. Two blocks over was the center of old town, a shady square that had been sodded, outfitted with a cupola and park benches, and tagged as "Olde Town Plaza in the heart of Tortuga's historic district" in the propaganda distributed to tourists by the Chamber of Commerce. Here, four freshly paved streets bordered the square, but the surrounding buildings were less compliant to change. Built in the mid-1800s when the likes of Billy the Kid and Kit Carson and Doc Holiday frequented their bars and brothels, the buildings stared balefully down over the grassy square. Their facades, more than any written history of Tortuga, documented the town's rise and fall, its hopes and failures, its dreams and corruptions, and its absolute refusal to march willingly into annihilation before the great drum roll of progress. The buildings had endured, but not before each succeeding generation left its imprint.

As I drove around the square, it was hard not to smile at the patchwork effect of the storefronts standing shoulder-to-shoulder around the park—some were little more than ruins, their original adobe or brick exteriors crumbling around missing or boarded-over windows; a few buildings had been plastered, painted, and outfitted with chrome-edged plate-glass windows; still others were hidden behind fifties facades of machine-made brick or the rough planking of barn wood. The latest developer, banking on the contemporary mania for Southwestern authenticity, had sandblasted four stories of brick on an ancient if plain-faced rooming house, tacked elaborate cornices above the windows, gussied up the downstairs with plush carpeting and wainscoting and lace curtains for a restaurant-and-bar combo, and furnished the upper rooms in faux Santa Fe. Such was the Rosita Inn—a hangout for local drinkers like Jaz, and a pricey attraction for tourists who veered off the beaten path.

A couple of blocks past old town, a state university extended across several blocks, known across the state for its open enrollment policy guaranteeing admission to everyone, no matter how badly they might have screwed up in some past life. The school served as a kind of dumping ground, a hybrid junior college where the lost, deserted, or burned-out wandered across the campus waiting for some Aztec god to descend with their degree—as opposed to attending class, reading, writing, or any other unreasonable expectation that might be made of them. During September and January, as each semester began, you could see them in front of the administration building, waiting in long lines to register, the school not yet having entered the computer age, and then they were herded like despondent cattle through their courses until their time was up and the graduation march was at hand.

I found a parking place in the lot behind the science building that was empty except for a battered '63 Cadillac and a rusted-out Brat pickup with a muffler tied up with bailing wire. I parked alongside the Brat, and Jones tagged along behind as I headed for an orange-painted stucco building that was trying to look adobe and historic. Jones sat to wait outside while I pulled open the heavy glass entrance door. Inside, the halls were dark tunnels with that kind of hollow emptiness that universities have during August when students are still holding on to their summer vacations. My boots were loud and echoed off the walls which were scratched with graffiti in between waist-high glass cabinets containing shelves filled with the bones of small animals with descriptive placards next to them. One cabinet housed animals indigenous to the area, and I smiled to recall how frightened I had been of them when I originally moved here, fresh from California. The Western rattler with its arrow-shaped viper's skull and apparently innocuous markings was actually a fair-minded creature who gave at least as much respect as he got, rattling a warning before he coiled to strike—more than he got from his human stalker who collected snakeskins to sell as hatbands and souvenirs. Arranged next to the rattler, the whiptail looked too much like its cousin, the scorpion, but in fact the lobed tail curled back over its body carried no worse poison than a bee sting. From an invisible filament, a shiny black widow spider dangled in midair, her red abdominal spot exposed; along one side of the cabinet, someone had glued a particularly large specimen of a centipede, a creature that even dead still sent a chill down my spine.

Mac's office was near the end of the corridor, and I could see a triangular wedge of light lying across the floor from his doorway. I had met him several years back, during a brief stint when I was so broke that I took on a creative writing class at the university. Between the long drive, the low pay, the general incompetence of the administrators, and the ineptitude of the students, I didn't figure I'd ever get that broke again. Technically, Mac was a professor here. Years ago, the university hired him ABD fresh out of grad school, back in the early eighties when every teaching job had five hundred out-of-work teachers begging for it. But while others like him had finished up their dissertations, racked up a few publications, and said *vaya con Dios,* Mac had stayed on, not so much undeterred by incompetent deans and lethargic students and miserable paychecks as merely oblivious to them. I walked toward his office and conjured him in my mind's eye—nodding, smiling his beatific smile, and taking copious notes at faculty meetings; not until I sat next to him during one particularly long and draconian meeting did I see that those "notes" were actually a draft of his latest article. It was the microscope and the research that engaged Mac's heart. So long as he had his laboratory, his computer, and interlibrary loan, he was one happy camper. I also knew he had achieved a substantial reputation in the international science community, but for all that, he had recently been denied promotion to full professor, the grounds being, as he confided to me, the dean's opinion that he had "failed to show adequate and significant publications in the area of research."

When I peeked around his office door, he was hunched over a computer facing the window. He wore his perpetual Dodgers baseball cap pulled down over frizzy blonde hair that straggled to his shoulders.

"I see you're not taking the summer off," I said to his back.

"Hey, hey, Jet," he boomed, not missing a beat on the keyboard. "When'd you get back?" He spun around in his chair. He was a big man, about six foot six, and powerful. He had been a star fullback at Louisiana State and had gone through college on athletic scholarships. Rumor had it that he was offered a contract by the pros, but Mac was a Scientist the way Hemingway was a Writer.

"A few days ago," I said, sitting in the ragged armchair across from his desk. Mac had crackling blue eyes, cherub cheeks, a frothy gold beard, and the kind of old-fashioned morality that kept him home at night. "How's the wife?"

"Yeah, well, you know," he drawled in Louisiana English, "hangin' in." He stretched his long legs out under the desk and leaned back with his hands clasped behind his head. His wife, Willa, was as high-strung as Mac was laid-back. While he was checking out microbes under the microscope and chasing down articles through interlibrary loan, she rode English on the horse show circuit, hung out with the Anglo money set, and spent lots of time in Santa Fe. It was good that a distant relative had left her a few bucks because Mac's paycheck wouldn't keep her in bridles and blower cuts.

"That's too bad." I stretched out my legs, leaned back, and clasped my hands behind my head in the ratted-out chair.

"Now, Jet, you just come on down off your mountain a little more and we'll talk." He grinned from ear to ear, slipping into our old style of banter. "Hey, what can I do for you?" he said, sitting up. "I know you didn't just come all the way here into town to pay me a social visit, did you?"

"You sell yourself short all the time?"

"Nope, I read minds." The computer was humming behind him, and then the screen suddenly turned to swimming fish. I also read minds—I knew that most of Mac's was on that computer.

"Okay." I stood up and took the bottle out of my jeans pocket. The growth had turned a darker purple, and the tentacles had hardened since I last looked. I handed it to him. "I want to know if you can find out what this is."

He took the bottle, turned in his chair, and held it to the light. He turned it sideways, upside-down, catty-corner, then right-side-up. He shook it gently, held it at arm's length, and then held it close up and back again.

"Well, I can't eyeball it for you. I've never seen anything like it, which doesn't mean it doesn't exist, of course." He chuckled at himself and raised his eyebrows. He looked at me and set the bottle on his desk. "Wanna tell me about it?"

"Rather not," I said.

He took off his baseball cap, squinted one eye at me, and scratched behind his ear. The first time I ever saw him do this, I didn't know whether to laugh or cry—his high expansive forehead just kept on going up and back and around into the most spectacular shining dome I'd ever seen. With his bald crown and the blonde fringe and curly beard, Mac is part comedy and part tragedy, like that place between the rock and the hard place the human animal has to live in.

"Suit yourself. So long as I'm not party to theft or blackmail or a sex scandal." He looked at me.

I didn't say anything.

"Am I?"

I shrugged a little and got up to leave, wondering if Mac was going to back out on me.

"Yeah, well," he chuckled, "let me know before the Feds arrive. When you want to hear about this?"

"When can you have it for me?" I wanted it yesterday, just like everybody else who comes around wanting you to do your job for free.

"Mmn, tomorrow do?"

"Sounds good." I turned to go and then stopped. "You want to take a running start up my hill or shall I visit the civilized world again tomorrow?"

"You call it, kid." Mac slipped into his Bogie impression, grinning in his come-on way through the beard.

"Hey, give it a shot. If you only make it halfway, it's a pretty walk." When I left, he was holding the bottle up and gently shaking it again.

When Jones and I got back to the truck, the yellow Brat was gone and there was a dent the size of a grapefruit in my rear fender. I was steaming, gritting my teeth. I would either have to live with this dent or fork out the cash since I had dropped my collision coverage. I didn't want to come up with several hundred dollars to pay for someone else's bad driving. Always assuming it *was* bad driving.

When I spotted the yellow Brat parked in front of the Rosita Inn, my good sense told me to go on past. Instead, I parked as close to the truck as I could get, touching the rear bumper. I let Jones out to wait in the park across the street and went steaming into the Inn.

The tavern section of the Rosita Inn is a long, narrow room with high ceilings and a bar that runs the length across one side and floor-to-ceiling windows looking out over the park on the other side. The windows are hung with see-through lace curtains and flanked by a row of small tables. Marguerite Sanchez was bartending this afternoon, so I took a barstool at one end near the door and waited for her to work her way down to me. Across the lobby from the bar was the restaurant section which had a pricey menu with mediocre food disguised as "authentic New Mexican cuisine." It and the hotel attracted the tourists; the bar drew a motley collection of serious drinkers that represented a good cross section of the town taken from the university, the local artists who exhibited in the galleries nearby, a few down-and-out drunks who came in to watch the free television and eat the free popcorn, and wealthy tourists looking for local color. This Sunday morning, the several tables lining the windows were mostly empty, but the bars in New Mexico fill up fast in the afternoon and evening, Sunday being the one day of the week when liquor sales are illegal anywhere except bars. You don't want to be on a New Mexico highway on a Sunday night. At a corner table, a fellow sat with his back to me, his dark hair splayed over the collar of his black leather jacket. Facing him was Metzo, a gay Hispanic who had been at Jaz's funeral yesterday and who owned the gallery next door. Metz was a good guy, a reservoir of gossip and other flotsam that sprang up around the town.

Several people sat on the bar stools staring up at an overhead large-screen television tuned to a local station giving an update on the Taos fire. Marguerite was doling out beer and a few mixed drinks. She was a hefty blonde with a wooden way of moving that discouraged sexual come-ons. I'd once thought this was an acquired device she had dreamed up for self-defense, but in fact Marguerite had a chronic spinal condition that made much of her life a misery. Maybe it was the pain that kept her taciturn and warned troublemakers away, or maybe it was her eyes, whose electric blue could shoot right through an alcoholic stupor.

I homed in on a fellow sitting at the other end of the bar, an oily-haired specimen with a sharp nose and small black darting eyes who had a fresh Corona and no empties in front of him. He wore a red muscle shirt with the armholes torn out and grease stains on it, and one hand rested on the beer bottle while the other kept up a rapid drumming on the bar. I thought about the centipede stuck on the wall of the glass cabinet.

Marguerite was wiping the bar, working my way. We were closer than passing acquaintances but not quite close enough to be friends. Like many of the white residents who somehow wound up in this town, her background had its twists. Married to a guy who behaved a lot better living high in Belize than he did broke in Santa Fe, she had moved with him to Tortuga, where they lived with his parents in a battered adobe without water, phone, or electricity. Marguerite had turned up at the local hospital a couple of times, once with a broken wrist and then with a fractured clavicle, before she moved out and took a job bartending at the Inn. Now she was turning out some better-than-average landscape paintings, several hanging in Metzo's gallery.

"So, Jet, California vacation over?" Her eyes were on low, and her voice had a deep, mellow tone.

"Coming from anybody but you, them's fighting words."

Marguerite wiped circles on the bar in front of me, then left her rag there while she went to pop the lid on a bottle of Perrier, setting it down in front of me with a slice of lime and a glass of ice.

"You remembered," I said, pouring the fizzing water over the ice. "What's the story on Mr. Clean in the muscle shirt?" I asked, not looking up.

"Bad news. Problem?"

"How long's he been here?"

"Few minutes before you." She took the cloth and began wiping circles on the bar again.

"What's he drive?"

"Yellow truck."

"Got a story?"

"Just your everyday ordinary local drug dealer. Small stuff. Vicious little motherfucker, though." She gave me a sharp blue look before easing off to set another Corona in front of a porky tourist who had his head turned straight up to watch a baseball game just starting up. Marguerite picked up the remote control and turned the sound off.

A hand settled on my shoulder, and I jumped, nearly choking on my Perrier.

"Jet." The only other voice in the world that sounded like this one belonged to Sam Elliott. Juan Falcon eased down on the stool beside me and put his hat on the bar. "You just get out of church?" he said, sliding his hand off my shoulder and taking in my jeans and T-shirt, the one that said "Wild Women Don't Get No Blues" in red letters. Marguerite, her eyes softened to a dreamy turquoise, snapped the cap on another Perrier and put it down in front of him. No glass, no lime. Juan took a long drink out of the green bottle as Marguerite watched him.

"Right," I said, still coughing. He was wearing the same outfit as yesterday—faded jeans, white shirt open at the neck, wedding ring. Either he had a whole set of those shirts and jeans, or he did laundry every night. His shirt was white as a cloud, and he smelled like bath soap and leather. He was looking straight ahead as he talked to me, leaning on the bar with his forearms, his hands clasped together.

"Seem a little jumpy," he said. "You okay?" His eyes scanned the room.

I caught my breath and decided to ask Juan about our friendly drug dealer. When I looked down that direction, the stool where he had been sitting was empty, a half-full beer marking his place. Juan had caught my drift, and we both looked at the empty spot with the abandoned beer.

"Friend leave?" Juan asked. Through the lace curtains at the window, we saw the yellow truck cruise by.

"You know that guy?"

"Don't travel in the same circles. You interested?" Juan looked around at me, and I began to imagine I saw nuances in his expressions. Was that a twinkle in his eye?

"You think I got a chance?"

He looked at me for a minute before he spoke: "I think you got about anything you want." He took another drink of his Perrier and set the bottle down on the bar. Marguerite was rubbing on some glasses in front of us, going over them for the third time if my count was right. She glanced up at Juan and then at me and smiled.

"Yeah, I'm a lucky girl." I waited for him to say something, but he didn't. "That guy just sideswiped my truck in a parking lot over at the university. What do you think I should do about it?"

"Think you ought to pretend he didn't."

"You know his name?"

"Yep. Trouble." He picked up the bottle of Perrier and held it in both hands.

"Hey, Juan, thanks a lot."

"Don't mention it."

He was watching the corner table where Metz sat talking to his buddy in black leather. The buddy twisted around in his chair and looked at Juan. He was very handsome, with a delicate face and high cheekbones.

"Okay. I won't," I said.

Metz gave us a broad smile and waved the tips of his fingers. His friend turned back around.

Juan took a long drink out of his bottle, and Marguerite had another one sitting in front of him before the empty hit the bar. She took up her place in front of us and started on the glasses again while I watched the ice cubes melt in my glass and Juan examined his new bottle. Finally, when a fellow sitting next to the porker raised an empty glass, Marguerite left to mix up some vodka and grapefruit juice for him.

"Those tire tracks you saw at Jaz's place? Can you match them?" I asked.

"Could. Haven't yet."

"Did you check out Kit's Jeep?"

"Yep. Not a match. Not with the set that came after you left that night. Did match another set, came maybe a day or two before." He swung around on his stool. "Didn't think they were all that neighborly. You had a chance to talk to her?"

Juan had the kind of deep brown eyes that made me want to crank up the air conditioning. He also had the straight dark eyebrows and facial bones that turned the heads of men like Metz's friend at the corner table and women like Marguerite who couldn't keep a distance. I had to look away to lie to him. "I'll try to get over there this afternoon," I said. Anything that I could tell him at the moment would make Juan even more suspicious than he already was. How could I expect him to believe Kit was innocent when I, her best friend, was having doubts?

Marguerite came back to stand in front of us and work on the glasses.

Juan kept watching me. I looked down at the bar where his left hand rested on the brim of his hat. It was the same golden mahogany color as his face, with large knuckles and square-tipped fingers and a latticework of veins, the hand of a man who works horses and defends himself when he has to. I reached over and touched the gold band.

"You still wear it."

He kept his gaze locked on me, but his expression was impenetrable. Marguerite cleared her throat and went to the other end of the bar to refill the corn popper.

"How long has it been now?" I asked, taking my hand back.

"Two years in October."

I nodded and traced the grain of the wood under the shellac on the bar with my finger. Where the straited lines of the oak met and outlined a large oval knot in the wood, I imagined that I saw a face rise to the surface, with its pale brow and narrow chin, and the faint smile that I remembered on her face as she stood in the center of the training circle and watched her husband ride by.

I stroked the ring around the pale face, and then I covered it with my hand.

"I'm sorry. I didn't mean to pry."

"It's okay. I'm not all that fragile." He looked out through the tall windows where the day lay behind the lace curtains. Above us, slowly rotating, a fan hung from the ceiling, circulating the refrigerated air forced from small louvered grates set into the walls. "Thing of it is, you're the first person that's ever mentioned it. Funny how you can see people shy away from the subject, kind of like a nervous horse. Think it's got more to do with the way they feel than it does with me. Or Grace."

Grace. The name spoken in the air seemed to call her up. I moved my hand and looked in her face caught in the filigree of wood. She had been the sort of woman that people, not only men, took pleasure in watching, not just because she was a pretty woman, but because she was compassionate and gentle and honest, and there was something about the way she would tilt her head slightly when she listened to you, or maybe the way her lips fit around the words when she spoke so that what she said seemed to cast her in a softer material than the rest of us. Maybe that accounted for her genius with horses. That and her patience. I once saw her take aside a stubborn horse, stroke it while laying her head against its mane and saying something into its ear, then mount and ride it around and around the arena until the horse became as willing and obedient as the family dog. Grace.

"Did you get married right out of high school?"

"Close. Right out of college." He looked sideways at me and grinned a little. "Indian folks do that sometimes, too," he said. "But we pretty much paired up from the time we could walk. Same tribe, lived down the road from each other. Back in Oklahoma. Bought a little spread in Texas after college, out in the boondocks where you could buy land for close to nothing a few years back, meant to raise horses. Struck oil. Damnedest thing." He shook his head. "Bought that spread outside of town here with the money."

"Nice place. I guess it's tough keeping it up and being the sheriff, too." I had never really thought before now about how his ranch had been affected by the loss of Grace and winning the election.

"Hired a fellow to watch it for me. Lives out there. Makes a mean enchilada." Juan looked around behind us as a group of people collected in the lobby and began to file into the restaurant. "By the way," he said, turning back around, "folks at the Lab say Jaz wasn't working for them. Also say they're considering a slander suit against your friend Kit. Seems like she's the one that called the TV folks and gave them some wild story about Jaz and the connection to the water development issue. Said he was involved in some kind of water experiments."

I shook my head. "I admit she's a hothead, Juan. I don't know that there's much they could collect even if they won."

"Don't think they're all that interested in the money."

"I see. Worried about their good name, are they? As far as the water issue's concerned, I've heard it's a done deal. They're signing papers or something this Tuesday?"

"Yep." He nodded at the Perrier bottle and gave it a half turn. "Just thought you might want to know what the scuttlebutt was on Kit, though. Might want to let her know before they dump it on her. Settle her down a little. Jaz is past history. Might as well let it go."

There was an innovative thought. I was trying to imagine Kit settling down when I told her she might be on the wrong end of a lawsuit.

"Speaking of Jaz," I said, "what was your take on this old flame that turned up?"

"Fine-looking woman," he said, drawing out the words. He leaned sideways in my direction. "How much detail you want me to go into?" He smiled briefly.

"I get your drift."

"Didn't think you were the type for X-rated descriptions."

"Didn't think you were the type to give them."

"Fool a lot of people." He gave a quarter turn to the Perrier bottle. "Something a little spooky about her, though."

"Spooky? What do you mean, 'spooky'?" Caroline Marcus had left me feeling that way too, but I wrote it off to the oddness of the hour. Juan had seen her in broad daylight the morning of the burial.

"Been trying to answer that myself," he said, frowning into the Perrier. "Reminds me of somebody back when I was a kid. This boy on the reservation, Willie Joe Figgen. Didn't know him real well, five or six years ahead of me in school. Used to show up at our door, wanting to do odd jobs, wash our car, fix fences, weed my mama's garden. His folks were like most the rest of us, on the poor side, but this kid, he never quit working, always on the move, bought his folks a television set when he was a freshman in high school. Kid was kind of an oddball, though. One thing, he was always clean, not like the rest of us out riding horses or running traps or hanging out at the swimming quarry. Except for after doing his odd jobs, you never saw Willie Joe that every hair wasn't in place and his boots spit polished. Another thing, Willie was a real good-looking fellow, like he just stepped out of a magazine ad, had a crowd of girls flocking after him all the time. And he made straight A's, starred on the baseball team right through high school. What I'm saying is, Willie was hardworking, handsome, smart, so he wasn't an oddball from lack of anything you could put your finger on. Yet the thing of it was, I never knew Willie to have a close buddy. Always kept his own company. Never saw him just sitting around shooting the shit, hanging out. When I look back and see Willie Joe, he's standing there all by himself, way across the room from the rest of us on the other side." Juan was looking down at the end of the bar where Marguerite was still fiddling with the corn popper, but I don't think he saw her. "It wasn't like we had rejected Willie Joe, it was more like Willie Joe had rejected us.

"He got a full ride to Harvard, graduated law school. Everybody thought we'd seen the last of him. Hardly anybody ever goes back to the reservation unless they got nowhere else to go. Well, Willie Joe came back right about the time I was setting off to college. Moved back in with his folks. Set up an office in town, and a few years later he was representing the tribe in one lawsuit after another. Ole Willie was one rich Indian. Tribe was doing okay too. Willie bought his folks a new house, couple of cars, did some work with disadvantaged kids. Never did marry. I went back to visit the folks couple years ago. They gave me an update on Willie Joe, reckon he must have been forty or so, just finished up a big case. Seems like he went berserk. They say he took a rifle and a .38 Special one morning, went out and parked his car by the side of the road where the school bus stops every day to let kids off. Willie took the rifle, climbed up in a tree and waited for the bus, then he started shooting, shot a bunch of kids riding on the bus. Climbed down out of the tree, went over to his car, shot himself with the .38. Nobody ever did figure out what got into him." Juan paused and look down at his hands, both of them spread out flat on the bar. "But I can tell you," he said, turning to face me, "there was always something a little sideways about Willie Joe Figgen, same kind of something I picked up from Jaz's ex, Caroline Marcus."

Juan stood up, drank the end of the Perrier, picked up his hat, and laid a five-dollar bill on the bar.

"Juan," I said, swinging around on the stool and looking up at him where he stood backlit against the window, "did animals like Willie Joe?"

He stared at me for the length of time it would take to say, "Have you lost your fucking mind?" with about the same kind of expression on his face. Then he said, "No," nodded at me and then at Marguerite, and left.

Marguerite stood, as though enchanted, and watched him till he was out of sight.

M ARGUERITE WASN'T THE ONLY ONE looking out
through the lace curtains when Juan Falcon's white truck
drifted by, Metz and his friend were looking in that direction, too.
The guys in front of the muted television watching the baseball
game were still staring up at the screen. Overhead, the ceiling fan
rasped slightly as it rotated. I leaned across the bar, picked up a
glass of cocktail straws, and was about halfway through a game of
pick-up sticks when Marguerite strolled over.

She had the dazed, sickly expression of a kid who's been into
the cake icing. "Are you all right?" I asked her.

"God," she said, sagging over the bar, "isn't he about the most
gorgeous thing you ever laid eyes on." She kept an eye on the window where Juan's truck had disappeared and swiped the cocktail
sticks off the bar and into the wastebasket. She took out a new box
and refilled the glass. "It's enough to make you want to go rob the
nearest Seven-Eleven."

"Stop-and-Go."

"Huh?" She saw me for the first time since Juan had left.

"Stop-and-Go. We don't have any Seven-Elevens in town." I
reached for the new set of straws.

Marguerite heaved an exasperated sigh that was part grunt and
moved the glass of fresh straws out of my reach. The porker sitting
directly under the baseball game raised his empty Corona bottle
without taking his eyes off the screen, and Marguerite took a cold
one from the cooler, snapped the lid off, and set it down in front of
him as she grabbed the remote and cranked up the sound. She grav-
itated back to my end of the bar.

"So. You guys looked pretty chummy. Anything happening there?"

"Marguerite, give it a rest. I've got ten years on him."

"So? Come into the nineties, Jet. Everybody knows men reach their peak at eighteen, and women at forty."

"I guess that puts us both over the hill."

"Not me." Two lines appeared between Marguerite's eyebrows as she leaned back on her elbows against the bar so she could talk while watching the customers. She had generous features that hinted at a lusty Italian in her family—full sensual lips with an odd wrinkle above her upper one when she smiled, a slightly oversized nose, a rich-colored complexion with large pores and flushed cheeks. Up close, her overpermed hair looked brittle, caught up with a barrette in back so that it fuzzed out in a brassy blonde puff. She wore a long shapeless knit sweater that hit her just above her knees, over a black leotard that went from neck to toe. I wondered whether she dressed this way for comfort, not wanting to aggravate her spine, or because it hid her body from the ogles that bosomy women attract in a bar. It wasn't the kind of thing I was going to ask her about.

"By the way," I said, "I saw you at the funeral yesterday."

She twisted around on one elbow and looked at me like I'd spoken in tongues.

"Jaz's funeral?" I reminded her.

She did a .38-caliber number with her eyes. "Oh yeah?"

"I was sitting back in the corner," I said. "By the door."

She went back to looking out across the room.

"I guess you got to know him pretty well. I heard he spent a lot of time in here."

Marguerite twisted around again. Her eyes revved up to .9 millimeter. "Yeah, stool next to the corn popper." She jerked her head toward the other end of the bar. "Used to call it 'his kitchen.' Come walking in around five, saying 'Hey, Mag, my *kitchen* open?'"

"*Mag*?"

Marguerite squinched her face up into a sour smile. "When he was really in his cups, it was 'Maggot.' Real nice guy." She drew a cocktail straw out of the glass and started chewing on one end of it.

"And you went to his funeral?"

"You bet. I was celebrating." She used her tongue to shove the straw to one side of her mouth and talked around it. "Couldn't have happened to a more deserving guy. I can tell you, my job got a whole lot easier without him mouthing off."

"I heard he got into it with Kit one night."

"Oh yeah. Big-time fireworks, those two," she smiled, switching the straw to the other side, "and ole Kit let him have it, I mean. She been wound pretty tight over that water thing." Marguerite shook her head and rolled her eyes at the ceiling. "Nutcases, both of them."

"I heard she threatened to kill him."

"Her and half the town." Marguerite shook her head and switched the straw again. "No big deal. Shit, before the night was over they had their heads together like buddies."

"Did you ever hear of him dealing?"

"Nah. Not his movie. Not that he wouldn't, he was just too busy with the schmooz and booze."

"I don't suppose you ever saw him writing in here?"

Marguerite pushed herself upright and gave me a full-body stare. "You're kidding, right?" She poured white wine into two glasses and carried them over to Metz's table. When she came back, I asked her how Jaz paid his tab. She shrugged and started polishing glasses again.

"He could be very charming, you know." She gave me a low-voltage look with a towel in one hand and a glass in the other. "Tourists, mostly," she said, holding up the glass to the light and rubbing it around the lip with the cloth. "He'd talk, they'd buy. He wouldn't start for the jugular till he was sure they were about to leave. I think what pissed him off wasn't that they stopped buying him booze, but that they stopped listening. He never really got falling-down drunk, no matter how much he soaked up, even when it was mescal. I never saw anybody could drink as much as him and still navigate. And sometimes when he came in, it was just a slow night. Nobody around. He'd come in for a couple bowls of popcorn and leave." She looked at me out of the corner of her eye.

"So you went to his funeral."

She took the straw out of her mouth and looked at the mutilated end of it. Then, with her eyes revved up somewhere around Uzi level, she said, "Yeah, that's right. I went to his fucking funeral. Good fucking riddance," she said, slinging the straw into the wastebasket. She moved over next to the porker and stood watching the television, her back to me.

I sipped on the dregs of my Perrier and tried to imagine just how charming Jaz might have been to Marguerite on nights when no one was around to buy him drinks. Charming enough to con her into running a tab for him and then sticking her with it? Hardly a motive for murder. I was deep into mental scenarios that starred Jaz and Marguerite, trying to figure just what Jaz might have said or done to provoke such hostility, when I suddenly realized I was looking straight into the eyes of the guy in the black leather jacket who was gliding my way. He was taller than I'd supposed and not as thin as his face suggested. I put him a little under six foot, and while his frame was small-boned, he had a certain flexibility in his walk that made him seem elegant rather than fragile. He wore a tight-fitting black sweater underneath the jacket, expensively tailored loose pants, and the self-conscious expression of a good-looking man who studies GQ and works out in a gym. His hair was the fashionable shoulder length that rebellious young men were wearing this year, and as he strolled past, he did something with his mouth that fell between a smirk and a seductive smile while his eyes did a slow crawl up and down my body.

After he'd left the bar and the double doors were swinging after him, I looked over to where Metz was sitting with his chin propped on his hands and his lower lip stuck out. When the doors stopped swinging, he lifted his eyebrows, pulled his hair with both hands, and opened his mouth wide in a pantomime scream. Leaping out of his chair, he balanced himself on one leg with the other stretched behind, leaned forward at the waist with his wineglass high in one hand and the other stretched out for balance. He was a better artist than he was a ballerina.

"Hey Jets, what's up?" he said, trotting over and taking Juan's stool. "You and the sheriff an item?" He wiggled his eyebrows and his ears at the same time. "How'd you like that sublime piece of mocha that just waltzed out of here? Some sweet patootie, huh?" He smiled hugely, the bottom half of his face showing large square teeth. He crossed his legs, the top one jiggling nonstop, folded one arm across his chest where he caught his hand under his armpit, and held the glass of white wine with the other. He vibrated on the stool, waiting for my verdict.

"He's a looker all right," I said, wishing I had a roll of duct tape to wrap around Metz, neck to toe. His manic phases would fry the nerves of a hyperactive six-year-old. "Where'd you come across this one?" I said, holding on to the bar with one hand to ground myself.

Metz spun around on the stool, lifting his knees up to his chest and working up speed. Then he leaned back, extended his legs, and coasted to a stop. He was wearing most of his wine; his trademark white jumpsuit was dotted with wet spots. He also wore moccasins, no socks, lots of heavy gold chains on his wrists, ankles, and neck, and a couple of plain gold rings in his right earlobe. His black hair was past his shoulders and so fuzzy that he looked electrified. He was Tortuga's best-known, and most successful, artist—which was a lucky thing, because if he'd been as poor as most artists in the area, his antics would have made him a prime candidate for the local nut bin.

"Oh Jet, that boy. He just wandered right into my web," he said, wiggling his fingers and bending back his head to reveal a substantial Adam's apple as he launched into a high-pitched maniac's cackle. The porker watching the television and the fellow next to him working on the grapefruit juice and vodka stopped watching the game and swiveled their heads in our direction. Marguerite cranked the volume up, and they went back to the game.

"Tell me, tell me, tell me," he said, kicking his feet, "what do you think, what do you think of him?"

"Solid, twenty-four karat glitz, Metz," I said. For some reason I never could comprehend, Metz set great store by my opinion of his latest paramours. He had occasionally gone so far as to bring them to dinner at my place, just so I could get an in-depth view. "You've outdone yourself this time. Really."

Metz glowed and vibrated on the stool. His eyes were large and set deeply into their sockets—he widened them so that white showed all around the brown irises. Marguerite came over and stood in front of us.

"Metz, you want some more wine?" Marguerite didn't usually encourage the clientele to drink. But I knew what she was thinking—neither of us would ever forget a few years back, when Metz had been persuaded by a well-intentioned friend to take lithium. Plagued by the memory of Metz medicated to the point of catatonia, sitting for days on end in his pajamas and staring out his bedroom window, Marguerite had opted for alcohol over lithium, and as much as I despised the effects of alcohol, I had to agree.

"Lay it on me, babycakes," Metz said. "Bring us the bottle, bring us the bottle." He spun around on the stool again, this time leaving his glass on the bar. Marguerite poured the wine into an eight-ounce water tumbler and left the bottle.

When he stopped spinning, I asked Metz about the funeral. He snatched up the glass of wine, downed it in several large gulps, and poured some more. "Oh, Jetso, Jetso. I can't bear it. I can't bear it. He's gone. You didn't know him, not really," he said, his eyes enormous. "Nobody did. I adored the man. I can't believe he's gone." Metz was wailing, drinking the wine.

"Well, there's a minority opinion. I ought to introduce you to his old girlfriend. She just got in from the West Coast."

Metz put down the glass and looked at me. He had stopped shaking his leg, and his eyelids were drooped at half mast. He was sitting perfectly still. Marguerite was refilling decanters, and she stopped in midair, holding a bottle containing a dark gold liquid. Metz turned toward the bar, folded his arms, and laid his head down on them. Marguerite looked at me and shrugged. I shrugged back.

After a while I touched Metz on the shoulder, but he didn't move. Then I felt tiny shudders coming from his body.

"Metz, hey Metz." I patted him across his back, in between the angles of his shoulder blades. "Hey, guy. Listen, I need to talk to you a few minutes. You got time?"

Metz kept his head down on his arms, but he nodded.

"Okay, well, let's go over to the gallery. Can we do that?"

Metz nodded again, but he didn't move. I put my hand on the back of his head and stroked his hair which was very soft. He pushed himself up off the bar, wiped his sleeve across his eyes and nose, and walked toward the door with his head down. I put some money on the bar, gave a wave to Marguerite and the boys, and followed him out.

8

I**T WAS EASY TO FORGET** in the conditioned air of the Inn that
a heat wave was happening outside, but when Metz shoved
open the lobby door to the street, we felt the impact as though we
were walking into a furnace. In the park, Jones leapt in the air for a
Frisbee, to the delighted screams of a swarm of children veering his
way. When he saw me, he paused for a moment, the fluorescent
pink Frisbee caught between his jaws, but as I passed by the truck
and followed Metz to his gallery, Jones pirouetted sideways to
evade an oncoming youngster and dashed toward the gazebo with
the children in wild pursuit.

Metz stood in front of the gallery door with its skewed "Closed for
Lunch" sign dangling in the window and began foraging in one of the
deep pockets of his jumpsuit. An elderly couple, bent and squinting
through the storefront window, straightened up and looked at us.
They were both squat, white-haired, and wearing turquoise polyester
pants suits; parked at the curb was a motor home three parking spaces
long. A small white poodle wearing a turquoise bow stared out the
window, barking as steadily and dispassionately as a metronome.

From the depths of his pocket, Metz extracted an enormous
wad of keys strung on what looked like a manacle and began sort-
ing through them. The elderly couple came over and watched him.

"Guess you eat an early lunch, huh?" said the man, wiping the
sweat off his forehead with a handkerchief and dabbing at his neck.
The woman, a white patent leather purse dangling from her elbow,
stepped closer to the man and took his arm, frowning as she looked
Metz up and down.

"No," said Metz, not bothering to look up, "I drink it." He selected a key from the ring, stuck it in the lock, pushed the door open wide, and with a grandiose bow and sweep of the arms, said *"Entrez."*

It was dark inside after the brilliance of the sun. The man approached the door and paused, glancing back at his wife and the poodle barking behind the window of the motor home. His wife tiptoed behind him and peeked over his shoulder. They both looked at Metz, who was still bent over, and then they looked at me. The turquoise man stepped carefully, one foot and then the other, across the threshold and entered the front room of Metz's gallery. The woman followed, drawing in her breath as she passed Metz. Inside, she rolled her eyes at her husband, who was surveying the room.

Maybe the couple had expected just another elegant salon in the mien of Santa Fe—acres of open space, polished oak floors, discreet indirect lighting, a scatter of woven rugs, sculpture displayed on elegantly slim pedestals. The front room of Metz's gallery was a study in artful disarray, every square inch packed not only with art but with antiques, tapestries, oddball crafts, and Southwestern kitsch. Metz played host, ushering the couple down a narrow aisle to an Art Deco sideboard laid out with coffee and a variety of teas, and then, cups in hand, the trio disappeared into the labyrinth of rooms behind the front one, Metz gesturing in the lead.

I wandered back to the sideboard and fished a Lemon Zinger tea bag out of a glass urn sitting next to a stack of blank forms requesting information from visitors. I dunked the tea bag and strolled around, waiting for Metz. The room looked more or less as I remembered it from the annual Christmas hoopla last year. In fact, draped high in one corner a particularly large and graceful spider web still sparkled with tiny silver stars. Immediately thoughts of Hilda, Metz's pet tarantula, sprang to mind, and as I turned to the cut-glass bowl she preferred for her afternoon siestas, I recalled it had been broken last year when a tourist lifted it to examine the fuzzy, dark contents—a shriek, a crash, and according to Metz, one Canadian tourist near cardiac arrest. In spite of the fact that Metz had pointed to the sign near the bowl warning tourists of sleeping spiders, the Canadian had threatened a lawsuit and left without reference to the $500 price tag on the smashed bowl. Luckily, Hilda survived unscathed, aiming a deft black squirt of ink at the fellow's pants leg. Tit for tat, Metz had said, and carried the spider to his apartment upstairs to set up her new digs.

But the storefront display stage was new. Along the front of the room, behind the window, Metz created what he termed "enviro-scapes." The new one held three stylized mannequins of indeter-minate gender dressed in haute couture—designer velvets, paisleyed turbans, trailing feathers, leather lace, silk scarves, and elaborate fringes of beads, the three figures posed among surrealis-tic paintings and elegantly carved pottery and black obelisk sculp-tures. The scene generated a certain 1890s ambiance, an elaboration of detail, all arranged on a magnificently decadent Oriental rug embossed with a Beardsleyesque portrait of a green parrot.

On one of the enviro-walls hung a landscape by Marguerite—a New Mexico desert vista with mesas receding behind a foreground of tortuously gnarled piñon trees, whose finely detailed branches and trunks, on closer inspection, resembled human limbs. But at the center of the stage was an elaborate surrealistic oil painting, mural-sized and arranged on an easel where two of the mannequins pan-tomimed delight. It was a spectacular example of surrealism—a sprawling landscape, a dried riverbed at the center with crusted mud detailed in an intricate web of cracks that were climbing the riverbank, crawling into the surrounding fields, beneath the houses, edging toward a freeway in the distance. Some of the cracks had invaded the sky and infected the clouds that lay desiccated along the horizon. Protruding from the dark crevasses in the riverbed, writhing hands of nightmare creatures groped for a hold, pulling themselves up into the picture, while blood oozed from the finer cracks near the banks and edges of the fields. As I stared at the lower left corner, which was almost entirely black, ghostly features of a creature began to form as though rising to the surface of a deep pool, its gaping mouth a hole into which the river's water had flowed and from which the subterranean creatures crept. This was the face of the beast, contorted in what might have been either great agony or great joy—it was Jaz's face and I knew before I looked that the signature in the opposite corner would be Katrine Melpine Willis.

"You've seen it," said Metz, rushing over as the turquoise couple left, the woman holding a large square box between her hands. "Isn't it *marvelous*? Have you ever seen anything quite so deliciously disgusting?" Metz looked at the painting, his enormous smile erupting ear to ear.

The price tag read $27,500 in scrolling font. "Had any nibbles?" I asked.

"Thing of it is, Kit sees it mostly as a little publicity. I'm beyond politics, you understand," he said, owl-eyed, "but if she wants to stick a price on it to keep it here, who am I to argue? It's absolutely *exquisite* with my new mannequins." He clapped his hands prayer-like under his chin. "I don't know what I'll *do* if it sells. I just can't *visualize* the scene without it. I mean, really, think of it," he said, moving to one side and cocking his head, his fingers spread across his chest, "what could you *possibly* imagine there that would give the right effect? Yes, well, *Guernica*, perhaps."

"When did she do this?" I asked, glad that his mood, having climbed and dived, had momentarily stabilized. "I don't remember ever seeing her work on it."

"Oh, just finished, paint's barely dry. I had it in mind as I did the mannequins. I've been nearly beside myself, popping up to the mesa to keep tabs on it. I really thought there for a while she was going to die on me. Oh, she got terribly blocked. But then, shazzam, she drove straight through to the finish. A veritable Secretariat. Just put it up Friday. I mean it's just *stupendous*, the effect."

I went to stand beside Metz, and we both surveyed the painting. "Mm, which part was she having trouble with?" I asked.

Metz waved his hand vaguely toward the painting, "Oh, here and there," he said, glancing at me and then looking away. "By the way, I've got a surprise. Back in the office."

I followed Metz through a winding maze of rooms which he had categorized according to his unfathomable system of genres— we passed through a room devoted to pottery, another to weaving, still another to portraiture. We passed through a room of wood carvings, of soapstone sculptures, of basketry and woven willow furniture, of abstract design, of masks. We wound and jackknifed through the innards of the building which, like the adjoining Inn, extended from the storefront backward to the rear alley, nearly half a block. It had two stories, and Metz used most of the upper rooms as living quarters, many of them outfitted as guest accommodations which he offered to friends and artists who came and went in dizzying succession. We passed through several rooms furnished only with reading chairs, floor lamps, and tables stacked with reading materials.

All the interior doors between the gallery rooms had been removed, but the door to Metz's office had not. I waited as he fished for the manacle of keys and opened two sets of dead bolts. When we entered the office, clearly the gallery with its extravaganza of Victoriana and Southwestern art was behind us: the floor was high-polished white tile, the walls a stretch of white as blank as a canvas. Along the back wall adjoining the gallery, a white leather sofa and two matching recliners were arranged around a chrome and glass coffee table. At the far end of the room, a latticework of white-painted shelves held rows of books interrupted with electronic devices—stereo components, a television, a VCR. The door that opened off the alley was fitted with several dead bolts, and next to it, another door stood slightly ajar, open just enough to reveal a stairway leading to the second story. I recalled that the wall along the alley contained a long bank of paned windows, though they were currently hidden behind white pleated blackout drapes drawn tightly together.

The last time I had been here, the room was a dingy affair that Metz used mainly as a passageway to and from his apartment upstairs, or the gallery downstairs, by way of the alley. But the shock was sitting on a long, white laminated desk, the front indented with a special inset shelf that held a computer keyboard. Above the keyboard, sitting on a raised pedestal, was a large monitor with a computer the size of a suitcase sitting next to it, the long expanse of the desk on either side completely bare except for the mouse pad, the mouse, and a stack of the same forms I had seen on the sideboard, these with the blanks filled in.

"Are you kidding?" I said, eyeing the computer in disbelief. "Tell me I'm hallucinating. Are you the same guy who lamented the loss of the quill pen as the preferred writing instrument of the twentieth century?"

Metz grinned sheepishly. He approached the monitor with what I could only call reverence and slid into the slim secretarial chair mounted on large gold casters. He flipped a switch, setting in motion a series of whirring noises and flashing lights. "Never let it be thought," he said, paddling himself around to face me while the machine chattered and hummed and beamed behind him, "that James Metropolitan Almanzar is not in tune with the times." He took the chair for a spin around the room and returned, coasting neatly up to the monitor. He held up both arms, shot his invisible cuffs, and poised his hands with their long curving fingers high over the keyboard. He bent his head backward to look up at me where I stood behind him.

"Ready?" he said upside-down, his eyes the size of eggs, the pupils dilated. I shrugged, and he snapped back upright, paused, then dived at the keyboard, hunched and pecking with his index fingers, sending the screen into paroxysms of images. Finally, a column of names and numbers appeared.

"This," he said, peering at the column and rolling himself aside to give me a clear view of the screen, "is the miracle of our decade."

"Mm." I waited. Nothing happened.

"It's a *database!*" he said, articulating the word in the hushed tones of an acolyte addressing the great unwashed masses. "Watch." He dollied up to the keyboard and began tapping. Beside the word LASTNAME in blue letters was a white box into which he typed "Butler." FIRSTNAME: "Jet." STATE: "New Mexico." RACE: "White." GENDER: "Female." AGE: he leaned his head back upside-down.

"Skip that one," I said, ignoring him.

He typed "Unknown." Immediately, the computer beeped and sent a message across the screen: USE NUMBERS ONLY. He typed in two zeros. The computer beeped: ILLEGAL ENTRY!

"Shit," he said. He typed in "25."

"Thank you," I said. The computer was silent.

"Isn't this wonderful?" Metz typed in "Writing" to the machine's SPECIAL INTERESTS.

"Wow," I said.

"Well, you have to understand that every sale I make, every person I enter into the computer, I can use in my database." ANNUAL SALARY: he looked at me upside-down.

"Skip that one, too."

"The thing of it is," he said, an edge creeping into his voice, "I can do *tons* of things with this information." He tapped on a few keys and the column of names reappeared. "I can call up the names and profiles of everyone of a certain age group, for instance."

"Mm. In case you have an Adults Only opening? Or maybe Kindergarten Art for the under-thirteen set?" Metz was scrolling down the column, and I recognized several names of local people who couldn't tell a Picasso from a Rembrandt. "Angel Torrez?" I asked. This had been the name I'd pried out of Marguerite as belonging to the driver of the yellow Brat truck.

"Oh. Well." Metz shrugged. "Jaz was the one who ordered the computer and showed me how to use it. We just put in everyone's name we could think of to start off. Besides," he said, spinning around on the stool, "are we a little on the snobby side? What's wrong with Angel?"

"I can't really say I know him," I said, not thinking of Angel Torrez. "*Jaz* set your computer up for you? What did Jaz know about computers?" I pictured his cabin, the candles he must have lit at night, not having electricity.

"I was thinking about buying one, and he offered to find out about them for me. He began researching them at the university library, then used the computers over at their writing center, got on-line, the whole smear. I mean, he just became *obsessed* with them. He picked this one out, absolutely state of the art. He reviewed lots of computer programs and ordered these." He nodded toward a shelf of thick books beneath the desk where the printer was housed. "He taught himself how to use them, and then he showed me. He was quite the computer whiz, actually." Metz's eyes began to brim. "Oh Jet. He was here so much the last few months. You can't imagine how much I miss not having him around." Metz's lower lip began trembling, and a tear wandered down his cheek.

"Sorry, Metz. I didn't know you were all that close to him. I've been gone, you know?" I patted his back and leaned over to squeeze his body against mine. He felt very frail.

"I don't mean he was gay," he said quickly, pulling away and looking up at me, "but he was very witty. No one could trash someone better than Jaz." Metz was smiling again, his eyes lit with memories.

"I don't guess you were at the bar last Sunday when he and Kit had their little skirmish?"

"I was, actually," he said, wiping his eyes with his sleeve. "Juan asked me that, too. I ranked it a notch or two above their usual melodrama, primarily because of the curse and the death threat, but Kit is convinced that the loss of water from the river marks stage one of Armageddon. When you believe something with that much conviction, the world's no longer a confusing place. It's populated with two species: those who agree with you, the Rights, and those who don't, the Wrongs. Jaz was definitely a Wrong in Kit's eyes."

"Wasn't it a problem for you, being friends with them both?"

"Not really. Artists are exquisite creatures. They sense when you're insincere. Always. And I cared very much about both of them. No one can resist being genuinely liked." Metz smiled and sniffed and wiped his eyes again with his other sleeve. "But Kit wouldn't come here to the gallery because she knew Jaz was around a lot, so when I needed to chat with her or keep tabs on the piece she was doing, I went up to her place. Your place. Whatever. I drove up last week, Tuesday I think, but she was still blocked."

"So I've heard," I said dryly, remembering Kit's confession. "What is this 'curse and death threat'?"

"Hah!" Metz slapped his leg and did an ear-to-ear. "Great stuff! Worth the price of admission. They were yelling at each other about the water stuff. Kit said he was a spy for the Lab, and Jaz told her she was an escapee from the nuthouse. Kit said she wasn't crazy enough to sit by while he helped the Lab dry up the river. Jaz said maybe the spics would go with the flow and get back to Mexico where they belonged." Metz took a breath. "Then Kit came up off her barstool like a spitting cat and told him if she found out he was helping the Lab she would personally blow his, ahem, motherfucking head off." Metz waited to see my reaction. I waited for him to go on. "Well, Jaz sat there kind of stupefied, looking at her, then he stood up on top of his barstool and pointed his arm down at her." Metz paused and closed his eyes, and then he went on as if reciting: "'From this day forth, may every foul word that leaves your filthy mouth become mother to a hoard of...mm...rabid bees, striking hence from where they sprang and plant your tongue with maggots. From this night forth, may your garden suck poison from the soil and may every object you paint turn fuchsia."

"You're kidding."

"I'm not. Jaz was. I don't think Kit was."

"You're making it up."

"Nope. In fact, I took out my pen on the spot and wrote it down on a napkin, Jaz's stuff that is. I collect curses."

I thought about Kit yesterday, sweating in front of her stove when it was over a hundred outside. Hadn't she said something about cleansing and a sweat lodge? Jaz had been ranting in high dramatic form with one eye on his audience, but I was betting Kit's superstitious side was hyperventilating.

"So what then?"

"That was pretty much the high point. They yelled a little more, nothing memorable. When I left they were talking pretty much like normal human beings."

"That must have taxed their acting skills," I said. "What about drugs? Was Jaz into anything?"

"Nah, he was an alcohol junkie."

"I saw some marijuana plants at his cabin."

"Oh, he grew a little grass to make a few bucks. I thought you meant *drugs*," he said, round-eyed.

"I heard something about Jaz doing some mushrooms?"

"Really? I don't think so. Anyway, he never said anything to me about it. What's got you interested in Jaz?"

"He died right in front of me. Isn't that enough?" I said.

"I thought it was just a heart attack, right?" He spun the chair back to the computer and closed the database program. A moonscape appeared on the screen, complete with tiny mountains, moons, and lakes, and dotted around the edges with small icons. "Is there something else going on?" he said, spinning back.

"No. I think you're right, his heart just stopped. Probably a combination of malnutrition and prolonged alcohol abuse." Juan had asked me to keep his investigation confidential, and what would be gained by telling Metz about the unidentified substance that had shown up in the autopsy? "But I've been hearing about this water thing ever since I got back from California. Kit gets nearly hysterical at the mention of it. I heard Jaz had some kind of connection to the people who were putting it through. Frankly, I can't quite get a handle on the whole thing."

"Depends who you listen to. One woman's Armageddon is another man's Eldorado." He got up and pushed the chair in my direction. "Have a seat," he ordered.

I sat down. "Was Jaz working for the Pecos Water Project?"

Metz scratched his head. "Jaz knew I wasn't interested, so he didn't talk to me about it," he said. "And neither should you. Here." He shoved me toward the computer screen and leaned over my shoulder to watch the screen as he ran the mouse over the pad, clicking on a series of icons to demonstrate a program that created graphic designs, another that scanned materials into the computer, and another that activated the computer's modem and surfed the Internet. "There are lots more," he said, straightening up, "but that will give you some toys to play with if you're so inclined. Got to get back to the shop," he said, stretching and yawning. "A queen's work is never done." He went to the door and then came back. He pointed to an icon that looked familiar, one that belonged to the same word processing program I used at home. "That one there is what Jaz used."

"What do you mean?" I said. But I think I knew then what he was going to say.

"In exchange for dragging me into the computer age, I let him use it for his novel." Metz slid open a drawer. He extracted a small square floppy disk from a box, handed it to me, and closed the drawer. "But he said he didn't like taking up storage space on the hard disk with it, so he always filed his work on the floppy. I can't imagine what to do with it. Thought maybe you could."

He handed it to me. Then he turned and left the room.

Morgan

THE UNIVERSE IS FULL OF HINTS, signs, clues. Transmitted in whispers and scents and images. We miss them because their language is not one we have created. But they are there all the same.

See: the first sign of rain is the circle around the moon. The first sign of a turbulence is the stillness that precedes it.

The first sign of trouble is impatience.

But you cannot recognize the early warning signs of impatience unless you have first recognized the beast. The animal that roams the labyrinthine coils of the human mind. That discovers the hidden trails, lopes to the sound of inner drums, tears away the flesh to reveal the truth in a dream's hieroglyph. An invaluable beast. Our thoughts are often its thoughts; our actions, its actions.

I pace before the double windows of the hotel room overlooking the park across the street. The carpet is deep, yet it might be some jungle patchwork of leaves and nettles and roots, some path familiar to the black jaguar, her muscles rippling, her tail snapping in boredom, eyes aflame with imagined mayhem.

Below, I watch the woman leave the gallery, cross the street, choose a bench below the sheltering arm of an elm, the dog leaving its game, lying at her feet. She sits on her bench, I on my chair. I watch them through the lace curtain from my side of the windowpane where the air is cool and the room is stacked with the paraphernalia required by the nature of my assignments and the file folder is spread open on the table beside me. Written across the front of it in black letters: Jet Butler. A name plucked from a box of Cracker Jacks. Yet here we sit, the both of us, incognito. She with her destiny deferred, I with mine. Our crossroads just ahead.

Also on the table, beside the file folder, is a book—the first one she wrote, the famous one. On the cover, a woman stands bound to a pyramid of burning sticks, her naked body licked by flames. LIVING DOWN UNDER. *Anna Lee Stone. 1969. The original cover had been half red, half black, the title in white, before the Indiana burning in 1972. Before the men returned home from the futile war on foreign soil, newly educated in the common-place banality of killing and cruelty so that their women, drunk on liber-ation, left home in droves and constructed menless communities across the continent, drawing on Stone's novel for their model. Even after the eighty-three women and children had been burned alive in their conclave of homes, by the time the investigation fingered the FBI, too many years had passed, public interest had wandered, and the other communities of women disintegrated, having learned the lesson of Indiana. It was then that the editions had appeared with the revised cover. A reminder, some said, of the penalties of women's disobedience.*

Anna Lee Stone, a.k.a. Jet Butler. The facts, the profile. Not to be con-fused with truth. For if the truth of Anna Lee Stone lies here between the covers of this Company folder, then my quarry is revealed before me— open and known and perfectly translucent in her essential elements:

BIO: Born 1947. Spencer, IN.
Father, professor of literature, Indiana University.
Mother: poet. Both killed in auto accident, 1951.
Raised by aunt (realtor), Nashville, TN.
BA/English/Berkeley, 1968; MA/English/Berkeley, 1969.
MA thesis/*Living Down Under,* pub. St. Martin's, 1969.
1969-72 course work for PhD/Berkeley. Withdrew 1972
following publicity surrounding burning of women's
community in New Harmony, Indiana. Living under
pseudonym, Jet Butler, near Tortuga, New Mexico.
Assigned royalties/*LDU* to Foundation for Homeless
Women, 1973. Occasionally teaches creative writing
course using given name in universities outside NM.
Taught one course in NM using a.k.a. Written 3 novels
following *LDU,* mysteries under a.k.a.

NEWS CLIPPINGS:
1) *Bloomington Herald-Times,* professor & poet-wife killed in auto accident, 1951; incl. pictures of deceased.
2) Publisher's PR picture of ALS for jacket cover/1969; incl. blurb.
3) *NYT,* review of *LDU,* 1969.
4) *SF Examiner,* interview w/ALS re. *LDU* on bestseller list, incl. pic, 1970.
5) *SF Examiner,* article/interview/pic of ALS following burning of women's community, 1972.
6) *NYT,* article re. disappearance of ALS, 1973.

CONCLUSIONS, RE. ASSIGNMENT:
Danger/level 5. Reclusive, but potentially influential re. media. Profile indicates past tendency to activism. Wild card, suggest caution.

Simon Cruz
8/6/93

A FTER LEAVING Metz's gallery, I wandered over to the park where Jones trotted up carrying the Frisbee, the swarm of children shrieking toward us. He looked frazzled around the ears, with the slightly hysterical glint to his eyes that some mothers get near the end of a long day. I took the Frisbee and gave it a flick, and we watched it soar above a group of teenage girls flattened out face-down on blankets in the sun, their bikini tops untied in back. The children followed the Frisbee, turning like a flock of swallows in midflight. I sank onto a nearby bench under the shade of a sprawling elm and watched the girls scream and scatter, holding both hands to their bikini tops as the children pinwheeled over them.

The sun directly overhead sent up waves of heat from the pavement. A group of women, about the right age for watching grandchildren, had spread food across a table on the gazebo, and they sat eating and smiling at the children chasing the Frisbee. I mulled over the new information I'd stumbled across in Metz's office. Not being as computer illiterate as he assumed, I resisted toying with the graphics program or surfing the Net. Instead, I opened the database and found the record for Angel Torrez. I made a note of his address—a post office box in Pueblito, a village not far from where Jaz lived. No phone. AGE: 30. RACE: Hispanic. None of this was very helpful—I had been hoping for a street address and phone number at the very least. Most of the other categories on Torrez's card, designed for tourists who had some interest in art and the money to buy it, were blank. Although the database program was one of the more elaborate ones, with all the bells and most of the whistles, Jaz had created the categories for Metz's gallery with an eye for clarity and simplicity—name, address, age, etc. One category, though, seemed odd: "OFC." I checked a few of the other entries, but the OFC space always turned up empty. I fanned through the stack of forms on the desk that Metz was preparing to type into the database. There was an OFC designation on those forms, but with the exception of an occasional question mark, the space was blank. Not wanting to sift through the entire database, I did a search on the category using the wild-card asterisk, but none of the cards contained an entry. Finally, I changed the program's file configuration system so that it would list hidden files and then repeated the search. Bingo. The computer tossed up fifteen entries, one of which was Angel Torrez. I called up the other fourteen names and discovered, like the one on Torrez, most of the data categories were blank. All seemed to live within a thirty-mile radius of Tortuga, and near the bottom of each card, in a text box labeled NOTES, all the cards except Torrez's had various dates typed in, the earliest in February and the latest on July 31, the day before Jaz's infamous argument with Kit. Only one card contained a name I recognized—Jim Becker—and the dates were spaced evenly at two-week intervals. I printed out the names, addresses, phone numbers, and dates and slipped the list in my pocket before I closed down the machine and left. On my way out, I saw Metz up in the display window with a large pink lamb's wool duster. I stopped by the sideboard and filled out one of the forms.

"Metz, what do I put in the blank where it says OFC?"

Metz hopped down off the stage with the duster held up in one hand. "Don't fill it in. It's just office stuff."

"Like what?" I asked.

"Oh, I don't know. Jaz said it was a space that the computer used to store extra information on each card if it needed to. Just leave it blank." He batted at the lamb's wool, sending up a puff of dust. I said good-bye as he disappeared into the back room.

Before leaving, I tiptoed up on the stage and circled around Kit's landscape to see how the light reflected off the paint at different angles. The lower left corner, the dark portion containing Jaz's face, had a slight matte caste to the surface, and when I drew my finger across it lightly, I felt the tacky surface of oil paint not completely dried. It had to be the last section that Kit had painted after her "block" had disappeared.

My reverie was interrupted when bells from the church behind the square began tolling the noon hour. The group of women in the gazebo had finished eating and were packing up the leftovers in paper bags when a flurry of shrieks brought them around just in time to see one of the youngsters make a head dive for the Frisbee which had landed in the midst of the sunbathing girls. The women gestured halfheartedly for the children to come, but they scattered wildly away, pursued by a girl with the pink Frisbee in one hand and holding up her bikini top in the other. The women shrugged to one another and returned to their packing.

The shade where I was sitting wouldn't hold out much longer against the heat, but for the moment, I stretched my legs, propped my head on the back of the bench, and gave myself over to the tranquillity that had settled over the park with the disappearance of the children. I was trying to fit together some pieces of the puzzle surrounding Jaz's death. What had started out as a simple venture to erase Kit's name from Juan's list of suspects had so far made her name more indelible than ever. According to Marguerite and Metz, two of the most reliable gossipmongers in town, Jaz wasn't dealing in anything more noxious than a little low-grade marijuana. If there had been any other illegal substances, Juan would have turned them up when he searched Jaz's cabin. And if Jaz hadn't been holding any mushrooms, then why would Kit have lied about it, especially considering the promise she'd made me when she moved into the guest house? And if she hadn't visited Jaz to buy mushrooms, why had she gone there? I remembered hearing that by the end of their argument Sunday night, Jaz and Kit had been sitting with their heads together, talking peaceably. Was it possible Jaz had lied to Kit about having the mushrooms in order to entice her to his place?

According to her story, she had driven to Jaz's on Monday, the day after their Sunday brawl at the Inn, because she had been blocked and unable to complete a painting she had been working on. Metz said that when he visited her on Tuesday, the day preceding Jaz's death, she was still blocked, yet on Friday afternoon, two days after Jaz's death, she delivered the finished painting for Metz to display. Somewhere between Tuesday and Friday, Kit had managed to complete the painting, and I wondered what it was that had started her creative juices pumping again. How significant was it that she had become unblocked at about the same time Jaz had died, and that what she had painted had been a none-too-flattering portrait of Jaz? I had lots of questions, not many answers.

However, I thought, toying with the floppy disk I still held in my hand, the mystery of Jaz's manuscript was solved, although the prospect of reading it weighed heavily on me. I sighed and closed my eyes, but all I could see were never-ending piles of student papers I had read over the years, forgettable every one. Of course, Jaz could be an undiscovered Joyce, but I wasn't much cheered by the thought of reading an unedited version of *Finnegan's Wake*, either. I decided to take a quick peek at the disk when I got home, mostly out of curiosity, and then pass it along to Juan, maybe make a copy for Caroline Marcus. Why not? It wasn't copyrighted, after all. And assuming Caroline Marcus was telling the truth, she probably had as much right to it as anyone else.

And then there was the surprise of discovering Jaz's technological accomplishments as a computer wizard. As Ms. McCarthy might have said, "Who would have thunk it?" I wanted to look more closely at the names on the list I had pirated from Metz's database, maybe even pay a call on a couple of them. The presence of Angel Torrez's name suggested that Jaz knew him, so the drug connection might have some validity after all. And then there was Becker's name—I remembered Kit saying she'd seen some apparatus in the river behind his house, and she'd seen something similar behind Jaz's. But the police had inspected his property, and Juan had said nothing about a suspicious gizmo in the river. I made a mental note to ask him about it. Kit had tried unsuccessfully to get a list from the Lab of people's names and locations of points along the river. Could this be the list of names she wanted? But why would Jaz have had it? And why did he go to such lengths to create a dummy category and conceal the files in the database? Was there any name on the list that might include someone who wanted Jaz dead?

Not that there weren't plenty of people falling into that category. Marguerite, for one. I didn't know what Jaz had done to inspire such hostility, but I read it clearly in her eyes. And if the chemical analysis came back showing that Jaz had been poisoned, who better to poison an alcoholic than a bartender? I recalled Marguerite's expression when she said that Jaz could be charming—judging from her last husband, Marguerite had a weakness for abusive alcoholics. Had she been attracted to Jaz? Had he slept with her to feed his alcoholism? Had she realized it and killed him, then attended his funeral for good measure? Women have killed men for less.

The park began to fill with white noise—murmurs of Sunday couples strolling along the pathways, after-church families gathering for picnics on the lawn. Nearby, a young couple set a large red-and-white cooler on the grass and began unfurling a blanket, flapping it in the air. The sunbathing girls sat up and began fastening the backs of their bikini tops, looking pleased as the group of middle-aged women filed down the stairs of the gazebo herding the pack of wild children before them. One of the girls sent the pink Frisbee soaring in their direction.

I went back to composing my list of suspects, thinking about Caroline Marcus and her odd surprise appearance. She had driven in from California just in time for the burial, she said, but she could easily have come sooner, maybe visited Jaz with some exotic, slow-acting poison laced through a gift bottle of mescal. I wondered if Juan had checked her tire treads for a possible match with the fresh set he found in Jaz's driveway. Could Caroline Marcus have visited Jaz after I left, taken the odd bottles for some reason of her own, and then shown up at the funeral to keep tabs on the investigation? If she was telling the truth and was an old flame who had never gotten married after her affair with Jaz, had she hated him all these years for abandoning her and, after she discovered his whereabouts, set out to kill him? I thought of Juan's story of Willie Joe Figgen and tried to understand what it was about Caroline Marcus that might have reminded him of Willie Joe. I dredged up a mental picture of handsome Willie in his lawyer's suit and tie, striding down Main Street on his way to the courthouse with a friendly smile for everyone he met, driving his Mercedes to the bus stop and climbing into the tree with the rifle. And then I tried to fill in the features of the shadowy woman I had met on my deck last night. I was so deep in midnight imagery that when Caroline Marcus stepped directly into my line of vision, I must have been looking her straight in the eye for several seconds before she came into focus. Although she bore little resemblance to last night's shadowy visitor, I recognized her immediately—maybe because she was already running through my mind at that moment, or maybe it was something else. Maybe it was her odd penetrating look of…what? Recognition? And something else—a brief shadow of something savage?

But if I hadn't recognized her, I could hardly have missed her—even in the pitiless glare of the afternoon sun, she was a "fine-looking woman," as Juan had put it. Unusually tall for a woman, pushing six foot in high-heeled Western boots, she was so darkly tanned that the white silk shell she wore tucked into faded Levi's seemed fluorescently white. In contrast, pulled back and tied with a white scarf, her hair was jet black, straight as corn silk, and hanging across her shoulder, nearly waist-length, in an undulating streak of black on white. The girls on the blanket had turned and were giving her a hard-eyed appraisal. The white noise in the park faded into a pall of silence for a moment as I sat on the bench caught in the grip of Caroline Marcus's electric presence.

Jones leapt from his spot beside the bench and raced to greet her, and then he turned with a jaunty trot and escorted her my way. She stood for a moment beside the bench, taking in the park with a quick, sweeping glance and a terse smile. The muted voices began to fill the park again.

"May I join you?" she said. The voice was unmistakable, filled with smoke. And now I saw what last night had concealed—that she had the kind of storybook face that has driven men to launch ships, write poems, forsake thrones—a composite of exquisitely modeled bones and chiseled lips and precisely etched shadows. But it was the eyes that stopped you cold. So pale a blue as to seem nearly colorless at first: not quite the color of a human iris, they seemed to reach from a darker, more interior place. She wore no makeup that I could see, and while she was not oblivious to the charged atmosphere her appearance excited, she seemed less flattered than mildly amused by it. After the first jolt of recognition, my heartbeat was settling back down to its normal pace.

"Sure," I nodded toward the empty bench. "I'm afraid that white silk won't last long around here, though." Between the drought and the afternoon winds, every surface wore a perpetual skin of soft red dust.

She shrugged and sat down. "It washes," she said, crossing her legs. Jones gave me a surreptitious look and inched a little closer in her direction. "I guess neither one of us got much sleep last night. I'm really sorry about barging in on you, it seemed like the thing to do at the time. Sitting here in broad daylight, I can't believe I really did it." She leaned down, and using both hands, stroked Jones from the tip of his muzzle to the top of his head, where she burrowed deep into his fur with her thumbs and began massaging around the roots of his ears. He gazed up at her with adoration from pale eyes that were a mirror image of her own.

"It *was* a little strange," I agreed. "I found a potted plant knocked over this morning by the front door."

"That must have been the noise I heard when I was coming down your drive. I thought maybe I frightened one of your animals. I should have mentioned it before. I'll be glad to replace it."

"Forget it. I repotted it this morning." I watched her and Jones, and I remembered the way Noche had taken to her. "You didn't seem to upset the animals much, even Jones didn't raise the alarm. That's pretty strange, too."

"Animals take to me. I don't know why that is." She kept stroking Jones, but she gave me a penetrating look. "Maybe it was a prowler. Can you think of anyone who might want to get into your house?"

"You've got to be kidding. I live on a mesa where you nearly have to be dropped in by helicopter. Outside of my computer, I don't own a thing anyone would be interested in, not even a television. I don't even lock my doors."

"I know." She gave me another look that hit the adrenaline button, and I was reminded of her parting words of the night before about keeping my doors locked. She must have known what I was thinking: "When I got there last night, I noticed your front door was standing open, so I closed it. I turned the knob to see if it was locked. It wasn't."

I looked at her in frank amazement. Not only had this woman, a perfect stranger, left her vehicle parked in the boonies a couple of miles from my house in the middle of a pitch-black night, but she had made her way through two miles of seriously rugged terrain and then tried the lock on my front door. Who was the nutcase here—her for doing it and telling me, or me for believing it? My mouth had probably dropped open too because she gave a deep-throated laugh.

I was doubly incensed. "I have to say that you have damned good night vision."

"It's true. I do," she said. She sent me another penetrating look. "My mother used to tell me it was because she ate pounds of carrots when she was carrying me. She said it was one of those urges pregnant women get."

I shook my head and laughed with her, mystified by the craziness of it all. I felt, for the first time since we'd met, that our conversation had left the twilight zone and stepped into daylight, and I felt the Sunday murmur of the park fold around us. In front of our bench, two magpies hopped along, stabbing at the grass with their long knife-like beaks, twisting their heads sideways every few seconds to aim a wary yellow eye at Jones. When the smaller junkos or robins wandered too near, one of the magpies would make a run at it with wings outspread, screaming "Mag, mag! MA-A-G!"

"Am I forgiven?" Caroline said, fixing me with a look of mock remorse and raising her right hand as though she were being sworn in as a witness. "I promise never to invade your mesa and knock on your door in the wee hours." Jones, his eyes half-closed in what looked to be ecstasy, was now leaning with one shoulder pressed against her leg and his muzzle in her lap.

"Okay," I said, "but don't be surprised when I turn up unannounced on your doorstep in L.A."

"Deal."

We both watched as a gleaming black raven, wings open wide, sailed down to settle between the two magpies who immediately sprang forward with a tumultuous beating of wings and a great clamor of "Mag! Yak! MA-A-A-G-G!!!" until at last Jones pried himself away from Caroline long enough to give chase. But the heat was thinning out the park. One by one, families were folding up their blankets and leaving.

"Looks like I'm going to be here a few days whether I like it or not," Caroline said, leaning over with her head propped in one hand. "Your sheriff asked if I could stick around till they get some kind of lab report back. I called my office, so officially I'm on vacation. It's not a problem, really. We always have several pieces ready for a backup, just in case. And, you know, I kind of like it here, in spite of the heat. I need a break."

"You're staying at the Inn?" I knew how expensive the rooms were, and I wondered whether editors of literary magazines were making more than they used to.

"Yes. It's very pleasant, once you get used to the weird mixture of antiques and plastic laminates."

I was on the verge of inviting her to stay at my place, but then I caught myself. This was a woman I had just been scrutinizing as a suspect in a murder. She had also, I reminded myself sternly, made an extremely strange, and not altogether satisfactorily explained, pilgrimage to my mesa in the middle of last night. The least I should do before getting too chummy was to see if Juan had run an I.D. check on her yet. On my way out of town, I would see if he was in his office and let him know what I'd turned up. Jones had returned from birding and stood contemplating first me and then Caroline. I had the feeling he was struggling to arrive at some monumental canine decision. Caroline stretched out her hand to him, but he lay down in the grass and put his muzzle on his paws, whining faintly. Caroline tucked her hand back under her chin.

"I'll take a run up to Santa Fe. Do some shopping. Sight-seeing." She seemed to be talking to Jones. She twisted around to face me. "What's up, anyway? I thought Jasper had a heart attack."

I didn't know how much information Juan wanted to share, but if you've instructed someone not to leave town while a murder investigation is under way, how secret can it be?

"My understanding is that some foreign substance turned up in the autopsy. The coroner's office here is pretty low budget, so they're sending it to Santa Fe. My guess is that it will show Jaz munched on some indigenous plant he shouldn't have. It happens around here."

"So they're thinking he might have been poisoned? And apparently," she said, "the manuscript hasn't turned up. That seems to be another problem."

I looked down at the floppy disk I was still holding, suddenly aware that I held in my hand precisely what Caroline Marcus had come looking for at my house last night. I knew that she wanted it badly, but who else might also be interested in it? And why? Was it possible that whoever stopped at Jaz's cabin after I left had been looking for the manuscript, not for the bottles at all? If so, that person would have known Jaz might be dead, something that only the killer could have suspected. If that were true, the manuscript must contain something that he, or she, did not want found. I had nearly forgotten that Caroline was sitting next to me, and when she spoke, I started.

"Do you write on the computer?" she asked, nodding at the disk.

"I do," I said, slipping it into my jeans pocket, "and if you'd asked me that same question ten years ago, I'd have gone off on a long I-detest-computers tangent. I was strong against them back then. These days, I have a hard time writing anything at all, even a letter, without one." The day was growing hotter by the minute, and only a few people were left in the park.

"I think I've probably already heard that tangent in one form or another from quite a few of the authors I work with," Caroline said, giving me a droll smile. "Mostly the older ones."

"I'm an addict now," I confessed. "It started back a few years ago when I was teaching at a place where every office came with a computer and an Internet account." I shook my head, recalling the time like a junkie remembering the first fix. "I really hated computers. At first, I was just filling in time between student appointments. I'd log on and fly. Then I discovered the magic of the word processing program, and now it's just second nature to write everything on the computer." I paused for a minute, thinking back. It wasn't that long ago, but it seemed like a different century. "It's like I was another person, you know? I can still vividly remember feeling this self-righteous contempt for computers. And for anyone who wrote on one. I don't feel that way now, but why not? The computer didn't substantially change, I did." I shifted on the park bench, lost in thoughts that were becoming more uncomfortable, but I couldn't stop.

"I think it's something to do with getting older, racking up enough of a past to look back across ten, twenty years and see how something you believed back then with absolute certainty wasn't even close to the way you see it now. And knowing that's the case, how can you absolutely believe anything this moment when you know how it can shift around on you? Somehow, something just happens, twists just a hair—now you see it, now you don't. It's kind of like those two pieces of rock that shift on an earthquake fault—one day things are lined up with all the little picket fences in a row, then out of nowhere, with no warning, something invisible moves slightly and suddenly everything's changed, devastated, out of whack."

"Yes. Yes, it's like that, isn't it?" said Caroline, although she seemed to be speaking from a great distance.

We were drifting into territory I had avoided for twenty years. I wasn't quite sure how I'd been transported there so quickly, but I was looking back over the strange terrain of my past as though it belonged to someone else, transfixed by the spectacle of it. Not quite able to turn away, yet loath to enter.

"You see," I continued, looking out across the park but not quite at it, seeing instead the superimposed image of the news bulletin flashing across my television screen, interrupting the evening movie as I sat munching butter-soaked popcorn in my living room in Berkeley, California, twenty years ago almost exactly to the day, "when that happens to you, you're not quite the same person anymore. Like the picket fences aren't really picket fences anymore. They're in pieces, broken and crushed. They're still wood, you might rearrange the pieces, build something different, maybe something better, you might even try to nail them back the way they were before. But whatever you do, they won't ever be the same tidy little enclosures they used to be." I had crossed over the border. I was traveling toward the interior now, rolling backward in time along that path, and maybe I was headed downhill, because I couldn't seem to stop. The park had disappeared and the television screen had filled with swift fragmented scenes of clapboard farmhouses, outbuildings, barns, women and children running between groups of trailers set among apple trees, loudspeaker voices shouting staccato commands, the dull pock sounds of rifle fire, and then the screams inside the orange flames that exploded across the nineteen-inch screen.

"What that means for a human being, for me," I said, barely hearing my own voice, "is that somehow you get to this place in the present moment, because that's the only place you *can* be, and you know that any opinion you embrace may have the devil in it. Or maybe not. But the thing of it is, you can't go on like you did before, all wrapped up in that white dense cloud of righteous certainty— call it innocence—because now you know that there is not just that one vision you've chosen as holy. There are other visions, maybe just as holy, so many of them that you can't even imagine all the possibilities."

Caroline Marcus said: "So you're stuck in this one spot, paralyzed by all these alternate heavens and possible hells? Unsure of the difference, you choose not to choose?" I was lost in my own thoughts, and when I didn't respond, she continued: "I think that's a safe little philosophy, but it seems to me that if there are a hundred ways to see something and it's impossible to distinguish the moral superiority of one over the other, then why does it matter which one you choose? If we live in an accidental universe, as opposed to one created by god, it's all guesswork, right? You can do anything, and it's okay."

I should have heard her that time, but I didn't. I was so far into the backwoods of my past that I was wandering lost. Could you become permanently lost in the past? Isn't the world full of people who do? And full of the wandering shades who never had the chance to live long enough to have a past? I could hear the women and the children screaming behind the flames.

"You have to be careful," I said to the fire raging across the park, "because whatever attitude you have, whatever conviction you're shoring up brick by brick, it could all be a lie, mirrors and smoke. It could appear strong, well conceived, beautiful enough to stand up through several centuries, but the least breeze or ripple can send it crashing down. And if you're blessed or cursed with some talent for persuasion and lean toward the social arts, say you're a composer or politician or journalist, you could bring the roof down on a lot of other people as well. All caught in the collapse and the falling bricks and..." I paused for a moment, breathless, wanting to stop, turn back, unable to.

"And fire?" said Caroline Marcus.

I heard her this time, but faintly. Not loud, not long. I heard her, but I wasn't listening.

"So what happens is this kind of paralysis of the will. You're still breathing, you're still thinking, the world's still spinning, the music's still playing, but somebody's turned the volume down. Down so low that all you can do is sit there in the empty air and wait to hear something again, get some idea of the direction you ought to take. And even when you're sitting there waiting and thinking, you know, really, the *music*'s there, it's just that *you* can't hear it anymore. It's like the computer—it's not the computer that's changed, it's *you*. But knowing this doesn't help either, because you still can't move. All you can do is sit there: you still can't bring yourself to assert one thing and not another." I was panting, trying to slow down. I turned and looked at Caroline Marcus. "And if you can't do that, how can you write a novel worth reading? Where's the conviction, the passion?"

It was then that I noticed the difference in her. She was leaning toward me, her strange, pale eyes only inches from my own, glassy and sightless as though she were in a trance. A sheen of sweat glistened across her forehead.

"Are you all right?" I asked, touching her arm. It was cold as marble. She flinched at my touch, blinked several times, and sank back on the bench.

"Not used to the heat." She wiped at her forehead with the back of her hand and closed her eyes. "You sound pretty intense," she said, opening her eyes to narrow slits. "Are you saying you used to write passionate books, and now you don't?"

Bang. There it was. And after I heard her ask that, I began to hear her other comments as well. What had started out with Stevens's "Sunday Morning" humming through my head had turned into a "Waste Land" kind of day. The heat was nearly unbearable, and not a soul was left in the park. The birds had given up their squabbles and taken themselves up to the green air among the leaves. The silence seemed to last a lifetime.

There was not a shadow of doubt in my mind that this woman sitting beside me on the park bench knew my real name and that she could probably tick off every book I'd ever written, first to last—not that it was a very long or very impressive list. The question was, *how* she knew. I had written three books after the first one, and none carried my picture on the jacket. She might have seen me on one of the campuses where I taught a course every three or four years, though that seemed unlikely. She was too young to have remembered my face on the couple of brief television interviews back in 1973.

I measured my words carefully as I spoke to her: "I guess that is what I'm saying. Have you got an informed editor's opinion about that?"

"Maybe you ought to try for a little passion in your life," she said, attempting humor. I wasn't biting.

"I moved here to get away from the passion," I said. "But you know about that, don't you?"

She looked down at her lap and rubbed at the denim. "Yes, I do," she said, meeting my eyes. "When I read the article in the paper about Jasper's death and you were mentioned as 'a local author,' I couldn't place you. In my line of work, I keep a close eye on new stuff coming out. So I looked your name up, also just curious—thinking maybe you were connected to Jasper somehow, maybe a girlfriend. Three mysteries listed for Jet Butler, but just on a hunch I also checked out the copyright and discovered your real name."

"And you rushed right out and bought them?" I knew the mysteries were out of print. Luckily.

Caroline gave a brief laugh. "I'd already read the first one, of course. Hasn't everybody? But the others—well, I have some friends who run a used bookstore. I put the word out and came up with them."

Neither of us spoke for a while. I was feeling humiliation; if she had any compassion at all, she was probably feeling pity. There was a good reason, besides just wanting to live an anonymous non-Anna Lee Stone life, that I didn't put my real name on them. They made a few bucks, not much, and then disappeared quickly. I wrote them because I was a writer, but they were fourth-rate, and at the moment, I couldn't gear myself up to write another. Writer's block was too exalted a name for what I was feeling.

But Caroline Marcus wasn't ready to leave it alone just yet. She went on, "I read *Living Down Under* back when I was a sophomore in college," she said. "Required reading. It's unforgettable, and apparently it made a big impression on a lot of women back then, when it first came out."

"Yeah. It did." My truck was the only one left on the street. It was as though the entire town had suddenly become deserted. The crooked "Closed" sign in the door of Metz's gallery was back up again. He would probably be over at the Inn, taking in the cool air. There were only a few flames left, nibbling around the edges of the trees in the park.

"I guess you don't want to talk about it."

"Sure I do. Why else would I have changed my name and moved to an isolated mesa in New Mexico?"

"I'm sorry," she said. "Have you given up serious fiction, then?"

"It's given me up, looks like."

"I guess you wouldn't think about doing the 'Writers in Exile' piece, now that Jasper won't be giving me his?"

I looked at her like she was brain damaged.

"Sometimes talking about it, writing about it helps. You know that better than I do. It's twenty years ago, after all."

"Some things don't pass."

"You sound like you think you're responsible for what happened."

"Do you think those women would have started up that community if they hadn't had a model to go on?"

115

"Probably not, but when we were discussing your book in class, I remember the professor pointing out that lots of women had joined those communities to escape violence in their homes. In fact, my best friend was taking the course with me, and she talked about this friend of her mother's who always had a black eye or broken wrist or something wrong with her, and it turned out to be her husband doing it. But he was prominent in the community, well off financially, and had her convinced that he would kill her and get custody of their daughter if she ever told anyone or tried to leave. Things kept getting worse. Eventually she managed to escape with her daughter to a women's shelter. It was there she came across your book and made a connection to join one of the women's communities. From what my friend said, her husband probably would have killed her if he ever found her. The professor said there were thousands who had something of the same story and that, in spite of Indiana, there were many more women whose lives were saved by leaving homes where they, and their children, were constantly under siege."

"I've thought of that. It's a kind of pretty logic, isn't it? It helps, but it doesn't substantially change the facts of what happened."

"And so you write novels that are safe. That won't influence anyone?"

"Did they influence you?"

She gave a brief laugh, "No, they didn't."

"There you have it," I said, leaning back on the bench next to her, both of us looking out across the deserted park. The sun was angling toward the west and we were losing the shade from the tree above. I clasped my hands behind my head, closed my eyes, and thought of being home, in the cool adobe shadows. I was right in the middle of a pep talk to get myself moving when Caroline spoke.

"This thing you were talking about, looking back and seeing something in a totally different light—I'm having a similar experience about Jasper. In my imagination, he was this perfect shining being, but now that I'm here talking to people who knew him, I'm beginning to see he wasn't at all what I'd thought." She paused and looked around at me with a feverish light in her eye. "I went through so many years believing in something that didn't exist, loving someone that I needed and made up, that I'm feeling..." Caroline sat up, her eyes shifting rapidly about the park and the odd assemblage of the buildings' facades that surrounded us. "I don't quite know how I'm feeling, actually. Like everything around me is a stage set, painted on, not quite real." Her voice, though still sultry, had taken on a new edge, like steel. Jones got up from his nap and came over, rested his muzzle on her lap, and looked up at her. She dug her fingers around his ears and went on in her normal tone, "I think I need to say good-bye to Jasper, really put an end to it. I was wondering if you would be willing to show me where he lived. I know it's a pretty primitive place, I don't care about that. I need to be somewhere that was his, and really let it all go."

I had been thinking of stopping by Jaz's cabin to check out the "gizmo" in the river that Kit had mentioned, but I wasn't looking forward to it. The notion of visiting with someone else in tow made the prospect a lot more appealing.

"Sometime tomorrow morning?" I said.

"Perfect. How about I meet you at your place around ten? I'd like to take that same hike again by daylight," she laughed.

"Date," I said, getting up. "Ten sounds good." I was just turning toward the sidewalk, heading toward my truck with Jones, when Caroline spoke.

"Just one thing."

I turned back.

"Your name? Does anyone else here know about it?"

"Just Kit," I said. And left her sitting there.

J UAN'S OFFICE at the edge of town occupied an upgraded adobe house with modular add-ons at each end. His truck was parked out front by the curb, under a wide-branched dusty oak tree, and a small older model blue Civic sat in the driveway beside the house. The front yard had been made into a low-maintenance plot of crushed red volcanic rocks with a wooden sign stuck in it reading "Sheriff's Office," embellished with a cartoonlike drawing of a smoking pistol that someone had burned into the wood. I nosed my truck in behind Juan's to catch as much of the shade as possible and left Jones to wait on the porch as I entered the office. What had once been a living room was now a large open square of grey linoleum with a balustrade and mismatched chairs across the front. Running across the opposite wall was a chest-high counter where a couple of clerks worked behind computers during the week. But today was Sunday: the lights were off, and except for the ceiling fans revolving slowly, the place seemed deserted. I caught sight of a slice of fluorescent light at the end of a dim corridor off the main room and followed it to an office with a plate glass window set into the upper half of the wall. Juan and Scott Emerick were bending over a desk scattered with snapshots. When they saw me standing in the door, Scott's long bony face turned red, giving his enormous freckles a greenish tinge; Juan's expression was inscrutable as he nodded me in and indicated the only available chair, an Early American model that looked like it had been filched from a fifties dining room set. Scott left with a wide, horsey smile revealing teeth the size of piano keys, closing the door after him.

I took the floppy disk from my pocket, laid it on the desk, and sat down, giving Juan a rundown of discovering Jaz's manuscript on Metz's computer.

"Well, I guess that takes care of that," he said, picking up the disk and examining it in that way people who don't like computers do. His dark face looked haggard under the artificial light. "You mind looking at it," he said, handing it to me, "give me your professional opinion, get it back a-s-a-p?" He seemed about as overjoyed as I did at the prospect of reading Jaz's book. I heaved a deep, silent sigh and took the disk from him, fiddling with it as we talked.

"Sure," I said. I told him about running into Caroline Marcus. "I thought I might make her a copy. Okay with you?"

"Let's wait till you find out what's on it and let me know. And hang on till we get the lab results back, maybe tomorrow. Might need her to sign a release." Juan settled into a battered chair behind his desk. "What'd you think of her?" He leaned back in the chair with a loud creak.

"'Fine-looking woman,'" I said, imitating his own description of her. "She mentioned you asked her to stick around. Have you done a background check?"

He nodded. "*Nada.* Works for a magazine called *Western Writer* in L.A. Talked to her boss, says she's on vacation. Never married, no kids. No record. Couple speeding tickets."

"But you still don't trust her?"

He shrugged and rocked in the chair, the bones of his jaw working. "Something odd, just can't put my finger on it."

"Did you check the treads in Jaz's driveway with her car?"

He nodded. "No match. All we've got at this point is the unidentified chemical, the tread marks showing Kit visited him recently, her threat to kill him. Lots of people wanted to, no problem with motive. That's about it. It's wait and see till the lab report comes back."

"Have you heard anything about Jaz dealing drugs? Not weed, but hard stuff? Maybe mushrooms?"

Juan shook his head. "Why?"

I couldn't tell him about Kit, not yet. "Just curious. Heard he hung out with Angel Torrez." I paused, unsure how much Juan would confide in me. "I was just thinking of the rumors about Jaz and the Lab. Did you see anything set up in the river behind his cabin?" I stuck my hand in my pocket, fishing for the list of names to show Juan. But at the mention of the Lab, his eyes went suddenly flat. I left my hand in my pocket.

"Had a little solar pump set up back there. Using the river water for his water source. That's all." He studied me a minute and leaned over his desk, the fluorescent light casting deep shadows under his eyes and cheekbones. "Forget the Lab, Jet. They're not involved, and they're starting to get annoyed at being drug into this."

I slipped my hand back out of my pocket, empty. "We certainly don't want to *annoy* them, do we?" I said, trying to read Juan, but his face was as blank as a piece of drywall.

"Let it go, Jet. It's a dead end. Exists only in Kit's imagination, and she's headed for trouble. You can't just throw accusations around like she's been doing and expect folks to like it. Especially *these* folks."

I was wondering just how well Juan knew "these folks." And how could he be so sure Jaz wasn't involved with them? And if he was sure, why not tell me how he got that way? I decided to keep what I knew about Jaz's computer list to myself. If Juan was in communication with the Lab and the list had anything to do with the information they had withheld from Kit, the less "those folks" knew about it, the safer I would feel. As I stood up to leave, my eyes lit on the snapshots spread across Juan's desk.

"Jesus Christ," I said, bending over to look more closely, "what the hell..."

Juan sighed and ran his hand over his head. "Pretty grisly, aren't they?"

"What is it?" I asked, turning one of the snapshots right-side-up and leaning closer.

"What's left of a female cougar and her young. Got a call out by Casita this morning. Old fellow lives out that way heard a racket, went to take a look, then called us. Torn limb from limb. No sign of being shot or ravaged, just pulled apart and left, but we can't figure what would have the strength to do that kind of damage.

Old guy's sure it's aliens." Juan cocked an eyebrow toward the ceiling. "We'll figure it out, but we're stumped right now."

The snapshots showed bloody pieces of appendages and body parts strewn beside the river's edge. I shuddered, sickened by the sight, and left the office.

I started the truck, flipped the air conditioner on high, and stuck the floppy disk in the glove compartment for safekeeping. As Jones and I breezed along the freeway, I saw that the black smear in the sky had deepened. Fat storm clouds hung over the mesas along the western horizon, but unlike typical Southwestern summers with their late-afternoon cloudbursts, this year the storms had drifted north. I switched on the radio and scanned the channels to find an update on the fire threatening Taos. Finally, half an hour later as I pulled into my driveway, I found a hasty bulletin wedged between two country songs, giving a "no-change" assessment of the situation and noting that the evacuation was still scheduled for tomorrow.

I spent the rest of Sunday afternoon playing catch-up—refilling litter boxes, feeding laundry into the washer and dryer, wiping down the last couple of days' installment of fine red dust. I had tied an old T-shirt around my head and was dragging around the Shop-Vac by the extension attachment with the brush nozzle stuck on the end of it, sucking up the last seven months of spider webs around the ceiling vigas, when I felt a touch on my shoulder.

I shrieked and jumped a couple of feet straight up.

Mac stood behind me, both arms raised, palms out, as though he were at gunpoint. I reached down and shut off the vacuum.

"Sorry," he said, lowering his arms. "I yelled and banged before I broke and entered." He was staring at me with an odd expression, stroking his beard. "I don't guess that would be what my grandmammy used to call 'pantaloons,' would it?" He pointed at my head.

"Oh, jeez." I snatched the T-shirt off and threw it on the floor. "What are you *doing* here?" I asked, irrationally angry with him. He had on his goofy grin, khaki pants, and this morning's bright yellow waffle-knit golfer's shirt of the sort worn fifteen years ago or so with a green alligator on the pocket.

"I got some info on your purple thang," he drawled, taking off his Dodgers cap, looking at the T-shirt, and scratching behind his ear, "and thought I might as well drive on up. Willa's in Santa Fe, won't be home till late. Looks like you're busy, though."

"I'm afraid it'll keep," I said, motioning him to the living room. I picked up the T-shirt, draped it over the top of the Shop-Vac, and left it sitting in the middle of the floor. A reminder. "Want some tea?"

"Tea?" Mac repeated, spitting out the word as though I'd offered him vinegar. "I always forget you're one of them yuppie types that've moved over to Perrier with a splash of Martinelli. Rot your gut." He collapsed into a rocker beside the sofa.

Mac had achieved some repute as a connoisseur of beers, although I'd never personally seen him drink anything more than a Dos Equis with his lunch. I was ticking off several other possibilities and had reached M for Milk, which sent Mac into a spell of mock choking and grasping of the neck, when Kit stuck her head in the door.

"Hey," she said, "I thought I heard that Caddy of yours. Are you *ever* going to get a new muffler for that car? I could hear it all the way from the village." Kit slid through the door, holding up a pitcher of amber liquid, and went into the kitchen, where she began setting up glasses and breaking open a tray of ice cubes.

Mac left off his coughing drama and perked up on the couch, watching Kit pour the liquid over the ice cubes. She had on a pair of purple Spandex tights with small flecks of silver that caught the light. Over that, she had on a loose, white sweater of some kind of fishnet material, her shapely breasts backlit against the kitchen window. Her hair was wound around in a loose knot at the nape of her neck, and she resembled some swan-necked, larger-than-life double for Audrey Hepburn. I had pretty much resigned myself to playing the part of homely dwarf when Kit was around. Pretty much.

She came into the living room and passed glasses around. I watched Mac drink and then beam at me. I took a sip. My taste buds puckered and withered.

"Jeez," I said, staring into the tea.

"Hey, Sunday night. How about I make stir fry?" Kit said, going back to the kitchen.

While Kit banged pots and ran water and hummed, I lay stretched on the couch, buttressed by several cats and feeling blessedly content. Deciding to postpone talk of the "purple thang" till after dinner, Mac and I exchanged summer school stories as he sat rocking beside me, smiling into his beard. From the front door, which Kit had left standing open, came the trickling sounds of the river. We sat in silence for a time and listened to it, and then I asked Mac for his assessment of the Pecos Water Development Project, signaling him to keep his voice low. His smile disappeared.

"Politics as usual," he said. "But I think we're going to be in for some serious problems. You take the drought, minus thirty percent of the water we have now, and you'll see fields that can't be irrigated, fires that can't be doused. You'll see more of the nasty bugs already living in the water, and they're always there, whether from natural sources or just the stuff people have always dumped in their rivers—the water'll be that much worse. That means problems with wildlife that live in the river, and those that drink from it."

"Why haven't you spoken out?" I whispered, glancing uneasily toward the kitchen. "With Kit's group?"

Mac shook his head. "Right or wrong, I'm not much of an activist in the usual sense. I like my ivory tower. But, in my defense, I think my articles and research make as much difference as walking picket lines. *The New Mexican* up in Santa Fe sent a reporter down when Kit was kicking up her heels. He stopped by for my opinion, and I gave it to him. Their next comment is always a reference to the official study that shows no effect on communities who access the river. I explained how the official figures can be skewed to look about any way you want them to. Even gave him a few examples. It's not even a matter of outright lying so much as just your everyday brand of deception. But I never saw the information I gave him included in his article. It's city hall. Nothing's going to stop it. It's all decided somewhere else, not here, not with me or you or Kit."

A few minutes later, the three of us sat around the living room, wielding chopsticks over wooden bowls of rice, watched intently by several cats. Beyond the windows, the sun was setting, shooting off spectacular rays across a turquoise sky. Mac and I offered the cats tidbits of mushrooms with the tips of our chopsticks, followed closely by Kit's "Ee-yyeew, gross," while the room gradually filled with evening shadows and the sky deepened to indigo.

Later, as Kit washed up in the kitchen, I switched on a couple of lamps, and Mac stood up and stuck his hand into his jeans pocket.

"I come up with some interesting info on this purple thang," he said, pulling out the small bottle with the lavender growth. "I did a little surfing on the Net and pulled up a bunch of stuff." He saw my eye light up at mention of the Internet and grinned. "You're welcome to surf at my office any time, password's 'dodger' if I'm not around. Get Kathy to let you in," he chuckled. He held up the bottle to the stained glass lamp hanging over his chair and peered at it, squinting one eye, then handed it to me. It had grown darker, nearly black, and looked vaguely like a charred piece of sea coral.

"I don't know where you got this," he said, sitting back in the rocker, "and I'm not altogether sure I want to know." He had dropped the clowning routine and his voice was serious. "I've not personally seen anything like it before, although I came across a reference to what I *think* this is in a journal recently, so a lot of what I'm going to tell you is conjecture, but it's *informed* conjecture. I stuck it under the scope after you left. Then I got on the Net, looked up a few articles over at the library. Let's slide on through all the scientific double-talk. Basically, what I think you got here is the byproduct of a fungus developed for biochemical warfare." Mac reached over and took the bottle from my hand and shook it again. He looked at it as though doubting what he was saying, a look of revulsion spreading across his face.

"Are you telling me that inside that bottle is something lethal enough to kill people? Is that what you're telling me?" I watched him shake the bottle again, hoping that he had a good grip on it.

"Something like that. But this would be a tremendously watered-down version, not the actual people-killing variety. That was never actually perfected or used, so far as anyone knows anyway, although it was developed back in the late sixties during the Vietnam years. This one here, if my guess is right, is relatively innocuous, or in any event, not lethal. It's like, say, the polio virus—when used in small doses, it's not only harmless, it can even have a positive effect in developing immunity. At least, that was the theory of some authorities. But the FDA wasn't buying it. Funding to develop this milder strain here was, officially at least, withdrawn by the Feds because of some of its rather nasty side effects."

Mac shoved out his chin, still fascinated with the contents of the bottle. What I had taken as an aesthetically pleasant toy, like one of those glass balls that makes a snowstorm inside when you turn it upside-down, had turned into a black, twisted, sinister-looking growth.

"Wait, wait, wait," I said, my mind spinning.

"This is sounding more and more bizarre, Mac," Kit said, coming in from the kitchen, where she had been listening.

"Hey, I'm out of my area of specialization here. I like to stay over in the good guys' camp, develop nonpollutants, stuff like that," he said, lapsing back into his drawl for a moment. "Coming across something like this is pretty creepy, even for me. It's hard to imagine this kind of thing turning up around here. Course, maybe Jet brought it back from the West Coast." He waited for me to respond, but I was still trying to sort out some questions.

"Wait, back up. What do you mean 'the funding dried up, *officially at least*'?"

"Surely," he said, using the exasperated look that professors reserve for their most hopeless students, "at your ripe old age and in this present day when you can't pick up a paper or turn on the radio or television without some new exposé concerning the government's concealment of all kinds of information—nuclear experiments, dump sites, you name it—you can't possibly, *possibly* believe that the 'official' story is necessarily the true one."

I already knew more about the federal government's duplicity than I ever wanted to know. I saw Kit flash me a look, and I knew we were both thinking of how the FBI whitewashed the Indiana burning back in '73. According to the Feds, the conclave was a militant stronghold of subversives plotting to overthrow the American government. When it came to light that all eighty-three of the casualties were women and children, the government rallied with information of a stash of M16 rifles and filmed footage showing the FBI under attack by rifle-wielding women and children. Neither, as it developed, was true, but by then the public interest had been diverted to more current issues.

I looked over at Mac where he sat in the rocker, and for a moment my heart raced in fear. I breathed deeply, closed my eyes, and wrote it off to paranoia.

"Jet," Kit said, coming over to me and kneeling on the flagstone floor, "are you all right?" Her hand was cool as ivory across my forehead. I nodded, and she sat on the floor cross-legged beside me.

"Okay, okay. I know the official story's not always the true story," I said. "but are you suggesting they're still doing experiments, or they didn't stop when they said, or what?"

"I'm a cynic, Jet. And I'm a scientist. I'm trying to speak as clearly and as truthfully as I can. I am merely telling you what I know to be the truth—that is, the government released certain information. I have no idea if the experiments really stopped or not. How could I?" He raised his hands, palms up, and shrugged.

"All right, I get your point. But *if* they didn't, how would you know?"

"That's an easy one. You wouldn't."

"Well, if they kept experimenting, what would they be after?"

"It's anybody's guess. Maybe to get the jump on chemical warfare in the next war. Maybe curiosity or just plain perversity. Maybe some senator's brother owns a pharmaceutical business. Maybe, maybe, maybe. When the government doesn't want you to know, you don't know."

"That's not true. Watergate, for example," Kit said.

"Kit, you can't disprove the rule by citing the exception," Mac parried.

This was getting us nowhere. And while I agreed with Mac on principle, being as cynical as he concerning government information, I wasn't nearly as convinced that there was nothing to be done about it.

"Okay, let's skip this one. What did you say about side effects, that the government had shut down research because of side effects?"

"Well, this part's pretty involved, but reduced to its simplest elements, the original intent here on the part of the government was to develop some kind of chemical to affect men on the front lines, increase their natural aggressive instincts—not to *change* the body's chemistry, but to *intensify* it. Instead of the boy next door out there in a foxhole, you got a man that wants to tear your throat out at the slightest provocation. What happened, from what I've heard and read, was that a kind of synthetic testosterone was on the horizon. In fact, depending on to what source you read, before the experiments lost funding and support, an actual chemical was developed. It was called 'plastosterone,' and it heightened the level of testosterone in men, making them more aggressive, even violent."

Kit and I looked at each other. She was taking the pins out of her hair and letting it fall around her, fiddling with strands of it. She often played with her hair when she was irritable or angry, tied it up when she felt mellow. We looked back at Mac who continued speaking, avoiding our eyes.

"Well, a leak or two got out somehow. Or, who knows, maybe it was all just rumor. The truth is, no one really knows if the chemical was finally developed or not, or what kind of experiments went on. Anyway, you probably heard stories back then. Fiction writers picked it up, had a lot of horror tales going with it."

"So this may all just be made up?" Kit asked.

Mac was still fiddling with the bottle, holding it in his large hands between his knees, tipping it forward and back as he spoke. It was starting to get on my nerves. I leapt off the couch and took it from him, putting it on the table beside the lamp.

"Mac, listen," I began, settling on the couch again, "if this were all a concoction and rumor, you wouldn't be here. Am I right? What was it you said about reading an article recently?"

"Right. In Europe, someone dug up some of the old research on plastosterone, apparently while trying to find something to slow the HIV virus, and discovered that in minuscule doses it was a hallucinogenic, a mind expander, highly addictive, and no doubt likely to become the new designer drug of choice overnight if the word got out. Didn't seem to have any effect on the HIV virus, though," Mac quipped dryly, giving his crooked smile.

"Are you saying it's like cocaine or LSD or grass?" Kit asked.

"More like LSD, but probably more potent, even in the smallest doses. But there's worse news." Mac paused here for effect, wiggling his eyebrows and pulling at one side of his beard. "According to the little-known report I read, there were some very unsettling possibilities that developed in the lab animals that were used. Evidence of psychic abnormalities with larger doses, of course, but even with the smallest doses, certain kinds of aberrant behavior developed over time."

"Like what?" Kit and I asked simultaneously.

"Well," he said, taking a deep breath and looking from Kit to me and then up at the ceiling, "there was marked aggressive behavior, heightened sexuality, sometimes hysteria accompanied by persistent or unrelieved erections. In some cases, the sexual need was marked by extreme violence on the part of the male test animals toward the female. In one case, the male..."

"Ee-yeew, stop!" Kit looked like she'd eaten a lemon.

"Okay, okay," I said. "What could possibly be the point of continuing this kind of research? What were they after?"

"That's just it," Mac said, "if the chemical could be perfected, the negative aspects eliminated, plastosterone would be a veritable Fountain of Youth for men—a cure for impotence, an aphrodisiac, a new lease on life for elderly men."

"I never noticed that their old lease expired," Kit said. "In fact, I think most of them need to have *less*, rather than *more*, testosterone."

"*You* may think so, Kit," Mac said, looking her up and down, "but there are lots of women out there who would like their men to have a little more of the beast in them. In fact, women would probably want this drug on the market as much as men."

"Are you telling me that this stuff is going to be available?" I asked.

"No, no. That's not what I'm saying. What I'm saying is that if such a chemical were developed, there is a huge, an unbelievably vast worldwide market just waiting. We're talking billions of dollars."

"What about women?" Kit had stretched her silver-spangled legs out in front of her and was leaning back provocatively.

"Women?" Mac cocked his head and looked puzzled. "What about women?" Kit had a disconcerting penchant for non sequiturs that always stumped Mac, the rational scientist.

"What happens if *women* take this?" Kit said, as though her question had been perfectly clear.

"Nothing in the article about that," Mac said lamely. "After all, the chemical involves enhancing male behavior."

Kit gave Mac a look of undisguised disgust. "*Enhancing*, did you actually say *enhancing*? Jesus." Kit rolled her eyes to the ceiling. "Well, as usual most of the testing for 'man' in the generic sense is done for 'man' in the gender sense. There probably *weren't* any female test animals. You know, *men* aren't the only human beings on this earth that like to be turned on. Or is that news to you, Dr. Williamson?"

Only the greatest male fool could have looked at Kit and not felt a stirring in his organ. Mac was no fool.

"I don't know about that," he said, twiddling his thumbs, crossing his legs, taking his hat off and putting it on again. "But I think we need to get back to reality here. Like, *if* this stuff is what I think it is, where did it come from?" Mac and Kit looked at me.

I looked at first the one and then the other…and then I shrugged.

After all, what did I really know? Not where Jaz came by these odd purple growths nor why he had them. Though we had not been friends, I probably knew him as well as, perhaps better than, most people. Unlike his other acquaintances, I shared with Jaz a background in and antipathy toward academia and its dispiriting inner workings, its constricted literary boundaries and bigotries. I couldn't believe that he harbored any particular interests in science or chemical warfare, or that he had established any connections with people who did. Even if he had, he was as little interested in the pursuit of big money as anyone I'd ever known. Nor did I believe that he was particularly interested in drugs as a pastime— he grew the cannabis on his windowsill, I was pretty sure, less for his own use than to generate a few bucks for booze. One of the rare topics Jaz and I agreed about was that marijuana was the most innocuous of controlled substances. His movie was alcohol, and he made no bones about his addiction to it.

I lay on the couch, mulling over what I knew of Jaz Blankenship as Kit and Mac sparred from their respective gendered corners. My body was numb with exhaustion, but thoughts were flashing across my mind wild as summer lightning. I knew that whatever methods of repulsion Jaz had harbored to keep a distance between himself and every other living soul of his own species, he was not inspired by greed, and wasn't that most often the source of meanness, cruelty, dissension? The only more potent source I could think of offhand was righteousness, that blinding sense of absolute conviction—thus the most bloody wars fought in the name of love, of one's personal god, one's chosen race. Of one's chosen gender. On the dark edge of sleep, I saw the exquisite face of Caroline Marcus rise up like some pale apparition from between the two desiccated lips of a parched riverbed, her sightless eyes wide open, bright with flames and exploding with the screams of all the women who have ever lived. I looked into the fire and saw the future, the next century, red with the blood of man against woman. From a great distance, I heard the voices of Kit and Mac carrying their separate banners.

M AYBE IT WAS THE SCREAMING behind the eyes of
Caroline Marcus's apparition that woke me, or maybe it was
another one of those thumps in the night that you don't hear until
you wake up with it clawing inside your head, like last night. I sat up
and looked around, feeling disoriented. Not counting the cats, I was
alone—even Jones was missing, probably spending the night at Kit's.
The lamp by the sofa had been dimmed down to night-light proportion, but the glass walls surrounding the living room were dark
and implacable—I felt exposed, as though someone were watching
from outside. I thought of Caroline Marcus's parting words last night,
"You really should lock your doors at night," and I switched off the
lamp, nearly knocking over the bottle with the dark growth in it.

I waited for my eyes to adjust and then tiptoed toward the front
door, where I threw the dead bolt and switched on the floodlights
outside. I could see no signs of a prowler, only the piñon and
juniper trees throwing black shadows across the ground. I took the
flashlight from beside the door, shined it around the dining room
and bathroom, then crept up the stairs. The bedroom was dimly lit
from the light reflected below, and I crossed the room quickly to
lock the French doors to the deck, vaguely noticing an odd smell,
perhaps something the cats had carried in. At the bedside table, I
took the snubnose .38 from the drawer. It felt cold and heavy
against my palm as I stood behind the locked glass doors looking
down over the floodlit trees and the black shadows below, thinking
that only twenty-four hours ago I had opened these same doors
with a naive curiosity that seemed impossible now.

Turning from the deck, I opened another set of glass doors leading into my writing studio with its third-story sleeping loft. The odor was stronger here, and I ran the flashlight across the room—my huge oak desk with the computer on it occupied the center, with bookcases built across every square inch of wall space not taken up by windows. A cat slinked around my ankles and slipped silently into the room. I had climbed the ladder to the loft and was shining the light across the bedroom, when I heard a tremendous hissing and clatter below. I brought the flashlight and revolver around simultaneously, just as a figure burst out from under the desk and pushed through the doors to the bedroom.

"Stop," I yelled, "or I'll shoot." I ran down the ladder and into the bedroom just as the figure was pausing at the dark stairwell, which was narrow and precipitous even in the best of light.

"Hold it," I said. "Don't move." I cocked the gun, and the figure stopped, teetering at edge of the stairs. I had dropped the flashlight during the chase, so I snapped on the reading lamp beside the bed.

"Raise your hands. Slowly," I said. "And turn around."

Angel Torrez stood before me, still bent over, his hands held at half-mast. He had added a torn denim jacket over the grimy clothes he'd worn that morning in the bar, and he squinted out at me from behind an oily forelock. I was wondering what I was going to do with him now that I had him. Without a telephone, I couldn't call the police, or even Kit, for help. If I merely forced him to leave, how was I to know he wouldn't come back—through any window? I fell back on an old habit that I knew would give me an advantage: motioning him toward my studio, I flipped on the overhead light and eased into the chair behind the desk while my intruder sat in the spare across from me. Ever the teacher.

Under the harsher light, Angel Torrez looked even worse than he had that morning. The lower half of his face was stippled with an uneven growth of beard, and at this close range, the odd odor I had noticed in the bedroom was overpowering—a fetid body smell composed of sweat, motor oil, and something reminiscent of a stale refrigerator. With his sharp features and small, darting eyes, he seemed ratlike, feral—an animal cornered and dangerous.

I sat well back from my desk, with my gun on him, trying to appear calm. When I asked him what he was doing here, he shrugged and blinked. I thought I was going to have to deal with a language problem as well. But then he answered.

"Hey, I jus' thought you might have a VCR," he said, "no big deal. I make a mistake, okay?" His English was passable, but his tone was uncertain, shifting between snarl and wheedle. I didn't believe him for a minute, and I sat trying to devise some way to bargain with him for the truth.

"So, hey, what you gon' do now? You gon' shoot me? Maybe you gon' *read* to me?" he said, smirking at the books and drumming on the chair arms with both hands. I remembered Marguerite saying that he was dealing drugs. I was betting he probably had a police record, judging from Juan's reaction to him.

"What I'm going to do is report an unlawful entry, attempted burglary, and trespassing." He glared at me. "That's just for starters. If you don't have a previous record, you'll have to appear in court. You'll be fined and do some probation. If you've been hauled in before, you'll do some time. On the other hand," I said, "I might work out a trade with you."

He looked at me suspiciously. "Wha' kin' of trade?"

"You tell me what you're doing here, and we'll both forget the whole thing."

"I tol' you," he said, drawing himself up and looking offended. "I thought you might have some stuff, a TV, a computer." He nodded toward my desk. Burglary was a way of life in this part of the country, and since I left my doors unlocked, possibly even standing open for all I knew, he couldn't even be accused of breaking, only of illegal entry. Of course he wasn't afraid. I tried a different approach.

"I saw you in town today at the Inn. I know your name is Angel Torrez, and I know you were buddies with Jaz Blankenship, and if you don't tell me what you're doing here, you are in serious shit." I took a chance. "I came across some things Jaz had stashed away, and I think I can prove you're dealing drugs." Based on Marguerite's information, I already knew he was dealing; the database list showed that Jaz had known him, and I could only hope

133

that Angel would believe Jaz had left incriminating evidence behind.

He began squirming in the chair, his eyes darting and his hands drumming on the chair arms. "What you think you got?" he snarled. "Jaz, man, he don' know shee-it."

"Fine. No problem then. I'll just go ahead and give the stuff I came up with to Juan Falcon tomorrow, along with my charges against you." I started to get up, motioning him toward the door with the gun.

"Hey, okay. I don' know what you talkin' 'bout dealin'. Okay? But I don' wan' no trouble. I tell you 'bout me an' Jaz, you gon' just let all this go by?"

"That's the deal," I said.

He drummed on the chair arms a little while, frowning at the floor. I waited. I could almost see the wheels turning as he maneuvered for position.

"Okay, okay. I don' wan' no trouble, okay? I'm not dealin' nothin'. Hey, little weed for Jaz, okay? He don' like to bother sellin' so he grows a little and I move it, okay? Tha's maybe what he wrote down that you thinkin' is drugs, okay? I jus' come by here lookin' for wha's mine." His voice had been wheedling, but now it became angry. He showed his teeth, snarling, "You the one takin' stuff 'as not yours. I'm jus' here to get it back. Downstairs, i's on the table by the lamp."

So he had been window peeping. My heart raced when I realized he was referring to the lavender growth. I pretended disinterest and asked him to back up and start from the beginning. Angel Torrez told about the bottles, how he was paid by someone he called "The Man," an elderly retired fellow near Santa Fe, to haul his trash away twice a month. When I asked why the man didn't put his trash along the street for the city to pick up or haul the trash himself, Angel explained the man lived in the country and that being both elderly and without a truck, he hired others to do his heavy work. Angel said that the old man had once been a famous gardener and still experimented with different varieties of plants. He was trying to discover a new type of rose and was afraid his secrets would get out, so he paid Angel seventy-five dollars a load to pick up the unsuccessful plants and bury them where no one would find them. He had been on his way home last Thursday with the old man's load in his truck when he remembered he needed to stop by a friend's house. He had been cautioned by the old man not to leave the articles in the hot sun for any length of time, that there was danger of explosion. Since he was near Jaz's cabin, he'd decided to leave them there while he made his visit, and pick them up later. When he returned, Jaz had been dead, stretched across the floor.

"So you retrieved the box of jars, but you didn't report Jaz's death?"

"Hey, wha's to report, huh? Man's dead." He looked at me curiously.

"It's a law, Angel. You find a dead body, you tell the police."

"I's not *my* law," he said.

"It applies to everybody. Do you think laws aren't for you?"

"I think they for people tha' can afford them." He spoke matter-of-factly, sounding neither angry nor submissive. "Look, Jaz's dead, man, he's gone. I din' do nothin' to make him dead, but I report a dead man, who the police gon' talk to firs', okay? They wan' know 'bout my load, and The Man tol' me *nobody* s' posed know 'bout this stuff. Especially no police, then everybody gon' know about it."

"All right, all right. Forget it. So what's this guy's name?"

"No way, can' give that out." He shook his head and held up both hands. "No way."

I didn't think Angel was going to budge on this one, so I backed off. "So how did you know I had one of the bottles?"

"Easy. I always count the bottles, jus' to be safe, okay? Had twenty-five. Only had twenty-four when I picked them back up at Jaz's place. Only two thin's could happen—either you took one, or the police. Din' hear nothin' about the police findin' anythin' but the weed. Mus' be you then, right?" Angel grinned at me proudly.

"Why is it so important that you have every single one if you're just dumping them? How will the old man find out? Why not just cross it off?"

"Hey," he said, looking wounded, "I take the man's money, I do the work, okay? He gave me twenty-five, I get rid of twenty-five."

Sure, and the tooth fairy lives. "And the bottles contain, what, rose sprouts?"

"Tha's wha' The Man says. I don' know nothin'. I just dump 'em."

"Well, Angel," I said, getting up, "tell you what. You remember that black truck you sideswiped this morning in the university parking lot?" I kept the gun on him, but he didn't seem particularly dangerous to me anymore, and I felt a little silly. He also hadn't answered my question.

"That was my truck. I'm going to keep the bottle and we'll call it a draw."

He looked at the floor for a minute, then back at me. He shrugged and pushed himself up out of the chair.

"Looks like you the boss, lady."

I followed him down the stairs and let him out the front door, bolting it behind him. The clock read 2:33 as I took the odd bottle upstairs with me, placed it and the revolver on the bedside table, and undressed. I did not worry about Angel Torrez returning—he knew that I had evidence against him for drug dealing, and he also knew I had a weapon. As I pulled the sheet over me, my mind was swirling with the new information. I knew Angel would have fabricated some details of his story, like the identity of "The Man" and his description of the growth. But I believed he had been telling the truth about dropping off the bottles at Jaz's and then finding him dead when he'd returned for the pickup. Juan could verify easily enough that the tread sample he'd taken matched the tires on Angel Torrez's truck. And did Angel's panic when I mentioned information Jaz had left behind indicate that he knew about the list I had discovered on Metz's computer? If so, what did the list mean and how could I find out? And if the list was related in some way to Angel, did that mean that it was not connected to the Lab after all? I drifted off to sleep with the list of names running through my mind, seeing Jim Becker's as though it were written in red.

THAT SAME NIGHT...

Morgan

*A*LL GAMES *are part situation and part soul. There are no exceptions. The few people who know this secret are those who can win at anything, against whom the odds are stacked in vain.*

Take love: my tryst with Cruz was closest in strategy to a game of chess. A most rational enterprise. Yet his dark king, weakened by an insatiable ego and the illusion of inviolate defense, fell as night to light, and just as predictably, at the hands of my queen. You must take in the soft underbelly of the board as well as its simple squares and its extended equations. And you must never believe yourself safe from entry merely because your doors are locked.

Thirteen years with The Company, fifteen counting the two at The Company School, gives me this perspective. Against all odds, they say, I remain the top research specialist, the first to violate the ten-year-limit regulation. My colleagues enjoy speculating about my success: some say my advantage lies in an erratic and therefore unpredictable ingenuity, or in unscrupulous diligence, or in the extraordinary number of lives some few are apportioned through fickle luck. And some will speak softly of the preferential treatment from Pasonombre, The Company's prime mover and my surrogate father.

So simple a matter: everything in the universe that surrounds us is reducible to this confluence of situation and soul. Having carefully, patiently excavated the former, one must then discover the latter. For this, there is no one law. You must bring your own candle. My own approach is symphonic—look back across the series of events, convert the actions to music, the dialogue to tonal riff, the recurrent oddities to leitmotiv. Set the situation to humming and you will find the note of discord if there is one. And finding it, you have the flaw to save yourself. To live another day.

To this end, I have returned late to my hotel suite, knowing now for certain after speaking with the Stone woman in the park that something is wrong. Somewhere I have heard the warning note: the merest exhalation of a summer's breeze, the one dissenting leaf within the green accolade. Yet the smallest treebreath divines the storm. I must listen again to the symphony I possess.

From my suitcases, I remove the pieces of the game. I take out the burgundy-colored folder that Cruz gave me and the forest green one containing the materials faxed to me by Pasonombre and place them in the center of the bed nearest the door of the suite. I take out several manila folders and position them in a circle around the burgundy and the forest green. To one side, I set the playback unit with the tiny microcassette surveillance tapes arranged in the order of their occurrence: the first records my telephone conversation with Pasonombre, the next my conversations with Anna Lee Stone and Juan Falcon, and then there are the final two which I have retrieved from the hidden place inside Juan Falcon's office. Beside the television and VCR, I stack the video cassettes. On the desk, beside the laptop, I place the CDs and floppy disks, and I string the extension telephone wire from the laptop's modem to the phone beside the bed nearest the window. On the table beside the window, within easy reach, I place my open briefcase and the Heckler and Koch Mark 23 automatic.

I begin at the beginning, as though I have entered the concert house and am listening to the opening Prelude: I fit Paso's tape into the playback unit, position the earphones comfortably, and lie across the bed nearest the window. I press the Play button and close my eyes; I follow the cadences of the voices. Our first conversation, recorded last Sunday, August 1, made from outside a coffee shop in the village near where I had been resting: when I speak, my own voice is leaden, as though the emotion had been burned away. Paso hears it too, all the way across the continent, at his home outside Milan. He responds, his own words scalloped as seashells offered to a small child.

It is too soon, figlia, *he says.* Ride the horses of your friends. Drink much wine. Take romance with a handsome stranger. Visit the city, lie beside the ocean. You must forget the world for a while. Time must pass between assignments. It is a good rule, no?

But I refuse to listen. I tell him I am bored, I must have work. I cannot live without work, I tell him. This time my voice rises, plummets, a hawk without wings. Paso listens, he hears me. Paso also knows about the music of words.

I will look around, Cordelia. *He speaks in immaculate granite-syllabled English, without his Italian accent.* A couple of days, you will call again?

A silence. Then the tape continues. I have called again, outside the same coffee shop in the village. Paso is happy when he hears my voice. His vowels are fat as marbles on his tongue.

Ah, figlia! You will love this. *I can hear him smile so that his eyes disappear above his cheeks.* The need and the desire, they have found each other! It is what you call karma, yes? You would like a return to Santa Fe? Your Cruz he has called for a specialist, is looking at profiles as we speak. *Paso describes the Water Project, the man who has died, the woman who is calling the media with lies about the Lab.* It is too simple for you, I know, Cord, I know. But it is a vacation, a working vacation. You will busy your mind, and you will relax. You have always loved Santa Fe, yes? And perhaps the Cruz still a little?

Paso's voice. Something flows along, lurking just below the words. I rewind the last part of the tape, listen again. I memorize the fretted undercurrent the way one memorizes the cadence of poetic lines, set it aside, marked clearly in my mind so that it will rise of itself like a refrain during odd moments of the day and night. Perhaps I did not hear it the first time because I was hearing the words Santa Fe, Cruz.

Next I review the written documents: I open the dark green folder that contains the materials Paso faxed to my friends' house where I waited in the country, attaching my modem and computer to their telephone line. I remove the contents: Paso's letter, a transcript of Cruz's telephone call, Paso's précis of the situation, a specification sheet on the assignment, a profile of a woman in L.A. named Caroline Marcus (including a voice sample and video clips, which remain on the computer disk should I need them). I review Paso's letter, Cruz's telephone transcript, the précis, the spec sheet.

The dark burgundy folder contains Cruz's materials: his précis, a list of local constituents involved in the water issue and brief bios, a stapled set of official documents itemizing the Lab's tests and test results of water in the Pecos River, a land survey map of New Mexico following the river.

Both the green folder and the burgundy one contain materials similarly detailing the Pecos Water Development Project, Cruz's more thoroughly because of his proximity. The test report is specialized, highly technical. It may or may not corroborate Cruz's public statement that supports the political decision to decrease the water by thirty percent and his conclusion that the decrease will not negatively affect community water usage. This is irrelevant to me.

In comparing the documents, I discover only one difference. Pasonombre has included the name of a man, Jim Becker, who is not clearly associated with the water issue, but whom Paso wishes to remain outside the public eye. Paso has offered no explanation, as is often his way. But I find no reference to this man in Cruz's documents. It is unusual that this same admonition is not present in his file.

The map of New Mexico has been colored in geological tones—greens for forests, for the valley that follows alongside the river as it flows south, then into Texas which remains uncolored, and from there into the Rio Grande and Mexico. The river inside New Mexico has been inked in red, so that the southward line looks like an angry crack, a raw fissure scratched into the earth's body.

The false note I seek ripples like a subterranean current below the river of words, as though what is most present is what is missing. I know it is here. I read again the folders Cruz has provided—one each on Jasper Blankenship, Juan Falcon, Kit Melpine Willis. Anna Lee Stone...

...Reclusive, but influential re. media. Profile indicates tendency to activism. Wild card, suggest caution.

Simon Cruz

8/6/93

AUGUST 9, 1993

MONDAY MORNING

I'D GOTTEN A SLOW START this morning, thanks to Angel Torrez, and by the time Caroline Marcus came hiking up the driveway with the errant Jones at her side, I was still brushing Fresca, who chewed dispassionately on her alfalfa.

"Morning," Caroline said, hoisting herself to the top rail of the corral where she sat looking down over me and Fresca. She had on a pair of stone-washed Levi's, a pale blue silk shell, and yesterday's cowboy boots. Her sunglasses were oversized, big enough to cover the top half of her face, and her hair was again pulled back tightly in a ponytail. "Nice horse. Arabian?"

"You bet. One hundred percent," I said, giving Fresca a final swipe and carrying the grooming equipment back to the tack shed. I was experiencing the same impulse that Caroline's presence seemed invariably to ignite in me—the impulse to confide in her, to spill out all the mystifying details and uncertainties that Jaz's death had generated, along with last night's installment about Angel's appearance. I had to admit that without Caroline's backup, I would probably have decided against on-site nosing around for Juan in the name of Kit's dubious innocence. And it would be so much easier to bring a colleague into the picture, one who might help piece together the puzzle of Jaz's death. Hadn't Juan's background check confirmed her story? And except for his weird parable about

Willie Joe Figgen, nothing indicated Caroline Marcus was anything other than who she said she was. And also, I admitted to myself as I shut the tack shed door, she knew me, Anna Stone; how could I resist reclaiming my own identity, if only for a few days while she was in the area? I shouldn't have been surprised this morning at feeling more kinship with Caroline than I had expected to, or than I wanted to, yet I again repressed the urge to confide in her.

"You ready for this?" I asked, climbing through the corral, thinking of Jaz's cabin and what Caroline would find there.

"Ready as I'll ever be," she said, jumping down. With her height, it was less a jump than a step. Jones sat watching in a patch of shade below a nearby juniper. I ruffled his fur and gave him the command to stay, and he lay dispiritedly with his muzzle on his paws watching Caroline and me leave.

I drove slowly down the winding road of the mesa, Caroline hanging on in the passenger seat as we bounced over the potholes, rocks, and cracked boulders. The morning air was already hot and dry. As we passed the silver MG parked to one side of the road, I noticed a coat of dust had settled over it. It was starting to look like it belonged.

"Do you think it's all right to leave it there?" Caroline eyed the car as we passed.

"Not too many people come up this far unless they know me or Kit." I wanted to reassure her, but the fact was that nothing along the side of any road in this part of the country was ever safe. It wasn't the high Hispanic population, as the white contingent was fond of saying, so much as the high poverty level that created a climate for theft and vandalism. But, on the other hand, those of us living in the outback were vigilant in protecting one another's property. The car was as safe here as it would be anywhere else, including the hotel in town.

The village slept under the heat as we drove by—curtains drawn, blinds pulled, doors shut. Crossing the bridge, I was again struck by how low the river was, its increased reduction measured by the widening band of dusty white film along the banks. The border of cottonwoods following the river appeared lifeless, their leaves coated with a thick blanket of dust. I turned north onto the gravel road that ran parallel to the river, with the cottonwood groves in between and the undulating ridge of low mesas to the east. Past that, on a rise, tiny cars and boxy semis moved along I-25.

The turnoff to Jaz's cabin was even more difficult to locate from the road than when I had come across it in the woods while riding Fresca. I doubled back along the gravel road twice before I finally discovered the two faint ruts that led to Jaz's place, snaking through the cottonwoods for a mile or so before ending at the sharp curve where his old Rambler was still parked as it had been last Wednesday evening.

I pulled in beside the Rambler and shut off the engine. Caroline and I sat for a moment, taking in the bleak scene. The little home-made cabin looked desolate in the clearing with its stubble of tree trunks. She got out first, and I followed, letting her lead the way. When she pushed open the cabin door, the overpowering stench of stale cigarettes and the trapped heat inside the dim room hit us like a solid wall. It was just as I remembered—the tangled bed, over-flowing ashtrays and piles of girlie magazines, the cluttered table and wine bottles and beer cans. The only difference was the chalk outline Juan's men had traced on the floor around Jaz's body. I left Caroline standing in the middle of the room with her memories of Professor Blankenship and went back outside, through the burnt weeds, and around to the rear of the cabin. A couple of PVC pipes from the sink inside jutted out and disappeared into the ground. I followed a path leading to the river, the trail from the buried pipes running along one side. The PVCs reemerged out of the river's bank, one sawed off and sticking out over the water where it drained off the contents of Jaz's sink.

The second pipe took a right angle through some hardy scrub brush beside the bank before shooting out across the river, where it took another right angle into the water. It was wired to a stake pounded into the riverbed as an anchor and attached to a contrap-tion that I took to be a solar-activated pump, probably the "gizmo" Kit had seen through her binoculars. When the river flowed at a normal level, the PVC pipe would have been concealed by the flowing waters, but as the water level had dropped, the pipe was visible and the end of it just barely reached the water. With some difficulty, I made my way along a gravely peninsula toward the setup. Looking down into the shallow water, I could see that the stake had been inserted in a sandy declivity surrounded by several large rocks, probably one of the few places Jaz had been able to sink the stake to avoid hitting bare rock. But in the present situation, the stake was in the center of a small pondlike enclosure, growing more and more shallow by the day, so that fish carried downstream were trapped in the pocket of water, their silver bodies floating on the surface, loud with breeding flies.

"Hey," said Caroline, walking up behind me. "Find anything interesting?" Her sunglasses were propped on top of her head, her pale eyes surveying the pipes and the setup in the river.

"Maybe." I wondered how she was handling the grim spectacle of her true love's cabin. She didn't seem much affected. "How about seeing if you can find a small bottle for me back at the cabin?"

In a few minutes she reappeared with a liter-sized wine bottle.

"Sorry. It's as small as I could find," she said, bringing it along the gravel bar to where I stood.

I unscrewed the cap, washed out the wine as best I could in the river, and filled it about a quarter full with the stagnant water from around the solar pump. When I held it up, it swirled and drifted like a macabre underwater carousel.

"Yeck." Caroline was also looking at the river water captured in the bottle. "That's what I thought," I said, screwing the lid back on and heading for the shore. Back at the cabin, Caroline took a last look inside. "Get what you came for?" I asked.

She nodded, avoiding my eyes, and we closed the door behind us. In the truck, I lodged the bottle of river water behind the seat, cushioned inside a blanket I kept there, while Caroline settled back into the passenger seat and stared out through the windshield, perhaps lost in memories of a younger Jasper Blankenship.

"You okay?" I started up the truck and switched on the air conditioner.

"Life's a funny thing, isn't it?" I could barely hear her over the fan, but I nodded anyway. I was trying to remember what Kit had said about visiting Jim Becker, that he lived further north down the road from Jaz. Why had he been so upset when Kit had stopped by, and what kind of "gizmo" did he have in the river behind *his* place? I backed the truck and maneuvered it around until we were headed back through the cottonwoods toward the gravel road.

"I keep seeing Jasper behind the podium that first day in class," said Caroline, her sunglasses back in place and her smoky voice drifting around the cab of the truck in the cold air from the fan, "and then here you are, too. I'll never forget reading your book all those years ago. It changed my life. When I closed that book, I looked up and saw myself and the world in a different way—it's like thinking all along you're a pawn on the board and then seeing you're the queen, with all that power. What happens to us that we're one person back then, another now? How can you write that stuff you're writing now?" She had been looking straight ahead through the windshield since we'd left Jaz's place. Now she turned to me, full face. "How can you do that?"

I had a premonition, as the truck coasted to a stop at the gravel road and I shut off the fan so that we sat there in silence, that if I turned north, I would be taking on more than Jim Becker; and if I turned south, I would be abandoning more than Caroline Marcus at her car. And so I cut the engine. I told her about finding Jaz, about the bottle I had taken, and about Mac's research into plastosterone. I told her about Juan's suspicions of Kit and Kit's suspicions about the water issue and a man named Cruz; about Angel Torrez's visit last night and about an old guy somewhere on down the road who had another gizmo in the river. I told her all this without ever once looking at her.

And when I was finished, Caroline remained silent, staring out her own side of the windshield. I started up the truck and turned north on the gravel road.

"His name's Jim Becker," I said, rolling down my window and letting the hot air in, glancing at Caroline out of the corner of my eye. "Kit said he lived on past Jaz, somewhere out this direction." I drove slowly, watching for a turnoff.

"Jim Becker?" Caroline's voice was sharp.

"You know him?"

"No. Was he a friend of Jasper's?"

"I doubt it." I told her about Becker, not only because I wanted her to know but because I needed to keep talking. I told her what everyone knew—that he was an odd fish, probably closing in on seventy or so, had lived most of his life in this area. He'd owned a chemical analysis business in town for years and had gone off to join the peace corps after his daughter's death some years back, and when he returned he had bought a place outside of town and was seldom seen. Occasionally I had run into him in the aisles of the local supermarket, picking through cans of corn and peas or hefting heads of lettuce in his hands. A towering, gaunt man, put together with bones at sharp angles, he was silent as a specter as he pushed his basket down the polished aisles. He was a man whose appearance made children stop and stare and think about Halloween, whatever time of the year it was. When his daughter had been found dead in her room above a local bar, Marguerite had watched her body carried out on a stretcher, looking tiny as a twelve-year-old's under the white sheet in spite of the fact that she was at least forty, plagued with anorexia. She had been a drunk, and so maybe the stories told in her alcoholic stupors were concoctions—stories about her adolescent years, an absent mother, a father who entered her bed from the time she was eight years old and sometimes offered it to his male friends as well. But after all, people said, her words were tangled, incoherent, full of self-pity and blame.

I turned off onto a couple of roads that petered out inside the wilds of cottonwood before we hit on the one that brought us to Becker's locked gate, hung with a large homemade "No Trespassing" sign in red letters and flanked by a barbed-wire fence on each side. We sat with the truck idling, looking down the driveway and through the tangle of trees at a trailer another five hundred yards or so beyond the gate.

"What now?" Caroline asked from behind the dark glasses. It occurred to me, just then, that for all she knew of my life, I knew almost nothing of hers. I imagined her living a sedate, scholarly existence back in L.A., reading the short stories and poems that hopeful writers sent to her magazine, corresponding with authors, spending her evenings editing manuscripts, the occasional dinner with a colleague, perhaps a trip to Las Vegas for some high life now and then. Sitting here in this wild and devastated countryside, she seemed fragile as a birdsong.

"I'll walk on up to the house, see what I can find out," I said, opening the door of the truck.

"What is it exactly you're looking for?"

"I'm not sure, really." I described the apparatus Kit had seen in Becker's kitchen. "But from the way he reacted to Kit's visit, I think there's something he's hiding. And what the hell," I said, pausing for a smile I didn't feel, "maybe I'm just bored and need a little excitement." I closed the door before she could insist on coming along. I figured Becker wasn't going to be any happier to see me than he had been when Kit dropped by, and if he became angry, even violent, I wanted Caroline out of his way. She didn't strike me as the type who had a lot of experience with explosive situations.

I climbed between two strings of barbed wire and followed the driveway on through the trees until I came to where the trailer sat facing the clearing with its back to the river. Actually, it was not one, but a jumble of several mismatched trailers pushed together into a single ungainly structure. The main section was a long, fifties-type model with square lines and turquoise trim that had long since faded and peeled. Several other smaller trailers, the kind with rounded corners used for camping, had been added and joined to the main unit with sheets of aluminum to cover the junctures. The overall effect reminded me of the pictures of homeless communities that sprang up in vacant fields around large cities. At the end of the driveway was an old brown Buick, and right behind that I saw Angel Torrez's yellow Brat.

Before I could react, the door of the trailer flew open and Becker stepped down on the aluminum step and then to the ground. He slammed the door shut and walked toward me with a gait that leaned slightly from side to side. He must have heard me drive up or seen me coming through the trees; this time he was prepared. I had lost my chance of seeing the setup Kit described.

"Hey-yuh," he said, as he neared. His voice was cracked and high-pitched. "What can I do for you?"

"Mr. Becker?" I said, extending my hand. He shook it, his long fingers strong as a vise. "I'm Jet Butler from up on the mesa."

"Yes. Ms. Butler." He had a face made of bones, as though the flesh had evaporated and left behind the eviscerated skin withering into its empty sockets, yet he had a baby's mouth, wet and pursed into a rosebud. On the bridge of his beaklike nose rested a pair of spectacles reflecting the sun, and wisps of pale hair, fine as spider webs, stood out around his head. He wore a faded red plaid shirt with long sleeves, a pair of Levi's several inches too short, and tennis shoes with mismatched laces. Between the hem of his pants legs and the top of his shoes was a spectacular stretch of Day-Glo orange socks. "Saw you on television the other day," he said, nodding down at me.

"I didn't think it was a particularly memorable performance myself."

"Oh well. We don't get much of that kind of publicity around here," he creaked. He edged around toward the gate so that his head was backlit against the sun, creating a distracting strobelike effect as he swayed from side to side. I guessed him to be well over six foot. "You handled that reporter right well," he said, clearing a wad of phlegm from his throat and spitting it on the ground. "What can I do for you, my dear?"

"I wanted to talk to you about Jaz," I said, wiping the sweat from my forehead. "Do you think we might go inside out of the sun?" I took a couple steps toward the trailer.

"Past a hundred last I heard." He walked toward the cottonwoods and squatted down in the shade. "Here's as cool as we get, I guess."

I followed him reluctantly and sat on a rotting log, manufacturing a story about Jaz's missing manuscript, wondering if he might have confided in his closest neighbor. It didn't sound too convincing, even to me, but it was the best I could come up with. I didn't expect I was fooling Becker, either. He sat watching several vultures circling above as he listened.

"'Fraid I can't help you, m' dear." He kept his eyes on the buzzards and rocked back a little on his heels. "Jaz wasn't too neighborly. Didn't have much to say to each other, if you know what I mean." He shifted his gaze from the vultures to me. Under the shade of the cottonwood, I could see his eyes behind the glasses— red-rimmed and raw with disease.

He pushed himself up and crossed slowly toward the gate, drawing me after him. When I glanced over at the knot of trailers, I thought I saw a curtain move in one of the windows, but I couldn't be sure. If, in fact, Angel was there, as the yellow truck indicated, what was his connection with Becker? The old man was at the gate, swirling the combination, pulling it open.

After he'd snapped the lock back in place, he walked away without a word. When I returned to my truck, Caroline was nowhere to be seen.

Morgan

SEPARATING ME *from the man in the living room is a gray nylon screen smelling of dust. The opening in the curtains on the other side of the screen is long enough and wide enough to see the back of the man in the red T-shirt who looks through another set of curtains to watch Becker and the Stone woman. I am in a scene thrice removed, and when I think of it this way, my head spins for a moment. To the far side of the living room, the kitchen holds the apparatus that Anna Lee Stone wishes to see. It is lodged in the sink, towering up across the porcelain drain panels, along the countertops and over the kitchen table: a miniature city of glass and aluminum—elegant skyscrapers and spires made of beakers, slender jars and crystal pitchers; crisscrossed with silver scaffolding, the pipes and columns and bands of shining metal accessories—a chemist's galaxy.*

I hear Stone's truck start in the distance. I estimate that I am eight miles from my own car, less if I cut diagonally across the river and mesa. The man called Becker enters the trailer. I slip the microphone, shaped like a silver stud, from my belt and hold it next to the screen.

BECKER: *The fucking cunt. [The door slams, shaking the trailer.] Damn her, and damn that Amazon that lives up there with her. Fucking bunch of lesbos. Fucking lesbo snoops.*

RED SHIRT: *Wha' she wan', man?*

BECKER: *Snooping. That's what she wants. [The sound of a chair creaking.] Snooping around. [Pause.] Who knows what she wants. Says she's looking for Jaz's manuscript. My ass.*

RED SHIRT: *Wha' manuscrip'?*

BECKER: *A manuscript, Torrez. He was a fucking writer. Think about it.*
RED SHIRT: *Hey, man. Okay, okay. But I di'n' see him ever write nothin'. Wha' he write? He no' keepin' it a' his place, okay?*
BECKER: *How do you know what the fuck he kept at his place?*
RED SHIRT: *Hey, I know the Jaz, okay? We do little bi'nez, okay?*
BECKER: *Fuck. [Loud sound.] Just get the fuck out, go on. Take the shit to the dump and get out of here. It's bagged already, around back. [Another sound, a crash.]*

I shove the microphone back in its place and retreat to the cottonwoods at the riverbank to watch the man in the red shirt, Torrez. He appears at one end of the shambling arrangement of trailers, beside a stack of black trash bags. He picks up one bag, heaves it across his shoulder and disappears, then returns to carry another, then another, until the pile is gone. I squat among the small suckers that flourish from the roots of the cottonwoods, knowing the insects, the curling pill bugs, the lizards that scuttle along the rough spines of decaying logs, the skeletons of decomposed leaves that look like a miracle of lacework across the palm. I am crouched inside a glade of slender green leaves, their oxygen heavy with forest smells, the cloying odor of earth and dust. A faint, odd scent glimmers below the other more familiar smells, like a musical phrase that starts and stops in whispers. Behind me, the water trickles across pebbles near the shore, while the mainstream runs brown with small dimples on its surface.

A door slams, an engine starts and after a few minutes fades away. Another engine starts, fades. At the riverbank, from a PVC pipe similar to the ones behind Blankenship's cabin, a stringy, mucouslike liquid drips into a narrow channel that meanders to the river. The odor is sharp here—rancid meat, citrus mold, and something else unnamable but familiar.

I edge around the trailers, knowing the Buick and yellow truck will be gone, and knock on the door to make sure no one is inside. The door is locked but simple to enter. Inside, the odd smell from the river has seized the room in the oppressive way that cigarette smoke or cat piss can. It lives in the corners and in the fabrics of the furniture and beneath every carpet; it occupies the room with the absolute power of that which exists because it has been given permission to exist. Its tyranny is absolute. When I enter the kitchen, its presence is overpowering, and it is then that I recognize the other ingredient that had eluded me at the river. It is the scent of evil.

From the kitchen, I pass through a doorless entryway into a closet-sized area containing a washer and dryer, and then a door that is closed. It is then that I hear the sounds, scratching, movements. When I open the door, the stench and the din knock me back. Row after row of animals—cats, dogs, rats, ferrets, rabbits, others, all packed into wire cages stacked to the ceiling with aisles in between, their masses of daily excrement falling through several stories of the wire floors, through the cages below, piled high in the bottom layer. Many of the animals fight one another through the wire mesh of their adjoining cages, savagely ripping away their own teeth and claws as they tear at the metal grids. In some of the cages, animals creep along the wire floors; in still others they lie motionless, perhaps sleeping, perhaps dying or dead. Hidden away in this dark and soundproofed room, the animals fight, feed, subsist.

Outside again, I cut through the cottonwoods to the edge of the woods where I can walk along hidden among the trees, watching the gravel road, ready to flag down the black truck when it appears.

16

AFTER LEAVING BECKER'S, I cruised up and down the gravel road looking for Caroline, going just slow enough to outdistance the funnel of dust I kicked up but not fast enough to help much with the one-hundred-degree-and-climbing temperature. I figured the heat combined with boredom had driven Caroline off for a walk along the river, but when Becker escorted me off his property, about the last thing I wanted to tell him was that a friend of mine was wandering around nearby. The man gave me a serious case of the creeps.

So I drove back the way we had come, straining for a glimpse of Caroline's blue shirt through the cottonwoods. At the gravel road, I turned south toward the village, trying to estimate how far she could have walked during the twenty minutes or so I had been talking to Becker and whether my revelations about the police investigation and my own complicity in it had been the last straw in her quest to lay the memory of Jaz Blankenship to rest. Maybe the heat hadn't driven her away; maybe I had. I was on my third pass, busy concocting images of her hiking up the mesa toward her car, and from there hitting the road back to California, when I saw Angel Torrez's yellow truck nose like a demon through the fan of dust in my rearview mirror, passing me in a blinding wave of grit. Unable to see for a moment, I hit the brakes and felt the truck skid sideways across the gravel. I steered into the skid, straightened the truck before it hit the ditch, and pulled over to the side of the road, coughing up dust, my eyes running. That was probably the best place I could have been, because just as I was starting to pull back on the road, I saw another cyclone of dust heading my way. I cranked up my window just as Becker's old Buick streaked past. I wondered what the rush was about and toyed with the idea of following along at a discreet distance, but then I imagined Caroline—wandering lost and possibly frightened in heat-stroke weather. So when the dust had settled, I rolled down the window and turned back toward Becker's turnoff, inching along scanning the trees, giving an occasional beep of the horn. I considered going back to Becker's, but if he returned, or if someone else were there, I didn't want to have to explain why I was still hanging around. I was trying to think where I could park the truck out of sight and circle back through the woods on foot when I saw her break out of the cottonwoods, running through the sagebrush and chamisa.

"Sorry," she said, opening the door and jumping in, "I thought I'd be back before you left. But guess what I found out?" She was wide-eyed and excited as a teenager.

I, on the other hand, was soaked with sweat, still coughing up dust out of my lungs and rubbing grit out of my eyes from the dirt bath Becker and Angel had pounded me with. I wanted more than a quick "sorry, but." Thinking that this was exactly the self-absorbed, irresponsible California attitude that made me see several shades of red, and that now she would launch into a rhapsody describing a particular species of duck-billed blackbird or double-tailed trout in the Pecos or maybe one perfectly shaped sunflower growing out of a rock, I didn't hear at first what she was saying. And then I did.

"You saw *what*?"

She described the exchange between Becker and Angel Torrez, the drainpipe dripping into the riverbed, her tour of the trailer, finding the apparatus on the sink, the odd smell. When she began detailing the animals in the back room, I couldn't take it.

"Stop!" My stomach was rising and turning, and I took several deep breaths. "Jesus, you just walked into his place and went through it?" I looked over at her, and she lifted a shoulder at me. But then I began to sense some pieces of the puzzle falling into place. I caught her excitement. "So Becker must be 'The Man'

Angel's making trash runs for," I said. "And that's where he got the bottles with the growths in them." I stopped the truck and turned to her. She looked cool as mint leaves in a mountain spring, not the distraught damsel I'd imagined climbing up the mesa to rescue her MG and beat a hasty retreat to California. "It's Becker, he's must be working on the plastosterone chemical."

"That's what I'm thinking, too. Probably Becker tosses all his failed experiments in the bottles into the trash bags with who knows what else—his coffee grounds, banana peels, dead animals. Whatever. Has Angel cart it all off. Angel stops down the road at Jaz's place, they sift through it all, take out all the bottles. Then Angel goes on to the dump, buries the rest of the stuff, however he has it set up. That explains why the bottles were sitting there where you found them, where Angel dropped them while he went off to dump the rest. He comes back, but Jasper's dead. He takes off with the bottles, later discovers one's missing, and knows you're the one who found the body. Who else could have taken it, right?" She looked behind us, and I started on down the road. "That water sample you took?"

"Yeah?"

"Do you think that friend of yours over at the college might be able to take a look at it? If you were thinking of having it analyzed, most commercial places aren't going to get to it for a week or two, maybe longer. And I think we ought to find out what Jasper might have been pumping into his sink, what might have been coming down the river from Becker's."

"I agree. Mac'll probably be around. Classes haven't started yet, so he'll have some time." I wasn't sure how happy he'd be to put his own research aside again, though. "What do you think we're going to find?"

"I'm not sure. But if Juan is looking for some unidentified substance shown in the autopsy, it makes sense to see what Jasper might have been drinking. *Drinking*. My god, do you really think he might have been *drinking* that stuff?" Caroline propped her boots on the edge of the seat and hugged her knees. In this kind of heat, most light blue silk blouses would be dark with sweat. Hers, even under the arms, was miraculously dry.

"Have you had your sweat glands removed or something?" I flapped the top of my own shirt to let in a little air and dry off, knowing that if I ran the air conditioner while cruising the back roads, the truck's engine would surely overheat.

She laughed. "It's just a matter of controlling your body. Any biofeedback lab can show you how."

Yeah, right, and I'm the Easter bunny. But getting up some speed on the freeway helped. By the time I pulled up next to Mac's old Caddy in the otherwise empty science building parking lot, I was down to a wet back and a few perspiration stains where the wet patches had been.

"You want to meet Mac?" I asked, shutting off the engine. "Or were you maybe planning another walk?" My sarcasm was wasted on Caroline; her attention was elsewhere. She was taking in the buildings on the campus, the cracked parking lot with its potholes which, according to local lore, were the graves of an old Indian burial ground before being asphalted over.

"It's not USC, is it?" she quipped, ignoring my question.

"That's the good news," I said, feeling a rush to defend our local institute of higher learning. If the students had been on campus, she could have had a real chuckle. Not a pair of Ray Bans or Calvin Kleins in the bunch. Pulling the wine bottle from behind the seat, I told her to leave a note if she decided to wander. "Ten minutes," I said, slamming the door and walking off.

I entered the science building through the same door as yesterday, but today was a workday. The overhead flourescent lights were on and Kathy, the department secretary, had her door propped open and a fan going. I stuck my head in for a quick hello.

"Having a good summer, Jet?" She was working on an exceptional wad of chewing gum and clicking away on her computer keyboard with fingernails the length of her eyelashes, both a deep bruised shade of purple, with matching lipstick and Big Hair that was black this week.

"Next question."

"Not so terrif, huh?" she said, talking around the wad. She hadn't missed a stroke at the keyboard. The word was that she could do one hundred and ten words a minute, talk, and chew gum at the same time, all without making a single mistake. Mac swore this was the truth. She blew a bubble and popped it, sucking the wad back into her mouth. "Too bad." She sighed and kept typing.

"So it goes. Mac around?"

"Yep. Want me to ring him?" Still hadn't missed a stroke, her eyes shifting to something handwritten beside the keyboard, the monitor, and me. I shook my head and wondered if she had a foot-operated speakerphone so she could chew, type, talk, and monitor the phone as well.

The hall was a lot less spooky with lights, and I could see that the centipede in the glass case was missing some legs. Mac was working with his back to the door, pecking at the keyboard a good deal more slowly than Kathy, and hunched over to see the monitor.

"Jet," he said, still typing, "you better get you some new boots if you're expecting to slip up on folks. You know your students used to could hear you coming from a mile away? You never caught 'em cheating, did you?"

Didn't anybody around here stop computing long enough to have a conversation? "Never tried," I said, walking in. "What kind of cheating can you do in a creative writing class?"

"Beats hell out of me." He swung around in the chair with his big, goofy grin. "You ever cheat in *your* writing?"

Just the topic I'd been wanting to talk about, my writing. "I pick up a line or two from Hemingway and work it in, " I said, sinking into the ratted out chair. "Got a minute?"

"For you, what do you think, schweetheart?"

I thought his Bogie imitation needed work. "I think you're lying through your teeth." That sent him into one of his booming laughs. "But it just so happens…" I held up the bottle of river water.

He stretched across his desk and took it, going through his routine of holding it up one way and then another. "May I?" he asked, his hand on the lid. I shrugged.

"Wheee—eeuw! You drink this stuff?" His face wrinkled up like he'd bit into a lemon, and I could smell the river water from where I sat.

"No, but I'm wondering what would happen if I did."

"Where'd you get this stuff? What is it?" He screwed the lid back on.

"River. Behind Jaz's place. He had a pump rigged up back there, and I don't know if he used the water for drinking or just keeping his place immaculate. Could you look at it for me, maybe today? Maybe, um, now?"

Mac looked back at his computer and then at me. "This wouldn't have anything to do with that last piece of work I looked at for you, would it?"

"Nope. Don't think so."

"Mmmnnyeel." He stuck his bottom lip out and looked at the water and then at me. "You just not the kind of woman that likes to wait, are you?"

"How many people do you know who like to wait?"

"Everybody. Us professors just waiting to *re*-tire," he said.

"It's a lucky guy that likes his work." I got up. "Say I stop back by in a couple hours?"

"Woo-wee. You *are* in a rush. Yep, come on by whenever and we'll see what obtains."

He was on his way downstairs to the lab when I left, and Caroline was still in the truck, sitting with the passenger door propped open and the radio on.

"There's a forest fire up at Taos. People are evacuating tomorrow." She swung her legs back in the truck and closed the door as I started the engine. "Have you heard?"

"Mm, you can see the smoke when we get back on the freeway," I said, thinking of how to spend the next couple of hours. "I think I'll stop by and see Juan for a minute, let him know what we found. How about I drop you at the hotel and meet you at the bar in an hour or so?"

I knew Juan had some misgivings about Caroline. This didn't seem like the best time to appear as the dynamic duo, and Caroline seemed willing enough to go her own way for a while. After I let her off at the Inn, I drove across town and parked down the street a block from the sheriff's office which, judging from the cars lining the street, seemed to be doing a thriving business today. Juan's big white four-by-four was parked in the lot beside the building, and the front office was buzzing. Under no-nonsense flourescent lights and ceiling fans revved up to high speed, three female clerks were perched on stools behind computer monitors, working with people standing at the service bar. Several more people sat in chairs arranged against the wall beside the door where I stood, and I wondered if I was going to end up waiting at the end of this procession. I cut across the waiting area toward Juan's office, the hall today lined with bright cubicles on each side, humming with activity. Several men stood at the end of the hall, and I could hear Juan's deep voice. I walked up and stood to one side, piecing together information about reports of more dead animals. The ranchers in the area, apparently, were convinced that the grey wolves recently released into the wilds in the southern part of the state had somehow made their way north to Tortuga and were slaughtering cattle and horses.

"Not likely," said Juan. "That's several hundred miles, not to mention they're being closely watched and the forest service sees that there's plenty of prey in that area for predators."

But the ranchers were angry and volatile. After they left, I poked my head around the corner of the door. Juan's dark face was clouded with worry.

"Looks like you've got your hands full," I said.

He looked up with his handsome, carved face. "One of those days. Come on in, take a seat. Got the lab report back this morning." He reached for a folder beside the phone and opened it. "According to this," he pulled a page out of the file, "Jaz had lethal quantities of amanitin in his blood. Looks like he ate the wrong mushroom."

"Mushroom poisoning?"

"Yep. We get a couple of these every year. Not always fatal, but it happens. Especially with someone as malnourished as Jaz. Popcorn and alcohol's not the best diet." Juan looked up over my head, and I turned to see one of the deputies signaling him. Juan asked me to wait and left the room. I heard the sound of footsteps moving down the hall, a door closing, and then only the mundane sounds of office activities. On Juan's desk lay the page of the lab report he had been referring to, on stationery with the lightning/mountain silhouette overlaid with the Zia. I recognized it as the same letterhead I had seen in Kit's living room, the logo of Sangre de Cristo Lab. I was squinting, trying to read upside-down and making out Jaz's name and references to "amatoxins" when Juan came back.

"Sorry." He sat heavily in his chair and paused for a moment as he picked up the folder again. "Taos is asking for volunteer fire fighters, just in case you know anyone. Jesus. Fire, drought, killer wolves. What's next? Pestilence?" He looked at the report and shook his head. "Anyway, I'm closing the investigation on Jaz. Death by accidental poison." He slapped the folder shut and dropped it on his desk. "So Kit's cleared. Good news, yes?"

"What about the tread marks at Jaz's place?" I told him about Angel Torrez's visit of the night before and Torrez's explanation—which meant I had to come clean about my own theft of the purple growth and what I'd found out so far about it from Mac. When I came to my visit to Becker's, I thought of Willie Figgen and decided to keep Caroline Marcus out of the picture. I pulled out the passive voice and danced a little: "So some kind of experimentation is set up in his kitchen. It looks like Mr. Becker's up to some serious chemical research."

Juan frowned at me, then sighed and shrugged. "So Angel stops by Jaz's, sees a dead man, leaves with the bottles. He walks into your house last night looking for the missing bottle, and let me guess—your door's not locked, am I right? So we haul him in for leaving the scene, illegal entry. He's out in a flash. And with all the problems we've got across the county right now, I can't spare anyone to give you protection because, make no mistake, Angel Torrez will be after you. I'll do what I can. I don't like it and you don't like it, but that's the way it is."

"What about Becker?"

"Not much we can do. Report possible animal abuse to the SPCA, but there's no law against having a chemistry set in your kitchen or doing experiments. And assuming you're right that Torrez is dumping for Becker, then he's arranged for disposal of his waste products, right? We can bring Angel in and try to find out if he's dumping illegally, but at some point you'll have to explain how you found out about the experiments to start with." Juan pushed himself back in his chair. "Right now, I got five men doing the work of thirty. The department's closing in on critical mass, and I'm afraid all this will have to wait till everything settles down a little."

"So that's it? What about the bottles Angel stole from Jaz's cabin?"

"Interesting problem. They weren't there when we arrived. What we have is your word and the bottle you stole from a crime scene. You want to think about how Angel's lawyer will present that in court?" Juan shook his head. "Even if you could prove he took them and that they are what you say they are, so what? He was apparently dumping them for another party. Basically, you've both removed possible evidence from the scene of a crime. You really want to go to court with that?"

"So that's the end of it?"

"Well, there's the issue of animal abuse at Becker's. You can go ahead and contact the SPCA. And as soon as I clear some time, I'll drive out there to have a look. That's as good as I can do right now, Jet," he said, getting up. "But I want to thank you for helping me out with this."

I got up, too, feeling dismissed. I mumbled polite things, then stopped at the doorway and turned back. "Isn't it an odd time of year for mushroom poisoning? They come up in the spring, right?"

Juan stood with his head cocked, his arm braced against the door facing, looking down at me with the shadow of a smile. "Yep. People dry them, freeze them, who knows? Sometimes you just can't figure why people do what people do." At this close range, I noticed that his soap smell was gone, but he still had that just-pressed look and I caught a whiff of leather as I turned to leave.

Outside, the air was almost too hot to breathe. I started up the truck and drove back to the Plaza square, wondering why I wasn't as pleased as I should be that the case was closed and Kit was in the clear. Even assuming Jaz died accidently from mushroom poisoning, none of the questions surrounding his death had been answered. What were Angel and Jaz doing with the detritus of Becker's experiments? What was the list Jaz had hidden on Metz's computer? The square was deserted in the early-afternoon heat, not a car or human being in sight. I pulled up in front of Metz's gallery where the "Closed" sign dangled on its string, and the front room of the gallery lay dark behind the display window. The cracked riverbed and doomsday landscape in Kit's painting looked sinister when viewed in the white heat of the empty sidewalk, and I looked again at the lower left corner where Jaz's misshapen face was frozen in some kind of agony—one day that corner had been empty while Kit fought her own demons. Then she paid a visit to Jaz last Monday, a week ago today, and went home to paint his face the day following his death. What had really happened the day Kit had visited Jaz?

The drought and the heat wave ended as I entered the hotel. Inside the lobby, the conditioned air soughed quietly down from the louvers in the walls, and through the glass door of the bar, I could see Marguerite leaning back on her elbows, looking up at the television. She pushed herself up, and I was barely seated before she arrived with a Perrier in one hand and a slice of lime in a glass of ice in the other.

"You getting to be quite the barfly," she said, setting down the bottle and glass and scooting a jar of swizzle sticks in my direction.

"Looks like not many of us flies around," I said, indicating the empty bar.

"Too hot for tourists, and the hotel people don't come in till around dinner time."

"You haven't seen a tall woman, long black hair?"

"Caroline Marcus?"

I looked at her, surprised. "You know her?"

"Mm." She gave me a meaningful blue glare. "Says she's Jaz's 'old flame'?"

I nodded. "And?"

"No way." She leaned back on her elbows and looked out through the plate-glass windows where you could see the deserted park and the pagoda behind the waves of heat coming up off the asphalt. Her voice was hard as steel. "I got to know ole Jaz a few months ago?" She gave me another of her meaningful, loaded glares. "You know how he let people know he'd left Berkeley back in the sixties, hinted he took off to dodge the draft. Truth was, he got *turned down* by the draft. Couldn't get it up. The big 'I'. Im-po-tent.

Some kind of prostate thing, whatever. Anyway, what the hell. What's in a dick, know what I mean? So we started up, did okay together. But here's the deal. No way he had a sweetie way back when. He told me about everyone from square one. We spent some quality time, I mean, trying to figure what worked for him and what don't. No wife, no kid, no sweetie, no fucking way."

I should have been more surprised than I was. I tucked the information aside for the time being and thought about Marguerite and Jaz as an item. "So what happened?" I asked, trying for an innocent, nonchalant expression.

She sucked on the inside of her cheek for a while, still looking out the front window. "Fuckhead. He got on to some kind of stuff, I don't know what. Some kind of miracle drug he come across. Shee-it." She picked up one of the swizzle sticks and started chewing on it. "I tell you what, though," she said, swinging her head around and looking up through her eyebrows, "whatever it was worked okay on his dick. It was his head that give him trouble, I mean. Made him one mean sumbitch. Started getting rough, knock me around while we did it, you know? Annh, I had enough of that shit." She had worked herself up to being pretty pissed, chewing down hard on the swizzle. "Asshole. I gave him the door. But her, Caroline? No way. Don't know who she is, but I know who she ain't."

"You say he took a miracle drug? Like what?"

Marguerite shrugged. "Dunno. Maybe a doctor give it to him, something new just out. He didn't say."

A man and woman came in from the lobby, the woman wearing a purple leather vest with long swinging fringe and a calf-length skirt to match, with high leather boots. The man had on a white T-shirt and a pair of blue athletic pants tied with a string around the waist. He followed her to a table in the rear corner, and Marguerite went to take their order. After she'd served them a Corona and spent several minutes making something dark red in a glass the size of a bowl, she strolled back over, still chewing on the swizzle.

"Could Jaz have been into mushrooms?" I asked. "Maybe psychedelic ones?"

"Don't think so. He had that weed Angel fenced for him, but he wasn't into drug drugs. No, what I figure is that he come across something over at the college library when he was helping Metz with his computer stuff. Maybe he found out about a new drug for his *particular problem*," she said, wagging her head at me and then suddenly collapsing into a loud cackling laugh. The couple at the table looked over. Finally Marguerite surfaced, holding on to the bar with one hand and wiping the tears from her eyes with the other. "I needed that. I really let that asshole get to me. One day he's giving some of the best head I ever got, and next thing I know he's got a dick the size of his arm and crazy to shove it where I did-n't figure it'd fit." She grabbed at the top of her turtleneck and pulled it down, revealing the surge of one huge breast where a livid red mark ran across one side. "Hey, the jerk pulled a knife on me. I was out of there before he knew what happened. He was drunk, or I'd been up shit creek, I mean." She let the turtleneck snap back up. "Yeah, you bet I went to that sucker's funeral. Good riddance." She spit the swizzle on the floor and headed over toward the woman in purple fringe who was waving her empty glass.

I sat in the cold hum of the air conditioning, trying to fit together what Marguerite had told me with what I already knew. But my thoughts were humming, too. They were a lot louder than the air conditioner and getting louder by the minute, flying in all directions. My cheeks burned, and I struggled to catch the words, to hold them and nail them into sentences, into a logical pattern: Jaz had been killed by eating a poison mushroom. Jaz had been impotent for years. Jaz had recently come across some sort of cure, was sexually active, was violent. Jaz was...what was it Max had said last night? That the plastosterone could cure impotence. Jaz must somehow have gotten hold of it, the purple growths in his cabin...

But I couldn't think clearly. The words and their meaning kept flying apart because there was something else behind them, a sound loud as a locomotive, coming closer. Growing louder.

It was the same feeling, the same sound I had heard as a child. I had been standing in the center of my parents' backyard in a sea of green, freshly mown grass, splashing in a wading pool where cartoon images of red and green and yellow fish grinned up from the plastic bottom of the liner. Out of nowhere, an eerie quiet had spread across the day. I stopped splashing and looked up at where the bright summer sky had been. It had suddenly dimmed to yellow, the sun hidden behind a murky film that was not quite clouds. At first, the leaves of the trees began to tremble, and then came a gust of wind, rolling like a wave through the branches, wave after wave, each larger than the last, rustling and shaking the limbs until the trees pitched first one way, then another. The wind tore at my hair, my eyes, knocking me backward onto the ground. But still I watched—frozen, unable to move. I heard distant voices, screams, until finally my father lifted me into his arms and ran.

"Hey, you okay?"

The voice was small, far away. It came from another room, another world. For a moment, Marguerite's face bobbed before me. I managed a nod as the thoughts began to rush faster, surging dark shards of sound that exploded and ricocheted and annihilated every shred of coherence I tried to grasp.

After my father had taken me to the basement, we watched from a high, narrow horizontal window. The wind at last stopped, and then a great, yellow silence descended across the yard. Just before the tornado struck.

My cheeks burned, and I could no longer hear the couple in the far corner or the humming of the air conditioner or the traffic along the street. And now Caroline Marcus's face rose up before me— nameless, shaping itself out of the darkness, the eyes pale as ice.

"Jet?" Marguerite again. I nodded, closed my eyes, and shook my head. I pulled myself back into the room where the air conditioner purred. On the wall, the clock read 1:15. Whatever else I might do, I could not sit here and wait for Caroline Marcus, or whoever she was. Before I could make sense of anything else, I had first to make sense of her.

I mumbled a hasty good-bye to Marguerite and went into the foyer where a young desk clerk gave me directions to Room 218. Climbing the stairs to the second floor, I realized that if Marguerite were telling the truth, everything Caroline Marcus had said was a lie—Jaz had never been her lover, had probably never been married, never had a child. One question was pushing everything else out of the picture: Who was Caroline Marcus?

Where to begin? Hadn't Juan verified her employment as an editor at the L. A. magazine? At least that much must be true. Maybe she had read a portion of Jaz's book as she said, recognized it as a potential bestseller, and when she heard Jaz had died, came to find the rest of the manuscript and publish it under her own name. Or what if Jaz had not written a novel at all, but some sort of exposé for the purpose of blackmail or revenge? Maybe Caroline was somehow involved in the negotiations, maybe she'd been sent to acquire the manuscript, even if it meant slipping Jaz a dose of poison. At the top of the stairs, I felt like I'd just climbed ten stories. I leaned against the banister and heaved a sigh that seemed to come from the very center of my bones. The whole thing sounded depressingly familiar, like the kind of seedy escapism I was having such a hard time bringing myself to write.

I stood gripping the banister, looking down the long dimly lit hallway. I didn't want to be here, had no idea what I would say to Caroline or what she would say to me. I was in alien territory, swimming hard against my lifelong aversion to confrontations. I had forced myself up the stairs when I yearned most to take off in my truck and leave the world to its deceptions and betrayals. It hadn't taken much introspection yesterday, following my unsettling talk in the park with Caroline, to admit that most of my life after Berkeley had been spent in withdrawal and retreat. Having discovered New Mexico, the one state in the continental forty-eight that most resembled a Third World country, I then climbed to the top of one of its most uninhabitable mesas, living a reclusive existence except when forced down into the world by economic necessity. I had chosen between fight and flight, had taken the latter, and had mistaken isolation for peace, autonomy for freedom. I saw with painful clarity, walking in the subdued half-light down the long corridor with its line of closed doors, that I had lived nearly half my life under a bell jar, and the fact that I had created it myself, rendered it aesthetically graceful and virtually invisible, made it no less paralyzing or suffocating.

I stopped in front of the door to Room 218 and stood for a moment looking at it.

Morgan

I KNOW, just before she knocks, that it is the Stone woman.

Cruz used to try to understand this quirk I have—of knowing the future a few moments before it arrives. At first he considered it lucky chance, and then after we had been together awhile, he believed it. He began his tests, those miracles of rationality, and took obsessive notes—what I had eaten the last hour before the Knowing, what I had eaten the last four hours, the last twelve; what I had dreamt, to whom I had spoken, what I felt in my body. He filled notebook after notebook. He thought genetics might be the key, and he complained bitterly that he could not speak with my parents, that I had no siblings, that he had no access at all to the years of my youth. Pasonombre forbade him that.

He said that was my margin over the others, why I peaked almost overnight as the top research specialist in The Company. But prescience is best observed with peripheral vision—some things resist direct scrutiny. The more Cruz documented, the more capricious the quirk became, as though something inherent within it understood that a capricious prescience is worse than none at all, and understanding that, Cruz would perhaps leave things as they were. For all the times I might open the door just as the hotel maid stood with her knuckles poised to knock or lift the receiver just as the caller a continent away pressed in the last digit, what of the occasional times when the sound came first?

Not just the sound, Cruz pointed out, but other less explicit data as well. I would nod toward a roadside park along the freeway or a weeded lot on a city street, or we would walk into an empty room congested with an invisible turbulence, all these being places where images of violence wheeled across the tortured air like dead leaves in autumn, visible to me alone, and I would see where the body had lain and know how it had died and sometimes even why. I would on occasion describe these images to Cruz, needing to share them, annihilate them, needing to be reassured by his daylight grip on the world. Sometimes I embroidered around them a tale of violence by which to entertain him, and at the end, he would shake his head and roll his eyes at my unruly imagination, and we would laugh together. Perhaps I might have remained living forever in that simpler world of subjugated women that I inhabited back then if I had not one day pointed, on the freeway just south of Denver, to a patch of trees along a river that sent a dark shriek of adrenaline between my legs. The Mercedes still echoed with words of my fabricated horror, punctuated by Cruz's laughter, as he pulled in beside the gas pumps at a convenience store, filled the tank, and disappeared in the sun behind a silver flash of glass door. When he reemerged, folding his wallet and shoving it in his pocket, he looked at me through the passenger-side window with his grey eyes muted. Later, many weeks later, he described how he stood waiting in line behind two local boys, listening while they recited the area's history of atrocities, including the rape and murder years back of two schoolgirls in the trees by the river. He told me how he began researching each of the images I thereafter revealed to him, and how each time he discovered their historical authenticity.

It was around this time that my relationship with Cruz began to change. His former attitude, that of solicitous husband toward the child bride, although I always refused him marriage, began to erode. He endured several predictable stages of accepting the unacceptable—armed initially with the heavy artillery of skepticism, he softened, lay aside a weapon or two, showered me with the patronizing overindulgence an adult offers a precocious five-year-old. Then, grudgingly, he became genuinely, fatally intrigued with that human being he saw me at last to be—and overnight his interest bloomed into a passionate, all-consuming obsession.

Yet, as Cruz occupied himself with tracking one image after another, I was merely amused by his absorbed analyses. For, after all, while these incidents were aberrations to the rational world he dealt in, they were as familiar to me as a glass of milk. I had grown up with them, experienced them daily for twenty-four years. The prescience I took as merely a useless *oddity, a parlor trick ("Jane, answer your phone," I would say just before it rang), of no particular value since tested at the racetrack or on the stock market, it was maddeningly unreliable. As for the less obvious if more insidious images, my intellect had for years shaken them off as instinctively as a wet dog shakes off water—giving the lie to those subliminal snapshots of bleeding corpses and torn flesh and strangled, broken women that drifted and wheeled airborne in the Seven-Elevens and the parking lots and the restaurants, along the freeways and the mountain paths, inside the hotel rooms. Stepping quickly between me and the image, my reason dressed itself in tweed jackets with leather elbows and waxed professorial, arguing handsomely, convincingly, commodiously that some indefinable similarity of landscape or slant of light through a window or smell or perhaps even a faux déjà vu triggered by lack of sleep had called forth a dormant image from a movie, a newspaper, a magazine. Voilà, he said lifting his right hand above the podium, your bloody image.*

But as Cruz's data accumulated, neither he nor I could deny the body of evidence. The overwhelming proof of some paranormal faculty shook Cruz to his very foundations—his life's work, as CEO of the Lab and one of Paso's primary directors, was predicated on a solidly rational substructure. While he was revising and reconstructing, I at first did not see how I was affected. My clairvoyant skills were limited—I could not predict the future more than, at most, five seconds away. What possible difference could that make? And as for the images from the past that leapt up at me, they were ghoulish scraps of memory anchored in the past, unchangeable.

Yet it was here that I, like Cruz in his way, began to recognize the peculiarities of my nature. I began struggling inward: perhaps some cellular mutation had transpired in my own odd skull pile, some prelapserian seed lost in the larger course of human evolution had taken root, harbinger of a future genetic structure. If so, then Cruz's scrutiny was merely the next step toward understanding and making public this facility. Yet I was haunted by an inexplicable feeling of shame, of some great offense I had unwittingly committed. I sensed that these images I had shared with Cruz were quintessentially private, and while I had no understanding of what their purpose might be, I was nevertheless their repository just as a museum shelters its ancient and sacred treasures. I began to wake in the night to the sound of my own voice telling tales to the air, hearing Cruz's laughter and the screams of tortured victims, all wed together in the darkness, and I imagined all the knowledge forbidden to the human mind lying articulated inside enormous volumes stacked high on the desk of some immutable prince of the galaxy. Had I, in my ignorance, stolen a page, revealed its secrets? Had the prince looked down at Cruz and me that day in the Mercedes, found our laughter offensive, blasphemous as we snickered at the screams and the odor of old blood flooding the air? But then the cloud of noise would fade, and I would lie sleepless, wondering if such thoughts were merely the vanity of my present madness, whether human lives were only a shallow tumble of accidents leading us first one useless direction and then another.

But I was young then. I did not know the business of the man with whom I lived, nor of the Italian man whom I considered my friend and benefactor. Yet I was on the edge of knowing.

I was listening to the darkness, to Cruz's even breathing and the cloud of noise above me when Paso phoned late one night to say he had arranged for me to begin classes at his private school. It occurred to me for the first time, just as I was reaching for the silent phone, that if the ringing had been the sound of a bullet, I might have avoided it entirely.

So I decide—in these moments standing before the door waiting for Anna Lee Stone's knock—whether to merely remain silent, or to call out that I am dripping wet from the shower and will meet her in a few minutes downstairs in the bar. I have more than enough forewarning to hide the piles of materials on the beds—the file folders, the audiocassettes and recording paraphernalia, the briefcase sitting open with the HK Mark 23 lying in it.

But I think I have known for a long time that when this moment finally arrived, I will do neither.

JUST AS I RAISED MY HAND to knock, the door swung open.

Caroline stood beside it, holding it wide. The room was L-shaped, covered in a deep mauve carpet, with a small living room at this end, flanked by the larger bedroom where double-wide glass doors stood open. The suite was furnished with the same jarring combination of period antiques and pressed wood junk I had noticed in the lobby—an authentic Provençal desk with an inlaid leather surface was shoved beside a plastic-veneered wardrobe whose open doors revealed a television and VCR combo; the double floor-to-ceiling windows overlooking the park were hung with scallops of lace, while the two king-sized beds taking up most of the floor space were covered with a fake quilted chintz.

But most of the decor was obscured by the mess. The place was a swamp of clutter, every surface stacked with papers, file folders, scribbled legal pads, wads of wires, and sinister-looking electronic gadgets, including a myriad selection of video- and audiocassettes. A laptop computer, its screen indecipherable from my angle, sat open on the desk, connected to the phone jack in the corner by a tangled cord strung across the floor and over the beds, one of which was a rat's nest of sheets—either maid service was taking a day off or Caroline Marcus had forbidden them entry. But the centerpiece of it all, the object that set off all my alarms, was on the small round table between the far bed and the windows. Lying inside an open briefcase was a very large, very oddly shaped stainless steel gun that looked nothing at all like my little snub-nosed .38 Special at home.

Caroline hadn't moved. She watched me taking in the room, and as our eyes met, I suddenly understood in a flood of recognition why she had reminded Juan of Willie Joe Figgen. They were both cases of concealed identity—Willie Joe, I was willing to bet, had walked hand-in-hand for years with his other self, never suspecting the repressed rage bubbling under his good looks and goodwill. I remembered thinking, as Juan told me the story, that Willie Joe had worked very hard to please his parents, to buy them a television, a car, a home; he had worked just as hard to be the best-looking guy, the star athlete, the brightest student. Willie Joe had acquired everything most people ever dreamt of. He had earned respect, envy, gratitude, and admiration, but he had not done it for women or money or fame. Poor Willie Joe, very simply, had done it for love. And when that was denied him, for reasons he probably never fathomed, something at last snapped. I didn't have any idea if Caroline Marcus cared a whit for love, if she'd ever had it or ever wanted it or even thought about it. What I did know, and what Juan must have sensed, was that in both cases the inside and the outside didn't match, that concealed behind their postcard smiles lurked something unspeakably lethal. And while Willie Joe had been tragically ignorant of his other self, Caroline Marcus struck me as one of the most fully conscious human beings I had ever met. I could feel the danger charging the air as if lightning bolts were rippling across the ceiling, and if the woman standing beside the door had made the slightest gesture, any invitation at all to draw me further into the room, I would have been back down the stairs in a flash. But she stood still as a statue, watching me from her pale eyes, without a word or even a smile, as I decided which direction to turn.

And somehow I was inside, the door closed, Caroline holding up one hand with a finger raised and with the other slipping a videocassette into the recorder. By the time images started rolling across the screen, we were sitting in the two chairs that had been beside the windows, and we still had not exchanged a word.

The video opened with a wide-angle shot of a three-story stone building. It was set back on rolling manicured lawns with wings of trees on each side and looked vaguely like a castle, in spite of the modern plate-glass windows and the concrete walkway. There was no background music, no sound track at all. As the camera moved in silently toward the double glass entry doors, it paused at a column of granite fixed with a bronze plate, zooming in to show the initials CO etched in plain type. Inside the ballroom-sized lobby, light flooded through the windows and across marble floors, empty except for a crescent-shaped desk where a woman was just replacing a phone in the receiver. Like the floors, she was polished, her chestnut hair cut just above the shoulder. At the approach of the camera, she rose in one fluid motion and walked around the desk for a full body shot. She wore a tailored business suit, mocha-colored, with a creamy silk blouse underneath, and as she pivoted in the direction of one of the hallways leading off the lobby with the camera following, she had the hip spring action of a professional model moving down a runway. Suddenly, the screen went black for a few seconds, and then the video resumed just as the woman approached a doorway and paused to give the camera a half-smile as she waited to usher it into a room the size of a warehouse, filled with people wearing white lab coats, bustling with activity, working with scientific-looking equipment, taking notes beside large, tubular microscopes. The camera cruised the aisles behind the woman, dollying in for close-ups over the shoulders of several white-coated figures. Again the screen went black, then continued as before, this time following the woman into another immense room where people sat in long rows in front of computer monitors on one side, and behind moving assembly belts of printed circuit boards on the other. The tour continued the alternating pattern of blackouts and scenes, following the chestnut-haired woman along the halls and into room after room, the scenes on the screen changing each time: lithe, hard-muscled men and women in black leotards performed stretching and breathing exercises; a man in a plain white shirt and black slacks stood before a classroom of adults, using a wooden pointer to indicate parts of the body, parts of a skeleton, parts of the human brain; in a basementlike room, people cleaned, assembled, disassembled, and operated various weaponry. I looked over at Caroline.

She hit fast-forward on the remote. "You need to see this," she said, never taking her eyes off the screen, "and then we'll talk." Images flew by with the woman running Chaplinesque down aisles, through more rooms. Caroline slowed the action as a door opened into a room walled from ceiling to floor in books, a fireplace, windows looking out over a flagstone terrace and a lush garden in full flower. After the preceding series of well-lit rooms, the light in this one seemed hushed, the room self-absorbed. Its wood floors were a burnished honey color, scattered with Oriental carpets and forest green chairs beside tables with open books, lamps with stained-glass shades, so that the room achieved a flavor of rustic elegance. At one end, at a desk beside open French doors, sat a man of tremendous bulk, his forearms folded across the desktop. The camera hovered in the doorway, surveying the room and the man, and then it moved slowly toward him.

Caught in the natural afternoon light, the man's face was broad and deeply tanned, so sleek with flesh that his age was indeterminate—somewhere between sixty and eighty. He had an immense overshot lower jaw, a sensuous mouth, and luminous dark eyes below a forehead that traveled up into a magnificent bald dome. His presence was imposing, even imperial, that of a man familiar with looking down from peaks and giving orders. Staring directly into the eye of the camera, a motionless Buddha, he waited until his face engulfed the entire camera's eye before he began speaking. I had become so accustomed to the long silence that I jumped.

"You have just taken a tour of The Company. My Company." His voice was a deep bass, almost resonating, and he had a barely perceptible accent that I couldn't identify. As he continued speaking, he measured each word with importance, and I found myself mesmerized by the way only his lower teeth were occasionally visible. But for all the man's charisma, his ten-minute soliloquy was a tissue of abstractions with about as much substance as the speech of a politician on the campaign trail. He mentioned the The Company's history, its reputation for quality, and its reliability and concern for its clients as individuals, but I didn't have a clue whether The Company made shoes or nuclear arms. As the camera angled sideways to begin its exit, I noticed a few snapshots arranged in a group at the edge of his desk, one of which vaguely resembled Caroline, though with light hair and dark eyes, and I guessed this man was related to her in some way.

Caroline switched off the television, set the tape on rewind, and turned to me.

She didn't speak, so I did. "How about letting me in on what's going on here," I said, indicating the room, the mess, the video. The large gun in the briefcase.

She nodded and dragged her chair back by the windows, and I did the same. She put the briefcase with the gun on the unmade bed, within easy reach of where she sat, and poured herself from a brown thermal pitcher what looked like a glass of ice water but probably wasn't, tossing in a slice of lime from a cut-glass bowl; then she pushed pitcher and bowl in my direction.

"I should warn you," she said, sitting back and taking a sip, "that revelation isn't my strong suit. I haven't had much practice. No practice at all actually. One of the very few things I've never done before is tell anyone what I'm about to tell you." She was looking a little frazzled around the edges.

"I'll keep that in mind," I said, taking the empty glass from the table and filling it with water from the spigot at the bathroom sink. I came back and sat down, waiting for her.

"Okay." She took a deep breath. "That video is about The Company, the company I work for."

None of the scenes looked like anything from a magazine publisher. "What kind of company?" I asked. She looked at me blankly, as though she hadn't heard. "What *is* the company?"

She rested her head back on the chair and smiled up at the ceiling. "What The Company *is* is what The Company *isn't*."

"You want to run that by me again?" I snapped, unable to keep the irritation out of my voice. I didn't have to come back to New Mexico to hear this kind of double-talk; I could have stayed at the university in California and joined the deconstruction camp.

She rolled her head over to look at me. "On the videotape? You remember the building in the beginning? The initials C-O? No one knows what they stand for. It would be like Paso if they stood for nothing. It's his kind of humor, such as it is. But because of them, everyone refers to the business as just 'The Company.' In reality, that building doesn't exist. Oh, maybe some photographer somewhere took some shots of somebody's country villa, went in and digitally made a few changes in the windows, the walkway, scanned in some trees. Who knows?" She shrugged and went back to talking to the ceiling. "It doesn't matter. And all those rooms? They kind of exist, I guess. A couple of them look familiar, maybe from the school in Milan, but they could be from anywhere. The point is, that video-tape is just a master that we use to splice scenes together, choosing the ones that most apply to a place we need to gain entrance to, and then we do a voice-over. Say we want to get inside a pharmaceuti-cal company. We use the first scene plus, say, the lab scene, the data research library, whatever applies, and then we approach the target company as though we were, maybe, bidding on providing them some type of service, or product, or whatever. It's just a way to take a quick peek, see the layout, get a sense of the personnel, the corpo-rate structure, whatever we need to know at that point. After that, we figure how to place one of our people inside."

She rolled her head toward me again as though she were too exhausted to lift it. "The main point I want you to understand here is the invisibility. The Company, Paso's Company, is everywhere. You don't see it. You never see it. It doesn't exist in any concrete way. Think of Paso as an international independent contractor. No individual, political, religious, national affiliations. Any person, any organization, any country, so long as they have enough money, can buy anything. And when that 'anything' seems most impossi-ble, that's when Paso and The Company come in."

"I take it you're talking about illegal operations?" I asked.

She smiled, stretching her long legs and looking back to the ceil-ing where the afternoon sun was reflecting off the table and pro-jecting a pattern of lace shadows. "Not necessarily, though that's what most people would think of first, I suppose. But on the global scale I'm talking about, debating what's *legal* and *illegal* would keep a team of crack lawyers busy into the next century. The kinds of services The Company provides have no pre-established limits. No universal rules." She leaned her head forward and drained the last of her glass and then held it up where the shaft of sunlight turned the ice cubes to diamonds. She turned the glass as she spoke. "Did you know that in some countries it's still legal to kill your wife? No trial, no questions? Now why do you think it shouldn't be legal to kill someone who does great harm? Or look closer to home—in this country, the government itself sanctions cold-blooded, premeditated murder. The fact that we're used to it, that we call it 'capital punishment,' doesn't change what it is." She poured herself another drink, squeezed the lime, got up, and began pacing back and forth in front of the window.

I wanted to skip to why she, apparently a representative of this company, was here. But I was also intrigued by her attempt to describe it. "So The Company is a vigilante operation? Is that it?" I asked.

"Oh no. I'm afraid I was inserting my own observations into this. The Company is much simpler, much more direct than that." She sat in the chair beside the window again and looked down into the street through the lace. "It doesn't deal with moral issues, or judgments, or evaluations. Nothing subjective or messy. It's all a matter of money, clean and simple." The air seemed chilled, and for a moment the only sound was the purr of the air conditioning. I glanced at the silver-barreled gun in the briefcase.

"Have you ever killed anyone?" I asked. "For The Company?"

She cocked her head sideways, half smiling. "This isn't about me. Not in that way. And the specifics, like who and what and when, are not only irrelevant here, but they could compromise other people. I'll be putting myself in danger revealing anything at all about The Company, but I'm not willing to put anyone else in danger. All that's important for you to know right now is that I work for The Company, for Paso."

"The guy in the last scene who looks like Marlon Brando in *Apocalypse Now*?"

"I wouldn't say that to him if you ever happen to meet," she said, laughing. "I just keep that last piece in for me. It helps sometimes when things get tough in the field. He's kind of like a father to me. Psichari Pasonombre. He lives in Italy. Nuts about horses, racehorses. Used to buy Thoroughbreds now and then from my dad back in Kentucky when I was a kid. When I was seventeen, eighteen, my dad and I used to meet him at the racetrack, take him around with us. He loved to watch his horses run, mostly win." Caroline leaned back in the chair, and I could tell she was adrift in memories. I waited. Finally she began talking again, watching the empty television screen as though she were following something on it that only she could see.

"As I said, Paso is a kind of contractor on the one hand, and on the other, he trains people in special ways. At the school in Milan. When he gets a call for services, he sends one of his people to handle it. I'm oversimplifying; he goes through a pretty complicated procedure looking at the job, deciding who to send, contacting key people at various locations. What you might call 'branch locations.'" Her voice, though it was still the smoky voice I had first heard late one night, had changed in some ineffable way. I couldn't tell whether it was because she was no longer in the role of Caroline Marcus, ex-lover of Jaz Blankenship, or whether it was because of the drinks. "Take me. Right now, I'm on assignment. Paso sent me here to keep an eye on the Pecos Water Project. Keep it out of the papers, make sure the deal closes quickly and quietly. At noon tomorrow, Cruz signs the final papers, the last step in the process. Then it's a done deal, and my job's over here."

We looked at each other for what seemed like a long time. I felt numb and the room seemed to tilt a little. I thought of Kit's suspicions, the barrier of paperwork thrown at her by the Sangre de Cristo Lab. I thought of how Caroline, or whatever her name was, had arrived on the occasion of Jaz's death.

"I didn't have anything to do with Jaz, his death, if that's what you're thinking. I really don't know what happened to him. But when he died and your friend Kit put her call in to the newspapers with accusations against the Lab, that started the machinery moving. The powers that be want to keep the whole water issue in low profile. My assignment is to keep an eye on things, keep the volume down, that's all. I'm kind of baby-sitting, you might say."

My thoughts were racing like wild horses in all directions. "But what about the job at the magazine? Juan checked it out."

Caroline went over to the mirror above a plastic laminated dresser and bent her head down over her cupped hand. Then she reached behind her neck and untied the scarf from around her hair, fiddling with something. When she turned around, she held a long black ponytail in one hand and two pale blue disks in the other. Her own hair fell like dark wings cupping her face, and her eyes were deep brown. Except for the color of her hair, she looked exactly like the woman in the picture on the bald man's desk.

"You call the magazine, give them my personal description, the number on the driver's license I duplicated, tell them I'm vacationing in Santa Fe. There *is* a Caroline Marcus, and all those things apply to her." She laughed as she watched my expression. "This is the computer age. Researching and duplicating an identity is child's play. The ingenuity comes in dressing for the part." Using her index finger, she drew one wing of hair back behind her left ear, a gesture that looked at once spontaneous and deliberately seductive. I realized the difference in her voice was caused by the southern accent that seemed to be fluffing up the vowels as though they were feather pillows.

"My god," I said. I felt the blood drain from my face, and my body went cold. If I had been closer to the door, I would have made a run for it, but she was standing between me and the only means of exit.

"I'm sorry I couldn't tell you before. Please believe that I wanted to." She tossed the ponytail on one of the beds and shook the contact lenses onto the table. "I shouldn't be doing it now, but I think something's happening here. I'm not sure what it is, but I think I'm going to need all the help I can get."

"Who are you?" I was still in shock, trying to match the person in front of me to the person I had been calling Caroline Marcus. But I was truly looking at a stranger, in every sense of the word. "What's your name?"

She gave a smile I had never seen before, one corner of her mouth pulled up higher than the other, and a bark of empty laughter. "First things first, huh? I guess it's as good a place to start as any." She stood over me for a few moments with her arms crossed, tall and trim as a nail, and perhaps because I was unaccustomed to her brown eyes, I felt her gaze to be alarmingly invasive, as though she were watching me think. Finally she reached for the chair beside the table, dragged it into the narrow aisle between the foot of the bed and the video cabinet, and flipped it around, straddling it, facing me across the backrest and effectively blocking a path to the door. "Cordelia Morgan. 'Cord' for short. Most people just call me Morgan. Or 'The Morgue,' in some circles. And there are really two stories I have to tell you. And after that, I'm going to ask for your help. Whether you give it to me or not, you'll be free to go. Deal?"

"What if I said I wanted to leave right now?"

"I'd say no. I want you to hear this, for all kinds of reasons, not the least of which is that I think it might actually do you some good, too."

"Ah, I see. Kindness, is it?" I was feeling surly, but I was also scared, right down to the tips of my very cold toes.

"Whatever you say." She tilted the chair forward and stretched her glass toward the pitcher. I thought about tossing the stuff, whatever it was, at her and did a quick estimate of my odds of getting around her and through the door. They didn't look good. I poured the last of the mixture, vodka was my guess, into her glass and squeezed some lime over it. "Thanks." She gave me a direct look and rocked her chair back into place. For a passing instant she was Caroline Marcus again, and then I felt a pang of loss and nostalgia as though she were someone I had known in a distant land. I nodded, shrugged, and folded my own arms across my chest, hoping that I didn't look as scared as I felt.

"Okay," she said, "two stories, then. Unrelated, but both bearing on the situation at hand. The first is about me, the person, and the other is about me, employee of The Company. Let's get 'me' out of the way first, the me who knew you, Anna Lee Stone, before I ever came here." She took a sip of the drink, watching me across the rim of the glass.

I jerked upright and cursed myself silently for ever coming up that flight of stairs. But it was too late for regrets; now I was trapped. I could only sit and listen.

"This part starts way back when I was a kid in Kentucky. Picture Clark Gable and Vivienne Leigh and Tara. I'm the kid on the pony, living the dream. Dad's folks had big bucks, turned the

Thoroughbred farm over to him after he married my mother. She wasn't quite what they had in mind, a little on the backwoodsy side, from the wrong side of the mountains, but she was gorgeous and Dad was smitten. It wasn't till years later, after lots of therapy, that I could remember much except the big-screen memories. The other stuff gets pushed back, edited out, you know?" She, Morgan, had her arms folded across the back of the chair, her chin propped on them, her eyes glittering. "Now I can clearly hear the nights, my mother screaming, pleading. I can see the bruises, remember a couple of discreet trips to the hospital. Turns out my father was a very jealous man, also drank too much. A few glasses of Jim Beam and a nasty imagination, and the nights turned into hell for my mother. I was fourteen, my father had gone out of town for a few days, and my mother, her name was Rachael, and I packed a couple of suitcases and drove to Louisville. I remember her frantically going through pockets, drawers, collecting change, trying to find enough money for gas to get us there because my dad controlled the checkbooks, the cash, all of it. In Louisville, she found a place for women, a 'safe house' it was called back then. She didn't explain her reasons to me, never said a bad word about my father. She just asked me to trust her, said that this was something she had to do. And so I did. It was as simple as that. But over the years, I nurtured the memories of my father, the good ones, the way I wanted him to be—handsome, loving, patient, strong, all the things a kid wants a dad to be.

"We stayed at the safe house several weeks. I realize now, though I didn't at the time, that my mother was recovering from injuries even then, and by the time she was well, we had made friends. It was strange at first, but then it was all right. There were kids my age there, and lots of women getting together behind closed doors for what they called 'group' and talking about things my mother never went into detail with me about. At one point, I realized that she was smiling a lot, that she seemed much happier, and we would talk at night before bed. She was very worried that I would hate her, that I would be miserable without the expensive clothes and the horses and tennis. We had our own room there, a small one, with twin beds beside each other. She would sit cross-legged on hers, straight-backed as if she were in a lotus position, and her hair was long and dark and wavy. She was a pretty woman. We sat and talked at nights like roommates. The place also had a large room on the ground floor set aside as a library, lots of materials on abuse, women, psychotherapy, relationships, that kind of thing. And there was a fiction section, too. That's where we first came across *Living Down Under*."

Morgan stopped talking, her chin still propped on one arm, the other hanging across the chair back, dangling the drink. I knew what was coming. I felt it crawling up my legs and along my arms, spreading up through my spine and across my scalp, a tingling sensation that electrified my whole body and set my hair on end. I knew that this moment was the one I'd been running from for the last twenty years. I sat gripping the seat of my chair, facing this woman who had positioned herself between me and the door, who had what looked like a very lethal weapon lying just a few inches from her left hand.

"Of course, everyone else there had already read it," she said, her eyes narrowing. "My mother read it first, then gave it to me. We were very excited, the two of us. We thought of the future, of being women like the ones in your book. We couldn't have been happier or more inspired if we had just been shown the secret of flying by holding our arms at a certain angle. My mother began asking the other women about the different communities around the country where women could live and work. Together, we decided on one close to home, the one in New Harmony, Indiana."

The room was quiet for a long time. The air conditioner still hummed. The room had gone from chilly to cold. Behind me, through the brick wall, I tried to imagine the hot pulse of the sun outside and how it would feel on my skin if I ever got out of this room.

"That was the summer of 1970. Your book was still the hottest thing around and several communities that had sprung up back in 1969 when it first came out were already thriving. By the time 1973 came around, my mother and I and Claire, a woman my mother loved very much, had been living in a little trailer out in the orchard for three years. She was beatifically happy. She did a lot of gardening, took care of the goats. She never left the grounds to go into town like some of the other women did. She traded them work in return for their taking her turn at buying groceries or doing other errands. When I graduated high school in '73, the community joined together and paid my way into Chicago and a month's rent at the Y till I could find a summer job. It was my first adventure off the collective, and I'd gotten a scholarship for my freshman year at Northwestern." Morgan lay her cheek against her arm, looking toward the wall over the bed where two framed pictures of plants hung. Then she sat up and looked back at me. "I was angry at you for years. Your book took us straight to that orchard, that fire. I don't mean I wanted to track you down, not like that. It was more like a smoldering in the pit of my stomach. Always there.

"I went back to be with my father after the fire. There was no reason not to then. And at first, he was just like the legend I'd built of him. I still had no memories of the nights, not then. We went everywhere together—we rode, he let me help out with training some of the yearlings for the track, and nearly every weekend we went to one track or another—Churchill, Hawthorne, Hialeah, Aqueduct. But I began to see a kind of hollowness in him, saw his anger at the horses, his quick temper when the jockeys lost. And the farm was beginning to sink. He'd mismanaged it, made some bad investments. I began to notice that when we went to the races, afterwards, as we ate dinner or had drinks with his associates, he would often leave dinner early, or excuse himself from the nightclubs we visited so that I was left alone to finish the evenings with one or another of these people, men who owned enormous fortunes. I was very uncomfortable, and I sensed something insidious, unspoken, embarrassing. He became more and more irritable as time went on. He would fly into rages at me over small things, but I started to realize what he was really angry about was that I had not somehow drawn these men into buying horses from him.

"It was during this time that I met Paso. I think he understood what was happening between me and my father. I was very depressed by then, very withdrawn, but without the slightest understanding why. Paso was sympathetic in that unconditional way that someone with that much power and that much intelligence can be. Occasionally he would bring other friends to the races with him. It was always a place of relaxation, a place to unwind like he could nowhere else. One of the men he brought was a man named Cruz, Simon Cruz."

"The guy from the Lab in Santa Fe?" And the one, according to Kit, who had thrown up a barrier of paperwork to avoid giving her the information she had asked for.

"The same." She propped her chin back on her arm. "I was twenty-four, Cruz was forty or so. I had just the previous year been wildly in love with one of the jockeys at the track, one who often rode for my father. His name was Johnney Cole. I knew my father would be furious and would have ruined him, so we kept it a secret. We figured in a year or two, after he'd saved enough to start up the breeding farm he'd always dreamed of, we'd get married and let the rest of the world take care of itself. But he was riding in a stakes race, riding one of Paso's horses who was famous enough that you might recognize the name, and the horse fell driving into the straightaway. Johnney was killed, died on the way to the hospital. He was probably the only man I've ever loved. Really loved." She sat up and drained the glass. "But there was something in the air between me and Cruz, that kind of sexual electricity. I was at loose ends, very depressed. I went to live with him, just outside Santa Fe, with the good wishes of both Paso and my father. We were together around two years, give or take. My dad committed suicide a few years after I left. The farm was in foreclosure. He was an unhappy, violent, hollow man. And when I heard, I felt nothing at all for him."

She rattled the ice cubes, then set the glass on the table. "Living with Cruz was a roller-coaster ride, but after a while, the electricity began to fade, of course. We became more like adversaries than lovers—always sparring, each trying to outdo the other, whether it was in bed or on the tennis court or at the chessboard or during cocktail party repartee. Then it started to extend into the work scene. You see, Cruz is one of Paso's key people, but Cruz also owns part of the Lab. I became interested in some of the things I saw Cruz bringing home, although he was very sly about keeping that part to himself. I suppose mainly I was just bored, sort of drifting whichever way the winds blew to keep occupied, entertained. It was Santa Fe, after all." She gave a thin, one-sided smile, a shrug. "So I decided to take Paso up on his offer to attend one of his schools. I didn't have a clear sense, really, of what was involved; no one really knows until they've spent a year or so in classes. Then Paso pays you a visit—you're in or you're out.

"Part of the curriculum, though, is that you're required to participate in your own psychotherapy—the idea is that you have to know yourself backward and forward just in case you get stuck in the field. You have to know your limits, what you can take, what you can't, you see?"

I didn't, but I didn't think I wanted to either. I nodded. My face felt frozen.

"That's when I got into psychotherapy. That's when I understood what had really been happening when I was a kid, what my father had really been doing to my mother before she ran for her life to the women's safe house in Louisville. People with that kind of background, that kind of repressed memory with all its snapshots of violence stuffed away and the screaming muffled for a while, I think maybe they..." She paused for a minute, holding on to the back of the chair and stretching her neck and head backward, rolling her shoulders. "I think maybe they have some unique intuition, some eerie sensitivity when there is any impending violence in the air around them." She had taken an odd turn in her confession, if that's what it was, so that now she seemed to be talking to herself, massaging the muscles at the back of her neck. But then her eyes refocused on me and she resumed. "While I was in therapy, I read your book again. By then, that must have been around 1978, '79 maybe, I understood that my mother would have been dead probably long before the fire, and that those few years of happiness were really what your book had given her. All that hatred I was carrying around shifted to my father. All the psychotherapy in the world hasn't changed that. I don't believe anything will ever change that.

"But the name Anna Lee Stone—it had been with me too long a time to simply disappear. I had come across a couple of photos back when I needed an image to hang all that hatred on. One was the PR snapshot on the inside cover of the book. You were partly in the shadow, maybe on a porch. Another was fuzzy, from a newspaper interview after the fire. So when I saw the list of contacts in the materials Paso gave me for the Pecos Water assignment, and your name was there, all that curiosity flooded back. I couldn't wait to get here. Probably, I wouldn't have taken the case without that lure, because this is one of those baby-sitting assignments they give you for a punishment, or in my case when they're trying to figure out where to pasture you. The kind of assignment where you just hang out and watch the players and try not to think too much about who you are or where you are or what else you could be doing if you weren't stuck in this godforsaken backwoods paralyzed with boredom.

"Here's where the two stories cross. The personal me, Cord Morgan, gets handed an assignment, comes across this name that she's been carrying around like it's some kind of key to the universe if she can only find the door it belongs to. And the other me, Employee Extraordinaire for The Company—but past the ten-year max for field work. Very high burnout rate. Somewhere before the ten-year point, burnout kicks in—you start to get careless, scared, crazy. They start to watch you pretty close around seven years, set you up for a desk job, maybe a country house somewhere if you've been prime. But I present The Company with a special problem— not only has Paso been like a father to me since I started working for him, but I've been the ace specialist for nearly as long as I've been out of school. Plus, just thinking of retirement sends me to the edge, and you can imagine how nervous that makes them. So Paso must have thought this assignment was just made to fit—here's my old flame, Cruz, to add some spice, and there's Santa Fe for a familiar stomping ground to play in. What he doesn't know is that I've changed. I'd be more entertained by Mickey Mouse in Disneyland than by Cruz in Santa Fe.

"No, if it hadn't been for your name in the file he faxed me, I would have kept pacing the floors at that mausoleum in the country where Paso had sent me to vacation with some of my gltizy friends. So I took the assignment. As soon as I got here, all I could think of was seeing you, where you lived, what you looked like. By the time I visited you the other night, I had already made a couple of trips up the mesa—once last Friday when Kit left to take her painting in to the gallery." She stretched sideways to reach the other bed, picking up a pile of tiny microcassettes next to a tangle of wires and a portable tape recorder. "I went to Kit's place and hid a couple of voice-activated recorders there. One in the kitchen and one by the window in the living room. She talks a lot to the plants." She shook her head and raised her eyebrows, holding up two of the cassettes and putting them on the table beside the pitcher. "But you were home that day, so I had to make another trip to cover your place. I did it when you were at the church ceremony at Jaz's funeral. In your kitchen, living room, bedroom." She held up three more cassettes and put them on the table with the others. "That's why I wasn't there until later, at the burial, but by then you were on your way home. I saw you go by in your truck."

I looked at the tapes, trying to remember what would be on them: my visit to Kit's place last Saturday, and at my house there would be Juan's visit, and Mac's, maybe Angel's, depending on when she'd retrieved the tapes. But I couldn't focus. My thoughts were whirling chaotically, and I couldn't seem to follow one train of thought for more than a few seconds.

"Want to hear one?" she asked, watching me.

"No, thanks," I said dryly. "I was there. I know what's on them."

"Maybe you don't," she said. She cocked her head sideways, and I felt myself being invaded again by her gaze. She shrugged. "Well, then, you might be interested in the ones from Sheriff Falcon's office." She put the last two on the table and raised her eyebrows a couple of times and grinned.

"You must be crazy."

"Just doing my job. And there's another tape that we will both be interested in. I left it at Becker's place when I went through. Just happened to be carrying an extra recorder on me." She gave me a wide-open smile this time, and for the life of me, I couldn't repress the surge of joy I felt at her use of first person plural. Maybe it was only because it suggested I had a future outside this room. Or maybe that wasn't why at all. "I already knew most of what you told me in the truck this morning, except for the part about the stuff Jaz put on Metz's computer. I think that's important, but I don't know how yet. I'll need to see the list...

"I should tell you," I interrupted, the words tumbling out before I knew they were going to, "that I also came across Jaz's manuscript. I didn't tell you, Caroline, because...well, you know."

"Good move. Yeah, I do know." She seemed to be lost in thought for a moment. "I don't have any professional interest myself in why, how, or if Jaz was killed. And it probably goes without saying at this point that I'm not interested in the manuscript. It was just a handy way to introduce myself to you, given my cover. Had nothing to do with the assignment here. But I can help you try to find out about Jaz's death if you're willing to provide me with some backup here. How about it?" She got up and dragged the chair back to the table, leaving the aisle open and the gun unguarded. I looked at the door and back at her. She was standing with her arms crossed over her chest, smiling.

"One thing I don't understand," I said. "You're here to keep down the publicity on the water issue, so the deal will go through?"

"Right."

"That means someone has hired The Company, *via* the Sangre de Cristo Lab, to monitor the water deal. Someone who has a lot of money. Someone who wants the water deal to go through very badly. Who? And why?"

"Good questions. Unfortunately, I don't have the answers. If the client's name were critical to the assignment, or to the safety of whoever handles the assignment, then it would be provided. The fact that it wasn't given to me means it's not significant. Not for my purposes, anyway. The cardinal rule at The Company is that anyone on assignment is never deprived of information imperative to success or safety. No exceptions, ever, for any reason. Sometimes the client's name is included, sometimes not." Morgan stopped talking for a minute and looked around the room. She held her head down and began massaging her temples with her fingertips. "But, I don't know, I..." she began, dropping her arms. She seemed to be undergoing some kind of transformation, yet another one, changing from The Company's star pupil into a creature more feral, less confident that this room washed in afternoon sunlight offered any kind of sanctuary. She leaned her weight on one hip and then began pacing again in front of the windows, her movements suddenly catlike, her voice no longer measuring its words but spilling them out in a kind of manic rush. "I don't know. Something is off key here. Can't quite put my finger on it. Something in Paso's voice. On the phone. And something else. In the files, but I can't find it. Don't know where it is. Until I understand what's wrong, I need to make sure I'm never where anyone expects me to be. I was thinking. Maybe you'd loan me a bed for a couple of nights?"

I listened for a while as she rambled and paced. The familiar confidence, even cockiness, had melted away and, so far as I could make out, left behind a woman overwhelmed by paranoia. I couldn't make much sense out of her reasoning, only that her anxiety seemed to have been caused by someone's tone of voice. "Maybe you're putting too much trust in an ungrounded suspicion, in the tone of someone's voice over the phone?" I ventured. "I mean, I'm not saying you're wrong, and you can stay at my place, but what if you're just feeling a little anxious because of the heat, or the history you have here from years ago, or maybe you really do need a vacation? What's so bad about that?"

She threw me an irritated glance and kept pacing. I thought of another possibility, something I wasn't all that eager to pursue but that needed to be said. I watched her pace for a couple of more minutes while I screwed up my courage.

"There's another possibility," I ventured, trying out the water. She stopped pacing and listened, so I went on. "Maybe you've finally tracked down Anna Lee Stone after all these years, and maybe there are still a few live spiders in all those cobwebs? I mean, maybe you're pushing some old buttons and you're more upset about it than you realize." I paused, gauging how far I should push my luck. Her eyes had gone rock hard, and I decided to back off. "All I'm saying is that If I were you, I'd want to be able to point to some hard-and-fast proof before I got into serious paranoia about the people you work for."

"Yes," she said in the low, smoky, familiar voice. She walked slowly toward me, slim and lithe as an ocelot, and stopped where I sat. Even though she stood in the sunlight, she still managed to look as though she were inhabiting the shadows. She stared down at me for a long time.

When she finally spoke, she said: "Yes. If you were me, that is exactly what you'd want." She paused, her eyes unfathomable. "And that is the great difference between us."

Cord Morgan was very tall. She towered over me where I sat, with the long rays of the afternoon sun hitting us through the lace curtains, surrounded by the morass of materials that furnished her everyday life—stacks of clandestine, secret documents; instruments of subterfuge and surveillance; the sinister gun with the several attachments lying next to it on the bed in this anonymous hotel room. Only a few short hours ago, I had been sitting at Becker's gate, thinking that this woman knew a great deal about my life while I knew almost nothing of hers. And I realized sitting here now that I knew as much about Cord Morgan as she knew about me—I was sitting in her living room, one that she occupied in any city in any country in the world. They would all look more or less like this one. For all her genius with animals, she had none to call her own, to lie beside her while she ate or slept, or to greet her when she came home at night. No person to share her life, no next-door neighbor, not one human being in the world that she could tell what she had just told me. This woman standing above me, lethal and poised for some action that I could not even begin to conceive, was the most utterly alone human being I had ever met. Maybe that was the real connection between her and Willie Joe Figgen.

I realized, too, that the danger I had felt in the room was coming not from Cord Morgan but from whatever dark and corrosive cloud followed in her wake. I understood that she had deliberately drawn me into this arena, had done so to banish Caroline Marcus, not because she had to, but because Caroline Marcus had been the last of the surviving barriers that had separated us for twenty years. Cord Morgan and I finally knew each other, and whatever voices this woman heard that were beyond my hearing were voices that, on whatever frequency she used, had carried her this far. That was, indeed, our great difference. I felt the cloud of my own ignorance thin slightly, as though it were a physical movement in the room.

"You said you had become a problem for The Company?" I asked, thinking of the man on the videotape she had called Paso. "How far do you think they'd go to remove you?"

Suddenly she raised an index finger to her lips. She seemed to freeze for a moment, becoming absolutely still in that rapt, fully absorbed way that reminded me of jack rabbits, who would halt their nibbling, their heads springing up and their ridiculous ears tuned to sounds beyond human perception. And then she became a blur of movement. Into a large green nylon bag she threw the cassettes, disks from the laptop, the ponytail and scarf, a stack of file folders, the recorder, and several other objects I couldn't identify. She fitted the gun into a separate zippered compartment, along with the attachments. She slipped the contacts into a tiny Velcro side pocket, snatched a pair of sunglasses as she whizzed by the desk, and opened the door in the wall adjacent to the entry door.

She looked back at me standing beside my chair and crooked a finger, signaling me to follow. "Morgan's Law, rule number fifty-eight," she whispered, as I passed through the door. "Always rent an adjoining room under another name," and she closed the door silently behind me.

We were in a suite the mirror image of the one we'd left—without the clutter, apparently unoccupied. Standing with her back pressed flat against the hallway door, her ear against the wood, Morgan locked eyes with me, holding her index finger to her lips again. I heard something, a low knock, from the room next door. A few seconds passed, and then Morgan opened the hallway door, the two of us flying past the room we had been in just as its door eased shut with a faint click.

I WASN'T COMPLAINING about the heat any more, even after sitting in my truck for twenty minutes in the science building parking lot waiting for Morgan to show up. The sign by the bank registered 103 degrees at 3:25 when I drove past, but the chill from the hotel room had crept into the center of my bones and taken root. I shivered a little and rubbed my arms briskly to increase the circulation.

I was also feeling irritable and cramped from being too long confined inside Morgan's room. I got out of the truck and stretched, then wandered around the lot, avoiding the crater-sized potholes, hoping a little activity might clear out the sawdust in my head. The lot was deserted except for Kathy's red Tercel, still basking in the priority parking of the faculty section. The space beside it, where Mac's old Caddy had been parked, was empty—odd, since Mac was expecting me back. A man who treasured his rituals, he seldom left his office before 5:00, and if he had errands in town, he saw them as opportunities to get in some jogging. I walked around to the front of the building and looked down the sidewalk in the direction of the hotel. No sign of either Mac's Caddy or Morgan. The hotel was only six blocks away, less than a five-minute walk. After we'd reached the bottom of the stairs, Morgan had headed toward a door at the rear of the lobby, yelling back to meet her at Mac's parking lot. Apparently, she wasn't much of a hiker, even though in her room she'd moved with the speed of lightning: in fifteen seconds, twenty max, she had filled the canvas bag with what she must have considered essential and was out the door. For someone like me who had trouble packing an overnight case in less than an hour, I found her speed and quick thinking just short of truly unbelievable. And speaking of unbelievable, how had she known that far in advance that someone was approaching her room? Was there a human ear made that could pick up footsteps from beyond the room's thick door? And even if she had, how could she possibly have known they were coming here? Did she have some high-tech surveillance equipment to tip her off? If so, I hadn't seen her check anything just before she was alerted. What then: a sixth sense? I wasn't buying it—too New Age for my money; I was definitely Old Age when it came to questions of how many senses we had. So why hadn't she shown up yet, I wondered, looking down the street for some sign of her. Had she gone back to the room for something and run into trouble? I considered walking that way, hoping to meet her en route, but given the circumstances of our departure, not to mention her impressive execution of it, I decided to follow instructions for a while longer.

The sky was flat and white as a dinner plate, except for the black fist of clouds that still hung over the horizon to the north. Above the mountains to the southeast, the smoke from the Taos fire drifted up and trailed south like a smear above the mesa skyline. Today was evacuation day. The two-lane highway leading from Taos down the mountain into Tortuga would be backed up for miles with pickups heaped with furniture, pulling livestock trailers, and flanked along the shoulders with milling herds of farm animals and gawking tourists. Tortuga residents would soon be feeling the effects of their dispossessed mountain neighbors; spare rooms would be offered to relatives, families would set up tents in fields, and people would camp alongside the river, joining together in communal groups to offer support to one another during the next few days as the fire threatened their homes.

I paced the sidewalk in front of the science building, waiting for Morgan, still reeling from her long string of disclosures. It would take days to fully digest the information, so I focused on my own response to Cord Morgan. And the disappearance of Caroline. These two women, in my mind's eye, seemed as different as east from west. I imagined them walking alongside me, one at each elbow. True, I had been oddly drawn to Caroline, but now it was no contest. I leaned toward Morgan the way a candle burns toward oxygen—even after the revelation of her mother's death, even after she had led me into the flames of my darkest nightmare where women and children ran screaming inside the fire trapped on my television screen all those twenty years ago. For how many years and through how many sleepless nights had the sounds of those screams, the roar of fire brought me straight up in bed? How often had I imagined a sister, brother, a grown child standing at my door, knocking, holding the book with its red and black cover? If dread could be measured in pounds, then I had lived the last twenty years under the weight of an ocean. And now, inexplicably, the weight had lifted. I felt a kind of giddy optimism, a great wave of relief, as though a punishing storm had passed across the earth and left it cleansed.

I came to the corner of the intersection where a truck and car with Taos County license plates sat waiting for the red light to change. The truck driver stuck his head out the window and called back to the woman driving the car behind him. Several goats with dog collars around their necks had been tied into the bed of the truck, all bleating "maa-a-a" at a teenage boy who sat morosely ignoring them, holding on to the truck's roll bar. The car behind was packed with children ranging from toddler to teenager. These were people, it occurred to me, who were fleeing a fire of their own, a more current and immediately threatening one.

I wandered back to my truck, the buoyant feeling replaced by a sense of impending disaster. I decided to hang out with Kathy, maybe find out where Mac had gone, and I poked around in the glove compartment searching for something to leave a note on for Morgan. I found battered maps, a salt shaker, assorted catsup and mustard packets, a wad of tissues, a Phillips screwdriver, two cat flea collars, a couple rings of keys, a package of smashed Saltines, several lint-covered paper clips and, at last, a crumpled envelope that had held a payroll check from the college I had left just last week. I pressed it out flat and began looking for something to write with. I looked behind both seats, along the edges of the gearshift box, and then I began scrabbling around underneath the driver's seat. I wedged myself into the foot space below the steering wheel, my left cheek pressed against the floor mat, and began working my arms in the narrow space between the seat springs and the floor, probing through ancient and mysterious clutter for anything resembling a cylindrical shape and trying not to think about what might be living in there. My posterior and legs were hanging out the door as I braced myself against the asphalt of the parking lot, pushing deeper into the mess underneath the driver's seat.

"Need a drink or a smoke?"

I jumped, banging my head on the steering wheel column. "Cute," I said, carefully extracting my hands from under the seat coils. "Did you go by way of Santa Fe or what?" I inched my upper torso backward, out of the truck, so that I was squatting awkwardly on the crumbling asphalt, staring at Morgan's knees. For all that, I felt a hot rush of pleasure as I pushed myself up.

"Mm. I hung around to see who'd paid me a visit." She was wearing her large dark sunglasses, the nylon bag slung over her shoulder.

"And?"

"Another ship in the night, what's a girl to do? My guess is that Cruz sent someone."

"But why? Isn't that who sent you?"

"Well, actually Paso sent me. I think Cruz had his own ideas about who to send, but there was nothing he could do about it. Outranked. I liked that part, but he was pretty pissed about it. It would be exactly like him to send someone to check up on me, let me know he's having the last word. But I don't know. There might be more to it than Cruz's obsessive megalomania." She looked around the lot. "So where's Mac?"

"He's not here, but maybe Kathy knows where he went." I locked the truck, and we walked toward the science building. "You know, I just remembered something. The last time Mac was at my place, he said if I ever came by and wanted to play a while on the Net and he wasn't around, to have Kathy let me in. He gave me his password, too." I grinned at her.

"I take it you've got more on your mind than surfing." She had legs a giraffe would have been proud of, and I found myself having to skip to keep up with her.

"Well, it gets us into his office, anyway. Maybe there's something there about the water analysis."

Inside, Kathy was beating a mean staccato at the keyboard and chewing a mouthful of gum at the same killing speed. Morgan and I stood for a moment watching her in action. Today's outfit was a flamingo pink Spandex top, edged with yellow nylon lace and cut low enough to display an impressive line of cleavage. Into her big hair, she had sprayed a swatch of hot pink color across one side. Her eyes darted back and forth between the monitor and the piece of writing beside the keyboard, her head nodding rapidly to some savage and internal drumbeat that kept her bruised purple fingernails and matching purple lips in sync.

"Whew. That is one seriously driven woman," Morgan said, shaking her head and walking off toward the glass display cabinets.

The hot pink was making me see spots, and when I pictured Kathy sitting behind the wheel of her red Tercel, I looked at the wall above her head and asked about Mac.

"Went off an hour ago with some guy. Didn't say boo." Tap, tap, pop, snick.

"Who was the guy?"

"Kind of old, maybe thirty-five, forty. Square." She made a sour face, not missing a beat.

"Um. Not from around here? You didn't recognize him."

"Nah. Looked like the type to watch TV in bed, you know?" She blew a good-sized balloon and sucked it back in with a loud snap. "Not my type." She cut a significant look at me from the side of her eye.

"What'd he look like, I mean dark hair, jeans, what?"

"Oh, you want a descrip. Short-sleeved white shirt, button-down, tie." She shook her big hair and rolled her eyes. "Black slacks, belt. Bor-ing. Maybe five foot ten, sandy hair." Tap, tap. Pop.

"Eyes?"

"Yeah." Tap, tap, pop.

I waited.

"Hah! Just kidding." Snap, pop, click. "Dunno. Didn't look this way." She shrugged.

"Mac said I could use his computer to play on the Net? How about it?"

"Hey, I could care if he doesn't. Key's over there." She nodded her head backward at an empty desk where the work-study student would sit to help out when the semester began. Beside it hung a long row of keys on hooks above a set of pigeon-hole mailboxes where the faculty mail was distributed. I took the one to Mac's office and headed down the long dark corridor with Morgan. Inside, the desk had been cleared, the stacks of books Mac generally had piled on every available flat surface were reshelved, and the file folders he used to organize his research materials and various drafts were arranged in a tidy pile on top of the file cabinet.

"Wow. Looks like the maid's been in. Mac will have kittens when he gets back."

Morgan shut the door and lowered the blind on its window. "Looks like a real tidy fellow. Not his usual habit?" She dropped her sunglasses on the desk on her way around it, flipped on the computer, opened desk drawers, folders, file cabinet drawers.

"Nope. Likes everything at his fingertips," I said, looking at the rows of tidily shelved books. "He's kind of a nut about it. No one *ever* touches his stuff." By the time the computer was done loading, Morgan had searched every drawer and opened every door in the place.

"Mm." She settled into Mac's chair, hunched over the screen like he did. She held her fingers poised over the keyboard and spoke without looking up. "Password?"

"Uh. Oh geez."

Morgan kept her fingers poised and looked over her shoulder at me. "Don't do this, Stone. Think."

Stone? Shit. I collapsed into the ratty overstuffed chair and stared at her. She had her head cocked at me, the odd sideways smile hiked up at one corner. "Come on. Come on. Don't flake out now," she urged.

"Hey, back off." I settled into the chair and closed my eyes, thinking about the night Mac had come by with the plastosterone information. I pictured him sitting in my living room, in the chair beside the lamp, and tried to bring back his words. No luck. "Shit."

Morgan heaved a deep sigh and uncoiled her fingers. She took the Dodgers cap off the top of the monitor and pulled it on backward and stared at the screen. Women wearing baseball caps reminded me of the preppy California college I'd just driven away from last week—wearing baseball caps was very "in" on campuses these days, and Morgan looked like a young college coed gearing up for a term paper. And then I did a double take—she was wearing Mac's Dodgers cap!

"Dodger!" I yelled. "Morgan, listen. Something's wrong here. The office, the Dodgers cap. Mac would never have walked out of here and left his Dodgers cap."

"Yeah, I've already put it together. It's a sweep. You still trying to remember the password?" She spoke dryly, propping her chin in her hand. "This is important."

"'Dodger,' goddammit! I told you."

"Okay, okay. Calm down." She grinned, spun the chair around, and began tapping. I came over and watched behind her shoulder. This woman knew something about surfing. Web sites flew across the screen before I could read them. After a few minutes, just when I thought maybe Morgan had been lured into a little surfing of her own, she sat back in the chair. "Holy shit."

"What? What is it?" A long, boring list of names was on the screen. I didn't see what the problem was.

"I've gone into the history, traced where he's been for the last few days. This morning, not long after you left, he logged on to the Sangre de Cristo Lab site, and I'll bet my left tit he made some inquiries. Let's look at the bad news." She leaned forward again and began tapping. Soon the Sangre de Cristo Lab home page came on the monitor, carrying the familiar mountain silhouette with the bolt of lightning and the Zia symbol. She tracked through several links to find the e-mail Mac had sent, and then a copy of his message came on the screen: "Doing research on plastosterone. Noticed you folks used to work on it. Unclassified? Still have your test docs? Would like to take a peek if possible. Thanks." Mac had included his office phone number and university address.

"That's it, Stone." She leaned back in the chair again, staring at the screen, her arms crossed over her chest. "These guys move fast. It's one of their M.O.s." She hit the Print button, shut down the program, flipped the machine off. I returned to the ratted-out chair, and we sat for a moment in the semidarkness of the immaculate office with the strips of bright afternoon light slanting through the mini-blinds.

"Are you telling me you think the Lab sent someone to abduct Mac because he's asking about plastosterone?"

"That's my best guess." She chewed on her bottom lip and then turned to look out through the mini-blind at the street. An old shambling pickup drove slowly by, stacked high with boxes and ragged pieces of furniture tied on with rope. In the cab, on the passenger side, a woman holding a sleeping baby looked in our direction, her face expressionless. "It's Becker," she said to the window. "Paso sent me here to watch Becker, but Cruz's requisition was for someone to monitor the Pecos Water Project." She seemed to be talking to herself, so I just listened, trying to follow what she was saying. "They must have a keyword red alert at the Lab, so when Mac's inquiry came in, the shit hit the fan. Someone would have called Cruz, Cruz would have sent out a couple of reps, probably two—that's who the fellow was who paid me a visit. Part of the Lab duo Cruz sent to pick up Mac. One would have escorted him back to the Lab, the other hung around for the sweep, cleaned the office like Mac would have done if he'd really decided to take a hike, and then the guy dropped in on me. Probably wanted to know if I had stumbled over the plastosterone info." She swung around in the chair and looked at me. "This probably means Mac's not coming back. Ever."

"Are you...I mean, are they going to..."

"Don't get into melodrama, Stone. This isn't the movies. Usually it's a pretty decent ending. Like everybody gets what they want. The key is mediation, not brute force. We're talking private enterprise here, professional, very low profile. Brute force creates more problems than it solves. Take Mac. Would you say he's a happy man? Has everything he wants? Loves his wife? His job?"

"Yeah. Good job. Gorgeous wife." I thought for a minute. "Well, his job gives him the time he wants to do research, which is his first love. He teaches because that's part of the package, and from what I hear, he's good at it. And Willa? She's got a little of her own money, likes to hang out with the gallery crowd in Santa Fe, though she can't really afford it. I think he'd like to slip out of that noose. Just my personal opinion."

"All right. Let's say that's the way it shakes out with Mac. The Company offers him all the time and opportunity to do nothing but research, offers to set him up anywhere he wants to go—the South of France, London, New Zealand. Chances are good that someone like Mac, into research, could be put to good use by The Company and paid top dollar. So they make all the arrangements, make it look like Mac's just flown the old marriage coop, taken a hike. Probably the wife's just as glad, Mac's set, the school is slightly inconvenienced, but profs are a dime a dozen. They can get a new hire for half what they're paying Mac with tenure. No problem."

"But people can't just disappear."

"Why not? You did. Happens every day." Morgan leaned back in Mac's chair, watching me across the immaculate desk where she had set Mac's cap next to her sunglasses. She had an amused expression on her face.

She was right; it was damned easy, and I hadn't even tried very hard. Filled out an official change of name form, chased off a few curious grad students looking for a dissertation topic now and then, used my real name when I taught a class, but came home under my alias. The hard part was working up to actually doing it. "But what if he didn't go willingly? There's his hat."

"He went willingly. Might not have known he wasn't coming back, but once they make their presentation, they'll have trouble holding him back. I've seen it happen a hundred times. A thousand times. There's a small chance he's being held against his will, but that almost never happens."

"Wait. What about the water sample I brought him? That's why I was coming back."

"That's probably why he was putting out the inquiry. Just a guess, but look at the time frame." She leaned over to the printer and ripped off the top sheet. "We left here this morning around, say, 11:30? He sent the lab an inquiry a little after noon. He would have had time to do some lab work on the water. I.D.'d the plastosterone, no problem, because he'd already identified it from the other sample you brought him, right?"

I nodded. She went on. "It was public record that the Lab had been awarded the state contract to do the water testing required by the Pecos Water Project, so he probably figured they had already run the standard analysis tests. Also, from the sound of his message, looks like he came across something to indicate the Lab had been involved in plastosterone research at some point."

"He said back in the sixties, during the Vietnam war, the government was trying to develop it for chemical warfare."

"So he went right to the source, wrote the Lab thinking they must have found traces of the chemical when they did their analyses, must have found it harmless since the deal was going through, thought he'd run it past them. Probably thought he was ready to give you some good news about the whole thing." Morgan stood up and set the nylon bag she'd brought with her onto Mac's desk and began rummaging through it. She dug out the contact lenses, the ponytail and the silk scarf. "Naive, but there it is," she said, leaning her head over and inserting the contacts.

"Naive?"

"Sure. Good ole everyday American Joe logic: the government's seen it, approved it, put their stamp on it; therefore, it must be okay. Not too many people will admit to believing this; people will say just the opposite. But the fact of the matter is, they do believe it. In spite of everything they've seen to the contrary. Never ceases to amaze me—the human animal gravitates toward good. Or, if you're a cynic, gravitates toward stupidity, vacuity, inertia, deliberate ignorance. You pick whatever word fits for you. Works to my benefit. Couldn't do my job without it." She gave me a Cheshire cat smile as she fiddled with her hair, attaching the long swatch of ponytail onto her own and adding the scarf.

She was Caroline again, with the ice blue eyes. Looking at her sent a chill down my spine. I thought of Willie Joe Figgen and hugged myself, rubbing my upper arms. "You're kidding. You think the Lab found plastosterone in the water, according to Mac a potentially very dangerous chemical, and didn't report it?"

"Right," she said, sitting back down in Mac's chair. "If they had reported finding the stuff in the water, it would have blown the whistle on Becker's research, stopped it cold, and the water deal would have been history. Texas isn't going to want polluted water. That's exactly the kind of action The Company has been hired to prevent. So you've got the Lab undertaking a government contract, a conflict of interest given Cruz's position in The Company, so he's caught between a rock and a hard place. Add to that Paso's directive to keep Becker out of the picture. My guess is, from what I saw at his place, the old pervert's up to his ass in this whole thing. Plastosterone seems to be his baby. So, you bet, the Lab's burying this information."

"Look, I don't think you understand how lethal this stuff might be." Even though she must already have heard our conversation on the tape she'd planted, I repeated what Mac had told me about the testing done on plastosterone, the aggression and violence it created. "And he was pretty sure that there was a lot more bad news that he hadn't uncovered yet. He was still working on it."

"Yep. Looks like."

"You're awfully calm about this. If Mac did find this stuff in the water, there's a good chance that the entire river may be polluted with a chemical that is potentially lethal. And another thing. Don't forget the water scheduled to flow in even larger proportions through the state of Texas starting tomorrow will be used to irrigate new areas that, at this point, are unpolluted. We can't just sit by and let this happen."

Morgan was staring at me through the pale blue contacts, but I didn't think it was me she was seeing. She seemed to be somewhere else.

I tried again. "Listen, remember my friend Kit, the one I told you Juan suspected of poisoning Jaz?" Her eyes came back into focus, and she nodded. I repeated Kit's suspicion that Cruz had deliberately created a paper chase to conceal information.

"She's probably right. It's the easiest way to handle the problem if you're just playing for a few days' time. One hundred percent foolproof."

"And the Lab," I said, remembering the logo on the chemical report I'd seen on top of Juan's desk, "they did the chemical analysis on Jaz's body to determine the cause of death. The chemical that the local coroner's office in Tortuga couldn't identify. Juan told me today the case was closed, that it was amanitin, poison mushroom. But what if it wasn't? What if it was plastosterone? The Lab covered up the presence of the chemical in the water, wouldn't they also cover up its presence in a dead man's body? Isn't that why they sent you here, to keep anything to do with the water issue quiet so the deal will go through?"

Morgan and I sat facing each other across the desk. Her body was a black shadow, a silhouette backlit against the strips of white light coming through the mini-blinds. The office was silent as a tomb, except for the echos—first of my own words, and then those of the woman sitting across from me:

Isn't that why they sent you here, to keep anything to do with the water issue quiet so the deal will go through?

Just doing my job.

It seems to me if there are a hundred ways to see something and it's impossible to distinguish the moral superiority of one over the other, then why does it matter which one you choose? If we live in an accidental universe, as opposed to one created by God...you can do anything, and it's okay.

You can do anything, and it's okay.

A door closed somewhere down the hall, a hollow sound in the empty building. Five o'clock: Kathy was leaving for the day. I heard the door to the outside open and then close. On the street, behind the brilliant slits of light, a low-rider cruised slowly by, the bass pumped up to full volume, pulsing and vibrating the glass in Mac's office window.

Morgan

THE LOOK on Anna Lee Stone's face: I have seen it many times, hundreds of times. I read the sequence of expressions like emotional flashcards—confusion, disbelief, awareness, fear. This used to be the point in every assignment I worked toward, as certain as shards of lightning in a summer storm.

As I watch Stone having her moment of truth, is it an accident that I am now having mine? Or is it more than accident—is it fate, are we that closely linked? Because if she has been running in place for twenty years, from the time my mother burned to death in Indiana to now, had all my assignments during those same years been merely a rehearsal for this time, this place? Had I believed myself Paso's consummate prodigy, obsessed with the chase, maneuvering every corner, to discover that all my previous assignments had been attempts to escape this one?

I sit behind the desk watching the Stone woman with the lines of bright sun cutting across her face. She grapples, trying to understand. What motive, what evil, she wonders, brings a person to kill a river, conceal the malignancy flowing there. And I wonder what star, what galaxy burst overhead to shower the planet, the human animal with madness, the birthright of our limited vision. So that only our ignorance never ages: yesterday a Greek king took a brooch and gouged out his eyes, today no one believes in such gestures for our skies are long empty and Olympus scaled to size. We chart our path in a different book, a sordid unsacred text—a guide to our accidental universe that brooks no god and never did and never will, so that the human beast manufactures its own seed, sows its miracles and reaps such reward or punishment as befits the season. We are creatures eternally damned, sentenced at birth to everlasting freedom.

I feed on this voided air in this predictable, knowable universe. I can calculate which square your king will land on, when he will arrive there, and just as he steps across the boundary, already too late, he looks up to see the Queen staring down the long line of access. It is my game, my life, my specialty. Only here, in this chessboard order, can I plot my course without interference from some divine busybody; only here can such men as Becker create their toys of imminent destruction, diddling fate as though she were a dull-witted child.

The Stone woman's face passes from confusion to disbelief. I am the orphan of her art, the only surviving child of the fire she ignited, yet still she cannot believe that I, even I, can smell the foul waters and leave them to their putrid flow down across the wasteland of this doomed continent. And this, even after I have read the papers that she has not, have followed the mainlines of Professor Williamson's discoveries of the chemical's unsavory composition, its lethal propensity to accumulate one-hundred-fold in the decomposing flesh of the river's dead fish and birds and all those who gather there to drink and feed. The river is doomed, the animals around it dying, the people as well, but so it would have been without me.

I have not come to save the river.

All the same, the air grows darker between me and the Stone woman, as though a storm cloud has slipped across the sun, dimming the brilliant slants of light that mark her face. The intervening lines are shadows, a different terrain where I stare in disbelief as a creature lurks into the uppermost frame of those horizontal dark ribbons. Between the hair and brow, between the eye and cheek, leaping now along the upper lip, it skulks as by a riverbed. Its coat is dulled by illness, its amber eyes blazed with madness. It hunkers against the river's bank. I feel its claws extend as though my own muscles flex them. I grip the edge of the desk where I sit and hear the distant downstream chatter of the dispossessed Taos families erecting their tents in the shady hollows of the riverside cottonwoods. The beast digs deep into the muddy riverbed, desperate to soothe its burning pads, its parched mouth. It laps the infected water, its tongue dry, lolling, unrelieved. It gives itself to the river, sinking to its haunches in the water, expecting heaven. Its muscles are swollen, rigid, itching and screaming for solace. Its penis is red and pulsing and hungry. But the water boils. It *is parched with fire and burns the skin. The beast turns, fixing me with its glowing amber eyes, just below the eyes of Anna Lee Stone: they smolder with bewilderment, disbelief. Eyes that burn, eyes more familiar than the beast's or Anna Lee Stone's, eyes that peer from behind the moving shadows of more ancient flames in the land of apple trees.*

I hear a door closing, and then another, and in the further distance the sound of children's laughter, tinkling like wind chimes on a summer's breeze. Two children are running along the lip of the river, a small girl pursued by a slightly larger boy who looks so sandy-haired and similar that he must be her brother. The little girl has a heart-shaped face, small spaces between the nearly translucent baby teeth; her hair is a mop of ringlets, her body still ripe with baby fat. Her arms and legs pump, her voice squealing in gleeful terror, her eyes squeezed shut in the sheer delight of her brother's chase. Just as he stretches his arm to tag her shoulder, just as she turns her head briefly to calculate his position, just then the beast leaps.

Even as it springs, I feel its need surge like adrenaline throughout my own body. I feel the beast's heart struggling to pump, its blood thickened to mucous. I feel its teeth as though they are my own: as shrewd as an addict's needle, aching for freedom, for respite. For blood. I feel its throbbing desire—the penis erect and blind and driving the body so that the beast hits the air flooded by rank desire, engorging the girl child.

The darkness lifts. Soon the sirens will fill the air, fading toward the river where the victims of the fire are camped. Too late.

I watch Anna Lee Stone in the striped light. Her eyes hold mine. They fill with the terror of recognition, with the knowledge that her future may be a shut door, painted black. I am used to this expression: it is the gold ring, the bouquet of roses, checkmate. It is possible only because I believe absolutely in an accidental, godless universe.

Yet can her moment of truth hold more terror, more recognition than my own? For rising just behind her eyes are the others: the blazing amber ones, the ancient ones that observe from among the flames. Anna Lee Stone and I are joined in our mutual terrors. I peer into her, straight through the darkness and into the past as though piercing through the pupil of an eye, making out shapes, moving shadows as though cast by firelight, on the other side. The familiar ingredients are all present: there is the recognition, the terror. There is the disbelief.

And where there is disbelief, there is hope.

THE CHILL had nothing to do with the air conditioning this time. Something sinister had darkened the air between me and Morgan as we stared at each other across the desk in Mac's office. For an uncomfortably long moment, I felt dislocated, a reluctant character in an improbable James Bond scene, waiting for her to pull out that silver gun from the nylon bag—or maybe something quieter, an exotic poisoned dart contraption—and do me in right there. So when she stood up and reached for the bag, I gripped the arms of Mac's ratty chair and felt the room spin. I braced for the worst.

Even after she shouldered the bag and stood waiting by the door for me to follow, apparently oblivious to my terror, I was stupefied with fear. My hands trembled and my legs quivered as I followed Morgan out of the building and into the searing hot air of the parking lot. Yet nothing about her manner indicated that something unusual had just passed between us, and outside, surrounded by the familiar sounds of a small-town rush hour, I thought of the moment sheepishly, laughing at my overactive imagination, exacerbated no doubt by the heat, nerves, and exhaustion from a poor night's sleep. But the chill wouldn't lift. My bone marrow had turned to ice crystals, and I shivered in fits and starts. At the truck, I gave over the wheel to Morgan and climbed in the passenger side, rubbing my upper arms and insisting that I had to find Mac, with or without her help. Her protests about the dangers and difficulties of entering the Lab, along with her reassurances of Mac's safety, only fueled my determination: I had gotten Mac into this, and I intended to see for myself that he was all right. At last Morgan threw up her hands in frustration and agreed to help.

"Pure lunacy," she said, shaking her head and giving her odd, crooked smile. "But, what the hell, it's about time I dropped in on Cruz."

Morgan was pushing the four-cylinder truck up the crests toward Santa Fe as fast as it would go—not much over sixty-five or so in my experience, except she had a way of keeping the momentum built up from the down slopes. I leaned over and checked the speedometer. Hitting eighty-five and climbing. Amazing. And she had a built-in radar detector that allowed her to slow a couple of times just before the highway patrol came up over a crest ahead.

"Well," I said, trying for levity, "if you decide to change jobs, you could always take up race car driving."

"Mmh. May not be my decision to make."

We had stopped by her room before leaving Tortuga. No sign of the mysterious visitor, nothing disturbed to show anyone had entered the room. While Morgan took a quick shower and changed, I waited by the window, looking down at the park across the street—a man walked his dog along a concrete path; an old woman sat motionless on the bench where Morgan and I had sat yesterday, clutching a paper bag against her breast and staring straight ahead. Sirens began wailing loudly nearby, then faded into the distance. Morgan came out of the tiny bathroom wearing skimpy black underwear, her body hard and trim. She pulled on a black silk shirt that made me hot just looking at it, black jeans, and the same Western boots she always wore. She wound a black silk scarf around the ponytail, and now, sitting behind the wheel with the hot wind blowing around us and the large sunglasses in place, she looked stunning—even though her Caroline Marcus disguise wasn't helping my chills any. As the countryside slid by, I felt as though I were standing on a high building, looking down from a distance.

Morgan was talking, eyes on the road, unaware of my vertigo and the gooseflesh that crept across my body. "I can get us by the front desk," she said, "and down to the basement, that's where they have the apartments, and while you say your good-byes, I'll drop in on Cruz. It's going to be a little tricky because I need to look at a few things without him around." She glanced at the wristwatch she'd strapped on before we left her room. "It'll be after six when we get there. The Lab shuts down at six, so he might be gone for the day. If so, no problem. If he's around, I'll have to dream up some distraction." She grinned, one arm propped on the window frame and one hanging over the steering wheel, and I wondered vaguely how she would get into his office if he had gone and what kind of distraction she had in mind if he hadn't. "Might get a little tense. You up for it?"

I shivered again, even though the wind whipping through the window was torrid. "Sure, what the hell." I sounded more willing than I felt. A lot more.

We flew past the Cerrillos exit, leaving Santa Fe behind. I didn't have a clue how to get to the Sangre de Cristo Lab, but a little while later, Morgan veered down an off-ramp, then turned southwest on a cracked asphalt road. Soon, after several switches to progressively more desolate back roads, we were curving through a remote countryside of the type generally populated by rattlesnakes and coyotes. No houses, no road signs to indicate a flourishing business just ahead—just miles of mesquite and chamisa for as far as the eye could see. I sneaked a sideways peek at Morgan, remembering the moment of terror I had felt in Mac's office, thinking that inside the nylon bag riding between us on the front seat was a gun the likes of which I had never seen before. I doubted that I would know how to use it even if I were quick enough to snatch it out of the bag. In fact, I was so deep into thoughts of escape, gripped by an escalating terror, that I didn't notice the stream of cars we had been meeting until Morgan braked at an intersection, the left-turn signal blinking.

She took off her sunglasses and twisted around in the seat. An amused expression played around her eyes. "Stone, you have to get over this. Relax."

I realized I was gripping the arm rest of the passenger door with both hands. I let it go and folded my hands in my lap, feeling contrite as a small child. It was then I saw the string of cars backed up on the left, waiting to turn. Farther down the road behind them, the second story of a large concrete building rose up over a stand of piñons at the foot of a low mesa.

Morgan went on talking as we sat at the intersection, ignoring the cars. "Obviously I've got a serious conflict of interest I'm having to deal with here. And I'm not going to make any promises about blowing the whistle on the people I work for. I'm not even going to make any promises about letting you do it." She stuck her sunglasses back on and turned left onto a corrugated washboard road that set the truck off into a grand mal seizure. "But I can promise you one thing," she said, as we inched along over the ruts. "I won't harm you. And I'll do my level best to make sure no one else does either. That's the best I can do, Stone. And I give you my word on it."

I didn't know if that made me feel better or worse, but did I really want to say what I was thinking, namely, "Your word isn't worth jack shit"? Probably not. I had known danger was imminent, after all, but this put an end to any question of how imminent. The road got worse, the truck vibrated like the front and rear had lost all hope of communication, and I grabbed the sissy bar above the passenger door with one hand and held my breasts with the other. Morgan drove past a smoothly paved entrance road that led to a parking lot with lots of cars and employees milling around. Car doors were slamming, engines starting. We followed the bumpy road around to the back of the building where it changed abruptly into a paved driveway with an automatic crossbar blocking the way to another smaller parking area with carports on each side. Taking a small plastic card from one of the zippered pockets in her nylon bag, she shoved it into a slot. The automatic arm flew up. She drove slowly to the end of the lot, rummaging all the while with her right hand in the nylon bag. She circled around, passing behind the rear of a silver Mercedes parked in the carport with the name Simon Cruz above it. Morgan extracted something from the bag, tossed it under the Mercedes, and drove smoothly back through the way we'd come. When we pulled into the parking lot in front of the building, only a few cars remained.

I was still looking back toward the rear lot, my head ducked down, waiting for an explosion, something, when Morgan pulled into a slot near the entrance and switched off the engine. She grinned at me, shaking her head.

I straightened up and looked around. Maybe because locals called it "the Lab," I had unconsciously connected the Sangre de Cristo Laboratory to the infamous lab in Los Alamos, cradle of the atomic bomb. But, I thought, this place was merely a local industrial analysis and chemical development plant. It looked like any office building in any city in the country, its institutional concrete lines and rows of windows familiar and innocuous. Its only peculiarity was the remote location, and although the nebulous connection to the bald-headed fellow called Paso and the apparent conniving of its manager, Cruz, suggested some kind of villainy, it was probably no worse than many such enterprises in a state rife with corruption and political intrigue. It was a way of life, had been for many years, and anyone who lived here very long got used to it or left.

"Doing okay?" Morgan asked, removing her sunglasses and inspecting her face in the rearview mirror. She put the sunglasses back on, readjusted the mirror, and rolled up her window. She turned to face me, her voice flat: "Listen carefully," she said from behind the black glasses. "We go in to the front desk. I do the talking. We go straight to the basement and find Mac. I'll leave you there and be back in fifteen minutes. Probably less." She dug into the bag and pulled out another wristwatch, glanced at it and then at her own, and handed it to me. It was digital and read 6:17. "Put this on. When I leave you at Mac's, look at it, add fifteen. If I'm not back by then, you come back to the truck and get out of here." She tossed me the keys.

"What about Mac?" I rolled up my window too, reluctantly. I wanted to drive out of here, but I buckled on the watch instead. "What about you? What if you're not back?"

"I'll be back. If I'm not, there's nothing you could do about it anyway. Listen, you don't want to mess with these people, Stone. I'm not kidding. Pay attention: fifteen max and you're out of there. Mac? You'll see. He'll stay. They'll have given him their spiel by now. You couldn't pry him out of here with dynamite. If I'm wrong, take him with you." She looked over at me, and I saw myself in her sunglasses. I looked as small and scared as I felt, but Mac was in this because he had done me a favor. I couldn't turn my back on him. Morgan checked her watch again and shouldered the nylon bag. "Ready, kiddo?"

I followed her through glass doors mounted with small cameras; then she inserted a plastic card in another set of doors, and they slid open. There were more tiny cameras, and I wished I'd brought along some sunglasses, too. The outside of the building didn't reveal much about the inside. I was not prepared for the elegant furniture, the deeply polished oak walls and floors. What looked to be an office building on the outside felt like an exclusive club inside. But before you could join, you had to pass the test that I figured the guard in the uniform behind the entry bar was going to lay on us.

"Hey, Mike. How you doing." Morgan removed her sunglasses, walked up to the bar, and leaned against it. The guy looked like a thirty-something Robert Redford: blonde, tan, wholesome as weekend baseball. Morgan lifted her eyebrow and gave him the odd, sideways smile. After a moment of confusion, he burst into a two-hundred-watt grin as Morgan set her sunglasses on the polished oak next to the book he'd been reading. *All the Pretty Horses*.

"Hey, Morg. Cool disguise! Didn't recognize you at first." His smile dimmed a little, and he looked at her uncertainly. "Cruz's in. Want me to buzz him you're coming up? He chewed my ass about the other night. Hell, I thought he'd like the surprise. You figure." He shrugged.

"Nope. I'm here to check on the new guy. Mac? Getting set up for The Company?"

"Oh yeah. Hey, nice guy. Dodger fan, too." His smile gained wattage. "Down in B-9."

Morgan started to walk away and then stopped. I bumped into her shoulder blade. "Oh, Mike." She went back to the desk and pointed behind him at the row of small monitors. "When I was driving in, I noticed some smoke coming from behind the building."

Mike whirled and looked at the monitor showing the back parking lot. Smoke was billowing from the grey Mercedes. "Holy shit! Cruz's car is on fire!"

As we left, he was dialing the phone. I followed Morgan through a labyrinth of halls, junctures, stairs, into and out of a glass-fronted elevator. We were moving fast, and I was trying hard to remember the way, hoping I wasn't going to have to get out on my own. At last we were breezing down a wide hallway that looked like an elegant hotel—wainscoting, fabric wallpaper, framed paintings. The building had appeared good-sized on the outside, but I felt we'd covered several city blocks by the time we were counting off door numbers.

"The building actually extends back into the mesa," Morgan said, as we passed by rooms beginning with A. "This is really a huge setup. Can't tell from the outside. That's the idea." We were into the Bs now, standing before an elegantly carved oak door with B-9 in bronze letters on it. Morgan knocked.

Almost immediately the door flew open and Mac was standing before us with a skimpy white towel tucked around his waist and the television on a baseball game in the room behind him. Amazingly, he had on his Dodger's hat, and the big goofy grin was spread all over his face.

"Jet! What the hell you doing here?" He looked from me to Morgan, who was checking out the towel with her sunglasses in one hand. Mac followed her eyes. "Oops."

Morgan laughed. "Don't worry. I have brothers." Not according to her story a few hours ago; I wondered if she might be a psychopathic liar. She looked over at me and then at her watch. 6:32. "Add fifteen." And then she was gone.

But she hadn't lied about finding Mac—he stood gawking down the hallway after her. "Whoo-whee! That is some pretty woman," he said, shutting the door behind us and tightening up the towel around his waist. He was more than willing to talk about his new job, as excited about leaving town as a kid going to Disneyland. "Hey, this is a dream come true. Four times the pay I make teaching, my choice of location at their expense, and full-time research. And who's going to care if I make a quick exit? Hell, ole Willa probably won't even notice for a few days. Then she'll drag out the insurance policy to see how much she can collect if she can convince anyone I'm dead. Wait, see if I'm not telling the truth. And the students? I should give my life for theirs, right? Hey. Cut the crap. They fed that self-denial stuff to teachers back in the fifties like they fed it to housewives to keep them smiling and dumb as rocks. Or close to. " He cocked his head at me, squinting an eye. "Hey, schweetheart, it's the nineties."

Maybe where he was going, he'd have time to brush up on his Bogart imitation. "So you're just leaving? What about all your research here?"

He nodded toward a desk in front of full-length drapes where a pile of floppy disks were scattered beside three grocery bags stuffed with file folders. He walked over and looked down at them. "I always keep backup copies of everything," he said, picking up one of the disks. "Even my notes. It's all right there." I went over and stood close to him, feeling his body heat and the odor of clean male skin. "This is it, Jet. My life." His smile was gone, and his voice sounded tired. He turned the disk over as though he might have missed something on the back side. "That's the whole ball game," he said, tossing it back on the desk. We stood for a moment without speaking, looking down at the folders and disks, then I pulled back the drapes behind the desk. A solid wall. We were standing in a room elegantly appointed and decorated to resemble someone's apartment, someone's home. But there were no windows, and in spite of the designer teals and mauves and the original Native American pottery and authentic paintings on the walls and the gold spigots I'd spotted through the door of the bathroom, this space was little more than an elaborately camouflaged mine shaft, a hole dug under a mountain pressing down on us with unimaginable weight from above. I thought of Morgan disguised as Caroline Marcus, of the Lab's institutional concrete facade that hid the richly appointed, almost voluptuous interior, and it occurred to me that the Lab, an auxiliary of The Company, specialized in disguises. A hit of adrenaline shot through me: a forewarning of some looming disaster or harbinger of a claustrophobic panic attack that had begun to jab around the edges of my skull. I replaced the drape and took a deep breath. Then I checked my watch.

6:40.

There was nothing at all I could say to my friend Mac Williamson. He had thought it all through. He had looked back on his life and judged it a pretty dull ball game, but still in progress with a few innings left. I knew the feeling. I couldn't change his mind. I didn't even want to.

"Where you going?" I asked.

He shrugged. "They say it's a 'no tell' on that one. I see their point. I'll play by their rules if I'm on their team. We'll have to say *adios* here, and you have to not breathe a word about this to a soul. In fact, I'm real surprised they let you in here. How'd you manage that?"

I didn't want to tell him about Morgan. Whatever Cruz's spiel had been, Mac had bought it, and I was beginning to understand that some of the information I was carrying around was not the kind you say too much about. Still, if I had any hope of stopping the water deal, I had to have some kind of proof, and Morgan hadn't exactly pledged to help. I tried an uneasy path between truth and fiction.

"I was worried when you weren't at your office. I found someone who thought you might be here, could get me in to at least say bye." While he was thinking about that, I pushed on. "I don't guess you found out anything about the water?" I asked, changing the subject and trying to sound nonchalant.

He took off his cap and scratched behind his ear, then pulled the cap back on. He squinted an eye at me and sat down in the chair by the desk, pulling out folders, thumbing through papers. He found a sheath of stapled pages and handed it to me. The first two pages were a bibliography of research he'd found on plastosterone, starting with a couple of citations by people connected to the Sangre de Cristo Lab back in the late sixties and ending with the recent study he'd mentioned to me about the fellow in France who had been doing research on the AIDS virus. Following that were several pages of excerpts from various articles, complete with underlined passages and Mac's marginalia. The last two pages were dated annotations of his own analyses, the ones he'd done on the purple growth and, I saw turning to the final page, the last one he'd performed on the Pecos River water I'd brought him.

6:45.

"That's everything I got. Even if I'd stayed, this is what I would have pulled out to document what I told you the other night. Plus," he said, pointing to the last page, "the presence of significant amounts of plastosterone in the water you gave me."

"But what about your new employers, what are they going to do if I go public with this?"

"They won't like it a bit, will they?" He stood up and tightened the towel. "But everything there is already public record. Anyone can run a computer search and come up with that same bibliography in about ten minutes. Anyone can take that piece of purple stuff that you have or a sample of the water in the Pecos River and have a test run. They'll find exactly what I did. I don't see any particular reason why you need to tell folks who you got this from. Or when you got it." He beamed down at me.

I took the packet and folded it down into quarters and shoved it into my back pocket. "So this is it, huh? You're really going to do this?" I looked at my watch as we walked toward the door.

6:47.

"I really am. And I tell you what. I'm looking forward to every minute of it." He gave me the big goofy grin as he opened the door. It was the last time I ever saw him.

I stood in the hall alone, looking in the direction Morgan had disappeared fifteen minutes ago. No sign of her. I toyed with the notion of searching her out, maybe finding someone to point the way to Cruz's office. But I was shaking with chills again, still wracked by a sense of disaster closing in. And the long hallway with its walls of closed doors, in spite of its elegance, felt more like a tomb than a public passageway. I heard Morgan's words, a husky whisper: "I'm not kidding. You don't want to mess with these people, Stone. I'm not kidding...not kidding."

But getting out of this place was going to be a lot harder than getting in—my sense of direction hadn't improved since I was eighteen and riding shotgun navigator for a friend of mine in a sports-car rally. We set off early from Louisville, were supposed to make a circle through several checkpoints and meet back at the same spot that afternoon. Under my direction, we pulled into the city again very late that night. Problem was, the city was Cincinnati.

Finally, lots of wrong turns and backtracking later, I was waving what I hoped looked like a casual good-bye at the guard at the desk as I walked across the lobby toward the glass entrance doors. His book had disappeared, he was wearing a uniform cap, and he didn't crack a smile as he glanced covertly away from the group of men standing with their backs to me at the reception bar. He pressed something inconspicuously, the glass doors slid open, and I was out of there knowing that the guy wanted me to disappear fast. I did my level best to accommodate him.

7:17.

The parking lot now held only a scattering of vehicles. The sun had sunk west far enough that a pale blue had seeped back into the sky, and long tangled shadows stretched across the parched desert wasteland. The only movement came from the rear parking lot where a fire engine sat with its red lights flashing, but there was no siren, no sound of any kind, not even a bird or plane passing overhead. I fished for my keys, shaking badly, and fumbled to unlock the truck. I started the engine and took a couple of deep breaths to keep back the panic. Forcing myself to drive slowly, I edged the truck around the back side of the lot, near the second entrance which was hidden from view of the lobby, and as I turned up the decrepit gravel road the way we had come, I craned to catch sight of Morgan. But, in spite of the fire engine and the group of men I had seen collected in the entry, the place looked eerily uninhabited. Even the long rows of office windows, made of dark mirror glass and fiery with the sun's reflections, shielded whatever eyes might have been watching me drive by as I bounced along the same punishing washboard road that we'd come in on.

By the time I was on the freeway, with Santa Fe falling behind me and the hot wind blowing through the cab of the truck, my shakes had subsided, even if my thoughts were still flying fast and wild as meteors. Was Morgan in trouble? How could I find out? What could I do about it if she were? Mac was launching a new life, or so he thought. But I didn't know where he was going, whether the story he'd been fed was true, or what might actually become of him. I was no closer to discovering who had killed Jaz, though I was pretty sure the chemical in his body had been plastosterone and not amanitin. More important, with the implications of severe water pollution by the plastosterone chemical and the Lab's cover-up, I had to figure out something fast to draw attention to the pollution before tomorrow, when the contaminated water would be released into Texas and the state's designated new irrigation areas.

I was leaning forward over the wheel, tugging at the folded sheath of papers in my back pocket with the Glorieta exit in view up ahead, when a loud ringing startled me so badly that I swerved the truck, nearly sideswiping a car in the left lane. I hit the brakes, checking the rearview mirror for an approaching police car or ambulance, scanning the dash panel for an emergency warning light, and veering off the freeway on the Glorieta exit ramp. By the time I reached the stop sign at the frontage road, the sound had stopped. And started again. I pulled onto the frontage road, parked on the shoulder, switched off the engine, and hopped out of the truck, looking for the source of the ringing. Somewhere around the floor. I stuck my head gingerly into the foot space of the driver's side and discovered a black plastic object wedged under the seat—a cell phone.

I snatched it, fumbling, pushing buttons.

"Hello."

"Stone?" Morgan's voice.

"Jesus shit! You nearly gave me a heart attack with this fucking thing! Why didn't you tell me you left it here?" My heart was racing, my voice trembling. Cars whizzed past on the freeway. One slowed, took the Glorieta ramp.

"No time. Where are you?"

"Where am *I*? Where the fuck are *you*?" Anger, I've found from past experience, feels a lot better than fear or self-pity. It was a temporary fix. Very temporary.

"Stone, we'll talk about this later. Listen to me now. Where are you? *Tell me where you are.*"

The tone of her voice made me forget my own predicament. "I'm at Glorieta. End of the freeway exit ramp."

"Alone?"

The car was cruising slowly toward me. It eased up to the intersection adjacent to where I stood and stopped. "Well, I guess. Kind of." I got back in the truck, slammed the door, and locked it.

"*Stone?*" Morgan spoke sharply.

The car was a grey late-model sedan. A man with dark hair and sunglasses sat behind the wheel looking around, ignoring me. He pulled out a map and began unfolding it.

"Uh, well, there's a car just pulled off the freeway near where I'm at. Guy looking at a map."

"Probably nothing, but watch him. Make sure he doesn't follow you when you get back on the freeway..."

"Follow me? Who..."

"Stone. *Goddammit, listen to me!*" Morgan paused and began again, speaking slowly, articulating each syllable. "In the glove compartment, you'll find a small handgun. If you need it. Now, get back on the freeway." She paused. "Are you listening to me? *Say something!*"

I mumbled, jammed the cell phone between my shoulder and ear, and started the engine. I pulled out in front of the sedan where the driver had his head buried in the map. Gathering speed on the entrance ramp, I flipped open the glove compartment and removed the small gun. I laid it carefully on the seat next to me.

"Okay, I'm on the freeway," I said into the phone, feeling a wave of relief at the hot air pouring through the window again. "Where are *you?*" I asked, keeping one eye on the rearview mirror. I held my speed at fifty, watching for the grey sedan to show up behind me.

But the line went dead.

"Shit!" I flung the cell phone at the floor on the passenger side. The grey sedan was nowhere in sight. Still, I pulled off at the next exit and watched the cars passing along the freeway for a few minutes, and then I drove along the frontage road the rest of the way to the village, certain that no one had followed.

No one, that is, except Morgan, who came flying up the driveway in a wild swirl of dust just as I was getting out of the truck, the cell phone in one hand and the gun in the other.

She hit the brakes and slid to a stop beside where I stood. She was driving a grey sedan, but not the one that had stopped at the Glorieta exit. Hers was a Mercedes S500. Cruz's car.

HALF AN HOUR LATER, polishing off Kit's leftover stir-fry from the night before, Morgan and I sat on the deck taking in the sunset. It is the most spectacular event in a northern New Mexico evening, when the last rays of the sun, just before sinking behind the western mesas, set the uppermost peaks of the Rockies on fire, then disappear in a great splash of shooting beams. For a few moments, the valleys glow, pines and cottonwoods and aspens tremble in a golden light, and the eastern slope forgets its trees and streams and meadows and turns so violent a red that the early Spanish settlers named the mountain range Sangre de Cristo, "blood of Christ." And then, just as suddenly, the spectacle passes. The sky deepens to turquoise, the first star pricks in the east, and a coral halo appears along the darkening horizon of mesas and craggy peaks.

Usually, the summer nights here are like those in the high deserts, arid and chilly, but tonight was different. The dark clouds looming in the north were moving closer, preceded by an oddly warm breeze that stirred in the branches of piñon and juniper. Toward Taos, the fire was no longer marked by a trail of smoke; now it was faint orange glow behind the mesas. With any luck, the clouds would keep moving in.

I watched the early stars beginning to appear as I listened to Morgan, leaning on monosyllables to hold up my end. I was paralyzed with exhaustion, but she was wound tight, impervious to a day with no food, no breaks in the nonstop melodrama, not even the solace of a private room to call her own. This was a woman who thrived on adrenaline. She explained that after leaving me with Mac, she went to Cruz's office, where his secretary welcomed her back to Santa Fe and said he'd been called away on an emergency, but to go right ahead and wait inside. By the time Cruz returned from the parking lot, where someone had played a practical joke, apparently tossed a smoke bomb under his car, Morgan had helped herself to his files and waved a cheery good-bye to the secretary. And, she grinned, what the hell, she decided to lift his spare set of keys as well.

"Hey, I needed a ride," she said, wide-eyed, feigning innocence. She used her chopsticks to distribute a few uneaten scraps of stir-fry to the circle of cats who sat on the table following every hand-to-mouth movement. "Besides, I always like to mix a little pleasure with business. Keeps the board interesting." On the deck beside her chair sat the nylon bag, ends of manila folders poking out the top.

"So you think Cruz is just going to let it slide? That's a hundred-thousand-dollar car sitting over there."

"Mmnh. Eighty-thousand, give or take. He tries to repress his flashy side." She leaned over and dangled a morsel over Grendel's nose. The cat batted it to the floor, pounced, and shook it hard for good measure. One dead mushroom. "Also, we play this game, kind of like chess. The rules are: we can take anything of each other's that we can steal so long as we don't endanger, humiliate, or professionally compromise the other person. So the car's mine. I stole it fair and square."

"You stole an eighty-thousand-dollar car from under his nose, and you think he's not humiliated? You can't be serious."

"I am. That's how I came by the MG, too. But that one was a theft of love, took some serious planning to make off with it. Keep it parked at a garage in Albuquerque for when I visit. But the Mercedes. Sssst. Thing is, I didn't even really want it." She shook her head and rolled her eyes. "Car's about as interesting as a piece of string. Only more boring vehicle is a BMW. Can't figure why anyone would want them."

"Status."

"Right. Maybe that's the joke. Make them well, but ugly as hell, see how far you'll go to impress your friends." She offered the last scrap to Mink who, after much sniffing and deliberation, caught it gingerly with her tiny front teeth and tugged it carefully from the chopsticks, hopping from table to chair to deck and disappearing down the stairs. Morgan shoved back her bowl and laid the sticks across it. The rest of the cats converged on cue, doing a thorough sniff-and-scratch before turning tails and stalking away. The sky had deepened to navy, crowded thick with constellations and whorls of stars and a dollop of moon. Behind us, Fresca gave an occasional stomp and snort, munching her evening flake of alfalfa. The ceaseless chorus of frogs drifted up from the river; an owl hooted intermittently from a nearby tree. Now, with a full stomach and lulled by the night sounds, I felt myself grow increasingly stupefied, dazed, barely able to sit upright. A pack of coyotes set up a din of howling and yipping somewhere far across the mesa.

"Hey, where's your dog?" asked Morgan. Her voice sounded far away.

I roused. "Probably at Kit's. That's where he stayed when I was in California. Haven't been home enough lately for him to make a habit of living here again." But I had wondered about it too. "Might be off hunting. Or maybe Kit's gone somewhere and decided to leave him inside her house." I considered walking over to her place, but I was wilted beyond revival. Morgan, however, wasn't having it.

"Okay, let's hit it. Tonight's a work night." She bounced up and stretched, heaved the nylon bag across her shoulder and headed inside. "I need to look through this stuff. Mind if I set-up in your study, maybe use the computer too? Might have to make a stop or two on the Net."

Morgan's high energy rasped against my nerves. With some effort, I pushed myself out of the chair and trudged after her, throwing the dead bolt on the French doors and joining her in the study, where she was unloading the contents of her bag across my desk.

"Hey, just make yourself at home," I said. If she noticed the sarcasm, she ignored it. I collapsed into the chair Angel had occupied just last night. "But no phone, no Net." I watched her arrange the file folders on one side of the desk, a couple of floppy disks next to them, a spiral notebook.

"No problem. You have a modem, right? I'll just hook up to the cell phone. And I'll need that list you took off Metz's computer, too, the one with the names Jaz hid in the file?" When I brought in the phone and the list and handed them to her, I noticed the computer had already booted up. "Thanks," she said, "and by the way, you should lock the downstairs door, too." She pulled out the long, lean, odd-looking gun that I'd seen in her hotel room. She placed it on the desk, at the right side of the keyboard. She looked over at me, eyebrows up. "Now."

"Do you think..."

She interrupted. "I don't think anything. Precautions are a good investment." She fished into a zippered pocket and brought out a handful of tiny cassettes and a larger playback unit. "Here, set yourself in front of your stereo or wherever and listen to these. Take a pad and pencil with you. Take notes on anything you find interesting, odd, important, anything at all that catches your attention. When you're done, come back up here. I'll be finished going through these files by then, and we'll compare notes, see what we've got." I took them, sighing. None were labeled. "Morgan, I can't..."

"You can, and you will. Incidentally, on my way here, I did a quick pass by Becker's. No one home. Picked up the one I placed there." She nodded at the tapes in my palm.

"Yuck." I wrinkled my nose in distaste, eyeing the cassettes.

"Tsk. An English teacher, too. You need to brush up on your expletives." Morgan grinned, sat down, and spread open a file folder. She was tapping away at the keyboard when I turned to go.

"By the way," I said, pausing, "what the hell am I looking for?"

She smiled and continued working, her eyes still on the screen. "You want to find out who did old Jaz in, right?"

"Mm." I stood for a moment watching her work. She was scanning the pages from the folder, typing, her eyes flying between the printed pages and the computer screen. I was still wearing the digital watch she'd given me at the lab. 8:47. "And what are *you* looking for?"

Her hands stopped moving across the keyboard, but she sat watching the screen for a few beats before swiveling the stool around. She ran her fingers back through the dark wings of hair, having removed the fake ponytail and blue contacts as soon as she'd walked in the house. She was still gorgeous, but with a chocolate-bar kind of warmth that the frigid blue contacts masked. She frowned past me through the tall dark windows that comprised the walls of this round room perched at the top of the house, out to where the night pressed black and opaque and the wind rose and fell sporadically. I was thinking of how we might appear to someone standing below, the two of us spotlighted in the night. I was reminded of an open-air theater-in-the-round where I had once witnessed a mesmerizing performance of *Medea*, especially the riveting end when a miraculous heavenly chariot descended to the stage and bore the heroine away from the bodies of her dead children and the impending punishment at the hands of her fellow mortals. Some renegades, it seemed, even those who had committed heinous crimes, were divinely appointed to discharge a justice beyond human understanding.

When Morgan turned back to me, her eyes glittered in that odd way I had noticed in her hotel room. The room sang with tension, sizzling the air, ignited by the manic energy she discharged. I imagined the odor of sulfur etching a visceral trail around the room. Yet for all that, I stood bewitched—her dynamic was irresistible, the simultaneous impulse of dread and anticipation that draws people too near the edges of cliffs, that makes them lean too far across the guardrails of tall buildings and marvel at the tiny cars, the miniature people below.

She opened her mouth to speak, sat like that, and then swiveled the chair back toward the monitor.

"Answers," she said, turning a page in the folder and beginning to tap the keyboard again, "just answers."

Downstairs, I tried to take my mind off the odd exchange with Morgan, turning from her eerie electrical presence to something more mundane. I bolted the front door, rattling the microcassettes in my hand like dice. I fitted the first one into the playback, shoved it into the cassette drive, and armed with pen and paper, sank into the sofa, put my feet up, and hit the Play button.

Three hours and some serious fast-forwarding later, I shut off the player and sat for a while in the late-night silence, letting it wash over me like ocean waves, soothing my nerves. Although my body felt numb, I had hours ago left behind the point of exhaustion and entered a different arena—the late-night kind where spectators smoked and drank and sneered at the friendly primary care practitioner's advice about food and sleep and exercise, one where men and dogs and cocks fought and sucked up adrenaline and whatever else will keep you moving forward in a world where demented winds howl and there are not enough candles to light one square inch of this planet. I closed my eyes, trying to dispel the depression that descended on me, but shadowy animals crept into the darkness, circling, their fangs flashing, tearing at one another's flesh. The silence that had been a balm reconfigured itself into a high-pitched keening, the kind of ringing we call silence but which is the echo of all our bad dreams and a forewarning of the future. My avoidance tactics were as futile as breaking a clock to stall time, and the voices from the tapes came pinwheeling back to me.

I discovered that Kit was a great talker. At first I was startled to think that so many people passed daily through her life, just yards from my own front door. But soon I realized that "Mootie" and "Carolita" and "Dimweb" were not visiting friends but the creatures among whom she lived her daily, solitary days—spiders, plants, possibly even purely illusionary creations. New Mexico lures those who put more than ordinary store in the spirit world, but Kit was not merely giving her cyclamen a pep talk, not with the expletives she favored, nor was she rehashing the past with dead relatives. Kit had created her own special collective of characters to entrust with her emotional outbursts. For the black widow spider she nurtured in a darkish corner of her kitchen, she gathered flies, ladybugs, other spiders and insects, and placed them in the web, watching the ensuing rejections and struggles, the maimings and slow deaths with the gusto and applause of a psychopathic sports fan. Her paintings aroused her most serious monologues. These were ongoing diatribes played out against the background tinkling of brushes against glass, scrapping against canvas and palate. Kit spoke to the objects that she nudged into shape, reviewing old wounds and elaborating schemes for revenge. It was here that I heard the detailed description of her infamous Sunday night scene with Jaz at the Rosita Inn, followed by a colorful narrative of how Jaz had nearly raped her in his cabin the following Monday. Then came a hair-raising revenge scenario. She explained to the canvas, or maybe some imaginary creature she was painting, that no pain and suffering were too cruel a punishment for such a beast, that although he had died, she wished him an afterlife of eternal misery. She elaborated a diabolically detailed scenario in which he was implanted alive and screaming in a sticky web, unable to move, watching the approach of an enormous salivating black widow, her belly shining black and blistered with a red decal, her delicate legs probing. I took a deep breath, sickened, and fast-forwarded.

I remembered Morgan saying that she'd hidden the recorders during Jaz's funeral, and while the tapes might show Kit certifiable in other areas, they revealed clearly that she had not killed Jaz. It wouldn't hold up in court, if it ever came to that, but I no longer had any doubt in my own mind. My misgivings took other directions. I thought back to that first day three years ago when Kit had driven up my driveway in her Jeep, bursting with excitement and happiness about living the life of an artist. The woman on the tapes was mean-spirited, angry, seething with resentments. Such were the dangers of insular living, and I kept close tabs on my own psyche. Or so I thought. Still, how far away was I from Kit, chatting with my cats, Jones, even a plant or two on occasion? True, I had not taken up spider-baiting as a sport, but neither was I producing the works I had always meant to write. Kit, on the other hand, had stepped over the line that separates creative seclusion from crazy-making isolation, and as much as the prospect saddened me, I knew the time had come for her to leave the mesa. I made a mental note to talk with her as soon as my days settled down and I had a few minutes to call my own.

If Kit's tape was an indictment of isolated living, the couple from Juan's office failed to prove that small towns offered any improvement. I heard some names I recognized, more I didn't. I glimpsed the sorrowful indiscretions of pathetic, sick people whose secrets I didn't want to know but now knew anyway. Through it all ran Juan's deep, steady voice, a wellspring of sanity in the chaos that flowed through his office. I realized that his curt summary yesterday of his overworked staff had been a gross understatement, and I felt a pang of guilt at how I had resented his preoccupation when I reported Torrez's attempted entry and Becker's animal abuse. His office was swamped with requests for help in the Taos evacuation, deluged with an unprecedented number of calls from hysterical women reporting domestic violence and from ranchers and rural residents with hair-raising stories of slaughtered and dismembered animals. Struggling to add more personnel to his force, Juan was holding ad hoc interviews and temporarily deputizing volunteers right and left. Unlike his predecessor, he resisted crash-and-burn tactics, but his even-tempered approach was being severely tested. He was keeping the shaky department above water, if just barely.

Morgan had picked up Becker's tape on her way over, so she couldn't have heard it yet. She had a stronger stomach than I, but even so, this one was going to push the envelope. I estimated the time frame, beginning when Morgan had hidden it, at around 11:00 today, give or take, and ending with when she'd picked it up, around 7:00. So the tape covered approximately eight hours, during much of which Becker was gone. I had passed both him and Angel after I'd left his place earlier today, flying along the gravel road as I searched for Morgan. But not to worry: Becker didn't need much time to leave an indelible impression. The tape began with the sound of a door opening and closing, and then another opened, followed by a mixed bag of odd, muffled animal noises. A brief pause, and then an explosion of sound that brought me upright on the sofa with my hair on end—an animal screamed, and then another and another. My living room was a hellish pandemonium of tortured shrieks and wails, apparently made by animals whose exact misfortunes I tried not to imagine. I stared in horror at the stereo speakers, knowing that I was both blessed and cursed by the limitations of sound. I was fortunate because I did not have to witness the abominations being executed; cursed because when limited to sound alone, the mind racks its own images—nothing can match an imagined disembowelment and dismemberment, a mental rending of flesh sliced and stripped, of organs and limbs shattered and displaced.

Becker's tape presented a portrait of the human animal still mired in its savage prehistory, before the psyche set about creating beneficent but rigorously vengeful gods. This was evil incarnate, and it lived and breathed its foul breath just below the veneer of civilized behavior. Even after I had fast-forwarded the tape, the memory of the animal screams shrilled through my veins, penetrated my nerves, stood every hair on end. The muted lamplight of my living room took on a bloody tint, the air stung with a sharp odor, an acrid metallic taste coated my tongue.

The rest of the tape was disturbing in a different way. It consisted of Becker's end of two phone conversations from which I pieced together what had occurred today after I left him. A man with a bad case of hair-trigger paranoia, Becker had been thrown by my visit this morning into a state of hysteria. To him, I was not a writer who lived in the area and minded her own business but "that Butler woman that's friends with that fucking nutcase that called the reporters." After I had left, his paranoia had kicked in, and he had rushed into town to use a public telephone, unaccountably fearing that his own was tapped. There, from what I could piece together from the ensuing phone conversation, he called Cruz who apparently reassured him that one of their agents was monitoring the situation and there was no cause for alarm. Becker then returned home, tortured a few animals to stem his anger, and when the phone rang the first time, it was the man Morgan referred to as Pasonombre. The high-pitched, excited squeal Becker used to answer the phone became immediately calm. He assured the man on the other end of the line that he was not hysterical, that Cruz must have misconstrued his simple concern about the Butler woman's visit. "I think she might be trouble, but Mr. Cruz says she's being watched, so..." His voice trailed off uncertainly, waiting for reassurance. Several mm-hmm's passed. And then: "I'm close, Mr. Psichari. I'm very close. Say, even a matter of weeks." More mm's and mmn-hmms. "Yes, he comes twice a month, sometimes more. No, no, nothing in the river. It won't happen again. There's no problem now. Everything's fine, Mr. Psichari. Everything is fine." Mm-hmm.

Suddenly his voice shot up to a nervous screech, with the words flying so wildly I caught only snatches: "...*a rotten lie...water's*

228

fine...a plot to get me...buries them...dump." Then, as suddenly, the pace slowed, as though Becker had reined in the runaway sentences. "You have to remember, the French exaggerate," he said in a calm, reasoning voice. "I think he's after publicity. He wants everyone else to stop so he can get first shot at the Nobel, talking about a cure for AIDS. This stuff won't touch AIDS. He's on to us, and he wants to get there first, get a ban on chemical development and then there he is." But his attempt at calm was a stretch; Becker lapsed into a whine. "He'll hit the market with this, and we'll have nothing."

My guess was that they were talking about the chemist in France whom Mac had mentioned, the one who had published the article on the dangers of plastosterone experimentation. But then the discussion veered back to Kit. It was clear that in her effort to capture public attention before the finalization of the Pecos Water Project, she had contacted the Albuquerque television people with accusations about the Lab.

"...but now everyone has her number. She's just a big-mouthed troublemaker." More mm-hmms. "Not a problem. Any reporters come around, I'll just tell them she's the local crackpot. I wouldn't be lying, either. That is one strange lady. Friend of that Butler woman, both got screws missing."

Yeah, right. And this guy is sanity in a suit coat. When the phone rang again, I got a good picture of just how tightly wrapped this old coot was. This time it was Cruz, so enraged that I could hear the crackle of his tinny voice as it came out of the receiver. It didn't take a prophet to figure this one: he'd just discovered his Mercedes missing and guessed the culprit. This call was definitely not going to help Becker's paranoia.

While Cruz raged, Becker tried to get a word in: "You what? Well, who....you mean the agent who's supposed to be...no, I haven't seen a, a...did you say Mercedes?" Becker's voice hit the top of the charts, moving at warp speed. "...my fault...can't...fucking car, some fucking cunt...stole your...*that's who's taking care of...Jesus fucking....*" Minutes passed, more squeaking of the tinny voice. Then Becker: "Okay, okay! Right. She comes by, I'll get right back to you...No, no one like that, but I'll keep my eyes open."

More squeaking. "No, no, not a good idea..." His voice lowered, became wheedling. "I don't keep that kind of stuff around here. No, Angel makes sure every last bit of it is...right, buries it, takes it to the dump." More telephone squeals, and then Becker's voice flew right off the charts: "...*sheriff coming here...the fuck is wrong with...what am I supposed to do with all this....*"

Cruz must have been worried that Morgan's theft was more than playful, albeit expensive, one-upmanship. Preparing for the worst, her defection, he apparently directed Becker to clean out his trailer, get rid of the chemistry setup at the very least, for I heard the clanking of metal and glass for a while, and then a door opening and slamming closed. I suppose the presence of mutilated animals was less incriminating than the presence of plastosterone. Cruz thought so, anyway. He must have called specifically to order Becker to clear out all signs of the chemical, and why would he do that unless he knew the consequences were dire? Unless their presence near the river might be important enough to abort the water deal? Cruz was in this up to his ears, and I had to alert Morgan right away. If they did a sweep on something as innocuous as Mac's office, what would they do on a setup like Becker's? I could feel the danger throbbing like wings beating the air.

I piled the tapes and the playback on top of my clipboard and notes. Upstairs in the bedroom, the reading lamp had been switched on low, and several cats lay curled sleeping on the bed in the muted light, but the study was dark. I stood in the ghostly blue illumination cast by the monitor which was still on, my heart pounding in my ears. The desk was a clutter of scattered papers and open folders, the cell phone was hooked to the modem, and the gun was still lying where I'd last seen it, but Morgan had disappeared. I checked the upper deck of the sleeping loft. Nothing there. My heart began doing triple time. Back in the bedroom, I unbolted the French doors, flipped on the floodlights, and strolled around the deck peering out through the darkness. Nothing. Leaving the floodlights on, I bolted the doors again, took the .38 from my bedside drawer, and returned downstairs, trying to imagine what might have happened to Morgan. I tried to reason my heart back down to normal speed, figuring that she had probably needed a little fresh air, come downstairs, found me listening to the tapes, and eased on out the front way.

The front doors, as I suspected, were unbolted. I grabbed a flashlight in one hand and the .38 in the other, and I wandered around the patio, up the walkway, toward the driveway, aiming the flashlight among the trees. Still nothing. Fresca nickered as I approached her corral, where Cruz's Mercedes, a pale shape in the shadows, sat parked beside my black truck. I stuck the .38 in my pocket and hoisted myself to the top rail, wondering what to do next as I scratched along the base of Fresca's ears. Her musky horse smell and the sounds of the night were familiar and reassuring; my pulse was slowing back to normal. A train chuffed in the distance, its whistle keening above the sleeping houses in the valley. The frog din rose like a contentious symphony from the river, and a sudden gust of wind swept through the trees. To the north, sheet lightning played behind the clouds. I inhaled slowly, counting to ten, filling myself with the brisk New Mexico evening. The sense of danger that had gripped me began gradually to fade.

But the tapes had sent my mood spiraling underground. I was bone tired, and suddenly I missed Jones with such a driving intensity that I jumped down from the corral and wandered across the gravel in the direction of Kit's place. I kept the cone of light aimed at the ground to avoid stepping on the desert rattlers who enjoyed hunting in the dark, cool hours of summer. The cliff walk leading to Kit's was a closer route, but it was precarious after dark, so I followed the road around the front way until it sheered off to the right and began the decline that comprised Kit's driveway. Her Jeep was nosed in among a shelter of piñons, and although she often painted at odd hours of the night, tonight her windows were dark. Disappointed, I stood debating whether to rouse her, still craving the feel and smell of Jones's thick ruff against my face.

"Hey."

She had the kind of voice that could sound like leaves rustling. Except that piñons and junipers have no leaves. I turned, expecting her behind me; her voice was that close. At first, I didn't see her among the shadows. Her long-sleeved black top and black jeans absorbed the darkness so well that she seemed a part of it, her face tanned, dark, a smudge against the textured evening. She stepped toward me, her form separating itself from the trunk of a gnarled piñon.

"Little late for a neighborly visit," she whispered.

"I was looking for you." I whispered back. "I thought I'd pick up Jones while I was here. Kit won't mind," I said, remembering the times we had swapped midnight visits over the years, turning to each other in moments of loneliness or sleeplessness. I began to walk down the driveway, toward the adobe cottage.

"Wait." Morgan's hand rested on my shoulder, light as a bird, pulling me gently back while she stepped in front of me. She stood with her face lifted to the sky. Slowly, she pressed a finger to her lips, cocked her head sideways, lay her arm along my shoulders. Minutes passed with Morgan's fingers resting against the curve of my neck, sensing when I was about to move, to speak, tightening her grip slightly, shaking her head, her ear toward the river. I strained, but I heard nothing. I braced my legs against the decline, trying to ease the aching muscles which had begun to tremble with exhaustion. Locking my knees, I leaned forward slightly toward Morgan for support. She remained motionless as a statue, and I seemed to feel the pulse of her wrist as it rested against the side of my neck. The breeze rose and fell, shuddering in the pines as we stood locked together in the driveway. It carried the body scent of this woman who sustained me in the darkness, and it brought too a lurking sense of danger that seemed to spring and ebb with the wind, flickering in the rhythm of distant lightning and the low, rolling thunder. Morgan shifted, leaned slightly toward me. Her cheek grazed my lips so that I could feel the down along her skin; her head shifted again, her ear aimed down toward the driveway, toward the dark cottage, the finger still at her lips so that the two of us seemed suspended in motion, her face against mine. It was the quiet of a breath suppressed, the dead silence that had hushed even the river's flow and the frogs' interminable racket. Morgan shifted again, her finger still covering her lips, covering mine. And when she removed the finger, there was nothing at all between us—not even the long vowels of the train whistle that had vanished from the chill night air, not even the wrist that stirred like a moth's wing behind my ear so that we became a single shadow, part of the darkness exchanging the long-held exhalation.

Suddenly, the silence cracked with a deep, guttural noise that began low, rising moment by moment. I jumped back, switching on the flashlight, aiming it across the darkness until I located the sound. Jones was crouched in the driveway, halfway between Kit's house and where we stood, maybe twenty-five yards away. The cone of light reflected off his pale eyes, turning them red; his muzzle was drawn back from his teeth, his tongue sporadically licking and gulping. The Siberian husky is, genetically, one-quarter wolf, and somewhere between when I had last seen Jones and now, the other three-quarters had followed suit.

"Don't move." Morgan's voice was sotto and even, the one I was beginning to associate with tight spots. Her movements were silk. She eased slowly toward the dog. His snarling increased, grew louder and more frantic, like an engine revving. His teeth gleamed below the contracted skin of his muzzle. He crouched low, lower still, preparing to spring as Morgan advanced.

"Stop. Come back!" I cried. Morgan was in front of me, and I ran to one side, tugging at the handle of the .38, which was caught in the lining of my pocket. "He doesn't recognize us. Don't...."

Jones was hurtling through the air toward Morgan, a fury of enraged snarls and gnashing fangs. Drops of spittle flew from his mouth. The seconds slowed, the scene drew out into slow increments of motion. I ran, the gun forgotten, reaching toward Jones as Morgan stepped sideways, both her hands streaking out as the dog flew past her slightly to one side, missing his mark. Her left hand flew up against the bottom of the dog's muzzle; the other hand, palm up and edge aimed, slashed sideways at its neck in a chopping motion. The dog hung impossibly in midair for a moment, his eyes fading back to blue, my own body stretching toward him so that as he arched toward the ground, the razorlike teeth sliced through the flesh of my upper arm.

Seconds later, we stood motionless, looking down at where Jones lay in the driveway, his head at an unnatural angle from his body. A rivulet of dark blood began seeping from his nostrils.

"Stone, I'm sorry, I...."

I knelt beside him; death was already dulling his eyes. I stroked the deep ruff of fur around his neck, but I did not bury my face in it. It was matted with something and unpleasant to the touch. But I stroked the side of his head. "It wasn't your fault," I said to Morgan, who had squatted beside me. "But I don't get it. What..." I tried to remember the last time I'd seen him, what might have happened to cause this. My brain was tied in hard knots.

Morgan put her arm back across my shoulder the way it had been before Jones appeared. "He wasn't sane, Stone. Something happened to his mind. I could see it in his eyes." Her hand found the gash on my arm. She took the flashlight and aimed it across the torn flesh. "He got you a good one," she said, "but it's just a flesh wound. I'll wrap it at your place."

She pulled me up, and we stood together for a moment staring at Jones. Then she played the flashlight around Kit's place, around the garden, the menagerie of stone animals peeking from the cactus garden near the front door. Which was standing open.

Morgan shut off the flashlight. She said: "Wait here. I'm going to check on your friend." I couldn't see the expression on her face, but she used the dead-level voice again. The night had turned black and opaque as soup as the storm clouds began to drift in. The flashlight beam appeared again in Kit's door as Morgan directed it inside, making the windows flicker briefly. I began walking down. Then the light disappeared, and I heard Morgan coming up the drive toward me. "Go back, Stone." I knew what she had found inside by her voice, and I suddenly realized why Jones's coat had been so heavily encrusted and matted. I whirled in the drive, my stomach heaving.

"Listen," Morgan said as she walked up, "it's not going to do any good for you to go in there. It's...the dog's been there for a while, at least a day. And the heat..." She didn't have to finish; I was getting the picture.

I thought back, remembering that the last time I'd seen Jones was Sunday, after coming home from town. He had not been around when Angel had shown up in the middle of the night. I realized that even then he must have been...staying...at Kit's. I heaved until my stomach stopped convulsing and then wiped at my face with my arm, the one that wasn't bloody. Morgan was right; I didn't want to go inside.

We turned to climb back up the steep driveway, Morgan circling my waist with one arm and helping me along. We walked in silence until, drenched in the bright glare of the floodlights, we paused at the front door and Morgan turned to me. "I'll dress your wound, and I'll make the call to the police. But I can't be seen here, and you're not going to be able to tell them I was here with you. Before they arrive, I'm going to be moving fast. I have to get the MG and the Mercedes out of sight. I don't know when I'll see you again, so I need to go over some things with you."

Inside, as she cleaned and dressed my wound, Morgan gave me an update. "The folders answered a lot of questions. But the news is bad. Real bad." I winced as she placed a folded towel under my arm and dribbled a bottle of peroxide over the torn flesh. "Kit was right about the Lab falsifying the results of the water tests. In fact, the water showed high levels of plastosterone contamination back a few months ago when they did the first preliminary tests. But no special equipment, like Kit thought. They simply used the system that was already in place where a designated member of each community takes in a water sample once a month. But instead of taking it in to the closest water analysis place, as they usually would, they sent it to the Lab for analysis. There are community checkpoints from the river's source to the Texas border. The tests were fine from the source point to right before Becker's place. Obviously, he had piped his grey water runoff into the river, which is illegal but lots of people do it, and dumped his experiment wastes in the river as well. The plastosterone has probably been in the water for some time, who knows how long, but because it's such a rare bird, the small community-based analysis didn't pick up anything.

"The odd thing, though, was that you'd have expected the plastosterone levels to be highest at the checkpoint closest downriver from Becker's dump site. But, in fact, the toxicity levels *increase* at each checkpoint between Becker's and the Texas border. When Cruz saw those first tests, he must have known that when the State Engineer's office saw this, the water deal was history. Texas wouldn't want any part of it. You can bet that somewhere around that time is when they were all over Becker to stop dumping in the river. That would have been when Becker got Angel to haul the stuff away. But here's more bad news—the contamination levels never improved, even after Becker quit dumping. In fact, they've gotten steadily worse.

"I couldn't figure what was causing the increase in contamination, so I called the fellow in France, Dr. Jullion. Mac had made a notation of the guy's phone number on the printout he gave you." She took up a cotton swab and bottle of iodine, and I turned away. "Here comes the really bad news. According to Jullion, the body retains this stuff over a long period of time, like permanently. But the effects it has on various test animals of the same species varies widely, and presumably the same would be true of human beings. In fact, that's one of the main problems they're having in developing it for human use, whether as a chemical for biological warfare or as an antidote to male impotence. For some people, it takes a very small amount to poison the system, often to the point of death, but always to the point of heightened aggression, generally leading to violence. Has some odd characteristics though. So far as anyone knows, women aren't affected by it directly." She dabbed the iodine-laden cotton swap gingerly along the wound. I bit my lip, grasping the edge of the table.

"Directly?"

"Right. If you were injected with this stuff, so far as the female test animals this French guy used, there would probably be no effect. But indirectly, you betcha. Two ways. First, the male injected with the experimental plastosterone becomes extremely volatile, but the aggression is only toward the female, and species doesn't matter. Like he's pushed into some kind of testosterone frenzy, needing release so bad that, in some instances, he actually kills the female before, during, or after sexual intercourse."

Morgan squeezed out a curl of salve from a tube and applied it thickly over a gauze bandage, which she eased over the wound. "Second, while a direct injection of the chemical didn't produce any effects in the female test animals, this guy says that when the female ingests the chemical into her system through secondary sources, like when the female eats something infected with the chemical, for example, or if maybe she's injured by the male during intercourse, the female becomes infected as well. But instead of becoming aggressive or violent, the female generally becomes extremely ill. No antidote at this point. Some recover, some don't." She began unrolling a gauze strip, circling it around my arm.

"Also, and this is the reason the river water is becoming progressively more toxic, the saturation level of plastosterone is greatly increased during the process of tissue degeneration in animals that have died from it, so as the decayed tissue of all those dead fish and other microorganisms are carried back into the river, the other life forms there are ingesting huge doses. Also, scavenging animals—dogs, bears, birds, cougar, you name it—that feed on these animals, whether living or dead, will become infected. That's what I think happened to Jones. He drank out of the river, maybe sampled a bite or two of rotten fish, and you saw the results."

She finished the wrapping and stood back, frowning and staring at the wall above my head as she followed her line of thought. "I think we've been seeing the results all around, but no one's realized yet what the cause is. You remember on the tapes from Juan's office, all those phone calls he was getting, all the reports of slaughtered animals? I'll lay odds the slaughtered carcasses were female, and that they're being attacked and killed by animals infected by the river water, just like Jones was. Same thing with those calls of domestic abuse. When I was looking over the list of names you came across on Metz's computer? The ones Jaz had hidden in a special file? Several of them were familiar, and then I realized I'd heard them on the tapes from Juan's office, men who were being charged with violence of one sort or another—wives reporting domestic violence, bars filing complaints of disorderly conduct. There were too many of the same names for this to be entirely coincidental."

"But Jaz must have entered those names months ago—how...?"

"Exactly. Months ago. Probably just about the same time as Cruz saw the first water analysis results and realized Becker was dumping in the river. About the same time as Angel was hired to cart the stuff off."

"You think Angel was giving it to Jaz? But why? And how does Jaz fit in?"

"We'll probably never know the answer to that for certain, but here's what I think happened. Probably Angel heard enough hanging around Becker's place to know this stuff was connected to correcting impotence problems, maybe overheard phone conversations Becker had with Paso or Cruz. Giving updates, that kind of thing. So he decided to do a little experimenting of his own. Decided to take the purple growths, the rejects, instead of dumping them, and see what would happen if he planted a little in his friends' drinks or dope or whatever. But he couldn't keep the stuff at his place. Obviously the police in Tortuga kept an eye on him, probably paid a little surprise visit now and then. He already had several arrests, right? So he let Jaz in on it with the idea of keeping it at Jaz's place along with the marijuana plants Jaz was growing, maybe getting Jaz to help him dry it out, powder it, whatever they did to process it. After Angel tried it out on his friends, saw it gave them a sexual high, he started dealing it. He might have been splitting the profits with Jaz in return for storage and for keeping records of deliveries he made to those names on the list. Or maybe in return for giving Jaz a little of the product—that would explain why Jaz, a fellow you say seemed to have no libido in the years you've known him, attempted to rape Kit a while back, just a few days before he died.

"I'll bet the delivery dates on the computer files coincide more or less with the dates Angel was picking up the stuff from Becker every week or two..."

"Hey," I said, remembering that information had been on Becker's tape. "How'd you know that? You just picked up that tape, so..."

"Hah! Funny thing about those Mercedes. They have tape decks," she said. "Anyway, he wouldn't have wanted to keep any records like this around his own place, and he must have been picking up and selling to enough people that he needed a written record to keep it straight. So Jaz agreed to keep track of the pickups and deliveries for him, and hid the records on Metz's computer where Metz wouldn't come across them. Angel must have stopped in the day of Jaz's death to pick up some product for delivery, or maybe just check in, discovered Jaz dead where you had left him when you went to call the police, and realized that the police would find out what it was and that he'd be in deep shit when Becker discovered he wasn't dumping the stuff like he was being paid to do. So he takes the stuff, the police are none the wiser, and even if you'd mentioned it to them, they wouldn't have had a clue what the stuff was or where it had disappeared to. It all worked out just fine for Angel, except he must have kept track of exactly how many bottles he delivered to Jaz, discovered one was missing, and realized that you must have taken it when he saw the news about you discovering Jaz's body with no mention of odd bottles. So he pays you a visit last night, hoping to get it back without you being any the wiser."

It had seemed far-fetched at first, but I was seeing how all the pieces fit. "And Jaz?"

"I came across a notation in one of the files concerning the analysis the lab did on the chemical found in Jaz's body. You were right, it wasn't amanitin. Cruz changed the results to conceal the presence of plastosterone. I think Jaz was one of the types who react strongly to the chemical, and he was seriously malnourished to start with, right? Probably he died as the stuff began to accumulate in his system. Might have been getting some from the river too, maybe sipped the water now and then in a pinch. Maybe caught a trout now and then for dinner. The symptoms you described of Jaz's death sound very much like those of the lab animals that Dr. Jullion described—basically, they die of suffocation. The chemical causes muscle paralysis in the last stages of toxic poisoning—the blood's supply of oxygen is shut off. It's essentially death by suffocation, and it can look very much like the symptoms of amanitin poisoning. When the local coroner's office in Tortuga couldn't identify the chemical, and they could have if it had been amanitin, they sent it up to Santa Fe where the Lab did the analysis. When Cruz saw the results, he knew the trail would lead to Becker, and then to the river. That would be the end of the water deal. So he falsified the results and reported it as a rare strain of amanitin, and when Juan saw that, he naturally closed the case."

Morgan sat down across from me, in the same chair Juan had sat in just two days ago when he'd asked me to help him clear Kit. She went on. "On the phone, Jullion said he didn't put all the test results of plastosterone in his paper, the one Mac must have read, because he wasn't finished testing it out yet. But, if I'm right, what this all means is that, if the river is as polluted from Becker's dumping as I think it is, and the Lab reports show that it is, I'd say what we've got here is the start of an epidemic the likes of which the world may not have seen, even including AIDS and the Ebola virus."

My arm was starting to pound, and the skin around the bandage felt hot. I wondered if Morgan had wound the gauze too tightly. I held my hand over the flesh above my arm to cool it and tried to concentrate on what Morgan was saying, but my head was throbbing and exhaustion was hitting hard. I fought to make sense of it all: "I don't understand why Cruz would falsify the water analysis. He apparently knew Becker was working on developing plastosterone for Paso; after all, he's the one who pulled Mac out of the picture, right? Wouldn't he have known how serious the water pollution problem was? He could simply have relocated Becker and given an honest assessment of the water. That would satisfy Paso and the terms of his contract with the state. Why would he conceal and perpetuate this level of water pollution going on? What's the point?"

"Ah, there's the central question." She stood up and began pacing back and forth across the kitchen, hands shoved in her pockets. "Cruz wants the water deal to go through, and he's willing to cover up the fact that the river is dangerously contaminated. But why? At first, I thought it must have something to do with Becker. But that's really Paso's little project. He's been subsidizing Becker for years now, ever since the late sixties when the government-sanctioned experiments in biological warfare fizzled out. Chemists like Becker got swept under the carpet, still getting government subsidies, but unofficially, off the record. Lots of them were relocated in private setups in the backwoods, like Becker. But in this case it was Paso who picked up the tab, gambling that for a relatively small investment, plastosterone would turn into the find of the century, just below electricity and the automobile. He would make billions marketing this stuff to any guy who had trouble getting it up and keeping it up. In fact, that was his priority when he sent me on this little 'vacation assignment' in my old stomping grounds. Killing several birds with one well-placed stone—I'm under the watchful eye of Cruz, my past lover still in Paso's employ, partially at least. I'm his best agent—who better to watch over this little project for him, make sure no one stumbles over Becker while thrashing around in the woods about this water issue and Blankenship's death?

"Yet when I arrived, very suddenly as far as Cruz was concerned, and picked up the assignment guidelines, there was something just a little out of focus. I couldn't figure out what it was at first. When I read over Cruz's requisition, he stipulated that the main purpose was to keep things quiet on the water project, not the plastosterone. At first, it seemed like all the same thing. It was an issue for a quiet, after all, so what difference did it make? But in fact, Cruz figured Paso would never know the difference one way or the other, as long as everything went smoothly and no one stumbled across old man Becker. And they wouldn't have as long as the water issue went smoothly. But that's what was bothering me: why was Cruz so intent on the water issue that he would deliberately override Paso's direct order, even in that small way? He figured it would never come up, of course, but nevertheless it placed him squarely at odds with Paso if it ever did come to light. This is one of the things you never want to do when you work for Pasonombre. *Never.* Cruz was not only risking his career; he was risking his life. It could only mean he had some private interest, and it wasn't Becker."

Morgan stopped pacing and gazed out through the kitchen window. I had no idea what time it was, but I expected the eastern sky would soon show streaks of dawn. The wind had increased and was driving through the pines, their branches churning against the kitchen window. I leaned back in my chair and closed my eyes. When I opened them again, Morgan was standing over me, her short hair wet and slicked back in what we used to call a "D.A." in the early sixties. She wore a fresh pair of dark Levi's, a plain navy blue shell, and the Western boots. For a moment as I stared into the buckle of her leather belt, I thought of Juan Falcon and the smell of soap and leather. Behind her, the bathroom door was standing open, and I realized that she had showered and changed clothes again.

"Listen," she said, kneeling so that I stared directly into her eyes. My head was pounding horribly, and I closed my eyes. She shook me gently, and I felt her cool hands on either side of my head. I opened my eyes. "*Listen*. You have to remember what I'm going to tell you. It's very important, and it will mean that you're safe from what happened to Mac. You wouldn't be quite as willing to relocate as he was, and what I'm going to tell you means that you never will have to. Okay?" Her eyes were large and brown, her hands cool against my face. I felt myself nod, and I squinted, trying to concentrate.

"I remembered that Cruz's dad left him lots of worthless acres in northwestern Texas several years ago when he died. We drove through it once, coming back from Dallas. Nothing but flat desert wasteland, as far as you could see. I came across a letter in one of the files from a company in Pecos County, which reminded me that was where Cruz was raised. The letter mentioned some transaction he has in the fire, a big financial deal for a land development project he's waiting to close on, the one provision being that the Pecos Water Project is completed, and thus the increased water supply will mean that all those acres of wasteland Cruz inherited aren't worthless anymore. That area's been apportioned a percentage of the increased water, which will turn it into highly desirable land designed to become a kind of oasis, a very pricey retirement community that will mean millions for Cruz. If anything happens to the plans for increased water flow into the area, he's lost big bucks. And Cruz likes his bucks."

"But that...water's..." I was trying hard to get the words out, but forming each one was like moving a boulder.

"Right, the water's a nightmare. But probably Cruz figures he can get it cleaned up, or at least get the irrigation in place and start the development after the deal closes. Outside of Dr. Jullion, probably no one knows how potentially devastating plastosterone is. If Becker knows, he probably wouldn't care. He certainly wouldn't want anyone else to know. That would be the end of the golden egg he's got going for him right now."

"And Cruz...Paso? Would they...stop this...if they...?" I was seeing an image of Jones, flying through the air with his crazed red eyes. I was seeing an image of my best friend lying ripped apart, an image more vivid because I was helplessly imagining it.

Morgan pulled a chair close and sat facing me, her cool hands holding my hot ones. She was shaking her head. "I don't know, Stone. Oh god, I don't know. I don't even know if this time last year, this time five years ago, I would have stopped it. You put those kinds of considerations in another compartment, someplace that doesn't interfere with whatever assignment you've been given. But it's true what they say about the ten-year max. Something starts to happen. The walls between the compartments turn to jelly. They collapse. Things begin to get confused, muddled. Or maybe just the opposite. Maybe it's always been a muddle, and this analytical approach to living just puts a comfortable mask over it. Maybe things are beginning to come clear, and it just seems like murk right now. I don't know. But I'm going to pull the plug on this one. That's why you have to listen to me. *That's why you have to remember*. Listen to me, Stone. *Listen.*"

There was a cold cloth across my forehead, and Morgan's long, cool fingers stroked the side of my neck. I remembered standing in Kit's driveway with her, just before Jones appeared. I thought of how cool her lips had been, and I leaned toward her. I felt like I would die if she left.

"I'm going to leave tonight. I'm going to try to stop the ceremony tomorrow. Whether I can or not, Cruz will know I've left the fold, so to speak. I'm going to have to go underground, so deep underground that you don't even want to know because he will spend every day of his life after this wanting to get me. It will be another kind of game for us, but I know all about disappearing. No one knows how to do that better than I do. And you're going to be okay because I'm going to let Cruz know that the minute he comes anywhere near you, I'm sending his requisition for this assignment to Paso. That will be the end of him. He won't give you any trouble. But you've got to remember. There's a postcard with a name and address; it's like a bookmark. It's stuck in the book up by your bed, the one you've been reading. Don't worry about the message, just drop it in a box if you even suspect the Lab's around. You got that? A bookmark upstairs, in that trashy novel beside your bed." I heard something like a laugh.

I was trying hard to keep my eyes open, but Morgan's voice came from very far away. I saw her through a haze when she stood up. Her fingers were cold on my arm just above the bandage. She tilted my chin up so I was looking into her face. It was smiling down into my own, coming in through the fog that had settled in my brain, but the words were loud and clear.

"You know, Stone, anonymity is a great treasure. I'm an expert on it. It's my business. It can give you unlimited freedom, mobility, even time. But it's got two edges. Try to hide with it by pulling the walls down around yourself and shutting the world out, and what you've got is one hell of a prison. The kind you make for yourself is a lot more escape-proof than the kind other people make for you." She placed her cool hand over my feverish one, touched it to my shoulder above the wound, leaned across and touched my forehead, my lips. "That novel Jaz Blankenship's been working on half his life? I took the floppy disk Metz gave you out of your glove compartment and took a peek at what's on it. It's on your desk if you're interested. It's a kind of lesson, that disk. Look at it and think twenty years, because that's about how long you've been around here, too, isn't it, Stone?"

She knelt and was looking directly into my eyes, very close. Her own were huge and dark as the night outside, glimmering as she spoke as though lightning were playing around inside them.

"You wrote one great book way back when, Anna Lee Stone. That book saved a lot more people than it killed. It created possibilities in the minds that read it where no possibilities had existed before. It created hope out of hopelessness. A vision of harmony and peace where a wasteland had been. The world needs another book like that, Stone. It's time." And then she was gone.

I sat at the kitchen table, paralyzed with fatigue as the fog dug in. Somewhere in the distance, upstairs, the French doors opened and closed, and I heard footsteps along the deck, along the stairs outside, along the flagstones. I heard them fade away in the distance.

Several days later, at the hospital, I was told that when the ambulance arrived, I was still sitting in that position, staring at the kitchen wall. Juan said that when he walked in the door, I looked up at him and said:

"It's time."

Morgan

*I*T IS EXACTLY *like the moment that precedes the ringing of the tele-phone, the knocking at the door. There is a suspension of sound, of thought, of movement—for an instant. So brief a time that it could pass across the still surface of a day's life without a ripple. Like this: the phone rings, you pick it up. Probably you do not notice that moment just before, when the world stopped turning. To me, that moment is an absence of time, an exploding emptiness, as loud as a jet grazing my rooftop.*

There is always plenty of time, so much time that, as I open the Mercedes door, I look up, surveying the darkness, seeing the man's out-stretched arm beneath a distant piñon, the soft glimmer of steel. So much time that I look up further still and see the outstretched heavens: these swirling and constellated stars, the thick mass of Milky Way down the center, a hint of dawn touching the eastern horizon. So much time that I see at last a creator's hand behind the elegant designs, though in some ways no more than a reflection of these below: lines of furrowed fields, ribbons of interstates flung across valleys and peaks, the artifice of new-born communities with their plotted homes, pools, buildings. How odd, how very odd, that we doubt a creator's mind above more than here below.

I stand inside the open wing of the Mercedes' door, holding it steady against the gusting wind. The lightning flashes, flashes again, again, leav-

ing a dazzle of afterimages on the retina: the graceful, three-tiered house poised at the edge of the cliff like a ship where Anna Lee Stone still sits dazed from the bite of her poisoned dog. The black, churning clouds bleeding now like ink across the stars. The Heckler and Koch Mark 23 lying on the seat next to my knee, its slim stainless steel muzzle pillowed against the car's mocha-colored, saddle-leather interior. The man standing not quite behind the gnarled trunk of a piñon pine fifty yards away, the barrel of his own HK 23 aimed directly at me.

And even then there is still plenty of time, as there has been so often before, in so many countries, for so many years. Time to turn; time even, when the situation is just right, to smile; to step aside if need be. Time to pick up and aim my own weapon in my own sweet and incontestable defense.

And by the time the thunder cracks, my assignment in New Mexico is ended.

I turn the Mercedes toward the precipitous and winding road, across the granite shoulders of enormous boulders and through pine trees that, in my headlight beams, churn wildly in the wind. As I pass the turnoff leading to where the dog lies in the driveway, growing rigid, I marvel again at how the earth creates and devours its creatures and how, in our brief span, we the creatures do likewise. I think of the paintings such as those of the woman called Kit whose last, leaning against the easel above the scattered remnants of her corpse, will surely precipitate the reputation that was the thing she most desired in life. Even without the spectacular circumstances of its inception and her own death, few could stroll by this portrait of a mammoth-sized black-widow spider, its head a Medusa-haired likeness of the artist herself, without staring in fascinated horror as the spider extends a long, slim tentacle to touch the cheek of the man captured in her web—the screaming effigy of Jaz Blankenship. For these are artists of the fringe. Like Kit, they nourish themselves by gazing into the void created by their own terror. They thrive in a spiritual vacuum, nurturing in solitude the monsters of their imagination. Few can sustain the weight of such visions. Yet there is the other type of artist, such as Stone, whose genius requires the misery of society to agitate itself into alternative speculations. These find solitude and the pastoral life so agreeable that, like complacent wives grown sedentary and plump, they lose the propensity for the sharp retort. Their pens grow limp and useless as willows.

The wind has set in with powerful battering gusts, ripping through the tree branches, and the Mercedes lurches as though pounded by great crashing waves. The thunder is closer, louder, the blinding strobelike lightning more frequent. Energy flows and crackles, effervescent. It excites my blood, pounds at my throat, and ahead, in the beams where the pine branches shake and leap like flames, I see the face of Anna Lee Stone emerge from the dissolving darkness, and behind her image a faded, more familiar one which seems to speak from a distant enclave of trees, of apple trees in some past orchard, uttering incomprehensible words, yet in a voice so like my own. Spellbound, I stop the car. I recognize the flickering likeness of my mother's face: her lips move in mystifying sounds among the thrashing branches, the crackling lightning.

I lean forward into the windshield, struggling to make out her words. I recognize the image that has often visited the edges of my dreams across the years: the fiery hair, the enigmatic expression. But although I have waited, motioned to her, she has never entered the dream, never spoken. The car lurches in the wind, the image flares. Her language is not of this world. She speaks a mother's tongue of crackling syllables, yet I read her meaning, the story of her own escape from my father's tyranny, her special genius passed through the mother line to me. Her presence dances across the mesa, spirited in the wind, the shadows, the storm's electrifying air. We are, she intones, the artists of invisibility, connoisseurs of escape. Her hair flares around her head fantastically; her lips at last give me their smile. We are, she hums, the perfect instrument of vengeance. And when the next lightning flashes, her image is gone and I am left alone in the storm, thinking oddly of how my father died—the house set fire, they said, by his own hand.

The car is rocked again, hard, by a blast of wind. The darkness has thinned to the color of dark steel. I switch off the headlights, preferring the virgin morning, and continue down the mesa. Behind me, I have left the stage with everything in place: the ambulance and Juan Falcon will be arriving soon, acting on the calls I made to their respective offices. On the table, beside Stone, is a note that appears to have been written by her, coming as it does from her computer. She explains that she is racing against time, infected with a chemical called plastosterone that is rapidly immobilizing her. The note explains to Juan the death of the woman called Kit, but not that of the man who lies beneath the gnarled pine with the HK beside him and the .45 caliber hollow-point in his chest. That one will remain unsolved on their books. The note also describes Becker's experiments and the subsequent pollution of the river water—even though it is unlikely that any trace of the old man or his experiments is still around. Lying beneath the note, in a manila envelope, are several research articles on plastosterone, a photocopy of the Sangre de Cristo Lab's original chemical analysis results of the river water identifying the polluting chemical as plastosterone, a photocopy of Jaz Blankenship's tissue analysis before it was falsified, and the microcassette from Becker's place. He will also find, in a sealed, legal-sized envelope with his name in my handwriting, a photocopy of the assignment that brought me to New Mexico—Pasonombre's issue for a quiet concerning Becker's experimentation. What he will not find is the other assignment—the one issued by Cruz for the quiet on the water issue. This one I keep for myself, although I will be delivering a copy to Cruz with a note stipulating that should anything happen to Anna Lee Stone, ranging from her disappearance to her death from the plastosterone poisoning, this proof of his duplicity will be delivered to Paso. I expect Cruz to make every effort to contribute to Stone's recovery. And, last, Juan will find two bottles appropriately labeled—the first, Stone's purloined purple substance, which she took from Jaz's cabin on the afternoon of his death; the second, a plain old sample of river water. When the two are compared, even the most elementary analysis will reveal the presence of the same chemical, whether the local Tortuga lab can put a name to it or not.

At the bottom of the mesa, I stop at the road running along the railroad tracks. If I turn right, the road leads to the village; if left, to a county back road that slices down toward the flat plains of southern New Mexico. I sit for a moment at the junction, surveying the countryside in the grey morning light. Spatters of intermittent rain pelt the windshield, and the sky is kept dark by the storm clouds whose bellies ripple with lightning. In the distance, the silhouette of the Rowe Mesa presses flat and black against the west. I feel a stirring inside my chest, like the flutter of tiny wings, a familiar racing that I have not felt in a very long time.

I breathe deeply, savoring these odd moments when nature rushes in like a green poet to fling her own unsubtle metaphors across our paths. Behind me is the tortuous road, and now I glance left and then right. I am beginning a new life, and I have not mapped out the direction. I flip on the windshield wipers, and as I sit contemplating my choices, their slapping *rhythm recalls an old recurring dream I had as a young woman, after my mother's death—I am driving fast along a deserted highway, speeding wildly through a stormy night, the headlights unable to keep up. Abruptly, without warning, the asphalt ends at the edge of an abyss. I wake upright in bed, not terrified and screaming, but wildly excited, my palms aching for the feel of a steering wheel.*

The wings are beating stronger inside my chest, and I embrace the sweetness of being a renegade. I am now in flight from The Company, the only home I have known for most of my adult life, and at odds with Paso, my surrogate father who knew this moment was near at hand. To Paso, the businessman, my defection will be no more consequential than a gadfly at dinner. Much greater is our other loss, the one that made us more than kin. He, too, had my strange capacity for apprehending the bursting sound of the empty moment, for seeing the images of past violence spread along his daily paths. He therefore understood it in me. His call that late night inviting me to his school had been informed by his own spectacularly executed assignments those many years ago when he first conceived his Company. We were alone together, Paso and I; never were two people more alone. And now we have lost each other.

The wind rises, bringing a deluge of rain, then recedes as the water courses along the road beside the tracks. A shard of lightning hits nearby, followed by a crash of thunder. I look down the muddied road, to the right and to the left, and it occurs to me that these junctures are only the appearance of choices, bones tossed at the human animal for purposes of diversion, illusions of free will to keep the beasts from decimating the planet. For the Old Bone Thrower up there knows how it will all end. And I sense that even he wearies of the watching as he stands looking down through the clouds. I hear him yawn from his rare height, bored. He turns, begins walking away.

But for all that, my palms still ache for the steering wheel, and I know a bone can be carved as well as gnawed.

I stand on the accelerator, driving the Mercedes full-speed straight ahead, flying up the embankment where the AmTrak rails run, tearing at the underframe of the car. The air is split with the sound of iron and steel colliding, thunder crashing in a blinding flash of lightning. I am over the tracks, flying high. I hang for a moment, the Mercedes and I suspended in midair.

And I think I hear him up there, the Old Bone Thrower. He pauses, turns back.

Then I am hurtling through the air, past the railroad tracks and over a twisted barbed-wire fence that sags precariously on juniper posts. The car tilts, skims the ground, touching down on a cushion of tangled, rain-soaked chamisa, and fishtails sideways. I angle the wheels into the skid, using the momentum of the car's weight to keep it moving forward through the muddy topsoil until I feel the tires grab hold on solid ground. I am in a field sprinkled with the dark shapes of cattle, their backsides hunched against the rain as they gaze around at the car with baleful eyes. I follow a lip of solid earth bordering an arroyo, a wide, sandy ravine that snakes across the pasture in a line roughly perpendicular to the railroad tracks. When I come to a place where the cattle have cut a trail into one side of the arroyo to cross over to the other, I stop the car and get out. The storm has subsided for a moment, but the air is still wet and chilled. Above the Sangre de Cristos, the morning sun struggles to break through the cloud pockets, and visible just above the crest where the train tracks run are the pulsing red lights of emergency vehicles heading toward the mesa.

I take the nylon bag from the Mercedes, set it on the ground, and then drive the car down into the sandy bottom of the ravine where I shut off the engine. I leave the HK on the floorboard, lock the Mercedes' doors, and hike back up the path, where the storm clouds are still boiling with jagged bolts of lightning around the mesa. I estimate the flash flood to be less than half an hour away; it is only a matter of minutes before a raging torrent of water will rush with the force of a locomotive through the arroyo, sweeping away everything in its path. By the time Juan has begun to search for footprints and tire tracks, they will be washed clean, and by the time the Mercedes is discovered and Cruz notified, I will be someplace that even I cannot imagine. The HK, that extraordinary weapon customized for The Company's representatives so that no two are alike, will tell him I've gone, really gone this time. It is a signal, from those of us on assignment, that we have come to the end of the road.

I shoulder the nylon bag, heading toward the train tracks and the stand of trees where yesterday afternoon I hid the MG. The field is spongy from the rain, and my boot heels sink into the earth. I take the small Smith and Wesson Airweight out of its boot holster to lighten my hike, and slide it into the bag. The wind has risen again, and the rain slants down across *the milky grey morning. When the lightning bolts begin to touch down across the field, I hold my face up to the sky and the turbulent adrenaline-drenched air, letting a great tide of joy flood through every cell in my body. I feel a movement, a rising motion from deep inside like a small hard bud of rapture, irrepressible and buoyant and light as froth on a sea wave. I feel it surface, blooming across my face, a smile as wide as a rainbow and bright as the solid rays of sunlight which are shooting from the east, between the surging black clouds. A silver thread of lightning leaps out of the clouds toward me, touches down where I stood just a second ago before I felt it coming. It is a sizzling, wickedly prankish kind of energy, too playful for the slow dancers or the faint-hearted. I run with it, around it, splashing across the muddy cow pasture as though we are two wild sisters learning the steps of some forbidden dance, measured out in ear-splitting claps of Wagnerian thunder.*

BETT REECE JOHNSON was born in Fountainhead, Tennessee, and lives in rural New Mexico. She is working on the next Cordelia Morgan mystery.

DON'T MISS OUT
ON THE NEXT
CORDELIA MORGAN MYSTERY!

B. Reece Johnson's next novel finds
Cordelia Morgan on the run in a gated
community near Aspen, Colorado.

**Yes! Please notify me of new mysteries by B. Reece
Johnson featuring Cordelia Morgan.**

Name: _____

Address: _____

City, State, Zip: _____

E-mail address: _____

How to Order Cleis Press Books
- **Phone:** 1-800-780-2279
  or (415) 575-4700
  Monday–Friday, 9 am–5 pm Pacific Standard Time
- **Fax:** (415) 575-4705
- **Mail: Cleis Press**
  P.O. Box 14684, San Francisco
  California 94114
- **E-mail:** Cleis@aol.com

Books from Cleis Press

DEBUT LITERATURE

The Little School: Tales of Disappearance and Survival, second edition, by Alicia Partnoy.
ISBN: 1-57344-029-9 14.95 paper.

Marianne Faithfull's Cigarette: Poems by Gerry Gomez Pearlberg.
ISBN: 1-57344-034-5 $12.95 paper

Memory Mambo by Achy Obejas.
Lambda Literary Award Winner.
ISBN: 1-57344-017-5 12.95 paper.

Queer Dog: Homo Pup Poetry, edited by Gerry Gomez Pearlberg.
ISBN: 1 57344-071-X. 12.95. paper.

We Came All The Way from Cuba So You Could Dress Like This?: Stories by Achy Obejas.
Lambda Literary Award Nominee.
ISBN: 0-939416-93-X 10.95 paper.

Seeing Dell by Carol Guess
ISBN: 1-57344-023-X 12.95 paper.

MYSTERIES

Dirty Weekend: A Novel of Revenge by Helen Zahavi.
ISBN: 0-939416-85-9 10.95 paper.

The Woman Who Knew Too Much: A Cordelia Morgan Mystery by B. Reece Johnson.
ISBN: 1-57344-045-0. 12.95 paper.

VAMPIRES & HORROR

Brothers of the Night: Gay Vampire Stories edited by Michael Rowe and Thomas S. Roche.
ISBN: 1-57344-025-6 14.95 paper.

Dark Angels: Lesbian Vampire Stories, edited by Pam Keesey.
Lambda Literary Award Nominee.
ISBN 1-7344-014-0 10.95 paper.

Daughters of Darkness: Lesbian Vampire Stories, second edition, edited by Pam Keesey.
ISBN: 1-57344-076-0 16.95 paper.

Vamps: An Illustrtated History of the Femme Fatale by Pam Keesey.
ISBN: 1-57344-026-4 21.95.

Sons of Darkness: Tales of Men, Blood and Immortality, edited by Michael Rowe and Thomas S. Roche.
Lambda Literary Award Nominee.
ISBN; 1-57344-059-0 12.95 paper.

Women Who Run with the Werewolves: Tales of Blood, Lust and Metamorphosis, edited by Pam Keesey.
Lambda Literary Award Nominee.
ISBN: 1-57344-057-4 12.95 paper.

SEXUAL POLITICS

Forbidden Passages: Writings Banned in Canada, introductions by Pat Califia and Janine Fuller.
Lambda Literary Award Winner.
ISBN: 1-57344-019-1 14.95 paper.

Public Sex: The Culture of Radical Sex by Pat Califia.
ISBN: 0-939416-89-1 12.95 paper

Real Live Nude Girl: Chronicles of Sex-Positive Culture by Carol Queen.
ISBN: 1-57344-073-6. 14.95 paper.

Sex Work: Writings by Women in the Sex Industry, second edition, edited by Frédérique Delacoste and Priscilla Alexander.
ISBN: 1-57344-042-6. 19.95 paper.

Susie Bright's Sexual Reality: A Virtual Sex World Reader by Susie Bright.
ISBN: 0-939416-59-X 9.95 paper.

Susie Bright's Sexwise by Susie Bright.
ISBN: 1-57344-002-7 10.95 paper.

Susie Sexpert's Lesbian Sex World, second edition, by Susie Bright.
ISBN: 1-57344-077-9. 14.95 paper.

LESBIAN AND GAY STUDIES

The Case of the Good-For-Nothing Girlfriend, second edition, by Mabel Maney. Lambda Literary Award Nominee.
ISBN: 1-57344-075-2 16.95 paper.

The Case of the Not-So-Nice Nurse by Mabel Maney. Lambda Literary Award Nominee.
ISBN: 0-939416-76-X 9.95 paper.

Chasing the American Dyke Dream: Homestretch edited by Susan Fox Rogers.
ISBN: 1-57344-036-1 $14.95 paper.

Nancy Clue and the Hardly Boys in *A Ghost in the Closet* by Mabel Maney. Lambda Literary Award Nominee.
ISBN: 1-57344-012-4 10.95 paper.

Different Daughters: A Book by Mothers of Lesbians, second edition, edited by Louise Rafkin.
ISBN: 1-57344-050-7 12.95 paper.

A Lesbian Love Advisor by Celeste West.
ISBN: 0-939416-26-3 9.95 paper.

On the Rails: A Memoir, second edition, by Linda Niemann. Introduction by Leslie Marmon Silko.
ISBN: 1-57344-064-7. 14.95 paper.

EROTICA

Annie Sprinkle: Post Porn Modernist—My Twenty-Five Years as a Multimedia Whore by Annie Sprinkle.
ISBN: 1-57344-039-6 $21.95 paper

Best Gay Erotica 1999. Selected and introduced by Felice Picano. Edited by Richard Labonté.
ISBN: 1-57344-048-5. $14.95 paper.

Best Gay Erotica 1998, selected by Christopher Bram, edited by Richard Labonté.
ISBN: 1-57344-031-0 14.95 paper.

Best Gay Erotica 1997, selected by Douglas Sadownick, edited by Richard Labonté.
ISBN: 1-57344-067-1 14.95 paper.

Best Gay Erotica 1996, selected by Scott Heim, edited by Michael Ford.
ISBN: 1-57344-052-3 12.95 paper.

Best Lesbian Erotica 1999. Selected and introduced by Chrystos. Edited by Tristan Taormino.
ISBN: 1-57344-049-3. $14.95 paper.

Best Lesbian Erotica 1998, selected by Jenifer Levin, edited by Tristan Taormino.
ISBN: 1-57344-032-9 14.95 paper.

The Leather Daddy and the Femme: An Erotic Novel by Carol Queen.
ISBN: 1-57344-037-X. $14.00 paper.

Serious Pleasure: Lesbian Erotic Stories and Poetry, edited by the Sheba Collective.
ISBN: 0-939416-45-X 9.95 paper.

COMIX

Dyke Strippers: Lesbian Cartoonists A to Z, edited by Roz Warren.
ISBN: 1-57344-008-6 16.95 paper.

GENDER TRANSGRESSION

Body Alchemy: Transsexual Portraits by Loren Cameron. Lambda Literary Award Winner.
ISBN: 1-57344-062-0 24.95 paper.

Dagger: On Butch Women, edited by Roxxie, Lily Burana, Linnea Due.
ISBN: 0-939416-82-4 14.95 paper.

I Am My Own Woman: The Outlaw Life of Charlotte von Mahlsdorf, translated by Jean Hollander.
ISBN: 1-57344-010-8 12.95 paper.

PoMoSexuals: Challenging Assumptions about Gender and Sexuality edited by Carol Queen and Lawrence Schimel. Preface by Kate Bornstein.
ISBN: 1-57344-074-4 14.95 paper.

Sex Changes: The Politics of Transgenderism by Pat Califia.
ISBN: 1-57344-072-8 16.95 paper.

Switch Hitters: Lesbians Write Gay Male Erotica and Gay Men Write Lesbian Erotica, edited by Carol Queen and Lawrence Schimel.
ISBN: 1-57344-021-3 12.95 paper.

TRAVEL & COOKING

Betty and Pansy's Severe Queer Review of New York by Betty Pearl and Pansy.
ISBN: 1-57344-070-1 10.95 paper.

Betty and Pansy's Severe Queer Review of San Francisco by Betty Pearl and Pansy.
ISBN: 1-57344-056-6 10.95 paper.

Food for Life & Other Dish, edited by Lawrence Schimel.
ISBN: 1-57344-061-2 14.95 paper.

WRITER'S REFERENCE

Putting Out: The Essential Publishing Resource Guide For Gay and Lesbian Writers, fourth edition, by Edisol W. Dotson.
ISBN: 1-57344-033-7 14.95 paper.

SEX GUIDES

Good Sex: Real Stories from Real People, second edition, by Julia Hutton.
ISBN: 1-57344-000-0 14.95 paper.

The New Good Vibrations Guide to Sex: Tips and techniques from America's favorite sex-toy store, second edition, by Cathy Winks and Anne Semans.
ISBN: 1-57344-069-8 21.95 paper.

The Ultimate Guide to Anal Sex for Women by Tristan Taormino.
ISBN: 1-57344-028-0 14.95 paper.

WORLD LITERATURE

A Forbidden Passion by Cristina Peri Rossi.
ISBN: 0-939416-68-9 9.95 paper.

Half a Revolution: Contemporary Fiction by Russian Women, edited by Masha Gessen.
ISBN 1-57344-006-X $12.95 paper.

 Since 1980, Cleis Press has published provocative, smart books—for girlfriends of all genders. Cleis Press books are easy to find at your favorite bookstore—or direct from us! We welcome your order and will ship your books as quickly as possible. Individual orders must be prepaid (U.S. dollars only). Please add 15% shipping. CA residents add 8.5% sales tax. MasterCard and Visa orders include account number, exp. date, and signature.

How to Order

• **Phone:** 1-800-780-2279 or (415) 575-4700 Monday–Friday, 9 am–5 pm Pacific Standard Time
• **Fax:** (415) 575-4705
• **Mail: Cleis Press** P.O. Box 14684, San Francisco California 94114
• **E-mail:** Cleis@aol.com